Miss
Nobody

Doubleday

NEW YORK LONDON TORONTO

SYDNEY AUCKLAND

Miss Nobody

TOMEK TRYZNA

Translated from the Polish
by Joanna Trzeciak

PUBLISHED BY DOUBLEDAY

a division of Bantam Doubleday Dell Publishing Group, Inc.

1540 Broadway, New York, New York 10036

DOUBLEDAY and the portrayal of an anchor with a dolphin are trademarks of
Doubleday, a division of Bantam Doubleday Dell Publishing Group, Inc.

Book design by Gretchen Achilles

Library of Congress Cataloging-in-Publication Data

Tryzna, Tomek.
[Panna Nikt. English]
Miss Nobody / Tomek Tryzna; translated from the Polish
by Joanna Trzeciak.
p.   cm.
I. Trzeciak, Joanna.   II. Title.
PG7179.R88P3613   1999

891.8′5373—dc21

98-7235

CIP

ISBN 0-385-48939-0

Printed in the United States of America

January 1999

FIRST EDITION

1   3   5   7   9   10   8   6   4   2

Look Father:

Chased by evil on earth

Away from your breath she wanders in vain

Looking for escape from bitter chaos

and knows not how to conquer it . . .

—HIPPOLYTUS

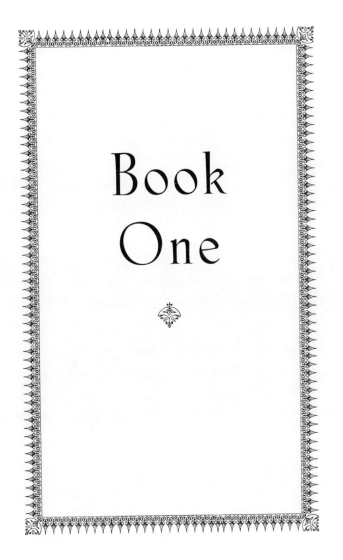

Book
One

Chapter One

I'M FOLLOWING MOM and, using a hoe, I'm covering the holes containing potato halves. Mom's nice. She never says anything when I cover them up wrong, she just gives me a look and I know I have to do it over. The earth is soft. Dad turned it over with a shovel. Now he's doing something over by the fence and Tadzio's tagging along. He's my younger brother. He's ten. He's a neat, cheerful kid. He always wants to arm-wrestle me, but I always pin him. Then he screams that I'm cheating, but I'm not, and that's why he screams. Maybe I should let him win sometimes, but, well, it's not right to cheat. I like him a lot. I took care of him when he was very young. I changed his diapers and fed him his bottle. Now I take care of Zenus. Zenus always sleeps, and when he isn't asleep, he's either crying or smiling. The air smells sweet. It's spring. All day long the sun warms your skin so nicely. Right now it's not so strong because the sun's setting. Our plot of land borders the woods. The woods are dark green and the whole field is dark gray. When the potatoes grow, the field will be green too. All morning I've felt like I have something in my stomach. Same thing yesterday, but not as bad. Someone's squealing. I look up and see it's Zosia. She's running away and Tadzio's chasing after her. Zosia's my sister. There's also Krysia. They're twins. They're five. They always play Chinese jump rope. I also used to jump rope, but I don't do it anymore because I'm too old for that. What's going on over there? Tadzio's approaching Zenus in the baby buggy and dangles a worm over him. Zosia's standing nearby.

From here I can hear her say, "Hey, give it to him, let's see 'im eat it!"

"He's too little to be chowing down meat," Tadzio says. Oh my God, I've been staring and listening too long and Mom's already so far away. So I cover the pits after her, swish, swish, next. Swish, swish, swish, swish. Tadzio runs beside me. Screaming "Score, score!" he jumps over the barbed-wire fence and runs to the top of the little hill. My eyes follow him and my belly starts to hurt and I don't know what to do. Maybe my guts got scrambled. Suddenly it passes. Thank God. A bird is flying in the sky. The sky's blue, the bird's white. Tadzio aims at him with a slingshot and shoots—"Bang, bang!"—but the bird keeps on flying and flying. Nature's beautiful when the sun shines, as long as it doesn't shine in your eyes. Again I've been staring too long, again Mom has gotten far ahead. So I grab the hoe and catch up with her and Mom stands up straight and speaks to me.

"Marysia, do you hear that?"

"What?"

"That."

Oh yeah. Zenus is crying quietly. He must have wet his diaper. I put down the hoe and head over to the buggy, which is standing by the woods in the shadow of the trees. But Zenus is sleeping. I put my hand under his diaper. It's dry. Maybe he was whimpering in his sleep, maybe he was dreaming? Oh well, I'm about to head back, but suddenly something twists in my stomach, and then untwists. I sit right down. I sit down and curl up because it hurts. Something very odd is happening in my stomach. Maybe I swallowed a tadpole in the water and it has now become a frog? Maybe it's hungry and is biting me in the stomach? I hit my tummy with my hand—maybe that'll scare it. It bites a little bit more and then stops. It doesn't hurt anymore. I sit on the grass. There are daisies all around me. I'd like to pick some and make a crown, but I have to go cover the holes. I'm about to get up when I hear a shout. I turn around and look. Maybe it's Zosia, maybe it's Krysia. But no, they're playing Chinese jump rope next to the tree.

Someone's shouting deep in the woods. It's high-pitched and sounds like a girl. I get up and walk over to the trees. I'm a little afraid, and a bit curious.

I'M IN THE woods. The trees are thick. It's dark; the sun doesn't reach here. I hear a bang far away. What can it be? I weave my way through the underbrush. I'm on a narrow path. I hear something like a squeal, or a neigh. There's a sort of clomping. I look over and see a huge carriage, all black, with silver stars, drawn by four black horses. It comes straight at me. The horses are foaming at the mouth. I jump aside and glue myself to a tree. I see the pretty face of a girl in the window of the carriage. She's about my age, I think. She has a golden dress on, and on her head a tiara made of pure gold, studded with diamonds. She notices me and wants to shout something, but suddenly a horrid black hand emerges and clamps over her little rosy lips. The carriage goes by. From the back two ugly hairy monkeys, dressed in tuxedos and baring their teeth, reach their ugly paws toward me, but I crouch so they can't reach me. They're gone. It's quiet. Something shines on the path. I squat down. There's a diamond lying there. It probably fell off the girl's tiara. Or maybe from her ring? Maybe she threw it to me so I'd have a souvenir and wouldn't forget. So beautiful—like the whole sun is hiding in there and shining. I hold it in the palm of my hand to admire it. Someone's moaning. It's coming from the same direction the carriage came from. I walk down the path, holding the diamond in my hand, getting more and more scared. What am I about to see? The moans grow louder. Finally I reach the place they're coming from. A young man lies there moaning, a spear piercing his stomach. He can't get up because the spear has nailed him to the ground. Beautifully arranged golden curls circle his face. He has on a red tunic embroidered with gold, yellow tights and beautiful red shoes. A broken sword and a feathered hat lie beside him. Oh, what terrible pain he must be in. Gripping the spear, he wriggles his body, like he's trying to climb up . . . He sees me. He begs pitifully, "Little girl, please help me. Pull this out of me, I can't do it alone. Please, pull it . . ."

I'd like to help him, but I can't. I don't know why, but I can't

move. I simply can't move. I feel ashamed because he might be thinking I don't want to help him, that I'm bad. But how can I help him
when I can't move? I'd like to tell him that, but I can't even move my
lips.

In great pain, he pleads, "Little girl, I beg you, pull it out of me.
Grab it and pull! Grab it and pull! Grab it and pull! Come on, little girl,
grab it and pull!"

But I can't do anything. Nothing—literally nothing. Nothing, nothing. All I can do is close my eyes; at least I can do that. I open them
once it's quiet again. I see the young man climbing the wooden shaft of
the spear, which is bent like a bow. The spear starts to tilt and the
young man falls on his side. The sharp blade of the sword is suddenly
sticking out of the ground. The young man is no longer moaning. He's
dead. A red ribbon slowly trickles out from under him. It flows down
the path to my bare feet. I'm standing in the puddle of blood and I
can't move. The red streams climb up my leg like little vipers. A ridiculous girl is standing in the forest shouting hopelessly. The girl is me.

"Mom!" I shout.

THE ROAD SWINGS away. Tadzio was chasing after us, but he got
tired. Mom's pedaling and I'm sitting in the cart attached to the bicycle,
on top of the empty potato sacks. Oh, here comes a car. It's getting
closer. There's a man and a woman inside. They look at me and pass
us. The sun shines to my left; it's low. To my right you can see shadows in the road—of the bike, of the cart, of Mom, of me. Mom's head
flickers against the tree trunks in the road. They're cherry trees.

I'm lying in bed. I have a bunch of cotton stuffed in my undies and
I don't feel like sleeping. Until today I was a little girl. Maybe that's
why I'm so tall, the tallest in my family. I'm five feet six. After me
comes Dad, five feet one. After him comes Mom, five feet on the nose.
After them, Tadzio and the girls. And last is Zenus. Dad's skinny but
strong. Stronger than Mom, but he weighs half as much. Mom's very
fat. Dad keeps saying she looks like a keg of beer. Mom says by the
time I've had as many kids as her, I'll be that way too. And our neighbor from the frame house, Mr. Kaminski, is about six three. When he

and Dad stand by the fence and drink beer, Mom laughs and says, "Marysia, look what we've got here, what a fine pair of boozers."

Mr. Kaminski likes a good, stiff drink. So does Dad, but he says that he doesn't drink at work, because if he did, he'd have fallen off the roof years ago. That's because Dad tiles roofs. A while back he used to do that full-time, but for about three years now he's been working at the coal mines in Walbrzych, then tiles in the afternoon when he gets off work. Thanks to the mine, we have a new apartment in Walbrzych in the Piaskowa Gora development. I haven't been there yet, but Mom went and told us it's really neat and there are even three rooms there. One is large, and two are teeny. There's also a kitchen, a full bathroom and a half-bath. Mom's very happy about that because if someone wants to use the toilet, he won't disturb someone who might be taking a bath. I suppose it's the same at our house, because the outhouse with the heart-shaped hole in the door is near the currant bushes, while the pump is on the other side by the storage sheds. Dad's having the hardest time leaving the rabbits behind. Mom's sorry too. As for me, I'm really happy we won't be raising rabbits in our new apartment. Dad won't be killing them anymore. We won't be taking Tabby with us, because cats get used to a certain place, and besides, Mom says, she wouldn't have taken him anyway, because he'd probably pee in our new apartment. Mrs. Kaminska will be feeding him. And we have no idea what's going to happen with school. I have less than three months left in elementary school. Same for Tadzio and the third grade. We had been going to school in Krzeszow. It's less than two miles away. And now . . . what's going to happen now? From our place it's twelve miles to Walbrzych and there's no direct bus. Dad goes to the coal mines on a bike, but he's a grown-up. The thing is, we haven't even got any other bikes, just Dad's. Dad said we shouldn't move to Walbrzych until summer vacation, but Mom said we should do it right away because squatters might break into the new apartment with an ax and by the time we got there they'd already be living there and wouldn't want to let us in. Dad offered to live there by himself for the time being, and the rest of the family could hook up with him when the school year ends. But Mom knows what's what. First thing you know, Dad's buddies would find out and turn the apartment into a hangout for drinking, and sleeping with women with VD.

It turns out that on Monday after work Dad will enroll us at a school in Walbrzych. I sure hope they take us. Maybe they won't want to so close to the end of the year. But maybe Dad can explain things and tell them about those squatters. Our new furniture's already there. A wall unit and a fold-up couch. I haven't seen them yet because they were packed up in cardboard and plastic in the storage shed. The day before yesterday Dad and Mr. Kaminski brought them down to Walbrzych in a truck. I really wonder what the apartment looks like. I'll be living in one room with the girls, with Dad and Tadzio in the second one, and Mom and Zenus in the third. Or, the girls in one, me and Tadzio in the other, and Mom, Zenus and Dad in the third. Mom hasn't decided yet. She says this, that and the other thing, always changing her mind. Then Dad laughs and says, "Like a kid in a candy shop . . ." See, that's the thing. Here, we fit into one room with a small kitchen, but there, we can't fit into three rooms, a kitchen and a hallway. We're sure going to have a lot of room to run around, though.

So I'm lying around, and all of a sudden I look down: I've got my thumb in my mouth again. Yuck. The minute I forget about it, I stick my right thumb in and start sucking on it like a pacifier. Everyone laughs at me—such a big girl and she sucks her thumb. I always swear never to do it again, and then I look down and I have it in my mouth. Zosia and Krysia, they're so small, but they don't suck their thumbs. Dad says he's going to smear it with cat shit, and then I'll really be in trouble. Each morning Mom tells me to show her my thumb, and if it's white and clean, then she yells at me for sucking it. Now I always wash all my fingers carefully at night so that in the morning you can't tell the difference. But even then, you can always tell if one's been sucked on.

Rats.

The sun has gone down and my folks aren't here yet. There were so many potatoes to plant and I'm here just lounging around, not helping at all. I'm sure Tadzio's covering the holes for me. I wish he was doing it well. "You got it wrong here, and here too!" I wish Mom could see that. "Ha, I'm gonna call her and show her how you did it!"

But Tadzio just laughs and sticks out his tongue. When we come down in the fall to collect them, there won't be a single potato there: the holes weren't covered right. Not the ones I covered—those will be fine. "Look, Tadzio," I say, "this is how you should cover them." I take the hoe and show him. I look over and Tadzio's standing on the hill shooting at us with his slingshot. *Taratatat.* I lie dead on the meadow and a bird sits beside me. It's white and blurry. I ask him, "What do you want?" He has something in his beak. He spits it out and flies away. It's shining. I stretch my arm out. The little light gets away and goes down into the ground. So I go after it. I crawl down on all fours into the mole's tunnel. Deeper and deeper into the darkness, underground. Again I see the little light. Someone's snoring very loudly. Here in a little room of a mole's family, the daddy mole's snoring on the cot. The mother mole is washing her fur over the washbasin, and over there, a girl mole is sucking her paw in her sleep. Two small baby moles are standing by her and whispering.

"Something tells me she's going to die soon."

"What are you talking about? Why would she have to die?"

"Grandma died, and for what? For no reason at all."

"She was old."

"And Marysia got bitten by a snake."

"Tadzio didn't find it."

"Because it bit her and escaped."

Dummies. They don't realize their older sister's just become a woman. I'm like Mom now. This is what God arranged with women so they could have children, so the human race wouldn't die out. I'll have children someday too. A boy and a girl. The boy will be called Pawelek and the girl Zuzanna.

IT'S MONDAY NOW. Seven twenty-seven in the morning. No, that's impossible, because it's Wednesday. That's just what my watch says. I got it last year for my name day from my godfather. It's gotten the day wrong several times now. But as far as minutes and hours go, it's never been wrong. I'm standing at a bus stop and I'm waiting for the number 8 bus. There are lots of people around. They're waiting, too. Some have umbrellas because it's raining. I have on a see-through raincoat with a hood. It's kind of warm and pleasant out here, although my legs are a bit damp. Last night was the first night we spent in the new apartment. Mom told us to remember what each of us dreamed, because dreams in a new place always come true. She dreamed that she was arguing with Mrs. Kaminska from our old frame house in Jawiszow, which is very odd because we're never going back there. Zosia dreamed about a hen. Krysia dreamed she ate porridge with milk and sugar and raspberries. Tadzio didn't dream of anything, but he never has dreams. I had a dream, something really beautiful, but I've already forgotten what it was, because when I woke up, I wanted to sleep a little longer so I could dream about it a little more, but when I woke up again, it turned out I didn't remember anything from that dream. Something about . . . No, I don't remember. Too bad, because it was really beautiful.

And we don't know what Dad dreamed, because everyone else was still asleep when he went to work. It's a quarter to eight already. I'm on a bus and I'm really nervous because I'm afraid I'll be late for school.

"Excuse me," I say. "I'm going to Maria Konopnicka Street. Where do I get off?"

"I don't know," the woman responds.

But another woman hears my question and says, "The stop after next."

"Thank you very much," I say. I smile at her and curtsy. The woman smiles back. The bus stops. Some people get off, some get on. The doors close with a hiss. I move closer to them. We start moving again. Something has splashed me. It must be from someone's umbrella. In three seconds it'll be twelve to eight. I don't know, maybe I'll make it. It's all because I'm not going to the same school as Tadzio, who got into the local school in our neighborhood. But there is such an overload of kids in the eighth grade there that Dad's foreman, who is on the parents' committee, found me a place in elementary school number 3 downtown. He told Dad it's the best elementary school in all of Walbrzych. From now on I'll be attending class 8A. I'm very curious about my new classmates—both girls and boys. When I went to school in Krzeszow, I didn't have a single close friend. I had one in the fifth grade once, but she left with her parents for Canada and never sent me a postcard, even though she promised.

The bus slows down and stops. The doors open, I jump out, straight into a puddle.

I was the only one to get off here. A woman is going down the street.

"Excuse me," I say. "Where is Maria Konopnicka Street?"

She points to the other side of the street. I run across, and once I'm on the sidewalk, I realize that I forgot to thank her. Oh, here's Maria Konopnicka Street. Boys with book bags walk by. I run after them.

"Excuse me," I say, out of breath. "Are you going to school number 3?"

One of them laughs and says, "Are you nuts? We're skipping school."

"So where is school number 3?" The boys point to the place that I came from. So I say, "But this is Maria Konopnicka Street."

"That's also Konopnicka Street," they say. "Two miles and you'll be at school."

I run back in that direction. It's six to eight. I'm not going to make it. I run across the street. I look around . . . there's no Konopnicka Street, only a dug-up square, full of puddles. But the street definitely continues on the far side of the square. I walk—it's muddy everywhere. I hope I don't fall down. I'm not going to get through—I have to circle around. Girls with book bags and umbrellas are passing by right then.

I yell, "Girls! Do you know where school number 3 is?"

"We're going to school number 3!"

They're walking, not rushing at all. I step out of the mud and join them. We cross the street together and we walk in the same direction that those boys went in, the ones who said they were skipping school.

"What grade are you in?" I ask the girls.

"Third grade," they reply.

"Just like my brother," I say.

"I'm a fourth grader," one of the girls offers.

"Do you get good grades?" I ask.

"I'm the best one," says the one with a red bow and red umbrella. "I made the Honor Roll."

"I made it too," says the other.

"But you got a B yesterday," says the one with the bow. We reach the school building. It's very large and there are lots of carved figures on the side of it. The girls take off; only one stays with me.

"I made the Honor Roll last year," she says. "But this year my dad died and I didn't make it."

We go in. Wow, what a large school. There's even a coatroom, but I don't know what to do, so I huddle in the corner. I take out my slippers and put them on my feet, wrap my muddy shoes in my raincoat and put them in my book bag. The bell's ringing. I run up to a lady who's shouting at kids to hurry up.

"Good morning," I say. "Where is class 8A?"

"And where did you drop in from?" The lady's surprised.

"I went to school in Krzeszow, but now we got a new apartment down Walbrzych way . . ."

"Run to the third floor," the woman says. So I run. Here it is. There are so many hallways. Where do I go? There? Or there? Or maybe there?

I SIT AT the last table in the row right by the wall. I don't know what notebooks to take out because I don't know what class it is. My cheeks are hot and my mouth is dry.

Here's what happened.

I enter the class and bang into some guy. He and I fall down. I get up, pick up my book bag, and he sits on the floor, feeling his teeth.

I say, "I'm very sorry."

He says, "Fuck off!"

Everyone laughs. I go to an empty desk and sit down. Someone says, "Hey, you, you sure you're not in the wrong place?"

I raise my hand and some girl stands over me. "Bogusia sits here," she says. "Get lost." I get up and she sits down. I'm standing, looking around.

I say, "Is there a free seat somewhere?"

"There's one here," I hear.

I look—and it's a fat red-faced boy. He points to a seat and I sit down beside him, but the boy who I crashed into gets up from the floor, comes over to me, hits me on the head and says, "Wait a minute, I sit here." I get up and he sits down.

"What are you doing, fatso?" he says. "Are you in the mood to pick up girls?" The fatso laughs and others laugh with him.

One girl says, "Look what fashionable tights she's wearing! Spotted ones!"

I look at my legs and my tights are splattered with mud. It's from when I stepped in the puddle. I'm standing and I don't know what to do. Everyone's looking at me. "Listen," someone says, "there's a free desk in the back."

I go there and sit down.

So now I'm sitting. The teacher's already here; he's quite young. He reads something and yawns. It's fairly quiet in the classroom. One of the girls raises her hand. She clears her throat. The teacher lifts his head and looks at her.

"What?" he asks. "Isn't it a little bit early to have to go to the bathroom?"

"It's not that," she answers. "But there's a strange girl sitting here." She points her finger at me. So I get up.

"What are you doing here?" the teacher says.

"I'm enrolled here."

"I know nothing about this."

"My dad enrolled me," I say. "He told me I was supposed to go to school number 3 on Maria Konopnicka Street. To class 8A."

"What are you saying?" the teacher asks. He cups his hand and puts it to his ear. "Louder!"

Everyone's laughing. My mouth is so dry I can't say anything else.

"Come closer," the teacher says. "Sit next to Klaudia!" I take my book bag and look around to see where I'm supposed to sit.

Then the girl who drove me away from her bench stands up and says, "But teacher, Bogusia sits next to me!"

"Why don't I see her?"

"Because she's in the hospital."

"Klaudia, answer this question for me then," the teacher says. "How can someone be in the hospital and be sitting next to you at the same time?"

"But this is her place."

"That *was* her place. It *was*! Now her place is in the hospital. Got it?"

The teacher turns to me and says, "You sit next to Klaudia, and the two of you, don't bother me if you don't want to end up in the hospital with Bogusia. So—what are you waiting for?"

I get up and sit in Bogusia's place. Klaudia scoots her chair toward the wall. "Excuse me," I whisper to her. "What subject is this?" She doesn't answer. I look around to see what books and notebooks are lying on the desks so I can figure it out, but there's nothing lying around anywhere. The teacher opens his grade book and leafs through the pages.

The girl sitting in front of me turns around and looks at me. She has large dark eyes and shiny short black hair. She's very pretty. She whispers to Klaudia, "Aren't you going to introduce your new friend to me?"

Klaudia shrugs her shoulders and snorts. She doesn't say anything. The dark-haired girl smiles at me and says, "My name is Eva. What's yours?"

"Marysia," I say, and smile back.

"Beautiful name. Where did you come from? Surely, from Paris. Am I right?"

"No. I lived twelve miles from here, and now we've got a new apartment down Walbrzych way . . . and . . ." I don't know what else to say.

"Down Walbrzych way?" Eva repeats my words slowly and makes a face like she's eating something delicious. "Hmm, 'cause, you know, you have such a beautiful dress on, I felt sure it was straight from Paris."

She sticks out her hand and feels the material of my sleeve with her finger. It's true. I'm wearing a very nice dress. Mrs. Kaminska got it in a package from the West and sold it to my mom, and then later our neighbor Marysia, Mr. Krzysiek's wife, altered it to fit me. I smile at Eva and say, "It might be from Paris because it came in a package."

All of a sudden, bang! The teacher slams his hand on the table. He looks at us and asks, "What is this? A lesson, or gossip?"

"So far, just gossip," Eva replies. "See, we were talking just now about our famed Polish postal service. Because our new friend here got a dress from Paris in a package. Only, judging by the cut of the dress, this package must have been lying around the post office for at least ten years."

The girls all start giggling. The teacher raises his finger.

"It's nothing to laugh about," he says. "Strange things happen in this country—things that philosophers and other philomaths had never dreamed of. Imagine . . . but there's nothing to imagine, these are facts. Last year I got a package from my cousin in Australia. I opened it, and of course there were all kinds of things inside. Among them, a tiny classy crock with a bright checkered top. What could it be? My wife's English is perfect, and she said it was raspberry jam. So, heck, I thought to myself, at least once in my life I'll gorge myself on raspberry jam from Australia, although who knows whether raspberries grow there . . . I twisted off the lid, I looked in, the jam was half-eaten, and you could still see the traces of someone's fingers in it."

The teacher laughs and the class echoes him.

"And my dad," some guy says. "He got a package too, from America. The letter said he was getting twelve pairs of men's underpants. There wasn't a single pair in the package."

"So your dad was a little surprised?" the teacher asks. "I would be too."

"We got a package from West Germany a month after Christmas and everything in it was rotten."

"Same here!"

"Our uncle from Canada sent us a package of clothing, but there wasn't any clothing inside, only an old coat, and even that was from Poland, because the label said Minsk Mazowiecki."

"Quiet. Be quiet!" the teacher says. "If we all start to list who did get what, and who didn't get what, we would be talking till our dying day."

The teacher stretches and yawns. He looks out the window and says, "Boy, is it pouring. So, guys, what're we going to do now?" He looks at me and motions to me with his finger. "You—the new one—come to the blackboard. We'll hear your confession."

I get up and go to the blackboard. I take a piece of chalk. The whole class laughs. The teacher does too.

"Are you planning on drawing us something?" he asks.

"Well, I could," I say quietly. They're laughing again, they're still laughing at me.

"Quiet," the teacher says. And then: "What are you going to draw?"

I shrug my shoulders. How am I supposed to know?

"If you don't want to," the teacher says, "then don't draw. No one's forcing you. But why the chalk?"

I don't know what to say. I set the chalk down on the rim of the blackboard.

"How about telling us your name?" the teacher asks.

"My name is Maria Kawczak."

"Oh man!" someone says, and the whole class starts to laugh.

"Kawczak pulled one over on us," someone else says. "That's his sister."

"She sure isn't my sister," says the guy I bumped into. "I don't even know her. There are tons of Kawczaks in the world."

"Most of them are in Shit Lanka," someone squeaks. Everyone laughs again. Bang, the teacher slams his hand on the desk. Things quiet down.

"I remind you, citizens, that this is a school, not a circus," the teacher says, and he asks me, "What was your time in the sixty meters?"

I don't answer. I don't understand what he's asking.

"What school did you go to?" he asks.

"To elementary school in Krzeszow," I say.

"Didn't you run there at all?"

"We ran."

"No one timed you?"

"I don't know."

It's quiet in the classroom. The teacher's not saying anything either. Everyone's looking at me. I'm standing and the buzzing in my head's getting louder and louder. The teacher nods his head.

"So," he says, "did you do the high jump?"

"I did."

"How high did you jump?"

"I don't remember."

"Show us with your hand." He raises his hand to the level of my head. "That high?"

"Not that high," I say.

"Maybe this high?" The teacher leans out from behind his desk and touches the floor with his fingers. Giggles everywhere. I'm standing there and can't think of anything. Someone's saying something, something's saying something in my ear, like buzzing, but who and what . . . How am I supposed to know when it's just murmuring and buzzing?

"Show us with your hand," the teacher says. "Don't you know how to stretch out your arm?"

"Sure I can." I stretch it out. There's a long ruler on the teacher's desk. He's gonna smack my hand with it. He's gonna take it and smack me. Oh my gosh, he's gonna smack me right away. It's better if he doesn't get up; it's not right for the teacher to come to me. I should go over to him. I go up to him with my palm turned up. Why is everyone laughing? Why isn't the teacher picking up the ruler, even though I'm waiting and waiting and my hand is shaking . . . ?

I hear crying. Someone in the class has started to cry. It's not me. The teacher turns away from me and looks elsewhere. Everyone's looking where he's looking. I look there too and some girl is crying violently at a desk in the middle row.

"What happened?" the teacher asks. No one knows. "Kasia, what happened?" he asks, louder.

The girl's weeping, her hands covering her face. All you can see is her hair. Blond. Falling in curls. Long. All around her. Suddenly she gets up. Her chair falls with a crash. She takes her book bag, walking toward us, toward the teacher and me. She passes us, still crying. Her eyes flicker as she looks at me. They seem familiar. Have I ever seen them? Probably not in real life, maybe in a picture . . . Maybe I dreamed them up?

She's walking fast toward the door. Her skirt is down to the floor, wide, bright, like a Gypsy's, like a fortune-teller's. Floating in the air are her hair and a large scarf, black with yellow flowers. She covers her shoulders with it. The door slams and she is gone.

No one says anything for a long time. Then the teacher says to me, "What are you doing standing around? Sit down." I go to my desk and sit down. "What happened to her?" the teacher asks.

Eva, the dark-haired girl sitting in front of me, says "You know" and taps her finger against her temple. The teacher sighs.

"Okay," he says. "Let's end this foolishness. It's time for a lesson. Get up!"

Everyone gets up. I do too.

"Stand by your desk," the teacher says. "Attention! Bend your knees, hands up, stand up, hands down. Let's begin."

NOW I'M IN physics. Last class of the day. I already got an F. I didn't know anything. Everything flew out of my head; the teacher wrote comments in her grade book. In Krzeszow I got an A in the subject.

This is the most horrifying day of my life. No one talks to me during the breaks. I go down to the second floor and stand by the window. Little kids from the first grade are running around right next to me. I don't know what's going to happen to me in this school. Klaudia moved away from me to the edge of our desk. I heard her telling Magda that someone here has fleas. She must mean me. What did I do to them? They're seeing me for the first time in their lives. Is it because I knocked over Kawczak at the beginning? Or because he answered me in such a mean way? Why was I in such a hurry? Because I didn't want to be late. Starting tomorrow, I'll leave the house earlier, around seven. How was I supposed to know it would take so long for the bus to come?

I talked with my homeroom teacher. She is young and pretty. She asked me about everything. She was surprised that I switched schools two months before graduating from junior high. I told her it was because of the new apartment, that Mom's afraid of squatters. Then the teacher laughed, stroked my head and left. She's nice. If she'd taught physics, I certainly wouldn't have gotten that F. Our physics teacher is impatient, and if you don't answer her quickly, she starts yelling right away, and when someone yells at me, I get tongue-tied. The physics

teacher's last name is Zelenow. The homeroom teacher teaches biology
and her name is Mrs. Turska.

I already know the last name of the girl who sits in front of me, the
dark-haired one whose first name is Eva. It's Bogdaj. The fat kid that
talks through his nose and shares his desk with Kawczak is Ziebinski.
There's a girl in the row next to the window who is even fatter and
taller than Ziebinski. She has breasts like balloons and during the
breaks always chases after this one boy named Zenek. Like Zenus.
When she catches him, she twists his arm and tortures him. He tries to
break loose and kick her, but she always jumps out of the way. They
all call her Nag, but she doesn't mind. She always chases Zenek. He's
two heads shorter than her. He has a high, squeaky voice and shouts,
"Buzz off, Nag, or else I'll kick you so hard you'll regret it!"

"You just try!" she says, coming up from behind and grabbing his
neck.

There are lots of pretty girls in our class. They dress nicely too.
They tend to wear black tights and tight denim skirts. Some wear them
short and some wear them long, to midcalf, with a slit in the back.

But the prettiest girl is Eva Bogdaj. She also wears a short denim
skirt and black tights, and a baggy, loose-knit black sweater. Her tan is
gorgeous. She sits in front of me, so I'm always looking at her. She also
looks nice from the back. She's always wiggling around in her chair.
Sometimes I see her face from the side. She bites her lower lip a lot. I
like to think back to how she smiled at me during the first class. She
has a beautiful smile.

She's kind of nervous, but whenever she says something to someone, she calms down right away. Her whole body stops and only her
lips move.

She likes to put her hand on the back of her neck. She always
strokes herself right at the nape of her neck. Her fingernails are long
and shiny, like they've been painted with clear polish. On her smallest
fingernail she has a pretty gold star. I never saw such a beautiful girl,
maybe in a movie on television or in a beauty pageant.

She hasn't spoken to me since she complimented me on my dress.
Sometimes she turns around and whispers to Klaudia. Klaudia's tall
and skinny. She has long straight hair and she always slouches. She

wears jeans. When she writes something, she sticks the tip of her tongue out. She has very pretty handwriting. I can see from here how Eva Bogdaj writes—fast but sloppy. The girl sitting next to her is Magda. She has a pretty, pudgy face with dimples and ash-blond hair down to her shoulders. She and Klaudia pal around with Eva during the breaks. Eva says things and they laugh. Eva walks like she's dancing, like a ballerina on TV. She has a nice body—she doesn't look like a girl who's still in elementary school.

The girl who started to cry during the first hour and never came back to class is Kasia Bogdanska. When they call the roll, Eva Bogdaj always comes first, and then Bogdanska, and when they call her name, someone always says she's absent. When the homeroom teacher called the roll, Magda stood up and said that Kasia ran out of the first class. The teacher said "Again?" and sighed. Then Magda looked at Eva, and Eva looked at Magda, and they smiled. Interference of light?

That's Marlena Pyzik stuttering in front of the blackboard. She's about to get an F. A car honks outside. It gets quiet and then starts honking again. Mrs. Zelenow makes an odd face.

"Very nice," she says to Marlena. "Sit down." Marlena returns to her desk. The teacher takes the grade book and says to the class, "Stay seated and remain quiet. The bell is about to ring."

She leaves. We're left alone. It's starting to get louder: everyone's packing their books and notebooks because this is our last class.

One boy, I think his name is Krempicki, calls from the window, "Hey, guys, hurry, it's her lover!" After a moment, almost the whole class crowds around the windows.

Someone says, "Fuck, he's really bald!" Eva gets up and throws her bag over her shoulder.

"Let's go," she says to Magda and Klaudia. "What are we waiting for?" They leave. The whole row next to the wall is empty. I'm the only one sitting there. There's a commotion by the windows. The boys are wrestling. I pull a mirror from my pocket. I fix my hair and put the mirror away.

IT'S GOTTEN WARM now: the sun has come out. The streets are all dry now. The wind is blowing hard, but it's warm. It's already past two. I wander around and explore Walbrzych. The houses are all nice and old. There are lots of stone ornaments on them. The windows are different on every floor. All the streets are either downhill or uphill. And there's a huge church here. I've already been inside; I said three Our Fathers and one Hail Mary, Full of Grace. Now I'm in the market square; there's a fountain in the middle. The splashing water shines in the sun.

Suddenly, I see . . .

On the bench, right by the fountain, sits a girl from my class, the one who cried—Kasia Bogdanska. Yes, it's her. She's sitting with her back to me, but I recognize her by the black scarf with yellow flowers draped over her back, and by her hair, which shines in the sun, just like the fountain. Her head is down, over her knees. Maybe she's crying again.

I come closer. I stop. Maybe it's not her? No, it's definitely her. I'll sit next to her: maybe someone in her family died. I had a grandmother who died, so I know what it's like. I cried all day long too. Maybe she doesn't want anyone to know that she's crying. It always feels better to get something off your chest. I guess I'll come closer. What if she doesn't recognize me? Oh well, then I'll leave.

I walk over. I look and she's not crying at all. She's hunched over because she's writing something in the little notebook lying open on her lap. Oh, I made a fool of myself. Lucky for me she didn't know I was coming toward her. I'm about to leave when she raises her head and looks at me. I feel stupid; I don't know what to say.

"Wow, look at the expression on your face!" she says, and smiles. She's not laughing at me—she's smiling. Oh, what a beautiful smile. I don't know why, but all of a sudden I feel really happy and I don't feel awkward.

"Sit down," she says, pointing to a place next to her. I sit down and look away from Kasia to the fountain, in which the sun is extinguished before my very eyes. I break down and look at Kasia. She's still smiling, and all the joy in me explodes like a balloon when someone's poked it with a pin. I begin to laugh, for no reason at all. Now we're both laughing. Loud, then even louder. We laugh and laugh, stop, and then start laughing again. We laugh and we can't stop.

Now we're not laughing anymore, just breathing loudly, all worn out from laughing.

"And what were you laughing about?" Kasia asks.

"I have no idea," I say. "I forget." Both of us start laughing again. We wiggle around, holding our stomachs, and can't catch our breath. Then all of a sudden . . . boom! Something hits me on the head. I look up and hard chunks are falling out of the sky.

"Let's get out of here!" Kasia shouts, grabbing me by the hand, and we take off. We run to the doorway of a building. There's a commotion in the marketplace: everyone's running away, hiding in doorways. The whole sidewalk's covered with bouncing, crackling balls of ice. I reach down and pick one of them up. I put it in my hand. Up close it looks like a small bird's egg. Kasia and I watch the way it melts. Now only a little bit of water remains. I wipe my hand on my dress.

The hail has rained itself out.

People are walking around again in the marketplace. It's white everywhere from the ice balls, which are becoming smaller and smaller. Kasia pulls at me to go somewhere. We enter some doors. It's a coatroom.

"Hand me your book bag," Kasia says. I give her my book bag and she gives it and her bag to the lady behind the counter. I look around: this is a café, we're in a café. I've never been in a café before.

"What are you doing?" I ask, a little afraid, but we're already inside.

"Get the number," Kasia says, and leaves me. She sits down at a table by the window. I go back to the coatroom. The lady gives me a metal triangle with a number on it: 42.

I go to Kasia's table. There are lots of people here and they're all adults. I sit down. Past the curtains, through the windowpane, you can see the marketplace.

Suddenly someone asks, "What would you like?"

Right by our table a lady in a tiny white apron stands and looks back and forth at Kasia and me.

Kasia says, "Two large ice creams with dried fruit, and two glasses of orange juice."

"We only have imported juice."

"I don't drink anything else," Kasia says. The lady leaves.

"I only have twenty zloty," I say quickly so Kasia has time to cancel what she ordered for me.

"I invited you, so don't you worry," Kasia says, brushing her hair back with her fingers. Her hair is beautiful, slightly golden and slightly rosy. She has so much hair you could share it between four little girls, or even five. With her fingers knit together, Kasia hugs her knee and, slouching a little, looks at me.

"You know," she says, "you make such funny and sweet faces that I might call you 'Mongoose.' Do you want that, Mongoose?"

"Okay."

"And my name is Katarzyna."

"I know," I say, "Katarzyna Bogdanska."

"How do you know?"

"Because they called the roll and I figured out it was you because no one else was missing."

Kasia smiles and starts to say something, but just then the lady comes back, puts the juice and ice cream on the table and leaves.

"Enjoy," Kasia says, and starts in on her ice cream. So I start in on mine. What a funny little spoon. This ice cream is really good. First I find some raisins in the whipped cream, then a cherry, then I fish out a piece of chocolate, and then, at the end, a little yellow circle with a hole in it. It's delicious, but I don't know what it is.

I've already finished everything in the sundae, and it's only now that I remember I'm in a café. I raise my eyes. Kasia's picking at her ice cream. She hasn't even eaten half of it. I look around. There's nothing terrifying about sitting in a café. Everyone's talking. No one is paying attention to me. What if some teacher from school walks by? Would she be angry at us sitting here? Who knows. I look at Kasia again. She's not eating at all; she's thinking about something, maybe about something sad, because she looks sad. She scoops some ice cream with the spoon and tips the spoon over and watches how the ice cream slowly trickles down. I'd like to drink some orange juice, but I feel kind of awkward reaching for the glass.

"Don't be shy," Kasia says, and, without looking at me, nudges my glass toward me and continues to pick at her ice cream. Oh my

God, I didn't say anything. How did she know what I was thinking? Kasia raises her head and says quietly, "Don't worry, that's how I am."

A strange smile appears on her face. I know this smile from somewhere, but from where? Someone has smiled at me that way before. But who, and when? Or maybe I dreamed it up . . . ?

God, am I dreaming all this up?

Kasia raises her glass and takes a sip. I gulp down half of my juice. *Ting, ting . . . !*

That's Kasia clanging her spoon against the glass. The sound's still ringing in the air.

"Do you remember how you laughed?" Kasia asks.

"Sure," I say, and quickly put down my glass because I'm about to start laughing. And the same thing happens to me that happened on the bench before the hail started falling. I laugh and can't stop laughing, though I know everyone's looking at me.

"Something sad!" Kasia cries out, through laughter. She, too, is laughing loudly. And I can't remember anything sad. I look at Kasia, and maybe she can't remember anything sad either, because she's almost doubled over with laughter. I cover my mouth: it's not helping at all. I might die any minute. The lady in the apron is standing at our table—ha, ha, ha—in such a small apron!

"Aren't we being a little loud, young ladies?" she says, and Kasia, shaking with laughter, cries out, "Check, please."

The lady pulls a tiny bill from a tiny pocket of her tiny apron and puts in on the table and says, "Three thousand, seven hundred eighty."

Oh my gosh, so much money. Where's Kasia going to come up with that much money? I could at least have not drunk my juice and returned it so we'd have one less thing to pay for. On the one hand, I'm worried; but on the other, I'm giggling uncontrollably now. Kasia throws a bunch of crumpled bills on the table.

"Keep the change," she gasps through the laughter. She jumps up from her chair, takes me by the hand, and we run to the coatroom. From the coatroom we bounce over to a doorway. No one's there; we can finish laughing in peace.

It's quiet in the doorway. I'm holding my stomach. It's a miracle we're still alive. You really can die from laughing.

"Our bags," Kasia says. "Do you have the number?"

"Oh Jesus, I left it on the table," I say, and I feel hot. How am I going to go back there? What an embarrassment.

"Don't you worry, I'll go." Kasia heads back to the café. Oh, she's so brave. And so happy. So why was she crying back then at school . . . ? There must have been a reason. But now she's so happy. Another thing is that when she's lost in thought, she turns sad right away. Why? I'd really like to know, but I'm not going to ask. Maybe she'll tell me herself. She paid so much money, but I only drank half my juice, and her even less, and she didn't even finish her ice cream. It's good that at least I managed to finish mine. Less went to waste.

"Mongoose!" someone calls. "Mongoose!" Someone is calling from the café. "Mongoose!"

It's Kasia's voice. I look into the coatroom and Kasia is standing by the counter waving at me. Oh yeah, that's right, I'm Mongoose. I walk in.

"Do you have that twenty zloty?" Kasia asks.

"I do." I pull my entire fortune out of the pocket of my dress.

"So pay the lady for the coat check," Kasia says. "I've spent everything I had."

I give twenty zloty to the lady behind the counter. Kasia takes her bag and I take mine and we leave. We're in the marketplace again. The sun has come out.

There's no trace of the hail: the streets are dry. We stand watching some children who are chasing each other around the fountain.

We stroll around, passing a bookstore.

"Shall we go in?" Kasia asks.

"We can," I say. We go in. I stop right by the door and look at the books behind the glass. Farther inside, Kasia's browsing through the ones on the counter. She waves me over with her hand. I go up to her.

She shows me a large art book and says, "I'm going to kill myself."

"What happened?" I ask.

Kasia opens the book. There are colorful pictures inside. "Look," Kasia says, in awe.

"Very nice."

"Brilliant. Too bad I don't have any cash on me. Damn, too bad."

She puts the album back on the counter. I look at the price. Three and a half thousand zloty.

"Jeez," I say sadly, "why'd we have to eat that ice cream and drink those juices . . . it would have been just enough."

"Don't worry," Kasia says. "You know what? Go up to this girl and ask her whether they have a book called *Gone with the Wink*."

"Okay," I say, and go over to the salesgirl and ask, "Excuse me, do you have a book called *Gone with the Wink*?"

"What?" the lady asks.

"*Gone with the Wink*—do you have it?"

The lady chuckles. She goes to the open door of the storeroom and calls out, laughing, "Zocha, some girl here is asking whether we have *Gone with the Wink*!"

From behind the door comes the laughter of an invisible other lady: "Tell her we used to have it, but it's gone with the wind!"

The salesgirl walks away from the door and, shrugging her shoulders, tells me, "It's gone with the wind."

"That means you don't have it?"

"No, we don't," the lady says, laughing.

"Thank you," I say, and return to Kasia. But she's nowhere to be found. I leave the bookstore. She's not in the street either. Has she gone somewhere? But why? No, there she is. She's standing in a doorway nearby. I go up to her. Oh my God, she's looking at that book. I feel flushed because I'm scared.

She took the book and didn't pay.

Any minute they're going to call the police, and they'll catch her, and they'll take me with her. God, it's all because of those ice creams and juices. But I didn't steal the book—she did. I don't have it, I don't know anything.

I look around.

No one from the bookstore has run after us yet. Kasia's looking at the book and doesn't see me. I walk away quickly.

I'm walking down the street.

Somebody's gonna scream at me any second.

I can't take it, so I dart into the closest doorway. I hide in the space between the door and the wall, sliding in as far as I can. It's dark here.

What if they search the nearest doorways?

Oh God, oh God, what am I gonna tell them? They're going to send us to reform school. They'll write us up in the newspapers. What am I gonna tell Mom? I've gotta run away from here. But when I try to run, they're gonna catch me for sure. They always chase somebody who's on the run. What if they're already standing there waiting for me to come out?

Why did I go up to Kasia? If only I knew she wasn't crying, I never would have gone up to her. How was I supposed to know she was bad news?

I should have known it. Normal girls don't dress like that. Every girl in the class was dressed normally; only she was dressed differently, like some kind of Gypsy. Oh yes, Gypsies dress like that. She's a Gypsy—that explains everything. A Gypsy once stole a sweater that was hanging on the clothesline from my mom. And I was wondering in the café where Kasia got all this money. She must have stolen it. But wait a minute—Gypsies aren't blond. True, but maybe she dyed her hair. Or maybe she was kidnapped by Gypsies when she was little. I thought I had made a friend—I was so happy—and now it turns out she's a thief.

The street's quiet. No one is shouting. Maybe they didn't notice. Thank God. I'll wait a little longer and then come out as if nothing happened.

She must have gone somewhere. It's a good thing no one from school saw me with her. We were together only in the café and the bookstore. But what am I gonna do if she comes up to me at school and starts talking? . . . Well, I'll say something and then pretend I'm in a hurry. But what if they've already caught her and she tells them I helped her steal? Well, there will be nothing left for me to do but commit suicide. But that's a mortal sin. Mom would never survive a funeral without a priest. I won't go to heaven; I'll fry in hell. "Our Father which art in heaven, hallowed be thy name. Thy kingdom come. Thy will be done in earth, as it is in heaven. Give us this day our daily bread. And forgive us our trespasses, as we forgive those who trespass against us. And lead us not into temptation, but deliver us from evil . . ."

Someone's entered the doorway.

It's got to be the police. I switch my school bag to my left hand. I cross myself quickly and close my eyes. Amen. But now my book bag is slipping out of my hand, because in all this mess I didn't hold on to it tight enough. I'm losing my balance and lean against the door. It opens, creaking.

She's standing in the doorway, a few steps from me. She's serious, quite different from how she's been up to now. She doesn't say a thing, just stares at me, puffing out her lips.

I lean over to grab my book bag. I feel really sad. A little while ago we were smiling together . . . and now . . .

"What are you doing here?" she asks.

"Nothing."

"I was looking for you everywhere," she says. "I was in the bookstore. I went around the old town square . . . Why did you hide?"

I don't say a word. What am I supposed to say? She's got to be lying that she was looking for me in the bookstore. But how did she know I was hiding here?

She comes over to me.

"You got dirty," she says. I look at myself. The whole sleeve of my dress is white from the wall. I start to brush it off. She watches, silent.

Brushing my sleeve, I say, "Bye, I've got to go."

"So go," she says. I'm already at the foot of the stairs when I hear her cry, "Wait!" She runs up, grabbing me by the arm.

So I say, "I really have to go. My mom told me to come home right after school."

"The whole back of your dress is white." I start to clean it in the back, at least where I can reach.

"No, no," she says, "it's not gonna help. I won't let you go like this. Come to my place—I'll give you a brush."

"Where?" I ask.

"To my place," she answers, and pulls me into the doorway. What does she want from me?

"Why here?"

"Because I live here," she says. She lives here? I go with her and it gets darker and darker. I stop in front of the stairs.

"You live here?" I ask in disbelief. She smiles.

"You hid in my doorway," she says, and grabs me by the hand. "Hurry up and go, before I lose my patience. Be Kind to Animals Week doesn't last forever."

She drags me upstairs. She stops on the third-floor landing, turning toward me. A sunbeam from a skylight falls on her. Her hair looks like it's on fire. She smiles strangely and her eyes are beaming. She pulls my hand toward her. I'm petrified with fear. I don't know what to do. If I jerk my hand and run away, she's going to catch me anyway, she's going to jump at me from behind. And with a changed, scratchy voice she says, "A little fortune-telling, missy?"

So I was right. She is a Gypsy. She turns my hand palm up and holds it up to her eyes.

"Ohhh, what a beautiful lifeline," she says in a screechy voice. "But why does it break off so suddenly?"

"I don't have any money," I say. My voice is shaking. "Really."

"Missy could pay me with an egg."

"I don't have any eggs."

"So what does missy have?"

"I don't have anything," I say in despair.

She pierces me with a fiery glance. She pants heavily, hoarsely. "Too bad. Such an elegant missy and she doesn't have anything. So maybe, at least missy has a soul?"

I feel my heart pounding. Oh, I wish I could wake up. But it's not a dream.

Suddenly she lets go of my hand. She becomes tiny. No, she's just squatting, browsing through her purse. She leaves, disappearing in the darkness. I can't move, I can't escape. The light turns on—she turned it on. Now she goes over to the large door and puts the key in the keyhole. I see a plaque on the door: INTERNAL MEDICINE SPECIALIST.

"C'mon," she says. I go.

"The man who lives here is a doctor," I say.

"Not man. Woman, and not just any woman—it's my mom."

That's right. At the bottom of the plaque is a sign: KAROLINA

BOGDANSKA, M.D. Doors open, we go inside. Here, in a gigantic room, beautiful paintings hang on the wooden walls. There are big light-colored armchairs around the table. A chandelier hangs from a high ceiling. It all sparkles as if with thousands of diamonds. There are doors here and doors there . . . but not a single window. And what a beautiful hallway.

She opens the closet and hands me a clothes brush.

"The bathroom is over there," she says, pointing to the door at the end of the hallway. "Can you find it on your own, or shall I show you?"

"I'll find it," I say quietly. I go up to the door and touch the knob. It's round and shiny, like it's made of gold. I look back and Kasia isn't there. She's disappeared. I turn the doorknob. It's dark in the bathroom. I go back out. Oh, there's the light switch. I flip it and the light comes on. I go in and close the door behind me.

It's so gorgeous here. This bathroom is three times as big as my room in the new apartment. The floor's made of white tiles and there are tiles on the wall too, only they're brown. And there are mirrors everywhere. I sit down on the edge of the bathtub. How stupid I was. I thought Kasia was some kind of Gypsy, but she's a normal rich girl, and on top of that, the daughter of a doctor.

There are various beautiful bottles with foreign labels on the tile shelves. There is a washing machine by the door—I think it's an automatic washer—and there are some other strange appliances. And over here on shiny racks there are towels hanging. Orange, pink and white. I look to the side and see myself. Some girl is sitting behind me.

I turn around. Another girl is sitting behind me there too. And behind that girl another girl, and another, and another. A whole row of girls. It's us sitting there—that is, me—but reflected in the mirror, which reflects another mirror. I raise my hand. All the girls are doing the same thing, all the way to the very end. There's so many of us, there probably is no end.

The whole dress is white in back. I unbutton it and take it off. I sit down on the white plastic stool, lay my dress on my lap and start brushing it with the brush.

I think I must be crazy. I thought Kasia wanted to do something to me, that she wanted to rob me or something . . . but it's me that could rob her. She let me into a bathroom filled with so many beautiful, expensive things, and she's not even afraid I'll steal anything. But why did she take that album from the bookstore?

Because she was afraid someone else would buy it. When her mom or dad gets home, she'll get some money from them and go back and pay for it. How could I be so silly and think that she is a thief? It's a huge sin to falsely accuse someone. I'll have to go to confession. I'll go tomorrow, right after school. To the church right next to the marketplace. The only thing is, I don't know what time they hear confession.

It's impossible to clean the dress without sprinkling it with water. I turn the faucet on and hold the brush in the stream of water. Yeah, now the paint is coming off. Maybe the priest will absolve me, but I'll never forgive myself. Kasia was so good to me. I never know how to talk to anyone, but she's someone I'd know how to talk to. Yeah, I have a funny feeling that with her I'd know how. Maybe I could even tell her I still suck my thumb and can't kick the habit. She's so wise, maybe she could advise me what to do so I won't suck it. Suddenly I hear music. It's coming from far away.

It's as beautiful as in church, but different.

Maybe Kasia turned on the radio. Maybe she has a tape recorder and turned it on. I like to listen to music in church. Sometimes on the radio they play nice music. Just like now. Like angels are flying across the sky.

Oh yes . . . I lost track of what I was doing, listening, and during that time the water trickled from the brush onto my dress and now I have a big wet spot. That's nothing. I'll go out into the street, stand with my back turned to the sun, and it'll dry out. I get up and put the dress on. It's soaking wet. I button it up, looking at myself in the mirror. I don't like this dress anymore. These shiny ribbons look so dumb. And to think that it was made in France. Eva Bogdaj said it was from Paris. But Paris is the world capital for fashion, so this dress should be nice. And is it really possible the package lay around the post office for ten years? Ten years ago fashion was different, and it's different today too. Now girls wear short and narrow skirts. But not

Kasia. Maybe her dress is from a package that took a long time to get here too.

I pull the bottom of my skirt high up above the knees. Even a little higher. I gather the pleats and hold them in back to make it narrow. Now that's something else—I look like the other girls in the class. If I were to dye my stockings . . . Mom has to have some black dye, no question about it.

I look at myself, I look and can't get enough of it.

At home we don't have mirrors this big. There's one in the closet, but you can only see yourself from the waist up. If I had a bathroom like this, I'd probably never leave it. Jeez, it's not polite to spend so much time in somebody's bathroom. What's Kasia going to think? I look at myself for a second and let go of my dress, which drapes past my knees again. I turn away from the mirror above the bathtub and see myself in the one above the sink. I've gotta go. I comb my hair, grab my book bag and leave. I forgot the brush. I turn back, take the brush, take one last look at the whole bathroom, close the door and turn off the light.

I walk quietly through the hallway and put the brush in the closet by the door. The music is even louder here. It's coming from that room where the door's open. But you can't see anything inside because right behind the door there's a honey-colored curtain. Kasia must be in there. She's sitting listening to the music. How could I think so badly of her?

Why am I like that?

I've never thought badly about anyone before, so why did I feel that way about her? Oh well, apparently I didn't deserve to know a girl who's that nice and good.

"Good-bye, Kasia," I say quietly, and I'm already pushing the doorknob when I decide I can't leave the door open, that is, unlocked, because a thief could come in and rob the apartment. There are so many of them around. I must go to her room behind the curtain and tell her I'm leaving. How can I look at her now . . . I'll probably die of shame. Too bad, I have to.

I walk up to the curtain, pull it open and enter the room. Loud music blasts at me and it's so dark here I can't see a thing. The windows are covered and only a small crack lets a little light in. I see the strip of lit-up carpet and nothing else. And the music is playing from over there and from over there.

"Kasia, are you here?" I ask, not hearing my own words because of the music. The music quiets down suddenly.

I hear Kasia's voice in the silence: "If it's too dark for you, please open the curtains by the window."

"Okay," I say. I go to the window, walking along the strip of light. There's music again. I raise my hand and pull on the curtain. It pulls apart some.

"Something's stuck," I say, but it seems Kasia can't hear me because the music is playing again. I look over . . . it's Kasia playing. She's sitting at the piano, playing. It's strange. She's sitting there, but the music is coming from over there and from over there. It must be from the speakers. And the thing Kasia is playing isn't a piano but something electric, something musicians play on TV. And it seems like someone is playing a drum. I look around . . . no one's here except Kasia, but she's not beating a drum, only playing the keyboard. She moves one of her hands away, turns a knob, and you can hear the wind. The wind moans, wails and then slowly dies down. It's quiet. Kasia looks at me, smiling, and I get sad because I have to go soon.

"I finished cleaning up," I say. "Thanks for the brush."

"It's the brush's pleasure," Kasia replies joyfully, and asks, "Want me to play a little more for you?"

I nod my head yes, I'd like that.

"So why are you standing? Sit down. You can hear it best from there." Kasia points to the rocking chair in the corner. I go over to it and carefully sit down. Something begins buzzing loudly.

"Just a sec," Kasia says. "I have to do something with this piece of junk."

She gets up from the piano and kneels down, pulling a wire from underneath. She examines it for a long time, then gets up. She looks around the room, scrunching up her forehead. She stands there, thinking. Suddenly she runs out of the room. I'm all alone.

I sit in silence.

Jeez, what an enormous room.

Curtains are draped along the walls and a huge black desk with lots of books and papers on it stands next to the window. On the other side is a black wardrobe with all kinds of faces and plants carved into it. There are suitcases lying on top of it and boxes stacked all the way up to the ceiling. And on the ceiling there are cartons like the ones you buy eggs in. Oh, what a strange bed. It looks like an antique out of some kind of film. I know what it's called. A canopy.

In the middle of the room is a black sofa with its back facing the door. It's covered in shiny black leather. Right next to it is a black box with white cable coming out of it running to the piano. Over there, in the corner by the window, are various shiny gadgets. There's one more electric piano and something like a table with a bunch of lights and switches.

Pieces of paper and piles of books are scattered all over the carpet. It's a terrible mess here. I'd make it so neat. It wouldn't take much. It'd be enough to stack the pieces of paper and stick them in drawers. The sofa should be moved so its back faces the wall, because how can you sit with your back to the door? And a prefab wall unit would come in handy. Just like Mom and Dad's room in the new apartment. We could stack the books on shelves behind the glass so they wouldn't get dusty.

Kasia's weird, and awfully messy. She really scared me on the stairs too. Why would she do that? I thought I was gonna die, I was so scared. Then she invited me into her house, gave me the brush and everything. Now she's going to play for me if she can get that piece of junk tuned up.

Jeez, she's been gone for a while.

I look at my watch. Wow, it's almost four. What am I gonna tell Mom? There's so much work to do at home and here I am sitting around rocking in a chair doing nothing. Suddenly Kasia walks in.

I jump.

"I can't find it anywhere," she says angrily. "Whenever you don't need one, there's always a whole bunch of screwdrivers to trip over!"

"What's that?" I point to the screwdriver in her hand. "Isn't that a screwdriver?"

"It's a screwdriver all right," she says, "but it's too big. I need a small one."

Before long she's lost in thought. She's been standing there awhile, not saying anything, her eyes closed. Suddenly she looks surprised and starts humming something strange. She sings in a high voice: "Though I'm not for writing, nor am I for drawing, proudly I am lying in this coffin I'm enjoying . . . !" She opens her eyes, looks at me and shrugs her shoulders.

"I asked him," she says, " 'Where are you, Mr. Screwdriver?' and he sang me this little poem. What's it mean? Did he die or what?"

She walks around the room, looking into everything. She knocks a few notebooks off the desk. "Oh," she says, turning toward me. "Hurry up and come here."

I run over and look. On the desk in an open pencil case are some pens and pencils, along with a small screwdriver with a blue handle.

"I was wondering why he was singing to the melody of that old Krakowiak folk song," Kasia says. "Look—that's why."

She takes out the screwdriver and closes the pencil case. On it there is a painting of a boy in a traditional Krakow outfit. Kasia kisses the screwdriver and says fondly, "You are a true poet, my nursery-rhyming Krakow boy. Are you going to help me unscrew this plug?"

She holds it up to her ear and listens for a while.

"He said he will," she says to me. She crawls on all fours under her electric piano. I squat down next to her and watch her unscrew the plug.

"When you're looking for something," she says, "it's best to close your eyes, imagine that thing and very politely ask it for its dwelling place. Remember this for future reference."

"My mother," I say, "prays to St. Anthony when she loses something."

"That's good too. The only problem with this Anthony is that he is a monopolist and has tons to do. That means you have to wait in line."

"That's true. Once Mom lost a thousand zloty and she prayed to St. Anthony and nothing happened. She didn't find it till two months later, when we were moving the wardrobe with Dad."

Kasia laughs.

"It sure was a long line," she says. She's looking at the plug she took apart. "Pretty soon I'm going to have to learn how to solder, or else I'm not going to have anything to play on." She wraps a little wire around the metal plate and screws the plug back together. She plugs it into the hole in the middle of all the other plugs in a tangle of colored cables. She comes out from under the piano and points to the rocking chair.

She sits down on the adjustable stool by the piano.

"Ladies and gentlemen, I will play for you my newest composition," she announces solemnly. "It's called 'The Household of Netophytites.' Due to circumstances beyond my control, you will not hear the thanksgiving chorus of the final movement."

She raises her hands, spreads her fingers and holds them motionless for a while. Then she drops them, touches something, and music comes out. Music, but not music. Like birds shrieking. Suddenly they stop shrieking.

Something is squealing quietly.

Now it's so loud my ears hurt. From somewhere, somewhere far away, something else is coming out, real music. Very quiet, like it's swimming outside the window. Now it's breaking through the squeal and coming into the room in waves. Every place is full of it now. The music is so beautiful.

It's almost so beautiful I can't take it. I feel paralyzed. I squeeze my eyelids shut. What's happening to me? Where am I now if I'm not here?

I can't breathe—there's music everywhere—and soon I'll drown in all these waves, in this music that's rushing and rushing over me. How long will I be able to stand it without taking a breath? I catch a breath, but instead of air, a glowing brightness fills my body.

I'm glowing like a giant lightbulb.

I'm standing on top of a tall mountain, radiating in the blue mist. I can't see anything except my own brightness. How light I feel here, crystalline, sweet.

I wish it would always be like this so I wouldn't have to go back.

But go back where? I can't remember anything except this one thing—that I've always been here. And I am here now.

I am.

My God, I am.

Boom, boom—something has whisked me away. I'm flying through the air in a rainbowy bubble. Oh, how sweet the air is. I can't tell myself whether it's more sweet or more transparent. My little stars, my sparks. My dearest little pearls, my beads! Here I am! Save me, catch me, I'm falling. I'm falling like a bead.

I'm falling, I'm falling . . .

I rise up once more, but once again I'm falling, falling to earth. To earth.

I'VE FALLEN DOWN. I'm sitting in a meadow. There are so many flowers around—daisies, forget-me-nots, blue cornflowers—but I don't know why, they repulse me more than earthworms and spiders.

Lost in a terrible and empty silence. Something's still playing over there. I take a look . . . clouds are playing, stars are playing . . . but I'm not there anymore, I'm here. Somebody's crying, a little girl is crying, she's crying louder and louder. I hear a voice, very, very close, somebody's voice . . .

"Mongoose, what's wrong with you? Mongoose, Marysia . . . !"

I feel someone touching me, stroking my head. I open my eyes, I look up, and it's Kasia who's stroking me and kneeling beside me. And me? I'm doubled over on the floor and I'm crying.

"Why are you crying?" she asks.

How am I supposed to know why I'm crying? It's not my fault I'm crying. It's not me crying, it's something crying inside me, but it's me crying and I can't stop.

After a while it passes.

I sit on the edge of the bed, with the canopy above me. I'm drying my eyes and face with Kasia's handkerchief because mine is so wet you could wring it out. I feel stupid.

I have the hiccups. Kasia sits beside me and looks at me.

"Why'd you start crying?" she asks.

"I don't know," I say.

"Were you reminded of something?"

"No."

"Then why?"

I have the hiccups. I really don't know what to tell her. "Something started hurting in me," I say.

"What hurt? Your leg, your hand, your stomach?"

"No," I say. "The music. It was so beautiful." And once again I'm about to cry. I feel new tears on my cheeks.

"That's why you were crying?" Kasia asks. I nod my head. She hugs me closely. "My sweet one, is that right?"

"Yes."

"You're wonderful, I adore you," she says. I can't hold back and begin sobbing like crazy. We sit for a long time. I'm crying and Kasia rocks me lightly in her embrace, just like I do to Zenus.

"Mongoose, sweetheart," Kasia says. "Do you want to be my sister?"

"I do," I say through tears.

"Dearest sister," she says, and tightens her embrace. I also hug her and caress her.

"Say 'sister,' " she whispers in my ear.

"Sister," I whisper. My God, oh God, how can I thank You. I have a friend and I'm calling her "sister." I've never been so happy in my life.

"I love you," Kasia says, wiping away my tears. "And you?"

"Yes," I reply. "I love you."

All of a sudden I hiccup. Kasia starts to laugh. I do too. We're both laughing, but not in the same way like that time on the bench and then in the café, but in another way, quietly, in sweet happiness.

I LEFT KASIA'S place at five-thirty, which means I've been walking for forty-five minutes. That's as long as one class at school. I could go by bus, but I spent the twenty zloty that I had on the coatroom. Walbrzych is a large city. I'm walking and walking and it's probably still a long way to my house. When I see someone, I ask for directions. I'm glad at least it's not raining or there isn't a hailstorm. There's just the wind blowing and I feel a bit cold.

Kasia Bogdanska is the most wonderful person on earth.

We were sitting down, drinking tea and eating cookies, not on the bed but on the black sofa. It's very comfortable; you don't even feel like you're sitting when you're sitting on it. We were just yakking and yakking away. She was calling me "Mongoose" or "Mongoosy" and I was calling her "Katarzyna," because she hates when anybody calls her by a nickname. She becomes furious when someone calls her "Ka-sienka." It's good I didn't blurt it out before she told me she didn't like it. Because in my thoughts I call her "Kasia" or "Kasienka." Katarzyna's a pretty name, but it's a bit too long.

She showed me her notebooks full of notes. She has lots of them. She came up with all of it herself and wrote it all down. She's a true composer. I never thought till now you could be a composer when you're fifteen. Well, it turns out you can.

She told me she'd teach me to play and that it's very easy. Gee, wouldn't Mom be surprised if I played for her! But how could I play for my mom? We don't have anything to play on. Kasia, however, has two pianos like that, she calls them synthe . . . sizers. On one, it is written in silver letters, KORG, and on the other one in gold YAMAHA. She also has a bunch of other appliances, and she even has her own computer. And some kind of table with knobs where you can mix music like a soup so it doesn't burn. That's what Kasia told me. She said she mixes the soup there.

On top of all that, she has a real grand piano, but she doesn't play it. She says piano is boring unless you're as good as someone like Keif Jarit, for example.

It's black and stands on a white rug in her mom's room, where everything's as clean and beautiful as the pictures in glossy magazines. And this piano's so huge it wouldn't even fit in my room. If I go to work, and get married, I might just buy myself a piano too. I'll put it in the living room next to the TV, because I'm also gonna buy a TV, a color one. I'll invite my mother and the whole family over and I'll play for her. She'll be so surprised and she'll ask me, "Where did you learn to play piano so well?" And I'll just say, "I learned."

I'll have a lot of sheet music. Because Kasia, Kasia plays from memory. Once she writes the notes down, she never looks at them again.

She says she forgets words after five minutes, but notes, never. It's the other way around with me. I remember every word I say or somebody else says, but then I can't forget it for a long time, even if I want to. If I've lived in the world for fifteen years, how many words would that mean I have in my head?

Unless I get really nervous. Then there's nothing in my head, and sometimes not even nothing, but something swooshing and buzzing like in the big shell Mom has. Mom has a shell that makes a really pretty swooshing sound. She got it from her fiancé. This was before she knew Dad. Then the fiancé married another girl, and Mom married Dad. She was lucky she didn't marry that fiancé because later he was killed on a motorcycle and left a widow and two orphans. Our dad is the way he is, but at least he is.

Mom used to be very skinny, even skinnier than Daddy. She didn't start putting on weight until after she had me. But she doesn't worry about it. She says that skinny women are evil, that it's the fat ones who have good hearts. This might be true, because Mrs. Kaminska is skinny. When I was little, she beat me with a stick because I stepped on her flower bed. I didn't step on her flower bed on purpose; Kazio Kaminski pushed me. Now he's in the army. Mrs. Kaminska's very happy about that. She says they'll straighten him out. When he gets out of the army, she wants him to go to a trade school or become a policeman. Then he'll have a good life. He'll have an apartment, money, a uniform and respect from people.

Once Kazio had a day off, came home and started drinking with Mr. Krzysiek and my dad. At first it was a lot of fun because they were sitting on the bench by the fence singing songs about the army, but then Kazio began to get in trouble and mouth off to Mr. Krzysiek. Mr. Krzysiek grabbed him by his coat, lifted him up and said, "Are you messing with me, boy?"

He pushed him onto a cage and the cage broke into pieces, but this was our cage and one of our rabbits got squashed. So Daddy said to Mr. Krzysiek, "Well, pal, looks like you just bought yourself a rabbit."

And Mr. Krzysiek said, "I ain't buying shit!" Then he started to beat up on Daddy. Dad may be small, but he's no pushover. He rammed his head into Mr. Krzysiek's stomach. Then Kazio Kaminski jumped in to help Dad and I don't know what would have happened if my mom hadn't come running out of the house along with Marysia, who has the same name as me and is Mr. Krzysiek's wife. Only Mrs. Kaminska hadn't seen anything because she was watching television.

The next day Dad made up with Mr. Krzysiek. The only thing was my father had a loose tooth for two weeks. We also had rabbit for dinner. We would have had leftovers the next day, but Tadzio crept into the kitchen that night and ate everything except the bones. Mom smacked him with a dishcloth when she found out it was him. Nobody would have found out except he took a bone to bed with him and fell asleep. When Mom was making the bed in the morning, she found it. And on top of that, his sheets were all greasy. We had pierogi for dinner, only Tadzio was sitting and crying because on the plate in front of him Mom had put two of the rabbit bones he had cleaned off.

"EXCUSE ME," I say. "How far is it to the Piaskowa Gora development?"

The lady in the blue coat stops. "What did you say?"

"To Piaskowa Gora . . . Is this the right way?"

"No," she says, and walks on. After a while she turns around and yells, "Come with me! I'm going to Piaskowa Gora too!"

I run after her. Now we're walking side by side. The lady's lost in thought and I'm looking around. Good thing I asked. I could have walked and walked and who knows where I would have wound up.

Clomp-clomp, clomp-clomp . . .

The woman's high heels are clomping. I wouldn't know how to walk in high heels. I'd probably fall down right away. She moves her feet very fast. For every step I take, she takes almost two. I'm beginning to walk like her.

It's kind of silly, but if you walk on your toes, it gets better. Oh, what a funny-looking dog . . .

All of a sudden the lady starts to run. So I run with her. The dog is following us and barking at a high pitch. She runs to the road and starts waving her arm. A taxi stops right in front of her. It's blue. She opens the door, stoops and goes inside. I turn back and she calls after me, "Hey, you, get in!"

"I don't have any money."

"Get in," she says. "Who asked you for dough?"

I get in the back. The woman sits next to the driver.

"To the Piaskowa," she says.

We're on our way.

Oh, that's the way I was just going. But now we're turning. I never turned, I was going straight. Good thing I met this woman.

"You don't remember me?" the driver asks the woman.

She looks at him and says, "No. Should I?"

"Have you ever heard this?" The driver starts whistling. I know the song, it's very pretty.

"I've heard it," she says. "What of it?"

"You were in my cab one time and you whistled this the whole way."

The woman laughs. "I must have been drunk."

"I wouldn't know," the driver says, "I didn't breathalyze you."

He starts whistling the song. The woman's also whistling. I start whistling quietly too. We're driving along, whistling.

"It was at night," the driver says. "Just you and me, Ms. Jadwiga."

"How do you know my name?"

"You really don't remember?"

The driver leans over and says something into the woman's ear. She looks at him. "Really?" she asks. The driver nods his head and laughs. Now they're both laughing. I look up and we're passing through the row of apartments. I think it's here.

I say faintly, "Is this Piaskowa Gora already?"

The woman turns toward me. "I completely forgot about you. What street did you want?"

"T. Rabiegi," I say.

"What number?" the driver asks.

"Twenty-seven." We go a little farther and the taxi stops.

"Thank you very much," I say, and look for the door handle. I can't find it anywhere. The driver turns around, reaches his hand back, and the door opens. I get out.

"Good-bye," I say, but the woman doesn't look at me. The taxi drives away and hides behind the apartments. One of those apartments has got to be ours. This one is 27. I crane my neck and look up to the ninth floor. Which of those are our windows? There are no balconies on this side, so the window of my room must be somewhere up there. I circle around the apartment complex.

There are lots of girls by the carpet rail. Boys are skating on the sidewalk. Our entryway is the second one. Oh . . . behind the glass is my little brother's face. He doesn't see me, he's looking the other way.

I go in and ask, "How come you're standing around? Why aren't you playing?"

He doesn't answer.

"You know," I say, "I came here by cab. You would have seen it, but it stopped over there."

"Buzz off."

"Why are you being so rude to me?"

He turns away from me without a word. His nose is dirty.

"Jeez," I say, "your nose is bleeding. Go home right away and wash yourself up."

He pushes me away. "Why don't you go yourself!"

"What happened?" I ask. "Were you fighting or what?"

"Watch out or I'll hit you too."

"Are you going with me or not?"

He doesn't say a thing. Oh well, let him stand here if he wants. I climb the stairs and press the elevator button. The red light comes on; somewhere up high something clinks. I lean my ear to the door. It's coming. Suddenly the window lights up. I go inside and press the button with number 9 on it.

I'm riding. Up and up, higher and higher. It's nice to ride in the elevator. I'm so glad our apartment isn't on the ground floor. On the other hand, it's too bad because people who live on the ground floor have their own small gardens by their windows. Some girl looks at me through the little window. Now she's gone, she's disappeared below. What a great thing we didn't wait to move until after the school year. If we'd waited, I'd never have met Kasia.

It's stopped. I step out of the elevator and walk along the long corridor. Doors everywhere. One of them is ours. If it weren't for the numbers, I wouldn't know which one. I knock quietly with my fingernail because maybe Zenus is sleeping. I knock a little bit louder. No one opens. Well, I'm not about to ring the bell, because of Zenus. Or could it be no one's home? Why wouldn't Tadzio have told me? In any case, I try the door handle. The door opens. I enter. It's quiet everywhere.

It smells like paint.

I peep into Zosia and Krysia's room. They're asleep. It's still light outside and they're sleeping in their dresses, covered by a blanket. Mom's lying on the new sofa in the big room. She's asleep and snoring. She didn't even cover herself. Zenus lies in the little bed and is also asleep. What's going on? Everybody's sleeping. And the doors aren't even locked—it's a good thing no one robbed us.

I leave on tiptoe and go to my room. It's as small as Zosia and Krysia's room. All we have is the old sofa Mom and Dad slept on in Jawiszow, and a table and two chairs for doing homework. We could use an end table and a bookshelf for school stuff, but for now it's fine the way it is. Only the day before yesterday all we had was a single room plus a kitchen for the whole family and no one was complaining, so why would anyone complain now? Still Tadzio and I argued on the first night over who would get to sleep by the wall. Because I wanted to sleep by the wall, and so did Tadzio. Finally we decided that one week he would sleep by the wall and the next week I would . . . and so on. One week him, the next week me. The most important thing is that each of us has our own comforter. We won't be fighting over one in our sleep.

We need to buy flowerpots and plant all kinds of flowers. We brought some with us, but they're not enough. We had our own garden there and a chunk of field, but here instead there are so many rooms and an elevator and a bathroom and even our own half-bath inside the apartment. When Mom buys me a straw mat to go around my bed, I'll cut out all kinds of colored pictures from the newspaper Mrs. Kaminska gave me and pin them to it.

I also have many pretty postcards, all with views of Szczecin. The walls are painted rather nice. My room is painted green with yellow patches. Like flowers growing in a meadow. The girls' room is painted the same way. The room with the TV is painted blue, also with yellow patches. There's a painting on the wall behind the sofa with a beautiful sign along the border: JESUS KRIST HAVE MERCY ON US. Dad's friend who painted it made a little mistake because it should be CHRIST, but it doesn't bother Mom because she says the sign fits the painting of Jesus and the Apostles that hangs right below it. It's really a beautiful painting, and old too, from before the war even. Lord Jesus and the Apostles are so rosy; only Judas is tanned and he's looking mean. You can tell right away he's up to no good.

Facing that wall, there's a shiny shelving unit, almost up to the ceiling.

It's so beautiful here.

I have to pee. I run to the bathroom. It's so nice and clean here. In Jawiszow we had only one outhouse with a heart-shaped hole in the wooden door for the entire frame-house unit. It smelled really bad and there were flies buzzing around. When anyone had any trouble and had to sit there for a long time, everyone else would have to go behind the currant bushes. Then, to wash our hands, we had to circle around the frame house because the pump was over by the sheds. Here we have it all to ourselves—a john, a sink and a bathroom with a bathtub just a step away. We always have hot water. It's so easy to wash Zenus's diapers. Five minutes and that's it. You can also take a bath whenever you want. I took a bath yesterday, another this morning, and I'll take one tonight too. God, how quickly one gets used to luxury.

I'M WARMING UP my dinner when Mom comes into the kitchen. She sits on the stool and sighs and yawns. She's groggy and a little angry. I'm standing quietly by the gas stove, not making a sound, just the lard sizzling under the potatoes. Mom scratches herself and says, "Who do you think you are? Is this any time to be getting home?"

"I was at a friend's house," I say. Mom doesn't say a word. I look at her and she's not listening to me at all. She's looking out the window where the sun is setting all orangy behind the apartment complex. Mom makes a face.

"I'm not happy," she says. "I'm not happy. This ain't no way to live. It takes a half hour in the elevator to go outside. I'm even scared to look out the window. This ain't no way to live. One day the gas is going to explode and everything's gonna go to hell. Where's your father?"

"I don't know," I answer. "He was gone when I came in."

"He got loaded again," Mom says. "Get me my cigarettes."

I walk into the big room. Zenus is still sleeping. I grab the cigarettes, go back to the kitchen and hand them to Mom. She lights a cigarette. I dish up some potatoes and sausage and begin to eat. Mom's smoking and watching me eat.

"I don't want to do nothin'," she says, yawning. "I gotta wash the diapers, but I don't wanna."

"I already did," I say.

"Yeah?" Mom asks in surprise.

"Yup."

"I was looking for the store for half an hour. There was plenty of folks but no one to ask. Just when I need you, you're not there. What were you doing for so long with that friend of yours?"

"She was playing for me," I say. "She's a composer. She's in the same classes I am."

"We were supposed to be hanging curtains."

"We can hang them right now."

"Now, so late at night?" Mom says. "Besides, they ain't even ironed."

"I can iron them."

"No, I'll iron 'em. You got yourself some homework to do." Mom looks around and listens. "Why is it so quiet?" she asks. Not even a second passes before we hear Zenus's cry from the other room. Mom puts the cigarette in the ashtray and walks out of the kitchen.

THE WHOLE DAY went by just like that. The girls got a lot of sleep and then they went wild until ten P.M. Dad came back half an hour later, when Mom was already asleep. He was buzzed, but not too much. I made him some supper and he went to sleep. Everyone's asleep except for me.

I'm lying in the bathtub in warm water and reveling in it. Only my nose, lips and eyes stick out of the water. I hear some faraway underwater noises. Someone's talking to someone else, someone's yelling something, but I can't hear what.

It's so strange.

When I close my eyes, I can remember what everyone in my new class looks like. I can see Klaudia, Magda and our homeroom teacher quite clearly. I can see Eva Bogdaj too, quite vividly, her hair, her black eyes, her beautiful face, and how she smiles. I even see the tiny star glued to the fingernail of her little finger . . .

But I can't see Kasia.

When I try to see Kasia, everything blurs in front of my eyes.

Is she taller than me, or shorter?

What color are her eyes? And what about her voice?

I don't know, I don't remember anything. All I can see is a shining light in the darkness.

I hear the music, which plays on and on.

It always plays the same thing. It says something, but you can't tell what.

"I tell you, I tell you, I tell you," the music says.

"What," I ask, "what are you telling me?"

And it says back, "I tell you, I tell you, I tell you . . ."

"Kasia, will you ever forgive me?" I ask.

"Forgive you for what?"

"I thought you were a thief."

"You should be forgiving me, because it's my fault. I'm never going to steal anything with you. You are so good and I am so evil."

"No, you're not evil at all. You're the best in the whole world."

"No, I am evil. All the world's evil is in me. You'll find that out some day."

It's not true, not true . . .

Underwater words are drowned by underwater music. It gets louder and louder. It's always the same and always different. I see a smile, yet I don't see it, blinded by the light. That smile is one of both pain and despair. And always the same music, although always different.

It swims straight at me and says, "I tell you, I tell you, I tell you . . ." Why is it this way? Why am I crying? And it says to me, "I tell you, I tell you, I tell you, I tell you, I tell you, I tell you . . ."

Chapter Two

I'M ALREADY AT school by twenty-five to eight. The only other person there is this large girl everyone calls Nag. She's sitting at her desk writing in her notebook. She must be doing her homework. So I pull out my book and notebook too.

But I can't concentrate. I get up and walk to the window. I look out. You can see the entrance to school from here. More and more kids are out in the school yard; there's a long shadow behind each one because the sun is low. Ten minutes pass and no sign of Kasia. Just noise, getting louder. So many kids swarming around.

"Whew, I got it done," I hear a voice next to me say. I look and Nag is standing beside me. She sits on the windowsill and says, "I wanted to do my homework yesterday, but it was impossible. My dad's name is Vacek. Get it?" She smiles and winks at me. I also smile, a little unsure, since I don't understand.

"It was his name day. They were rowdy until four o'clock," she says. "I was already asleep. Suddenly I wake up and some guy's sitting by me and holding me by my boob. He smells like a brewery . . . I don't say a word, I pretend I'm asleep. He slides his hand and grabs my pussy. It turns out to be a friend of Uncle Romek. Do you smell it?"

Nag blows at me.

"No," I say.

"Guess what it is."

"I don't know."

"Wine," she says. "I went to the bathroom this morning and there was a bottle there. It was still half-full, so I drank it. It was super-sweet."

You can hear a *vroom-vroom*. I look down.

Two motorcycles drive up to school. Eva Bogdaj is sitting on the big black one. The other one is smaller and multicolored. Klaudia and Magda get off of it.

"Oh," Nag says. "The princesses from Szczawno have arrived."

All three take their book bags and enter the building. When I see them, something weird happens to me. I have trouble breathing. I walk away from the window. The classroom is already full of guys and girls. I'm gonna wait for Kasia downstairs by the coatroom. I run downstairs and Klaudia and Magda walk toward me. I feel my heart pounding.

"Hi," I say quietly. I hear them laughing behind me. They're saying something among themselves; they must be laughing at me. What did I do to them? Klaudia likes me the least. Maybe it's because I sat in Bogusia's place who's in the hospital. But the gym teacher told me to sit there.

They're so dressed up, different from yesterday. Eva especially. She's wearing a black leather jacket and a skirt. And she has such cool shoes. She shines all over. I've never seen such a beautiful girl in my life. I'm sure she'll become a model or an actress.

I'm also dressed differently from yesterday. I have on a white pleated skirt that comes to just above my knees, a white blouse and white tights. I was keeping the white tights in my dresser for the last day of school in case it was cold, but oh well, I already put them on today. I also have on a black sweater. I stole it from my dad. It's loose and looks like the sweater Eva wore yesterday. The only difference is it's not a crewneck but a V-neck. I was up until one A.M. thinking about how I should dress today. I quietly took all my clothes out of the closet and tried them on. I only have a few things these days because lately I've been growing a lot. I looked at my reflection in the kitchen window. At night it reflects almost as well as a mirror. And I twisted a single pin curl. The curl turned out so-so, but I pinned it with a bobby pin and you can barely see it, just a little bit. And the dress I wore yesterday I'll never wear again, maybe just when I'm cleaning. I don't understand how I could have ever liked it.

It's two minutes to eight and still no sign of Kasia. Maybe she's not going to come today at all. I thought I'd be going back to class with her, but unfortunately, I'll have to go back alone.

I enter, and look . . . Eva Bogdaj, Klaudia and Magda are looking at my Polish notebook and are laughing like crazy. Why did I leave it in plain view? I'm standing by the doors waiting for them to put it back. Klaudia notices me; she whispers something to Eva. I take my seat. Magda places the notebook in front of me.

"We're admiring the color of your pen," she chirps with exaggerated praise. "Truly beautiful."

"It's ordinary," I say, and try to smile, but somehow it doesn't come out right.

"Oh, it's not so ordinary at all," Eva says. "It's as wild as the eyes of a homosexual lover at night with a full moon."

Magda giggles and adds, "Like Queen Jadwiga's dress after taking her corpse out of the coffin."

"Like an alcoholic's tongue when he's loaded on rum," Klaudia says with a sour smile. Suddenly she sticks out her tongue and hiccups. That gives Eva and Magda the shivers.

I take my pen out of my book bag. I have to do something with it, only what? I could click it. I click it, and at that moment I get over it. "I didn't know I had such a famous pen."

"Oh," Eva says, and raises her brow.

"Oh," Magda says.

"Famous squamous ignoramus," Klaudia says slowly. She holds her nose with her fingers. "Famous Seamus stinking squamous freaking wreaking ignoramus."

Magda starts laughing. Eva looks at me and waits. What am I going to say to Klaudia? I know she's waiting, but I don't know what to say back. They're looking at me like I'm a fish in a tank.

I'm saved by the bell. Kasia Bogdanska enters the class just as the bell rings. Oh God, what great hair she's got. There is so much of it! She's braided a tiny braid to the side and tied it with a blue ribbon. It looks great.

She smiles and comes up to me. She leans over and kisses me on the cheek.

"Hey, sweetie," she says. "You look great. Take your books and go to my desk."

I take my book bag, my book and my notebook and follow Kasia. I turn around to get my pen. I see their astonished looks.

I come up to Kasia's desk.

"Lily," Kasia says sweetly to the girl sitting there. "Be an angel and go to Klaudia."

"Why?" Lily asks. She's surprised, a little off-guard and starting to get angry.

"Because I'm asking you politely. Mongoose and I have something important to talk about. Do I have to say it twice?"

"As you wish," Lily says, offended. She takes her bag, gathers the stuff from the desk and leaves. She sits by Klaudia and immediately begins to whisper to her.

Eva Bogdaj looks at me from afar. There is something strange in her eyes, like she's angry, but no, it's not anger, it's something else—very strange.

I turn my head as Kasia takes me by the hand.

"I don't know whether I should," she says, "because it was supposed to be a surprise, but I think I'll tell you because if I don't, something horrible is going to happen to my tongue. Imagine"—she snaps her fingers—"yesterday I wrote a fantastic, brilliant, almost unimaginable piece of music, even better than halvah. I call this little miracle, listen . . . 'Moods of My Mongoose.' It's about your faces and about the way you make them. Do you like the title?"

"Uh-huh," I answer.

"It starts with bells," Kasia says, her face aglow. She spreads her fingers, starts moving them, closes her eyes, nods her head and smiles wonderfully.

I know she hears it now, everything she composed. From Eva and

Klaudia's desks you can hear giggles. They're probably laughing at Kasia, at the expression on her face, and they're laughing at me for having found such a crazy friend. Oh well, I don't care. I keep on smiling. I'm only worried because Mom asked me to come straight home after school. We need to hang curtains and in general there's a ton of work, but I'm going to go to Kasia's after school to listen to her composition. I'll get home late again and Mom's gonna yell at me. And she'll be right. Maybe it won't take Kasia long to play it, maybe just an hour, then I'll tell Mom we had seven classes.

Kasia opens her eyes; they're undeniably green.

"You'll hear it for yourself," she says. "I added the flute part in the morning. I only slept four hours."

"Gosh."

"Don't be worried. Once I didn't sleep for three days and three nights and nothing happened. You know, your faces are brilliant, better than wild berries with whipped cream. Mmm, does that sound good?"

"It sure does," I say, the taste of berries in my mouth. Kasia smiles.

"This face is even sweeter," she says. "That might have been the princess of your faces. If it were possible to eat princesses, I would have. I'll have to buy myself a muzzle."

I feel embarrassed. I lower my eyes, feeling a blush coming to my cheeks. I always feel them coming on. Because blood pulses in them. I force my lowered eyelids open.

I see Kasia's face in front of me.

A wonderful living sculpture.

In the morning, when I was walking to school, I was even thinking that I might have dreamed Kasia up, that really she wasn't there, that she was just a beautiful dream that had ended. But no. Kasia exists. She's sitting by me and looks at me and I look at her and try to memorize her face so I'll never forget it.

Her eyes are very round, with big circles under them. It's because she slept so little. Is she pretty? I don't know, I don't know. She's simply marvelous. She has a scar on her cheek, thin and pink. Almost an inch long. It must have hurt her, oh gosh. I also have a scar like that, but on my knee, from the time I scraped it on a nail.

Kasia touches her cheek and says, "Once when I was young, I decided to iron my face. I got only part way. Do you want to touch it?"

"Yes," I reply. I stretch my arm and gently touch Kasia's scar. Suddenly it gets awfully quiet in the room. The door slams, and right after: "Good morrrrning!" A whole chorus. The Polish teacher has come in.

"Good morning, eighth graders," she says. Clomping her heels, she walks up to her desk. She straightens her skirt and sits down. She's completely gray, but looks young. She's wearing a white blouse and a ladybug brooch. She looks around the class with a smile.

"Why is it so quiet here?" she asks. "Don't worry, dictation isn't for another week."

And the class says, "Woohoooo!"

The teacher raises her hand. It's quiet again.

"I hope we don't burst out laughing," Kasia whispers in my ear and immediately covers her mouth. Something is beginning to happen, something in me is about to burst out laughing. I can't hold it now. Holy Mother, help!

I burst out laughing, like a bang, a roar in the overwhelming silence. Although right away my fear flies in and locks the laughter in a cage, it's too late, I've already laughed out loud, everyone's already heard me, and now they're looking at me.

"Who's laughing?" the teacher asks. I get up, lowering my head. I feel stupid. Something starts swirling in my ears, like I've fallen into a seashell.

"Why did you laugh?" the teacher asks. What shall I tell her? I feel like crying. I don't know what to do. I'm about to cry any minute now.

Suddenly I hear the quietest whisper: "Tell her you were happy." It's Kasia. I raise my head.

"Because I felt happy," I say, and looking at the teacher a bit dumbstruck, I smile. Whatever will be will be. Oh well. Wait a minute, I see a smile on the teacher's lips.

"That's very logical," she says. "How did such a logical girl find herself in this class? I'm afraid we don't know each other."

"My name is Maria Kawczak. I've only been here since yesterday. I only came to Walbrzych with my parents, brothers and sisters the day before yesterday."

"Do you have a lot of brothers and sisters?" the teacher asks.

"A little less than a hundred," I say, "and a little more than three."

"My guess is you have four," the teacher says.

I nod my head. "That's right."

"Where did you come from?"

"From Jawiszow," I say. "It's a tiny settlement southwest of Walbrzych. Before that I was in Paris, where I got a terribly unfashionable dress. Fashionable, unfashionable . . . those are such relative notions . . . completely unfashionable."

Oh my God, what am I blabbing about? Who's blabbing through me? Everyone's staring at me. I think I've gone crazy.

"That's interesting," the teacher says. "I know Jawiszow. I was there once when I went to visit the Dwarf Rocks, which aren't too far from there. I just had to see something with such a great name. What was your grade in Polish?"

"May I lie?" I ask.

"Go ahead."

"I got an A."

"And what's the truth?"

"The truth is, a B," I answer. "But I always dreamed of getting an A."

"Let's see," the teacher says. "Maybe I can help you realize that dream. Tell me one more thing. What have you read lately?"

What have I read? What have I read? And then in my head I hear the quietest whisper, like it's Kasia's: "Pascal's *Pensées* . . ."

"Pascal's *Pensées*," I say. The teacher whistles at that.

"I'll give you your first A for courage," she says. "If there are any more to come, they will have to be for assigned reading and grammar. You may sit down."

I sit down. Kasia smiles at me. Thanks to her, I was bold in front of the teacher and the whole class. Thanks to her, something in me snapped and gave me courage. From now on I'll be like that forever. Brave and smiling.

Kasia gently raises her brow like she knows what I'm thinking.

And what if she does know all my thoughts—each and every one of them? Even those which . . . Some are bad. For example . . . Yuk, I'm not going to think about that.

Suddenly I feel like a whole swarm of bad thoughts has flown into my head.

Kazio Kaminski's peeing in the currant bushes. I'm looking at him and see it all. He's also looking at me and sees that I'm seeing it and doesn't even do anything. And I don't do anything either, except keep looking . . .

Zenus is screaming nonstop and I'm standing in front of him with a pillow. And I swear I'm gonna choke him if he doesn't stop . . .

Or else . . . I'm touching myself down there and I'm all sweaty. I don't want to touch myself, but I keep touching myself and touching myself . . .

I'm nothing but a repulsive pig. Why don't I just die? Kill me, Kasia—I don't deserve to be your friend and adopted sister.

But Kasia isn't even looking at me. She's playing with her pen, staring out the window. She must be thinking about her compositions. How great it must be to constantly think about compositions, about music. I don't have anything like that to think about all the time. I just live and think about whatever I'm thinking about, and that's it. The only people who focus on one thing all the time are great people like scholars and inventors . . . Or else if you're a mommy and you have a little baby, then you'll also be thinking about only one thing. And when you get spanked, you think about it until the pain goes away. Or when someone says something bad . . . or something good, then you think about it for a while.

When not too long ago for the first time in my life I had my womanly cycle, I was thinking and thinking, Why is it that this blood needs to flow out of me for so long? That it could have been alive but has to die every month. It's like a river that flows and flows, but there are no fishes in it because it's the river of blood that flows through all the women in the world.

I kept thinking about it and thinking about it, but when it ended the day before yesterday, I forgot all about it.

I'm sitting at my desk thinking about something. What was it? I forgot. It's already the third class of this beautiful day, a drawing lesson. Second period was math—just like at my previous school, sad and boring. The teacher is tiny, completely bald, and is always saying, "Let's say."

We're drawing a hawk. Our drawing teacher brought it from the zoology lab. It's real, only dead and stuffed. I'm drawing its beak. Curvy and sharp. To have a beak like that and see it in front of your eyes all the time and not be able to turn away from it . . . that's terrible.

I glance at Kasia. She's drawing a hawk in flight. It's a bit strange, but pretty. Mine is sad and angry, and hers simply flies.

Kasia's wonderful. During the breaks we walk through the hallways and talk. I told her about the twins, about Zenus and about Tadzio. She really wants to meet them. I also want them to meet her. The girls will be very embarrassed at first, but then they'll get used to it. I got used to Kasia right away. Well, maybe not exactly.

Sometimes Kasia looks at me like she's someone different, someone I don't know at all. Like she's a grown-up and only pretends to be a fifteen-year-old girl. But in general it's wonderful to sit with her at the same desk, to walk along the hallways, to talk with her and to be silent together. And just think . . . Yesterday morning we didn't even know each other, and today we're together talking and laughing.

Those girls I was sitting with yesterday—Klaudia, Magda and, of course, Eva Bogdaj—also walk around together talking and laughing, but it seems a little phony to me. Especially Eva. She's so pretty, walks so beautifully and smiles so nicely, but she does everything like she's acting in a play, with a lot of people looking at her. Whenever she walks by with that flock of hers, I get the chills. She hates me, I can feel it. I don't know why it's that way or how I know it, but I do.

What did I ever do to her?

With Klaudia it's different. She's simply repulsed by me. I don't know why, but I understand her. Take my godfather, for instance . . . he has really bad breath. Whenever he kisses me hello, his breath makes me feel faint. And though he's a very nice guy and always gives us chocolate, I don't like it when he comes from Szczecin. So I know what it's like to be repulsed by somebody. I'm a little repulsed by Klaudia too. She always has a sour grimace on her face and sniffles all the time. Even though she's pretty, she's not pretty.

"Has anyone finished drawing?" the drawing teacher asks.

I have. I raise my hand and get up. "Me!"

"Come and show us," the teacher says. So I grab my drawing and run up to her, but suddenly—boom!—I'm lying on the floor and see Ziebinski, the fatso, pulling his leg back. Everyone laughs and gets up to see what made such a splat. It was me. I'm the last to stand, since I'm getting up off the floor. My elbow hurts.

"What happened?" the teacher asks.

"Nothing," I say. "I tripped."

"Poor thing," the teacher says sweetly. I bring her the drawing. It's ripped because I was holding it with both hands when I fell down and neither of them let go. The teacher straightens it out.

"Don't worry," she says. "It's very pretty—you get an A."

She takes her pencil and puts an A in the corner of the drawing. Meanwhile, Kasia has walked up to Ziebinski and says, "Why did you trip her?"

"What business is that of yours?" Ziebinski asks. "Anyway, what are you—transparent? Get out of the way. You're blocking the model."

He moves Kasia aside with his hand and at that moment Kasia slaps him in the face. What a smack. Ziebinski jumps from his desk in order to hit her back when—boom! That's horrible. Kasia hits him another time; this time with a fist right in the middle of the face. In the nose.

Ziebinski falls backward onto Kawczak. The girl sitting in front of them starts shrieking in horror.

"He got blood on me!" she yells, and wipes the blood off her face. It's Ziebinski's blood, which has splashed all the way from his nose. The drawing teacher grows pale and runs out of the class. Ziebinski lies down, sobbing. There's blood coming out of his nose. Kasia leans over him; pulling roughly on his clothes, she shouts, "Why did you trip her?!"

"Because Magda told me to," Ziebinski mumbles. Kasia lets go of him and turns around. Just then I see her face. If I didn't know it was her, I wouldn't have recognized her. I want to tell her to calm down, but somehow I can't move. I'm standing like I'm paralyzed, and my mouth is dry.

Kasia makes a fist and walks up to Magda.

"Is it true?" she asks. "Did you tell him to do it?"

Magda is no longer sitting at her desk. She's backing up toward the door.

"Not at all, he's lying," she says, and flees the classroom. Ziebinski groans and asks someone to give him a handkerchief, but Kawczak doesn't have one and no one else wants to give him one. They're all afraid he's going to stain it with blood. Kasia pulls out her handkerchief and throws it to Ziebinski. By now she's calm, yet really serious. She goes back to her desk, sits down and leans over her drawing. She's the only one in the classroom who's doing any drawing.

The door opens.

Mrs. Turska, our homeroom teacher, enters with the drawing teacher. Magda slips in behind them, terrified. "Quick, get him to the nurse," the homeroom teacher says, seeing what's happened to Ziebinski. Kawczak and Magda take him to the door. He's crying and dripping with blood. They leave.

"Kasia," Mrs. Turska says. "Could you tell me why you hit him?"

Kasia lifts her head up from her drawing. She gets up and quietly says, "I just hit him."

"But why?"

"He tripped Maria Kawczak," one of the girls says.

"That's no reason to beat him up so mercilessly," the homeroom teacher says. "Maria could have complained to Ms. Szot."

Kasia interrupts her: "And Ms. Szot would have said, 'Oh, Ziebinski, Ziebinski, you know it isn't right, don't do it again.' And that way he would never trip anyone. I know the type."

"You could have injured him."

"That's why I hit him."

"So that's how justice looks according to you?" Mrs. Turska calmly asks, although you can tell she's getting upset.

"Not only does it look that way," Kasia replies. "It is justice."

"Maybe according to the laws of the jungle."

Kasia nods her head. "That's right."

"We are not in the jungle. We are at school."

Kasia laughs. "It's only a matter of words. You could even call wisdom stupidity, and stupidity wisdom. I imagine no one would see the difference."

"We're not going to talk this way," the teacher says.

"Oh, I'm sure you know other ways," Kasia says ironically. "Human intelligence is endless."

"I'd appreciate it if you saved your jokes for another occasion," the homeroom teacher says.

"My pleasure," Kasia replies. "I already have. Any other questions? If not, I'd like to finish my drawing."

"Kasia!" the drawing teacher says indignantly. "How can you talk like this?"

"I talk the way I talk!" Kasia says loudly. She takes her drawing, crumples it into a ball and throws it on the floor. She tosses her books and notebooks into her book bag, and raising her voice even louder, she says, "Why should I care about any of this? What's all this 'Kasia, Kasia'? Get the fuck out of here, all of you!"

She takes her book bag, passing by us, since all three of us—Mrs. Turska, Ms. Szot and I—are standing by the table. She stops by the hawk, pointing at it with her finger.

"Here it is," she says. "Here's your example. It's standing politely right where it's been put. Only problem is, it has a bird brain and it's stuffed. I promise you ladies that I won't let myself get stuffed. By *anyone*. Good-bye."

She leaves, slamming the door. The teachers stand stupefied. Me too. It's quiet in the classroom.

"She's gone way too far," the homeroom teacher says. "I'll have to have a talk with her mother."

"I think the whole thing's just scandalous," Eva Bogdaj interjects. "She ought to be placed in some kind of an institution before she kills us all. That'd be nothing to her!"

"Eva, sit down," Mrs. Turska says.

"Sure I'll sit, but could you tell me how it's possible for her to come and go whenever she wants?! Is Katarzyna Bogdanska a sacred cow? What is this—India? As far as I know, her grade for conduct hasn't even been lowered. You said a moment ago that school isn't a jungle. And yet, she seems to have different rights than we do. Or maybe they're the same. If that's the case, can we skip school too?"

Mrs. Turska shrugs her shoulders and walks out.

"If she's crazy, then we should place her in the mental ward," Eva finishes. She sits down and begins to whisper with Klaudia.

"Go back to your seat," Ms. Szot says to me. "And be quiet. You have only ten minutes left to finish your drawings."

I take my hawk and go back to my desk. Everything happened because of me. I should have calmed Kasia down beforehand. I'm a coward and a dork. I could have told her that Ziebinski didn't trip me.

But how was I supposed to know it would end this way? She was so calm and spoke so quietly. And this Ziebinski, he's so fat and strong. She wasn't afraid of him at all. She just hit him. So hard it went *smack*. He started crying like a little baby. I'd never be able to hit anyone, even if I was angry. I never hit anyone, though I've been hit more than once. We were so happy, it was so much fun to draw.

Why did I jump up with that drawing? If I'd just sat there and kept drawing, Ziebinski wouldn't have tripped me, I'd be sitting here with Kasia, and everything would be fine. I can't believe Magda told him to trip me. Why would she do that? I've never done anything to her.

I'M ON MY way home from school and still thinking about it. I thought Eva hated me. But it's Kasia she hates, and she only hates me because I'm friends with Kasia. She was saying awful things about her . . . How you would have to hate someone to say such things about them.

Kawczak is following me around. He's walking beside me and says, "Maybe we're cousins and don't know it."

"Maybe," I say.

"Supposedly there are a few Kawczaks in the world. But who knows, maybe . . ."

I stop.

"What do you think?" I ask. "Is it possible that Magda told Ziebinski to trip me?"

"It's possible," Kawczak replies. "Because he has a crush on her. But probably not a big one, because he told on her right away."

"Maybe he was only lying."

"Ziebinski doesn't usually lie," Kawczak says after thinking about it. "Although he likes to lie sometimes. You never know with him. Supposedly he's my pal, but one time when the math teacher asked who farted, he blamed me, even though he was the one that did it. He deserved it. Bogdanska gave him a good licking. It's been a while since someone punched him like that." Kawczak laughs. "And we got a bit of entertainment. He lost about five liters of blood."

"What are you talking about?" I ask. "Five liters is all the blood a person has. If that much came out, he'd be dead already."

"Someone so fat and so red in the face must have at least ten liters. He must have half of it left. Listen, have you ever really been to Paris?"

"I have," I say. "What of it?"

"Because, you know, we're in Paris now."

"What do you mean?"

Kawczak points to the sidewalk under our feet.

"The place we are standing right now, this neighborhood, is called Paris," he says. "It says so on any map. Bye, cousin. I'm taking off."

So he takes off. I wanted to ask him something, but he pulled the wool over my eyes with this Paris thing and I forgot. Strange thoughts come into my head. Because this is how it is: yesterday I bumped into Kawczak and I almost knocked out his tooth. Today Kasia smashed Ziebinski's nose. Ziebinski and Kawczak sit at the same desk, and Kasia and I sit at the same desk too. But when I bumped into Kawczak, I didn't know I'd be sitting with Kasia, I didn't even know her. But if we hadn't been sitting together today, then Ziebinski would never have gotten punched.

There were two girls in my class that I liked right away. Kasia and Eva. And it turned out that their last names are so similar. Bogdanska and Bogdaj. Strange. As if everything went in pairs. Because Kawczak has the same last name as me . . .

I walk along not knowing what to do. Maybe Kasia doesn't want me to come to her place. Maybe she's holding a grudge. Maybe I should have taken my book bag then and run out of the class after her. But it would have been impossible. I can't do stuff like that. I've never skipped a day of school in my life. Even when I was sick, I never told Mom and I went to school. Come hell or high water, I would go. And it's not that I like school that much. Simply: when you gotta, you gotta.

The day started so beautifully and was so great until third period. And then . . . Kasia went away and I was quiet again and afraid of everything. When I'm with Kasia, I feel like I'm a different person. Older, wiser, more cheerful. Normally I'm not so cheerful. I never laugh as much as when I'm with Kasia. With her, I even know how to talk with adults, for instance with Ms. Trauman, the Polish teacher. Normally I don't even know how to talk with Mom very well. As for Dad, I hardly talk to him at all. I'm afraid of adults.

What a nice city Walbrzych is. Especially here, around the marketplace. Some of the brownstones are really dirty and gray, but still they're beautiful. Like they are enchanted. And the streets are so narrow and steep. In the winter you can go sledding. I feel like I'm reading a fairy tale.

And there are all kinds of stores here. And so many people, each one going their own way, with their own thing to take care of. Like ants. I really like looking at anthills. I could spend hours standing in front of an anthill, watching them move around. Only thing is, as soon as they start climbing up your legs, you have to run away.

I also like molehills. I like to think about all those underground corridors. Once I found a tiny mole. He was so sweet. I petted him and put him on the molehill so his mommy could find him. He was moving his head in such a funny way. The next day I came back and he was still lying there, dead. My mom told me he died because of me. Because I petted him and caressed him, and that's why his mom was afraid to come up to him, because she smelled a human scent. But I didn't know you couldn't do that. That's the way it is sometimes. You can hurt someone unintentionally.

Oh, I'm already at Kasia's doorway.

Here are the doors I stood behind yesterday, when I was so terribly afraid. That was so stupid of me. I walk up the stairs and remember how I thought Kasia was a Gypsy. And here is the place she pretended she wanted to tell my fortune. I stand there, stretching out my hand, and stick it into the sunbeam falling through the skylight. I also remember how Kasia told me I could pay her with a little egg for her fortune-telling.

I ring the doorbell. Once, and then again. I wait, I wait . . . nothing. Maybe she's not home. Maybe she's in a café eating ice cream. Maybe she was sitting by the fountain and I wasn't looking. I'll ring the bell one last time and then I'm going to go. I ring the bell. I put my ear to the door. Silence. If she is playing, she won't be able to hear me ring the bell.

Okay, this is really the last time I'm going to ring it. There's a noise. The door opens. Kasia is standing in the doorway.

"Come on in, quick," she says, and runs back in. So I walk in, close the door and lock it. Oh no, I didn't wipe my shoes off. But it was dry outside. I set my book bag on a dresser and walk into the room behind the curtain.

It's really bright out today.

The curtains in the window are pulled apart and Kasia is standing by the synthe . . . sizer hitting the keyboard with her fingers, but you can't hear anything, no music, only the banging of her fingers on the keys. Oh yeah, that's because Kasia has headphones on and can hear everything.

Now she's taking them off, and turns on a tape recorder. Right next to it there is another one just like it.

"I'll be done soon," she says to me. "Give me fifteen minutes."

She sits behind the table with the knobs and puts the headphones on. She turns both tape recorders on—they're the reel-to-reel kind—stops them and then rewinds the reels by hand. I'm standing next to her, watching what she's doing. The reels spin again.

"This isn't worth sh—" Kasia says. "One more time." Again she reverses the tape and again the reels start turning. Kasia smiles and nods her head. "Okay," she says. She glances at me. "I dubbed in a flute track at the beginning and I just came up with the idea of mixing it in as a second track at the end. That's right, I haven't told you anything about it. When I was waiting for you, I got it all on tape. We'll listen together. Is the fatso alive?"

"Yes," I say. "He's all right. Only his schnozz is swollen."

"I was a little afraid I broke his nose."

"You didn't," I say. "He felt it and said it's in one piece."

"Did anyone say anything about me after I left?"

"Not really, just Eva . . . but she didn't say much."

"Eva?" Kasia wonders. "What did she say?"

"That you often skip school, but that everyone else has to come, and is that justice?"

Kasia laughs.

"Look at that," she says. "Ms. Bogdaj, an egalitarian? Pretty amazing. And now plug your ears because I'm going to be banging."

She runs to the corner and pulls a sheet of shiny black plastic off something, drums of some kind. She goes back to the reel-to-reel tape recorder, turns it on, puts the headphones on and runs back to the drums.

"The percussion has to be live," she says to me loudly, "because the percussion in the computer is like a butterfly in a watchmaker's display case. And now quiet!" She sits motionless for a while and then suddenly starts beating a drum with the drumsticks. I'm standing still, afraid to move because Kasia is recording it with a microphone.

She's so talented. She can play anything. She's beating the drums so quickly. And now, slower and slower and slower. She needs to bang one more time and that's it. She runs over to the tape recorders, rewinds the tape and starts listening on the headphones.

"If you're bored," she says, "you should read some Pascal. You were bragging to Ms. Trauman, so now you should read. It's lying around on my desk somewhere."

I go over to the desk, I'm searching among the books. It's right here. It's spelled "Pascal." "BLAISE PASCAL." I open it and can't read anything.

I look at Kasia.

"It's not in Polish," I say. Kasia slips off her headphones.

"What are you saying?"

"It's not in Polish!"

"I'm sorry," she says. "I forgot. So find something else to read."

"And what if Ms. Trauman asks me tomorrow about this Pascal," I say. "What is it about?"

"Do you think I remember?" Kasia asks, motioning to me. "Show it to me."

I come up to her and hand her the book. She starts leafing through it.

"Oh," she says. "Here is something. When you read too fast or too slow, you can't understand anything. And check page sixty-nine. Two infinities, the middle. When you read too fast or too slow, you can't understand anything."

Kasia looks at me.

"Do you understand?" she asks.

I shrug my shoulders. "No."

"Well," Kasia says, "it's about the fact that a man must suffocate in the middle, because, unfortunately or fortunately, infinitudes are not for people. Got it?"

I sigh. "And that's what I should tell Ms. Trauman?"

"You could finish her off with something like that." Kasia laughs. "You might also add that 'you live alone and you die alone.'"

She hands me the book, puts on her headphones and begins to turn the knobs. I go back to the desk. A man has to suffocate in the middle, because, unfortunately or fortunately, infinitudes are not for people. You live alone and you die alone.

And it's true that if you read too slowly, you can't understand anything. When I was learning to read in the first grade, before I managed to put the letters of the third word together, I would forget the first.

I'm looking at that Pascal book. On the first page it says, "Paris."

It has to be in French. I pick up another book. When you look at it from the side, all the pages are red. I open it: they are white. There is this "Paris" again. You live alone and you die alone. Maybe if you're single?

This Paris just won't stop persecuting me. First Eva Bogdaj talked about it yesterday—that I must have come from Paris. Then Kawczak tells me that we are now in Paris. Now all these books from Paris. What was it I was thinking of asking Kawczak?

Oh, what a wonderful figurine, so small. I pick it up and put it right back down, and brush my hand off on my sweater. I've got the shivers, like I just picked up a black leech in my hand. Yuk, this is a little devil, terribly contorted. Yuk, yuk! I think Kasia is saying something to me.

I turn around. No, she's not talking to me. She's humming to herself, leaning over the table with the knobs. Kasia is home alone again, just like yesterday. I've never seen her mom or her dad. I'm curious to know what they look like and which one Kasia looks more like, because I look like my mom when she was young.

"Come over here quickly," Kasia says. I go up to her. Kasia moves a mike to my lips and says, "I need you to laugh, but loudly."

"I don't know," I say. "I never laughed into a microphone."

"Try."

"I'm not in the mood."

"Try to remember something funny."

Something funny . . . Let's see, can I come up with anything funny? One time my godfather brought me a mask. It was a mask of a monkey's face. Really funny. He put it on; it had an elastic band. He began to jump, hunched over like a monkey. He was waving his arms. Everyone was dying of laughter. Then Tadzio put it on and ran into the garden and we looked out the window.

Mrs. Kaminska was outside picking radishes. Tadzio leaped from the bushes and shouted, "Whoooo."

Mrs. Kaminska saw him and ran away. Then she said it was a miracle she didn't fall over and die when she saw this monster. Nobody wanted to believe her and we never told her. That was a long time ago.

"Ready?" Kasia asks.

"Yup," I say, and start laughing, but it's kind of sad and fake.

"Look at me," Kasia says. I look and she's making a really funny face, swaying her head in a goofy way. I burst out laughing, Kasia presses a button on the tape recorder, and immediately I'm not in the mood to laugh.

Kasia lisps in a high voice, "And now, ladieth and gentlemen, I am pleathed to announth Mth. Mafter, a spethialitht in laughter." She makes googly eyes at me. And I'm laughing out loud, laughing and laughing. Kasia is recording . . . Suddenly, the doorbell rings. Kasia looks at her watch.

"That must be Miss Zenobia," she says. "I wonder if she forgot the keys?"

The doorbell rings again. Kasia runs to open the door. I hear her opening the door. Someone asks, "Hello, Kasia, is your mom in?" The voice sounds familiar.

"I'm sorry," Kasia answers. "Mom is going to be home late in the evening."

"Aren't you going to invite me in?" the same voice asks, only now I recognize it. It's Mrs. Turska, our homeroom teacher.

"Of course, come on in," Kasia says.

I hear the door slam and Mrs. Turska's voice: "Can we talk calmly for a while?"

"With pleasure," Kasia replies. But what's going to happen when Mrs. Turska sees me here? She'll probably ask me to leave, but it's been so nice here. I'm not gonna leave. I hide behind the curtain by the window and hear them come into the room. Jeez, what have I done? Kasia is going to call for me and I'll feel so stupid when I come out from behind the curtain. I know, I'll pretend we were playing hide-and-seek.

I stand there barely breathing.

"So this is your kingdom," goes the teacher's voice.

Then I hear Kasia laugh and say, "If we were going to call it anything, I'd call it a small, ruined principality. Would you like some coffee? Or maybe tea?"

"You know," the teacher says, "I could go for a cup of coffee."

"I'll get it," Kasia says, and I hear her leave. Now I hear the teacher walking around the room.

What if she comes over to the window?

I hear her cough. Far away from me. I look down to check

whether my feet are sticking out from under the curtain, but it's long and it's resting on the carpet.

I hear Kasia's footsteps and a quiet rattling.

"Back so fast?" the teacher asks.

"The coffee's from a thermos," Kasia replies. "Is that okay?"

"Of course," the teacher says. I hope Kasia figures it out and doesn't look for me. I look off to the side. In the windowpane I can see Kasia's and Mrs. Turska's reflections. Unclearly, though, because you can see other houses and windows through the windowpane.

I see Kasia putting down the tray on the table next to the sofa. "Help yourself," she says sweetly. Mrs. Turska sits down, as does Kasia. She offers the sugar bowl to the teacher. Mrs. Turska takes some sugar and stirs it with a spoon. She moves the sugar bowl toward Kasia.

"No thanks, I don't take sugar," Kasia says. The teacher lifts the cup to her lips and takes a sip. I look . . . a chimney sweep is walking on the roof of one of the other houses. I can't touch the buckle of my shoe, because if I did, they'd know I was hiding.

"It's very pleasant here," the teacher says.

"Thank you," Kasia says, sighing loudly.

The teacher sighs too. The two of them start laughing.

"That's the thing with serious conversations, they're hard to start," Kasia says.

"Maybe I'll start this way. Kasia, I really like you. And if I say something unpleasant, it's only for your own good."

"I like you too," Kasia says. "You're such a nice, even-tempered, elegant woman. And I, as you see, am only a small, ill-tempered, messed-up girl who really regrets having caused trouble. I place my symbolic hand on my symbolic heart and apologize deeply."

The teacher smiles. "You put it so beautifully."

And Kasia: "I keep promising myself I'm going to stop messing with reality, but then I forget about it."

"Yes, I know it's difficult," the teacher says. "I have the same problem too every now and then. You would like to say everything, but oh well, you're an adult and you have to live with people."

"I promise I'm going to train myself," Kasia says. "I'm gonna walk around with a bottle of water. If I'm about to flip, I'll take a little sip and hold it in my mouth until my tongue cools off."

Again they are laughing. They're talking to each other so nicely. All in all, our homeroom teacher is really neat.

"Because you see, Kasia, I'm really worried about you," the teacher says. "I remember when you were such a happy child—"

"Oh yeah," Kasia interrupts her. "I was happy and upbeat like the girls in the Soviet Union."

"Don't mock me, Kasia. Whenever I used to come to your place for a lesson, I was always happy to see your sunny face."

"Oh well," Kasia says. "Supposedly I'm going through adolescence. It's the period when all kinds of strange questions fly into my childish head from all directions, and there's no ready answer to most of them."

'That's true," the teacher says. "But I promise, I know it from my own experience, that the time will come when you'll find answers to all these questions."

"I wouldn't be so sure," Kasia replies.

"You should simply live and rejoice in everything that each day brings you."

"I rejoice, but in my own way."

"Oh, I know, you're interested in music, you have talent. I really envy you. It's wonderful to have talent. It's a great gift."

"I would rather say that it's terrible to have talent."

"I don't understand. Why?"

"I don't like that word, it's very superficial, but let's say it's called talent. Do you know what it is? It's a live, oozing wound that you have to constantly scratch and scratch."

"Why scratch?" Mrs. Turska wonders.

"Because otherwise it will heal."

"You know, I don't know much about it. I teach biology. But for my modest brain, if I had talent, I would be very, very happy. To be able to do something that so few people can do . . ."

"You're absolutely right," Kasia says in a strange tone of voice. "It's a great pleasure to be on the side of the minority. So you see I'm still really childish, and make a mountain out of a molehill." Kasia smiles. "It's repulsive to brag of one's suffering. I disgust myself."

"Don't say that. You're a wonderful, wise girl, and with your intelligence you'll outgrow your peers. You'll be famous someday, I'm sure of it. Only you have to understand, dear, there's a time for everything. Now you're in elementary school. You have high school and college ahead of you. For a few years you're going to have to reconcile school and your extracurricular interests. We forgive you a lot as it is. I counted that out of a hundred and ninety-two days since the beginning of the school year, you've skipped eighty-seven, nearly half. And you only brought a doctor's note once."

"It would have been ridiculous. You know where my mom works. I know all her colleagues and all her friends."

"I understand your intentions, Kasia, but those are unexcused absences. I really ought to lower your conduct grade. I fight with the principal over you at every conference."

"Am I a bad student? Have I ever once even gotten an F?"

"What's that got to do with anything? Please understand, we have our own statistics. Not to mention the fact that you present a bad example to other students."

"I know, you told me already."

"So you see?" the teacher says. "Kasia, promise me you'll come to school every day until the end of the school year. It's only two months."

"I promise. Please don't worry about me. I can take a C for conduct."

"Believe me, Kasia, with a C in conduct, you'll have serious trouble getting into prep school. No one likes truants. I know what I'm talking about."

"They won't need to like me. I'm not going to any prep school. Mom promised me she's not gonna bother me about it. Elementary school is required—okay, I'll finish it because I don't like police. But that'll be the end of my education."

"Kasia, quit joking," the teacher says.

"I'm completely serious."

"And what are you going to do without high school?"

"Let high school worry what it will do without me," Kasia responds.

"No, no, Kasia." The teacher raises her voice. "You've got to be kidding. Don't you want to acquire more thorough knowledge?"

"Oh yes, I really want to," Kasia says. "But I certainly won't find the knowledge I'm after in school."

"School provides the basis for all kinds of knowledge."

"Certainly. I've learned how to read and write. That's enough for me."

"That's a very childish point of view," the teacher says. "You can read a million wise books, but without a degree, not to mention a high school diploma, you'll be nobody to other people. Do you understand? Nobody!"

"I don't want to be somebody to other people," says Kasia. "I want to be somebody to myself."

"Tell me why every wise person has gone through formal education."

"How would I know? We should ask them about it. Still, to my childish mind, it seems there are far, far fewer wise people than there are university graduates."

The teacher begins to laugh. She stops. Sighs.

"Oh, Kasia, Kasia," she says. "One day you'll grow up and understand. Let's hope it won't be too late."

"For me, it's been too late for a while," Kasia says.

"Our discussion makes no sense. I say one thing, and you say another."

Kasia sighs. "I'm in complete agreement with you. But was I the one who started it?"

Now the teacher sighs.

"I'm tired," she says. "I really don't know how to talk to you . . . Someone has to explain a few things to you or you'll never make it. If I were your mother—"

"My mother is also very intelligent," Kasia says. "I assure you of that."

"You don't have to assure me." The teacher laughs. "And what does she say to you?"

"More or less the same thing. She got tired long ago and shrugged her shoulders at me."

"I'm not at all surprised. Tell me, was there a single person at any time who managed to convince you of anything?"

"I don't understand why anybody would have to convince me of anything," Kasia says. "Everyone has their own life and their own brain. Even their own fate, which you cannot foresee. To be honest about it, nobody knows what's good for them or what's bad. I often think about it. You do something wise and it comes out dumb . . . Take, for instance, humanity. M.A.'s by the billions, professors by the millions. And what has wise humanity, with its practical reason, done to the planet on which it lives? Do you want more examples?"

"You're right," the teacher says. "But we're not talking about ecology or philosophy. We're talking about you and school."

"Everything is ecology, everything is philosophy." Kasia raises her arms and stretches. "Great causes have their own small reasons. All of this makes me want to laugh, because there's no way out." Kasia laughs. "I'm curious, what would you do if I were to try to convince you of my way of thinking? Would that feel pleasant?"

"If you could put forth well-thought-out arguments," the teacher says, "then you could try."

"Well, in that case, could you answer this simple question for me?"

"Go ahead."

"Are you happy?" Kasia asks.

"Me? You know I am."

"You're lying. How can you be happy when you're repulsed by your own husband?"

Oh my God, what is Kasia talking about?

"Who told you that?" Mrs. Turska asks, raising her voice.

Kasia laughs quietly. "It's my secret. Let's say that I read it in your eyes. You got married because you were tired. Because you wanted to have a child, a family . . . Now you have them and you're not happy."

"You're being rude," the teacher says. "We probably should end this conversation."

"Just a second, let me tell you something else. You also hate your work. Working with children wears you out. Every day is torture to you. You can't tolerate the noise during breaks or the boredom of repeating the same thing for the thousandth time. Am I not right?"

"Kasia," the teacher says loudly. "Do you realize that you're behaving like the worst brute?"

"Call me a brute if you want," Kasia says. "But you, you're a liar. You're dishonest in the worst kind of way, because you, you're dishonest to yourself!"

Mrs. Turska gets up suddenly. "What is this 'you, you' business, you snotty girl!" she shouts, completely losing her temper. "What is this 'you, you'!"

"Maybe you're also gonna tell me that we're not on a first-name basis?" Kasia says. The teacher is about to hit her, but Kasia leaps nimbly away, grabs her by the hand and pushes her onto the sofa. Mrs. Turska sits vehemently. Behind the curtain I'm biting my fingers in nervousness.

"You sit down and listen, because I'm not done yet!" Kasia commands. "As you see, I'm stronger than you."

"You must be crazy," the teacher says, her voice breaking. "I'm going to scream!"

Kasia snaps her fingers.

"Be my guest," she says. "I'll gladly listen. This room is sound-proof; no one except me is going to hear you. And I'm mentally ill, I'm a nut, I can calmly kill you. So scream."

"Calm down, my child. Calm down, I'm asking you."

"You calm down."

"Do you know what you're doing?"

"I know," Kasia says, standing over the teacher. "We're having a little chat. First about me, and now about you."

"Kasia, I'm your biology teacher and your homeroom teacher. Let's not forget that."

"And you, you should try to forget about it for five minutes. Try to imagine that ten years have passed, that we're both adults and we're talking like friends."

"Okay, let it be, only calm down!"

"I'm perfectly calm," Kasia says, and sits down. She takes the coffee cup. "May I call you by your first name?"

"All right, go ahead. My name is Anna."

"So listen, Anna, sweetie," Kasia says sweetly, laughing quietly. The teacher sighs.

"I must be crazy myself," she says.

"You were trying to convince me," Kasia says, "to form my life according to the accepted norm. Of course, you had my happiness and well-being in mind, is that right?"

"Yes, Kasia. I wanted to spare you a lot of disappointment. Black sheep do not have an easy life."

"How do you know what kind of lives black sheep have if you're not one of them? And what does the easy life mean? Do you know what happiness is? Happiness is being true to one's self, it's a harmony of internal demons. I wanted to tell you all this, but you got upset."

"Because you stuck your nose in my personal life."

"And what should I have stuck my nose in? Into sixteenth-century sociopolitical relations in Portugal? Should I have criticized your dress? It's a very nice dress, it's inoffensive to me. We were chatting about the means for a good life, for happiness, so to start with, I wanted to show you where the way of a white sheep leads one. Because you consider yourself a white sheep, is that right?"

"Go on," the teacher says quietly. "I'm paying close attention."

"First tell me, are you happy in your marriage?"

"The fact is, I'm not," Mrs. Turska replies. "You were indeed well informed. School also gets on my nerves. But what does this all amount to?"

"So why aren't you going to get the hell out of it?"

"Okay, let's say I grant you that. I leave my husband, my home, my work. Where would I go? Onto the street? Do you think I'm going to find happiness around the first corner?"

"So you're going to torture yourself like this for the rest of your life?"

"Probably. Or rather, certainly."

"I don't understand," Kasia says. "We have one life and our moral obligation is to live it according to our own inner nature. Or maybe you're a masochist?"

They look at each other in silence. And I'm spying on them in the windowpane. I feel a terrible scratch in my throat, but there's no way I can cough. The silence grows longer and finally the teacher says, "The moral obligation to live in happiness . . . quite an interestingly formulated postulate."

"I didn't use the word 'happiness,'" Kasia says. "I said 'living according to one's own nature.'"

"Ah, yes . . ." the teacher sighs. "When you're young, you have great plans for your future. Then life comes along and that's the way it is. You have to get up every day and do your thing . . ."

"Your thing?"

"You wouldn't understand it. Well, maybe someday . . . Even I, when I first started majoring in biology, I wanted to be a famous scientist, I wanted to discover new laws of nature . . ."

"Then what?"

"Then nothing. I barely passed my last exams. I had something else on my mind. I was madly in love. It turned out to be unrequited. I begged him, I was on my knees in front of him, but he left and I had nothing to live for. Look." Mrs. Turska pulls up the sleeve of her dress and shows Kasia something on her wrist. "If my friend had come back to the dormitory any later . . ."

Kasia takes her hand and holds it to her face. She kisses it.

"Oh, poor thing," she says quietly. The teacher brings Kasia toward her. They're sitting in silence, hugging, and I already can't stand it. God almighty in heaven, help me, do something so I'm able to cough, because I'm going to go mad any minute, it's scratching me so much. Oh, I wish Mrs. Turska would go, or thunder would strike.

A chimney sweep appears from behind the chimney on the roof of another house. Over there, he can cough as much as he wants. If only I could switch places with him. As long as I could cough, I could even fall off the roof later, I wouldn't care. I can't stand it any longer. I have to, I have to, I have to.

The teacher says quietly, "If not for Antek, if he didn't take care of me at that time, I would have done it again."

"Antek is your husband?" Kasia asks.

"Yes. He loves me very much, we have a beautiful son . . ."

"I'm a fool. Don't be angry with me. You know I'm nuts."

"I'm not angry. I like you a lot, Kasia. Once I was just like you. That's that, we've talked quite a bit. I'm going to go now."

They get up from the sofa.

Hurry up! I wish they would leave! I'm gonna start coughing soon and I'll be exposed.

"I'm sorry," Kasia says.

"Don't worry," Mrs Turska says, kissing Kasia on the cheek. "The most important thing is that you come to school every day and temper your tongue a little bit. Do you promise?"

"I promise," Kasia replies. They leave the room, I hear the bang of the front door. And it's strange, I don't want to cough at all. Kasia returns to the room.

"Mongoose, where are you?" she asks loudly. I emerge from behind the curtain. I feel kind of stupid that I was eavesdropping, but Kasia smiles at me. She fans her hand in front of her face.

"Open the window," she says. "What awful perfume. That hag must have poured a whole vat on herself. I know, it smells of school."

I open the window.

"Did you turn on the tape recorder?" Kasia asks.

"Me?" I wonder.

"Ohhh no . . ." Kasia laments. And she cries out, laughing, "Do you know what happened? This entire idiotic conversation got recorded! Excellent, I'd like to hear it again."

She rewinds the tape and presses the button.

"So why aren't you going to get the hell out of it?" Kasia's voice sounds in the loudspeakers.

And then the teacher's voice: "Okay, let's say I grant you that. I leave my husband, my home, my work. Where would I go? Onto the street? Do you think I'm going to find happiness around the first corner?"

Kasia turns off the tape recorder and says, "Maybe she would find it around the second or third. I'm a total idiot. How can you talk a cow into flying if it can only chew the grass with its muzzle close to the ground? Come to the kitchen, let's eat something, because I'm going to die of hunger soon. Miss Zenobia stood us up today."

"Who is Miss Zenobia?"

"This is our extra special cook-for-hire. I really don't know what could have happened to her. Maybe she got hit by a car, the poor old woman."

Kasia smiles mockingly. And I say, "May I hold you by the buckle?"

"Go ahead," Kasia says. "But why?" I grab her by the buckle and with the other hand point to the window. On the roof of the house across the street, the two chimney sweeps are walking.

We're sitting at the kitchen table eating sandwiches. I'm eating a ham sandwich and Kasia is eating a cheese sandwich, because she doesn't like ham. How can you not like ham? And on top of that, with tomatoes and cucumbers.

And we are drinking imported orange juice.

"I noticed a very interesting thing about myself," Kasia says. "When I talk to someone stupid, I immediately become even dumber than them." I must have made a face, because Kasia looks at me and says, "You're not stupid. You didn't manage to become stupid. I had in mind this poor idiot who can't deal with her own life and messes with other people's."

She rolls up the sleeve of her blouse and with a finger points at her wrist.

"Look, my child, at this big bloody scar," she says loudly, with exaggeration. "This is a souvenir of my luckless love. Oh, if not for Antek, my fat corpse would have decayed long ago in the grave!"

Kasia bursts out laughing. I don't say a word. She gets serious: "You fell for her slashing her wrists?"

"But she really might have," I say quietly.

"Yes, and what of it? One time I visited my mom in the emergency room. They brought in three of them like that during the night. This is what's called emotional blackmail. If you're gonna leave me, I'm gonna kill myself. The guy was lucky he left her. To be stuck with such a dodo your whole life . . . Yuck. I suppose that according to you I'm the biggest bitch?"

"Not at all," I say very quietly.

"You shouldn't pity her," Kasia says. "You'll see, she's going to hate me. She's starting to hate me right now."

"But she was so good when you were saying good-bye."

"Because it didn't penetrate her noodle that she'd been led into a trap. And by whom? By some know-it-all snot. I can come to school every day and sweep the classroom for an hour after class and water the plants and lick the blackboard clean with my tongue and I'll still get a C for conduct. Mrs. Turska will see to it. You don't believe me?"

I am silent.

"I'll show you my report card, then you'll see," Kasia says. She looks at me like she expects me to say something. What can I say? I lower my eyes, and suddenly Kasia backs her chair away from the table. She gets up. She throws her sandwich into the sink and goes over to the window. She stands with her back toward me.

"Kasia," I say quietly. She shakes her head.

"Shit," she says. "One big yucky shit. On top of that, I get smeared in it because I wanted to believe that that's not the way it is, that it can be different. So this is the world? This smelly pond?" She spits on the windowpane, then turns around and looks at me.

"I thought that at least you were different," she says loudly. "But you're just like them. If you don't like me, go away. Get out, I don't need anybody." I put my sandwich on the plate.

"You don't have to do it right away. Finish eating first."

I am sitting by the table with my face down and my tears going *pling-pling* on my plate. I didn't tell her anything bad. I feel Kasia embracing me.

"My little one, forgive me," she says, "I'm despicable. Truly, I didn't want to . . . please forgive me."

I want to tell her this is nothing, that I'm not angry, that she's wonderful, but I can't because I'm crying.

"Mongoose, don't cry. You're all I have in the world," Kasia pleads, and kisses me on my wet face. My nose is dripping, but she's not repulsed. She's kissing me. "Are you gonna forgive me?" she whispers.

"Yes," I say. I look and she also has tears in her eyes.

"My dearest, my sweetest sister," Kasia whispers. Her hair smells so wonderful. Even nicer than a freshly mown meadow on a bright sunny day. And it's such a sweet feeling. Oh, how sweet it is to cry and be hugged by someone you love.

"Don't cry, I beg you."

She leaves me. She takes a knife from the table.

"If you're not gonna stop," she says, "I'm gonna cut off my tongue with this knife." With the fingers of her left hand she grabs her tongue. She puts the knife next to her tongue. I quickly wipe away the tears.

"I already stopped crying," I say.

Kasia lets go of her tongue and says, "You're lucky. You would have had to eat a tongue sandwich. Or maybe you like sandwiches with human meat?"

I laugh. "This is called emotional blackmail."

Kasia is also laughing. She puts the knife away and sits in front of me.

"We're such crybabies. Yesterday we cried, today we're crying again. If we go on like this, before the week ends . . . 'Extra, extra, read all about it!' " she cries, her rolled-up hands at her mouth. " 'Two crybabies drown in a sea of tears!' "

"But we were laughing even more," I say. "Yesterday and today."

"And tomorrow and the day after tomorrow," Kasia says. "Really. We either laugh or cry. You know, it's fantastic that it's like that with us. Because in general, according to my philosophy, when someone cries or laughs, then he connects with something . . . that something . . . Oh, I'm not gonna bother you with my philosophy."

"Tell me."

"Maybe another time. Mongoose . . ."

"What?"

"I have a big favor to ask of you."

"What?"

"Swear you'll never hate me."

"I swear," I say.

Kasia turns serious.

"Do you swear by everything?" she asks.

"By everything."

"And do you know what is contained in the word 'everything'?"

"Sure I do," I say. "It contains everything."

"It's a very abstract word," Kasia says. "Better you should swear on somebody's life, on the life of someone who you love the most in the world."

I know I will never hate her. I raise my hand and feel my heart pounding inside me and I say, "I swear on Zenus's life."

"Is that the brother of yours who's still small and in the baby buggy?" Kasia asks.

"Yes, it's him."

"Thank you," Kasia says quietly. "I'll never forget this."

She brings her hands to her face. She covers her eyes and sits silently for a long, long time. Motionless. The whole house is silent. Only something somewhere far away ticks quietly. Kasia takes her hands from her face and looks at me. Her eyes glitter as beautifully as the stars. "I cannot take this oath for free," she says. She's very, very serious. "So in return, sister, I will save you."

"From what?" I ask.

"From the kingdom of the poor, from the heaven of the innocent," she says solemnly. "I promise you that you'll go straight to hell."

I WAKE UP, I look . . . there is a canopy above me. I'm lying on the bed in Kasia's room . . . Kasia is sitting by me. She's placing a wet towel on my head.

"What happened?" I ask.

"Oh, Mongoose, I was so worried."

"What happened?"

"I don't know. We were sitting in the kitchen eating and suddenly you fell on the floor—you fainted. I took you in my arms and brought you here. I was about to call my mom so she could come with an ambulance."

I want to sit up, but Kasia holds me by the arms. "No, no. Lie down a little longer. You look really pale. Does this happen to you often? Do you faint a lot?"

"I've never fainted," I say.

"You need to lie down. Let me sit with you."

So I lie down and Kasia sits on the edge of the bed looking at me sadly. I close my eyes. I've caused her so much trouble. At least she didn't wind up calling her mom.

I'm lying down, and suddenly out of nowhere I recall how one time I saved my whole family from death.

And this is how it was:

I had a dream. I am in the lobby of a movie theater. Everyone is waiting for them to let people in, but they're not letting us in. There are a lot of people; we're standing . . . Suddenly the door opens and a horrible monster flies in from outside. Everyone starts screaming, and with his teeth the monster—chomp—grabs the head of some man—munch, munch—and leaves the waiting room. And again we stand and wait. Other doors start opening. Again the monster darts in, with His eyes peering straight at me. I back off and He grabs some lady, her head in His jaws—munch—and disappears. And again nothing happens and we all keep standing and waiting to be let into the theater. Everyone is laughing, talking and eating candy because they've already forgotten. Only I remember because I know He always darts for me, wants to chomp on me, and if He hasn't chomped me yet, it's because He's made a mistake.

Again He darts in, but through a different door. He leaps out at me. I squat, hiding behind people. He grabs someone else and darts out. I squeeze through the crowd and stand with my back to the wall where there is no door. He's not gonna find me here, He's not gonna surprise me here. Suddenly there's a crash, rubble, a racket and a jolt. I jump away from the wall. There's a huge hole in it. The monster darts in, opens His jaws and leaps after me. I jump back . . . and wake up. My head hurts. There's smoke everywhere. It's black all around.

That's because poison gas had been leaking from the stove. Miraculously, I got up from my bed, everything spinning around me, and I fell down. I crawled to the window, broke the windowpane, caught a little bit of air and began to wake up Mom and Dad. But by now I couldn't wake them up. I couldn't wake up Tadzio and the girls either. They only woke up when I opened the door and there was a draft and it was cold. Everyone's head hurt. I told them my dream and Mom said we all owed our lives to the monster, because if He hadn't gone after me in the movie theater, I wouldn't have woken up and we all would have been gassed to death.

Then I thought about how I'd been afraid of Him and was fleeing Him, but He was really my great friend and He kept scaring me so I would wake up. Thanks to Him, everything ended well. The only thing is, Mom was pregnant then, and when Zenus was born later, it turned out he was born completely blind and would be like that for the rest of his life, because he had a damaged optic nerve and it's quite possible that it was because of the poisonous gas that leaked . . .

I feel Kasia stroking my hand. I open my eyes.

I smile at her. I feel so light and happy.

"I feel better," I say.

"That's wonderful."

"What time is it?"

"Five to four," Kasia says. Why did I ask? I have my own watch. I look, and there is quarter after four on mine. Is it running fast? I must adjust it. I need to go home, but I don't want to.

"I'm going to make us something hot to drink," Kasia says.

"I don't want a drink," I say, sitting on the bed. "Do you know what I want?"

"What?"

"To play the drums." I point to the drums in the corner.

"So," Kasia says, "go for it."

I sit on the stool behind the drums. I pick up the drumsticks. "Here's the foot pedal," Kasia says. I press it down with my foot and hear a stick with a huge head boom on the drums.

Again it's quiet. I beat delicately with the drumsticks and they jump away by themselves, like I'm holding a couple of thin lizards by the tail. I hear the rain behind the window; it's not a normal rain but a dry rain, light and dry, every drop a raisin. I feel a sweet taste in my mouth.

Drip-drop, drip-drop, golden buttons.

We need to offer some hail to the earth. I drum faster and faster, stronger and stronger. I'm drumming with all my might. Kasia runs to the synthesizer. She touches the keys . . . A high-pitched sound flies through the speakers and begins to chase my boom-boom-boom. I'm drumming faster, and fleeing, and after me, after my drum, harnessed to two lizards, Kasia's sounds fly. They catch up with us, go round and around and giggle.

I prod my two winged dragons. We fly up, high, higher, and even higher. I look back . . . Kasia's sounds, colorful bubbles, are chasing after me.

I lose my strength and sit down on a cloud.

And there, on another cloud, sits Kasia. She's blowing bubbles at me and I'm hitting them back with my magic drumsticks. Every bubble makes a different sound, bursts into shiny bits and falls to the earth. The entire earth is already colorful and shiny.

"Come to me," Kasia cries from her cloud. I put away my drumsticks and run up to her.

"Take Yamaha, I'm going to harness Korg!"

I press on a key and hear *pliiiiinnnggg!!!*

A silver-and-gold fountain gushes. I press the second button and a second fountain starts to gush. There are already so many of them everywhere, buzzing and glistening, and all my fingers are at work, and each finger works on its own.

Fountains, fountains everywhere, all mine. Between them happy streamers fly. It's Kasia's music playing with mine. A gold-and-silver foam is all over the place. Kasia beats it, and it grows, a huge egg-white cake, growing up to the sky, sweet, crunchy, transparent.

God, how wonderful it is to play.

I COME HOME and Mom is mad because it's already after seven.

"Where were you?"

"At a friend's house."

"I'll show you a friend's house! It's been a while since you've been spanked."

Dad is sitting in the kitchen drinking *kompot*. "Hello, Daddy," I say, and go to my room to unpack my books. Mom follows me and behind her in the doorway stand my two little sisters, Zosia and Krysia.

"You're supposed to be my helper, not my prodigal daughter," Mom says. "I couldn't cook dinner because of you, because I ran out of vegetables."

"I really couldn't come earlier. I really couldn't."

"Why? What were you doing that you couldn't?"

"We . . . were playing and listening to music," I say, and I feel really stupid.

"You're going to hear music when I hit you in the ear!" And she smacks me in the ear. I'm holding my ear because it hurts. Mom says, "What's with you? Did you steal Dad's sweater?"

"I had nothing to wear for school."

"And that's why you had to wear Dad's sweater? Dad, did you hear that?!"

"What?" Dad shouts from the kitchen.

"Hey! Take off your pants. Your daughter has nothing to wear for school!"

Zosia and Krysia are giggling. Mom also laughs and asks, "What kinda tights you got on?" She's looking at my legs. "Take them off this instant. Get on with it!"

I sit on the sofa and take off my tights.

"I didn't buy 'em so you could run around in 'em," Mom says. "I bought 'em so you could wear 'em to graduation and for the trade school exam."

"That's not until June," I say. "It'll be too warm".

"Last year it was cold. Who knows, it could be like that again this year." Mom takes my tights and leaves the room, saying, "Put some- thin' on, we gotta hang the curtains. Here you are, scurrying around like you was in an aquarium."

I'm hanging curtains in the TV room. Zosia and Krysia are helping, holding the bottoms so they don't get dirty on the floor. Mom sits at the table, with one eye on the television and the other on the way I'm hanging the curtains.

Dad is snoring in his clothes on the sofa.

Zenus is playing in bed with a rattle.

All the curtains have been hung. I jump off the windowsill onto the floor.

After a while something below goes bang. We're looking at the floor. Something's banging.

"What's that banging?" Mom asks.

"It must be the downstairs neighbor pounding the ceiling, because when I jumped, something banged above their head."

"They're still banging," Mom says. "How long are they going to be banging?" And she stomps her foot on the floor. And again.

And from below: bang, bang! Mom gets up.

"What is this?" she asks. "What is this? Ain't I got a right to walk around my own apartment?"

She goes onto the balcony, leans over the railing and cries, "Neighbor! Neighbor!"

"What's going on?" a high-pitched voice calls from downstairs—it's a woman.

"What's all the banging about?" Mom asks. "Where's the fire?"

"It's you that's banging on the ceiling all the time!"

"What? Me? All the time?" Mom wonders. "And who was it that banged first?"

"It was me banging on the ceiling. Because of all the banging at your place."

"The banging was probably in your ear!" Mom says loudly. "And don't you bang no more, because we know how to bang too!"

"What a bitch!" the neighbor says, and you can hear her closing the balcony door. Mom comes back in the room.

"What a hag!" she says, and bangs her slipper on the floor. We are listening to see whether the woman is going to bang back, but for some reason she's not banging; it's quiet, except for the guy on the TV yakking. "Good," Mom says triumphantly, and sits on the chair. "Let her bang now."

"Let her bang," Zosia says. "She's going to flake off her whole ceiling."

We're laughing, all three of us. Zenus hears us laugh and begins to gurgle happily.

"Enough giggling for today," Mom says. "Girls, go to the bathroom, and you, do your homework."

She stretches, yawns, elbows Dad. "Wake up, Dad, time to pull out the bed."

I'M PARTLY DOING my homework and partly lost in thought. I have headphones on because Kasia lent me a tiny tape recorder with batteries. I'm listening to Kasia's music. It's about me. This composition is called "Moods of My Mongoose." Kasia recorded it for me so I could listen to it.

The music is first happy, then sad. And then something else, but I don't know what. It changes constantly. Kasia says that it's like my faces. But I don't even know I'm making them.

I'm going to go look at them in the mirror, which is hanging in the john above the sink. It's small, but if it's enough for Dad to shave in, then it'll be enough for me to make faces in. As I'm going to the bathroom, Mom shouts from the kitchen, "What's that on your head?"

I come up to her. Tadzio is eating supper and Mom is smoking a cigarette.

"These are headphones," I say. "And music flies from this." I pull out Kasia's Walkman from my pocket.

"Where did you get it?" Mom asks.

"Kasia lent it to me. You know, my friend who's a composer."

Tadzio stretches his arm and grabs my headphones. He puts them on.

"Man, so much noise," he says.

"Show me," Mom says. I take the headphones and put them on Mom's head. Mom screws up her face, I turn down the volume, but I'm just guessing because I can't hear it myself.

"Kasia's composition is on," I say.

"That's a composition?" Mom wonders. "Some buzzing, some hissing . . ."

"That's because it's contemporary music," I say. Mom takes off the headphones. Tadzio picks them up again and puts them on.

"There's no melody. This is just fooling around," Mom says. "Now Kasia Sobczyk, that girl could sing. About a melancholy moon making magic in an empty night."

"Sounds like someone scattering nails!" Tadzio says loudly. He laughs. I take the headphones back from him.

"Is that any way to do your homework?" Mom asks.

"The music doesn't bother me when I'm doing homework. When something is playing, I can think even better."

"You got a point there," Mom says. "I used to listen to the radio while doing my homework, and your grandma would always turn it off."

I go to the bathroom and lock myself in. I look at the mirror: there is my face, the heroine of Kasia's composition. I put on the headphones and I start making faces to the music.

Now I'm making the face that Eva Bogdaj always makes when she's listening to someone. I puff my lips, I suck in my cheeks, and I raise my brows slightly, a bit ironically. How weird I look now, not like myself, like some other girl. And what shall I wear tomorrow? Kasia has it good. She always wears the same blouse and that skirt that goes all the way down to the floor. Why does she dress so weird? Her mom and dad are so rich, they could buy her anything she wanted. Maybe all the money went to her synthesizers and tape recorders.

We also had all kinds of expenses. We had to buy more furniture, and it's so expensive. And we had to make the down payment for the apartment. There was a time when I had more dresses, but I was half as big. Now I can count them on the fingers of one hand with one finger cut off. Yeah, and I have two skirts.

I had a pair of pants, but now they're too tight for me, and still too big for Tadzio. I have a sweater, but a stupid-looking one with a huge collar . . . When I go to trade school to study light tailoring, I'll sew a ton of dresses for myself. And a bunch for the girls and for Mom. You can't buy anything for Mom off the rack because she's too fat, and the tailors want a ton. But I'm not going to be able to sew Dad a suit or pants because when you study light tailoring, you don't make pants.

Maybe I'll make friends with a guy in heavy tailoring and we can swap—I'll sew his mother a dress and he can sew my dad a suit.

In any case, it's interesting that when I was going to school in Krzeszow, I never worried about my clothes, though girls there dressed nicely too . . . Maybe I am like that now because I've become a woman?

Someone rattles the doorknob. I hear Tadzio's voice: "What are you doing in there?"

"I'm taking a poop."

"Hurry up, I need to go too!" Tadzio farts behind the door.

"You pig," I say.

"You're a pig, I'm a hog."

Oh well, tomorrow I'll steal Dad's black sweater again. And maybe I'll put on this navy winter skirt. It's quite narrow, but it's too long, it covers my knees. I know, I'm not gonna close the zipper. I'll pull it up as high as I can and I'll tighten the belt so it doesn't slide down. I'm going to pull it up in the elevator—of course if no one rides with me— because if Mom sees me going to school showing so much . . . Oh, if only I had black tights to go with that. Maybe tomorrow I'll be able to persuade Mom to give me some money to buy black dye? I'll tell her that black tights won't get as dirty.

TADZIO'S WATCHING TELEVISION with the volume off, because Mom and Dad are already asleep, and I'm ironing in our little room. I've ironed a brown polka-dot blouse—it'll go great with my shoes; they're brown too.

Now I'm ironing the page with Kasia's drawing of the hawk on it. She crumpled it up and threw it out, but I picked it up during the break and put it in my book bag. I wanted to give it back to Kasia, but I forgot. I'm going to pin it to the wall and pin my drawing underneath. That'll make two pictures on the wall. One hawk, Kasia's, will be flying, and the second one, mine, will be standing watching the other one fly.

I wonder what Kasia's doing now. Maybe she's sleeping? Or maybe she's composing and thinking about me? What's she thinking? Maybe she's laughing at me? She'd been talking to the homeroom teacher so nicely toward the end, and then she started laughing at her and said the homeroom teacher was a cow with her muzzle low to the ground.

Maybe I'm just such a cow, just standing where they put it on a chain, doing nothing all day but chewing the grass.

"THIS MORNING MOM told me to show her my schedule, and said since lessons end at one-thirty, she wanted to see me home at ten after two at the latest."

"You should have written in two extra classes," Kasia says.

"How was I supposed to know she would ask me to show it to her?"

We're sitting at the bus stop, just the two of us. It's after school and Kasia really wants me to come to her place. The second number 8 bus has already left; it's almost two.

"C'mon, come over. You'll come up with something."

"But I have to do some shopping for Mom."

"She's probably already bought everything."

"Kasia, you've got to try and understand . . ."

"Don't call me 'Kasia!' "

"I'm sorry, Katarzyna, I forgot," I say. "Try to understand: if I don't show up soon, Mom's gonna kill me. Her varicose veins hurt her, and she can't go far, and those stores in our development are so far away. And on top of that, there's Zenus. And you can't count on the girls to help, they're still so silly."

"What are we going to do?" Kasia asks.

"I don't know."

I really wish I could go to Kasia's, but today I certainly can't. At least it's good that Mom didn't look at the schedule for the other days of the week . . . So I'll add a class or two a day.

The bus is coming. It gets closer and closer, and it's a number 8 bus. I get up from the bench. "I have to go."

"So go," Kasia says.

"No really, I have to." The bus stops, the door opens. "So bye, see you tomorrow!" I shout, and jump inside. There's tons of people.

We're going. I take out my ticket and push my way to the dater.

There's no way I could have stayed with Kasia; it's not my fault. We spent a lot of time with each other as it was, because during the lessons and breaks we were together constantly. Today Kasia didn't argue with anyone and she stayed till the last bell. It was wonderful. Ziebinski was walking around with a swollen nose, but he didn't try to start anything with Kasia or me. Eva Bogdaj had a different outfit on again. She had on a dark green dress with buckles, really beautiful. And Kasia was dressed the same as yesterday and the day before yesterday. The homeroom teacher didn't have class with us, but we met her in the hallway. She smiled at Kasia and even winked at her, and Kasia winked back.

Bus stop. A guy with a child gets off. I stand in his place by the window. I'm looking at the streets and the people and how they walk. I've gotten used to people a bit, to the fact that there's so many of them everywhere. And to the number 8 bus too. I have twelve bus stops from home to school. So on the way back it's probably just as many. I have to count. Soon there'll be a second one.

Suddenly someone puts their hands over my eyes.

I turn around, frightened. It's Kasia, standing in front of me. How could it be that she's here riding the bus?

"Is that you?" I ask.

Kasia laughs. "I got in up front. I thought that we could do the grocery shopping together. Are you happy?"

"Yes," I say. "Very."

"Are you gonna invite me home?"

"Sure, you'll see everybody."

"You see how silly we were, that we didn't come up with this right away?" Kasia says.

We're riding, holding hands, and we look out the window at the streets rushing by. To be honest, at the bus stop I was thinking Kasia could come to my place today. But I didn't tell her anything about it because . . . I was a little afraid. Of what Mom might say about Kasia and her outfit. And you know how Kasia is. Mom might say something silly to her, and then Kasia might even yell at Mom. But oh well, whatever happens happens. I'm really happy that Kasia will finally get to see the girls and Tadzio and Zenus. And Mom. She's not going to be surprised how fat she is, because I already told her she's very fat.

"Ladies, may I see your tickets, please," someone says. We turn away from the window and it's a man in a cap, tall and old-looking, with a large nose. Gee, where did I put my ticket, did I lose it? I find it in the pocket of my blouse.

I hand it over, the controller tears it, and then he looks at Kasia. But Kasia looks out the window. The controller touches her shoulder. "And you, miss?"

Kasia turns around and looks, standing on tiptoes. She points to a man standing far away from us, by the door.

"The guy in the checkered coat," she says. "He's my daddy. He has my ticket."

The controller squeezes through to the man in the checkered coat and Kasia whispers to me, "Do you have a ticket?"

Oh my God, she doesn't have a ticket. I open my book bag and, with shaking hands, I look for a ticket for her.

"Hurry up," Kasia whispers.

I remember they're in a book behind the plastic cover. I pull one out and hand it to Kasia. She places it in the dater and quietly punches it. Then she puts it away in the pocket of her blouse. A minute later the controller is back next to us. Angry.

"That's not nice, miss," he says to Kasia. "School ID, please."

"But why?" Kasia asks, surprised.

"Because you have to pay a fine," the controller says, opening his ticket book for fines. "That man over there does not have a daughter."

"Daddy!" Kasia screams. Everyone is looking at us, including the man in the checkered coat. "Oh, Daddy, Daddy, is that nice? Not to acknowledge your own daughter?"

Kasia waves a finger at him, but in a joking way. The man looks surprised. Kasia says loudly, for the whole bus to hear, "He must be ashamed to have such a big daughter!" People are laughing all around us; only the controller is still angry.

The other man finally gets the joke and says, "I'm not a woman, I don't have to hide my age. What, is it wrong to joke?"

"You see?" Kasia says to the controller and hands him her ticket.

"But you told me your father had your ticket."

"I got mixed up," Kasia replies. The controller tears the ticket and . . . looks suspiciously at me.

"Show me your ticket," he says to me.

"I already did."

"Show me, show me!"

So I show him the ticket, he checks it carefully, hands it back to me and leaves. I sigh. Things turned out well. Oh, Kasia's so smart. I wouldn't know how to do what she did. I think I would have burst into tears.

We're approaching the Piaskowa Gora development. We're standing near the door because the bus stop is coming up. From the seat by the window the man in the checkered coat says, "Bye, Daughter!"

Kasia turns around, blows him a kiss and says, "Bye-bye, Daddy!"

We jump off the bus. "Was that really your dad?" I ask.

Kasia bursts out laughing. "What are you saying? My papa wouldn't wear such an elegant sports coat!"

We're right near our apartment complex. Zosia and Krysia swing with other girls on the carpet rail.

"Look," I say. "Those are my sisters."

We walk up to the carpet rail.

"Can you do it like this?" one of the girls asks. She lets go of the top rail, flies backward and hangs off the lower rail with her knees bent. Her head swings two inches above the concrete, her hair sweeping it.

Zosia and Krysia let go of the top rail too and swing their heads above the concrete. They slide off the rail.

"I recognized them right away," Kasia says. "How funny, they're so similar."

I look and Zosia's tights have a hole in the knee.

"What did you do?" I ask, coming up to her. "You walk around with those on?"

"It's an old hole," Zosia answers.

"It's from sledding," Krysia says.

"You're lying again. I would have seen it when I was mending them. Come over here. This is my friend Katarzyna. Can you say hello?"

"Hello," they say, and snuggle with each other. Whenever they are embarrassed, they always snuggle. Kasia smiles.

"You know what?" she says. "You guys are precious. Which one is Zosia and which one is Krysia?" Kasia squats in front of them.

"I am," they say together. Kasia and I laugh.

"How do you tell them apart?"

"Very easily," I reply. "They only seem identical at first."

Krysia points her finger at Zosia and says, "She has more freckles."

"Not true, you have more," Zosia says.

And Kasia asks, "Do you like cookies?"

"We do."

Kasia begins to rummage through her book bag. The girls come up to her and look inside the bag, curious about those cookies. Kasia takes out a thousand zloty and hands it to Krysia.

"Go ahead, buy some," she says. "Use all the money so you can also give some to your friends."

"We don't know where you buy them," Krysia says, taking the money.

"I know," says one of the girls on the carpet rail. "It's not far."

"I know too," another girl says. "I can take you there."

Kasia and I remain alone by the carpet rail. The girls all run after Zosia and Krysia.

"It's fantastic to have two such funny creatures at home," Kasia says. "I really envy you."

We enter the apartment at two-thirty on the dot. I'm a little bit afraid of Mom because I'm twenty minutes late.

Mom is sitting in the kitchen, and with who? Mrs. Kaminska from Jawiszow.

"Oh, Marysia's here," Mrs. Kaminska says when I enter the kitchen. "I was at Kazio's boot camp and he was asking about you. He wanted me to say hello. I was just telling your mom how nice it is here. Nothing like the old frame house. Your place is really classy."

"Hello," I say. Kasia follows me into the kitchen.

"Hello," she says, coming up to Mom. "I'm a friend of your daughter's. My name is Katarzyna Bogdanska." She sticks her hand out toward Mom.

Mom gets up and sticks her hand out to her and says, as if embarrassed, "Mrs. Kawczak."

"Very happy to meet you," Kasia says. "Mongoose has told me so much about you." Mrs. Kaminska also gets up and extends her hand to Kasia.

"I'm Mrs. Kaminska," she says.

"It's a pleasure," Kasia replies.

And I see that Mom is looking at Kasia's skirt, all the way to the ground, so I say quickly, "Mom, I'm a little late because the bus was late."

"Yup, yup," Mrs. Kaminska butts in. "It's one big joke with these buses here. The devil can take you before one comes. One time in the winter I came here. I'm waiting and waiting and nothing happens. When it shows up, I'm already gone. All there is is an icicle."

"I ain't been ridin' 'em," Mom says. "Since we moved, I ain't rode a bus once. I ain't done nothin' but walk around the development a bit."

"This is a very nice place," Kasia says, leaning against the stove.

"Eh, it's just a hole in the wall." Mom shrugs her shoulders. "They stick folks in a high-rise and let them sit. So you sit, like you're on a pole, what're you gonna do? You're even afraid to go up to the window."

Kasia laughs: "You're right," she says. "You put it very nicely. But I'm sticking with what I said earlier. With all the horrid monstrosity that passes for contemporary style in the construction business, this development is really pretty. What a wonderful name. Piaskowa Gora."

Mom nods her head. "That's right. It's a nice name."

"And look, what a view." Kasia points to the window. Mom looks out the window and so does Mrs. Kaminska. I pull Kasia by her hand.

"Come on," I say. "I'll show you Zenus."

"Excuse us for a minute," Kasia says to Mom, and we leave. I take her to the large room. Zenus is not sleeping. He is sucking his pacifier and scratching the blanket.

"How beautiful," Kasia exclaims, and leans over the bed. "May I touch him?"

"Go ahead."

She takes his hand. "What itty-bitty fingers. And look at the fingernails!"

"Yup," I say. "I'm the same way with fingers and fingernails."

"What a sweet little face, and what eyes," Kasia wonders. "Hello, hello. Mr. Zenus, please look at me!"

Zenus spits out his pacifier; he begins to google and move his head to all sides. Kasia makes sweet faces at him, and I somehow can't bring myself to tell her that Zenus cannot see.

Kasia turns to me. "Your brother is sweet as sugar. Yum, yum, I could eat him."

I take her to my room. "This is where I live with Tadzio. It's a bit cramped, but somehow we all fit."

Kasia looks around and notices the drawings on the wall.

"My hawk," she says, surprised. "How did it wind up here?"

"I picked it up and ironed it," I answer. Kasia nuzzles up to me and kisses me on the cheek.

"Mongoose, you don't even know how happy I am that I came to your place," she says. "Now I know where such a wonder like you came from."

I feel ashamed. Kasia sometimes says things about me that make me feel odd. No one has ever praised me before, but she does it all the time. We're standing and looking at our hawks on the wall.

"You know," I say quietly. "Don't call me 'Mongoose' in front of my mom, because she's gonna laugh at me afterward."

"Sorry, sweetie. I won't say it again. Listen . . . maybe we should do that grocery shopping. Get it out of the way."

"All right," I say, and go to the kitchen. "Mom, what shall I buy?"

"It's already bought," Mom says. "Eat your dinner. Maybe your friend wants some too."

"We already ate at school," Kasia suddenly says. I turn around and she's standing behind me. Why is she lying?

"Why eat in the cafeteria when you got dinner waiting for you at home?" Mom asks. You can tell by her look that she's not happy. "How much does the cafeteria run you?"

"We ate for free," Kasia replies. "Somebody didn't come and they had free tickets."

"That's a different story," Mrs. Kaminska says. "Never look a gift horse in the mouth. Ain't that right, Mrs. Kawczak?"

"Could be," Mom says.

And Kasia says, "As a matter of fact, I want to talk to you about something very important. The principal asked me personally to find out whether Marysia could come to rehearsals."

"What rehearsals?" Mom asks.

"Rehearsals for the celebration at the end of the school year, because the vice minister of education is supposed to come to our school. Today they were selecting the most talented and Marysia was picked for recitation. I'm going to play the piano. There will be choral and dance numbers."

"Marysia got picked?" Mom wonders.

"Yes," Kasia says. "She has very good diction, the best of all."

"Just look at her," Mom says, and looks at Mrs. Kaminska. "Just look, we're gonna have ourselves an artist here at home."

"So you agree to it?" Kasia asks.

"I'm not gonna say no," Mom answers. "If the principal chose her, then he ain't gonna let her go."

"Rehearsals start today at three-thirty, and it's almost three . . ."

"So go," Mom says. "Don't you be late."

"So I should say good-bye," Kasia says, and, turning to me, "Let's go quickly, maybe we'll make it."

Slam, bam, and we're out the door, we're in the elevator going down.

"What do you think, wasn't that a good idea?" Kasia asks me.

"Yup, yup."

"You can come to my house every day, and if something comes up, you can say that you were at rehearsal. Or maybe you don't like me anymore, maybe you don't want to come to my house . . ."

Kasia makes a sad face.

"What are you saying?" I ask. But, you know, it all happened so fast . . . I can't believe it.

WE'RE SITTING AT a table covered with a white crocheted tablecloth, and the restaurant isn't big, but it's really beautiful. Beautiful paintings in golden frames hang on the wall. And everything just shines. Elegantly dressed people sit at other tables and talk quietly.

We came by taxi. It took a long time, but we got here. It is ten miles from Walbrzych. As we sit here, the taxi driver is waiting the whole time in the car so he can take us back, and his meter is on the whole time. Oh, Kasia is so rich.

A waiter comes up to us. He's young and handsome, with black curly hair. He has a white napkin hanging over his arm. He bows and says, "My respects, Miss Katarzyna." And to me: "Hello, miss. Welcome to our establishment."

"Hi, Wojtek," Kasia says.

"Hello," I say, feeling a blush coming over my cheeks.

"Are the ladies ready to order?" asks Mr. Wojtek.

"Two borschts, with those . . . devilettes," Kasia says.

"*Devolettes.*" Mr. Wojtek laughs.

"That's right," Kasia says. "For me, an omelet with peas, and for the lady, the house special. And of course ice cream."

"As you wish, ladies," Mr. Wojtek says, and leaves, bowing.

YUM, YUM.

Not even a half hour has gone by and we've already finished dinner. Now we're eating ice cream, a hundred times better than the stuff we had in the café the day before yesterday. Mr. Wojtek scurried around us like we were princesses. And he joked with Kasia the whole time. They know each other really well, since Kasia comes here very often with her mom. It's a privately owned restaurant, the best in the entire region. That was a lot of food, all very tasty, I don't even know what it's called. I ate everything on my plate. Only I didn't finish the coleslaw because the tray was so huge, like half the table, so Mr. Wojtek took the rest away. So much went to waste. I practically can't move—it's even difficult to eat the ice cream, but it's too good not to finish.

"I'm going to play something just for you," Kasia says. She gets up. She goes over to the platform where the piano is standing. She sits on the stool and opens the fall board. She looks at me from afar, smiles and begins to play.

Very quietly, some beautiful, sad melody. Not like the ones she plays on her synthesizers, but a normal one. I look around: no one's eating, everyone's listening carefully. Mr. Wojtek also listens, standing by the cupboard full of dishes. Even the cook in the huge white hat is leaning through the curtain, listening.

The sadder the melody Kasia plays, the more beautiful it is. It bores straight into my heart and it hurts. Suddenly I remember my grandma, the one who died. I really loved her. When the girls were born, I spent the whole year with her. We were still living in Ksiaz Wielki near Krakow, at Aunt Jasia's place—Dad's sister—only then Mom had a bad argument with her and we left for Jawiszow.

Granny had a small hut near the woods two miles from my aunt's house. The hut had only one little room. Grandma was very little. She walked around practically bent in half; she couldn't straighten up. She was very nice. Every morning I helped her put on her stockings and combed her hair. It was gray and long, down to her knees. And I carried water from the stream in pails on a yoke.

That was the most beautiful year of my life. In the evenings we would sit in the hut, there'd be a fire in the stove, and Granny would tell various interesting stories from her life. What I liked the best was hearing about my grandfather, who flew a balloon and had even been to Brazil. He was very tall, over six feet six, and afraid of nobody. When Granny married him, he was already fifty years old, but built like a tank. Right after the wedding he left for Brazil and Granny was supposed to join him, but for the time being, there was nothing there to go to and it wasn't until ten years later that Grandpa got rich, built a beautiful house and went back to Poland to bring Granny with him. They never managed to leave because the war with Hitler broke out. At the end of the war Grandpa was killed. My dad was about to be born when two Germans came on bikes. Grandpa was in the resistance, but he happened to be visiting Grandma and was asleep because he'd been walking through the woods all night. One German stood by the window, the other by the door, and the first one said to Grandpa, in German, "Hands up!" Grandpa woke up, got up, put his hands up and left the house. Suddenly he grabbed the German by the throat and, boom, threw him against the wall and choked him to death. He never got a chance to kill the other German, because the other German shot and killed Grandpa. Why didn't he kill Grandma? Who knows? Maybe he took pity because Grandma had my dad in her tummy, and Aunt Jasia and Aunt Pola were small, and sobbing.

If only Grandpa had come to get Grandma a bit earlier, he would have lived for years and years, but in Brazil, and my dad would have been born in Brazil, and I would have been born in Brazil too. We all would have been Brazilians. Tadzio and the girls and Zenus. Wait—but then Dad wouldn't have met Mom, because he would have been in Brazil and Mom in Poland, so I would have had a different mom, a Brazilian mom . . . Or I wouldn't have known Dad, because Mom would have had me in Poland—a Polish mom, that is, my real mom—but then I would have had a different dad.

Or maybe I wouldn't have been born at all if the German hadn't killed Grandpa? Some other girl would have been born instead of me.

And what about *me*?

Where would I have been then?

I remember a terrible thunderstorm. It was bright everywhere from the lightning, and I was kneeling with Grandma in the middle of the night, and we were praying to Lord God so He would spare our hut. And He spared it, and a sunny morning came. Many pears that the wind had knocked out of the trees were scattered on the ground in the orchard. They were lying one next to another, and I thought the whole earth was made of pears, juicy and fragrant. And then Grandma died and was lying in a coffin. That was the first time I saw her straightened.

Four years have passed and still I remember her and the taste and smell of the pears that lay in the orchard after the storm.

Kasia keeps playing the same melody. It seems that it's about to die down, when it starts getting loud again. Maybe it's a melody with no beginning or end, and though no one plays it, it plays on its own and nobody hears it, only Kasia.

Grandpa was tall, and all his children, that is, Dad and my aunts, were so tiny. I'm the only one in the whole family who's tall. Maybe I take after Grandpa. Maybe I'll fly a balloon all the way to Brazil too?

Kasia plays more and more quietly, until you can no longer hear anything, she's not playing anymore. She closes the fall board with a bang.

Everyone in the restaurant begins to clap. Kasia returns to our table, and I'm very proud that I'm the friend and adopted sister of such a remarkable artist.

"Did you like it?" Kasia asks.

"Very much."

"That was 'Night on Bald Mountain,' " Kasia says, and drinks the pink liquid from her melted ice cream straight from the cup.

I'M DYEING MY tights black. It turned out Mom had some black dye, and she agreed I could dye my tights and on top of that gave me two worn-out pairs of Zosia's and Krysia's to be dyed.

Mom really liked Kasia because she was so bold and knew how to talk. Not like me—only Mom was surprised Kasia dressed so stupidly, like some kind of Gypsy, and was even more surprised when I told her that Kasia goes to school like that. I told her that her mom is a doctor and that she's very rich and this outfit is the newest Parisian fashion.

Tadzio runs into the kitchen. "What are you cooking?"

"Black soup," I say, and with a serving spoon I pull out tights that are dripping black. I show them to him.

And Zosia, sitting here chowing down sauerkraut straight out of the jar, says, "Marysia is cooking cream of tights."

"I'm dyeing my tights black," I explain.

"What for?" Tadzio wonders. "Are you going to a funeral?"

"Knock on wood, stupid," I say. "I'm doing it so they won't get dirty so fast."

"Can I stir?" he asks.

"Go ahead, but be careful."

I pass him the serving spoon. He stirs. He pretends he's trying the black water.

"Good soup," he says. "Only there's not enough pepper."

"And mayonnaise," Zosia adds.

"What are you talking about?" I say. "You don't add mayonnaise to soup."

"What if we cooked dumplings in it?" Tadzio offers. "You'd see, they'd get all black."

"I wonder who would eat them," I say.

"I would," Tadzio replies.

"Yeah, I'd like to see that."

"I would too. I ate a jar of glue once, so what are black dumplings to me?"

"Once he ate half a worm," Zosia says. " 'Cause Krysia and I had fifty zloty for candy, and he told us that if we paid him, he'd eat a worm. So we agreed. He only ate half, but he took the whole fifty zloty from us."

"I dropped the other half. It got dust all over it," Tadzio says. "Did you want me to eat it with dust?"

"Yuck," I say. "You shouldn't eat such yucky things."

"That ain't nothin'. I'd even eat a snake, but only if I was hungry, and for a thousand zloty—not a penny less."

"Would you eat a frog?" Zosia asks.

"For three hundred zloty. A toad for three fifty."

"And a crocodile?"

"Even a crocodile—but only for dollars. And not all at once. I'd eat it over a whole week."

"And we had cookies and cream cakes," Zosia brags.

"As for cake," says Tadzio, "I'd bend the rules and eat it for free."

Krysia runs into the kitchen. "Evening cartoons!" she shouts, and runs away. And just like that, the kids are gone from the kitchen. How good it is to be left alone with my own thoughts.

The most important thing is that Mom didn't find anything wrong with Kasia.

And Kasia liked Mom too. What she said about her is that she's very proud, the household's truest queen. I would never have thought of Mom as a queen, but it's true. She really is proud and never lets anyone get her goat. Even Dad is afraid of her.

Except when he drinks, then he's a bit more brave. When he's drunk, Mom never argues with him, she just won't do that. Instead, she just doesn't talk to him. Not a word. Like she doesn't even see him. Like drunken Dad is air. Once Dad was blaming her for something and yelling, and Mom said to me: "Marysia, close the window. A fly must have gotten in here and is buzzing around my ear." So Dad got pissed and went to bed. And he was snoring so bad we couldn't watch television because he was drowning it out. Besides, Dad is either asleep or not at home, because he works all the time. Mom says that if he didn't drink, we'd be millionaires and drive a fancy car. Whenever Dad gets drunk, the next day he always promises Mom this is the last time, and then his friends talk him into a drink, since Dad has a weak will and can always be persuaded.

Mom, in turn, smokes cigarettes and can't kick the habit. She never used to smoke, but once she went to the doctor because her chest was hurting and it turned out she has a really bad heart. The doctor sent her to rest for a month at a miner's sanitarium, because Dad was already working at the mine by that time. Mom met girlfriends there who smoked and they got her started. By the time she came home, she was already hooked.

At first she hid it and smoked when no one was home, but then it turned out that everyone knew she smoked, only Mom didn't know we knew. Now she always has to have a pack of Popularne handy and sometimes even a pack a day isn't enough. But it's really bad for her heart and her varicose veins. Once I talked to her about it and asked her not to smoke, because I was really worried about her. Mom said she knows she's doing the wrong thing, but what can she do, since the cigarettes got her hooked and when she doesn't smoke she doesn't feel like living?

Cigarettes are totally gross. You can't do anything about it once you start smoking. She told me she'd kill me if she ever saw me with a cigarette in my mouth. Because having a father who is a drunk and a mother who is a smoker is enough for the whole family. Poor Mom. She's got the whole world on her shoulders. A husband who's a drunk and five children. And on top of that cigarettes. How could her heart not hurt?

Chapter Three

⁂

DAYS CAN BE a strange thing. Sometimes a day can go on and on when it feels like it should be ending, even though it still has a long way to go to the end. And at other times the day passes by so quickly, it's like you wink, open your eyes, look around . . . only to find it's not only another day, but another week, or even another month.

Katarzyna says that time is bubble gum.

And you can do all kinds of tricks with bubble gum. You can chew it, you can hold it under your tongue in a little ball, you can blow it into a bubble and pop it, you can inadvertently swallow it. You can even stretch a thin thread from your mouth to the pole on the other side of the street. It's too bad we didn't get this apartment in Walbrzych last year, in September for instance. Katarzyna and I would have known each other since the beginning of the school year and we would have spent so many days and months together. But oh well. It's a good thing we were able to meet at all. Because I might have gone to the school in our settlement and then we never, ever, ever would have met. Now we're like sisters to each other, even more than that, since true sisters are born that way and sometimes they're only together because they're sisters, but we chose each other, so we're something more than sisters.

And it all started with the time we were laughing by the fountain in the marketplace. We were laughing and laughing so hard that the icy cloud above us couldn't stand it and crumbled and fell as hail.

Katarzyna says it was a sign from heaven.

And already a month has passed. Too bad it passed so fast. It's May now. If I could I'd step on every day's tail, but these days go by so fast because they're happy and interesting, and they're like that because Katarzyna and I spend them together.

Right after school we go to her place and eat dinner cooked by Miss Zenobia. Then I start doing homework, while Katarzyna composes and plays various works and listens to them on headphones in order not to disturb me.

That makes it loud for her and quiet for me.

Sometimes I look up from my notebook and watch how she composes. It's clear she's not in the room, but her whereabouts are unknown. Sometimes she'll even scream or say something . . . I'll look because I think she's saying something to me, but she's talking to herself, darting her eyes all over the room. Then I get the feeling that sounds are flying all over the place, and that she sees them and catches them in her synthesizers like butterflies in a net.

Once I told her that, and she said, "That's because they *are* flying. Don't you see them?"

But I don't. I look as hard as I can to see whether there are any flying anywhere, but no, for me there's no sound flying in the silence. I only see them a little bit when Katarzyna plays and you can hear them in the speakers.

Every other day at five I zip over to church for catechism. The church is very close by, so I can get back quickly and still spend an hour with my sister.

Katarzyna is very dissatisfied with what she composes. She says she should train worms instead of composing. And I comfort her and tell her she's talking nonsense, since I like her music a lot and think it's the most beautiful music in the world and no one composes as beautifully as she does. Then Katarzyna laughs at me and says that I don't know much, which of course is true. She plays tapes and records of various modern composers, but I like their works much less, although some are very pretty and interesting. I like it when Katarzyna plays operas. I especially like arias in which a soprano sings. When I listen to a soprano, something pierces straight through me. One time we were trying out my voice and it turned out I have a warm alto. Katarzyna promised she would write a song for me, and I'll sing it and it'll hit the top of the charts. But so far she hasn't written it, since she doesn't even like songs and doesn't write any.

What she composes are suites. The longest of them goes on for fifteen minutes and thirty-six seconds. She's constantly trying to compose something longer, but nothing comes of it. One time a suite lasted half an hour, but Katarzyna said it was a piece of shit, just repetitions. She dreams of composing a great long work that would fill both sides of an LP. Too bad. After fifteen minutes she's short of breath. And when she tries to put together things from several pieces, it turns out that although they are okay by themselves, together they begin to clash and you can see how they spark at the ends.

I really like it when she can play something she likes a lot, and when she can't it's a pity to look at her, she's so sad. At times she even gets so angry she could yell at me, but I don't worry about it like I did at first, since I know she's like that because things are not going well for her.

I remember once I was doing homework and she was playing . . .

Suddenly . . . she throws her headphones on the floor and shouts, "Jigi, you idiot: what's going on with you? Jigi, please! . . ." She throws her arms up in despair and, with tears in her eyes, says, "Why do you torture me? I've already given you everything! I don't have anything, so what do you want . . . ?"

Now she isn't saying a word, she's just looking straight ahead and looks like she's listening to someone invisible saying something. And she shouts again! "No, not that! Not that. Buzz off, you moron! Do you hear? Buzz off!"

She falls onto the floor and starts crying hard. And I look at her in horror, afraid to go near her, tears forming in my eyes. But Katarzyna gets up, happy and laughing.

"Great," she says. "So we'll both kick the bucket, no big deal. But you too, you too, you too!" Suddenly she notices me and starts to grow angry.

"What are you doing here?"

"Me? I'm doing my homework."

She looks at me, confused, like she doesn't recognize me, like I'm a stranger.

"Oh, so it's you," she says at last. She sits beside me on the sofa and chugs a whole glass of Coca-Cola. She puts her head on my knees, snuggles her face against my tummy and pleads sweetly, "Pet me . . ."

I pet her hair.

"Mongoose, sweetie, I feel so safe around you," she says softly. I look down at her and she's fallen asleep. I sit, gently stroking her hair, afraid I might move and wake her up. When you can't move your legs, they go to sleep right away. And when you're free to move them whenever you want, you can sit still for two hours even and nothing happens. So I sit like that, my legs asleep, Kasia sleeping on my lap, and it's almost five and I should go to my catechism . . .

SHE DIDN'T WAKE up for forty-three minutes. She didn't play at all that day. We only talked and laughed. What made her yell and cry? I didn't find out then because she didn't mention anything about it and I was ashamed to ask. I was a little afraid to ask because it might happen to her again.

Mom has already gotten used to me never being at home. Because I have either catechism or those rehearsals at school. It feels a bit strange to lie to Mom like that. I never lied to her in my whole life and now I'm doing it more and more often. Well, I have to lie so I can spend as much time as possible with my Kasia.

Anyway, the girls take care of Zenus. Mom says that it's high time for them to get used to it because I'll finish trade school soon and of course get married and start my own family. And when Tadzio was small like Zenus, I too was five years old like they are now and I did everything having to do with him. I changed his diapers and Mom would let me bathe him. And look at him, he's grown up to be quite a kid.

Once Kasia came over to my house for dinner. She complimented Mom a lot and she said that pierogi like these are only made in heaven.

Mom waved her hand dismissively, but I could see she was happy with the compliment. Mom says that getting to know rich girls will come in handy in the future, because when I'm done with tailoring school, I'll want to sew at home, and rich, educated women pay the most.

And I finally met Kasia's mom.

She's beautiful and looks like a young girl. Though she's my mom's age, she looks like she could be her daughter. Katarzyna calls her by her name, Karolina. They talk to each other like they're friends and not mother and daughter. They only see each other rarely, because Mrs. Bogdanska is always at the hospital or in the emergency room, and I can hardly believe that such a young and scatterbrained woman is a doctor helping people.

Once I saw her on the street in a very nice car. She was sitting behind the wheel and beside her sat a very good-looking young man. I mean, a man, but a young one.

Katarzyna doesn't have a dad.

Or rather she does, but her dad is very far away, all the way over in Africa, and Katarzyna has never seen him, and he's never seen her either. They know each other only from pictures. But they love each other. They write long letters to each other, but not in Polish. In French. Because though he lives in Africa, he's not an African but a Frenchman.

They call each other a lot. Once he called when I was there. They talked for about half an hour, but I couldn't understand a thing Katarzyna said, because she was speaking French.

I even managed to learn how to speak a little French. "Wee" means yes, "noh" means no. "Jamay"—never. And "jettem"—I love you. "Mohshare"—my dear. And so forth. Kasia's dad is very rich. He's always sending her money and presents. He also bought her all the equipment she plays on. All these synthesizers, computers and tape recorders cost more than ten thousand dollars. And in zloty that's many millions. I could work my entire life without making that much.

Katarzyna's mom and dad met in Tunisia, and he really loved her, but she didn't want him, even when she got pregnant and Katarzyna was about to be born. She fled to Poland, he came after her, but she chased him away and he left, started a different family and now has different children, but loves Katarzyna the most and is always asking her to come visit him because he wants to see her. He's old, he's already sixty. Katarzyna wants to meet him too, so she's gonna visit him right after graduation, which is not too long from now.

I don't know what I'm going to do with myself without her.

Katarzyna is trying to talk me into going there with her and she wants to pay for my ticket, but there is no way Mom will let me. That's one thing. Another thing is, what would Katarzyna's dad need a strange girl in his house for?

Katarzyna's mom doesn't want her to go visit her dad because she's afraid that once she gets there, she won't come back. But it's up to Katarzyna to decide, and if she does decide to go, her mom isn't going to oppose it. Lucky for me and for Mrs. Bogdanska, Katarzyna is wavering a bit on whether to go this year or next year. Because she doesn't want to go empty-handed, she wants to bring her dad a real record of her music, including her grand composition.

It's all because one time she bragged over the phone that she just finished her composition and that they were supposed to release her record, and she even played part of it for him over the phone. She was sure then that she would manage to compose it any day because she had such a great start . . . then it turned out that it was only a beginning and nothing more. So she might be going to Africa in a year, because even if she composes her beautiful piece soon, then she would have to wait a long time for the record anyway. Maybe that's why she gets so upset when her composing isn't going well, because the piece is standing between her and her dad. There are days when she's totally down. I have to console her and snuggle with her. She plays records of famous composers and says that, after all, it's so simple, but it's only simple because it's already been composed. And other times she says she couldn't care less—about music, about her dad, about her mom and about the whole world. She gets very cheerful and everything makes her laugh, but I can tell right away it's a fake cheerfulness that ends in tears. Then she and I cry together.

Once I even spent the whole night with her.

I didn't want to, but Katarzyna gave me money for the round-trip cab fare, so I went home and I lied that I had to stay with Kasia all night because she had kidney stones, and her mom was on call in the hospital, and if things got worse, I'd have to call her. Mom got all worried and believed me and I went back in a cab that was waiting the whole time for me in front of the apartment. The only true parts were that Mrs. Bogdanska was on call that night in the emergency room and Katarzyna was afraid to stay home alone.

What a strange night that was.

Katarzyna says that if I hadn't been there, she wouldn't have made it through the night and I would have had a dead friend on my hands.

It was the first time I saw her wear something besides her usual Gypsy outfit. She was wearing pajamas. I had the same ones on too, only in a different color. When we looked in the mirror, we looked very much alike, only she had on red pajamas with yellow flowers and I had blue ones with white flowers. She gave them to me for keeps, and now every night I sleep in them.

We braided our hair. Kasia's braids were long and thick and I had two funny-looking pigtails. Only then did I see how thin Kasia's face is, because her hair always covers it. Kasia bathed first and then I did. I took a quick shower, but I didn't know where the detergent for cleaning the bathtub was, so I ran out from the bathroom in a towel in order to ask.

Kasia was just putting on her pajamas in her mom's room and the light was off. I walked in and said, "Katarzyna . . ." She screamed, "Get out of here!" so I got scared and ran back to the bathroom. A minute later Kasia came in and apologized to me. She said she screamed because she didn't want me to see her naked. Once when she was little she had a terrible car accident and now her whole body is covered with burn scars.

Then we went to bed and Kasia asked me to stroke her and to tell her a story. So I stroked her and told her how I once painted my grandma's room white in her hut by the woods. I was ten, and I decided to surprise Grandma when she came back from picking wild berries. I was whitewashing it with lime for half a day. When I finished, I was as white as the walls. I washed the floors and waited for

Grandma to return, and because she didn't come back for a long time, I went to look for her.

I wandered through the woods calling, "Grandma, Grandma!" Suddenly I looked and standing in front of me was a horrible dirty pig, and around her small piglets, also dirty. I came up to pet them because I liked to pet small pigs a lot, but they ran away and the large one also ran away.

When I finally found Grandma, I told her what I saw, and it turned out that it wasn't a dirty pig but a wild sow with babies and it could have killed me.

So Kasia says, "Oink-oink . . ."

"What are you saying?" I ask.

"You said that you like to pet piglets," Kasia answers. "Oink-oink, oink-oink . . ."

So I stroked her and stroked her until she fell asleep. Somehow I fell asleep too and I didn't even turn off the night-light. Suddenly I wake up in the middle of the night because someone is screaming in terror and choking me. It's Kasia. She embraces me and hugs me so hard that my ribs are crackling. I scream, "Kasia, Kasia!"

She wakes up all wet from sweat and tears. She lets go of me and starts to cry.

"Sweetie, what's going on with you?" I ask.

She holds me and begs, "Save me, save me."

"What am I supposed to do?"

"Save me, save me," she keeps repeating, and starts twitching and thrashing all over the bed. I grab her by the hands and squeeze. Though she does everything to break loose, I'm stronger. I don't know where all my strength is coming from.

"Kasia! Kasia, calm down!" I shout. She starts getting weaker. I'm straddling her and holding her hands.

"Are you over it?" I ask. She's lying under me, her eyes are bulging, and she's staring at me. She makes an awful suppressed squeal, like a rat's. I feel pins of fear piercing my head. An awful scowl comes over her face.

"Kasia!" I shout in despair. Underneath me lies some horrible living corpse. It gets stronger and stronger, I can no longer hold its hands.

It's not Kasia, it's someone else, someone not from this world. This something grunts and drools. It gives me a horrible look and squeals in a terrifying high-pitched voice, "Let go, you whore!"

God help me. Grandpa, help. Grandpa! Suddenly I feel a great strength coming over me.

"I'm not letting go," I say. I grab the wrists of the monster. Because it's definitely not Kasia I'm holding, but someone else. And although I don't know how I know it, I know that it's Jigi lying underneath me. And I also know that if I let go, something terrible will happen.

"Fucking barbarian, holy bitch, let go!"

And he howls, wriggling underneath me like a snake captured in a pitchfork. I'm holding him and I'm not going to let go, because I'm stronger. I'm even stronger than my grandfather; there are a hundred of my grandfathers in me. I'm so strong I could even twist iron bars.

Jigi spits at me. I gather the saliva in my mouth and I offer him the same.

"I'm gonna kill you!" he squeals.

I laugh right in his face. "Ha, ha, ha, kill me, be my guest!"

He kicks up his legs like a wild horse, but what are wild horses to me? I'll tame the whole herd of them at once. He starts howling louder and louder, more horribly. I'm not worried about it, because I know the room is soundproof and no one except me can hear this howl.

Things have calmed down, the monster's gone. Kasia lies underneath me. So weak and so pale. I let go of her hands, I lie down beside her. I draw her toward me and say sweetly, "All right, my dear, everything is all right." She sobs quietly in my arms and I feel like I am a mom holding her tiny daughter, awakened by a terrible dream.

I kiss the violet rings, the traces of my fingers on her wrists.

"Don't be afraid, my little one," I whisper into her ear. "Jigi already left, he's already gone."

"How do you know his name?"

"Because I know," I say. "Because you quarreled with him once."

Kasia hugs me even closer.

————

WHEN SHE FINALLY calmed down, I went to the kitchen and made two cups of tea. I brought them—we were sitting in bed—and Kasia told me about Jigi. It started a long time ago when Kasia was tiny. Her mom was traveling around the world because she worked for UNESCO. Kasia was brought up by her grandma, who was the head of a bar association in Wroclaw and was always busy. Kasia was left alone for days on end, with only her grandma's old servant. She conjured up a little boy. She called him Jigi and played with him, and when she did something wrong, she always blamed it on him.

Then she went to school and forgot all about him. She began to play piano in music school and turned out to be a prodigy. When she was nine years old, she composed her first piece and everyone was awed by it. Years passed, Kasia played better and better and composed better and better pieces. Then she decided to become the greatest composer in all of music history. And that's when the trouble began. She would sit down at the piano and feel empty; nothing would come into her head. It lasted for weeks, months. She was repulsed by the piano and music, and left the music school, terribly down.

One day about two years ago she had a dream. She dreamed about a very funny boy, really ugly, with large ears. He told her his name was Jigi and that it was he who was the author of all her compositions and that if she wanted him to continue to write for her, she would have to invest in electronic equipment because he'd grown tired of using the piano. Kasia laughed at him in the dream and threw him out the door, but when she woke up in the morning, she wrote a long letter to her dad and soon after she received a new synthesizer and money for the rest of the necessary equipment.

Once again she began to compose, and it went better and better. But also more and more often she had the feeling that she wasn't alone in her body, that there was someone sitting inside of her helping her play. Then she understood that Jigi was making her aware of his presence. At first he was nice and she got to like him a lot. In her imagination she had long discussions with him about music and about life, and she was even able to read other people's thoughts thanks to him.

Suddenly he started demanding all kinds of strange things from her.

One time he ordered her to start dressing like a Gypsy, but she was always dressed in sporty clothes, in cotton shirts and jeans, and more than anything she was repulsed by Gypsies and their colorful rags. So she didn't listen to that order, but from that day forward she stopped having musical ideas. She would sit at the synthesizer and play some of her own old pieces, until finally she went to a tailor, ordered a somewhat tasteful outfit in the Gypsy style, put it on, sat down at the synthesizer and . . . nothing. All she heard was the giggling of Jigi and his words: "No Gypsy? No music. Gypsy? Music." Then she understood that you can't deceive him. She went with a friend of her mom's to a Gypsy camp and bought a whole bunch of silk rags and cretonne in the most horrible patterns in the world. She washed them at home, put all of them on, like on a Christmas tree, and in an hour she finished her most beautiful suite, which Jigi called "Gypsy Princess." He also told her she had to dress like that for the rest of her life.

She had trouble with it at school and at home with her mom, but when she threatened to stop going to school altogether, they backed off and even got used to it. Her closet is almost bursting with great clothes—her dad constantly sends her new ones—but Kasia has to wear these tangly draped curtains and can't do anything about it, because if she dresses in something else even once, Jigi will hide the key to the Land of Music forever.

Of course, the story didn't end with a dress code. Jigi found fault with Kasia's hair as well. Until then she wore short hair, but Jigi ordered her to never cut it for the rest of her life. And her hair grows so fast, and it's so tangled, that it's getting harder and harder to comb it.

Every now and then Jigi has new, idiotic whims. Kasia has to obey them. And especially now, when she wants to create this great piece for her dad, Jigi makes almost impossible demands and they always argue with each other . . .

"You told me you wear such a long dress because your legs are burned," I say. "So you don't have burned legs?"

"Of course not," Kasia says, annoyed. She rolls up the cuffs of her pajamas and shows me her calves. They're as smooth as mine.

"So why did you yell at me?" I ask.

"It's because of him," Kasia replies. "Because he told me to go to you in the bathroom and . . ."

"And what?" I ask.

"I can't tell you."

"Please tell me. Please, tell me."

"Don't ask me, I can't tell you. In any case, I resisted him, and then you walked into the room and it was like he sent you there . . . I shouted at you because if you hadn't escaped, then . . ."

"Then what would have happened?"

"What would have happened was that I could never look you in the eye. Oh, Mongoose, if you only knew what a monster I am."

Kasia snuggles up to me. I embrace her and stroke her head.

"You're not a monster," I say. "You're wonderful."

"And what happened afterward was his revenge. Do you know what he wanted to do? He wanted to come out of me. I don't know anything anymore, I only remember that it hurt a lot. Tell me . . . what did I do?"

"Nothing much," I reply. "You just thrashed around the bed some and shouted at me."

"What was I shouting?"

"All kinds of bad words, I've already forgotten what."

Kasia sighs, snuggles with me even tighter. Poor thing. Why did she get involved with Jigi? He came out of her, I saw it with my own eyes. But I can't tell her about it—it's better for her not to know. Maybe it's bad that I was holding him. Maybe if he'd come out altogether, he would have gone away and left Kasia alone. But then what would have happened to Kasia? He wasn't separate, he was also Kasia, he had Kasia's body and all, only I think he might have had his own voice. I don't understand any of it. How can it be that someone else could sit in you and persecute you . . . it's impossible.

"Kasia," I say, "can't we do something so that you can get rid of him?"

Kasia sighs and says quietly, "Maybe I don't really want him to leave. I know he's horrible and malicious. But there are also some moments when he's wonderful. Thanks to him, I got to know a lot of mysteries. Once he took me somewhere so beautiful . . . so beautiful I can't even describe it to you. If not for his awful whims, I could even fall in love with him, even though he is so ugly. Do you know that all the dead listen to him? He's their ruler. Once he promised he would lead me there . . ."

"God, Kasia, don't say things like that!"

"Don't worry, he told me I'll come back. If not for him, I would have been an ordinary fifteen-year-old girl."

"So what?" I ask. "What if you were! It's not so bad to be an ordinary girl. Look at me. I'm an ordinary girl. I live, and I'm satisfied. No one's trying to talk me into anything or choking me at night."

Kasia smiles sadly. "You don't even know how much I envy how little you need to be happy. But think, maybe it's like you don't know what you're losing being like that. If you could once in your life taste this sweetness, this grandeur, this sensation of being one with a billion spirits . . . maybe you wouldn't be so darn pleased with yourself."

"I'm not," I say. "I often find fault with myself, and I'd spank myself if only I could. But how can you spank yourself?"

"Very easily," Kasia says.

"How?" I ask. "If I hit myself once, it would hurt and I wouldn't be able to do it again."

"You could put your finger on a hot iron, for example, It hurts a hundred times more."

I look at her. I gingerly touch the scar on her cheek near her mouth with my finger. Kasia nods her head, answering the question I couldn't manage to ask. She nestles into me. She's silent, and so am I. I reach over and turn off the night-light. I look outside the window. It's dawn. Why did she punish herself like that?

WHEN THE ALARM rang, I somehow struggled out of bed. I washed quickly and made breakfast. Miraculously, I managed to wake up Kasia. She was saying she couldn't care less about school and the whole world, but I shook her and shook her until she got up and trudged to the bathroom, unconscious. While she was taking a shower, something came over me and I put on her Gypsy clothes. I was standing in front of the mirror and couldn't stop looking at myself. I looked so great and felt so fine in this outfit. Kasia came out of the bathroom at the moment I was doing a pirouette in front of the mirror and all those slips and skirts whirled around me fantastically. She laughed a great deal and wouldn't let me get changed. She just ran from the room and came back as a Gypsy. We stood in front of the mirror. Now we looked like two sisters from the same Gypsy camp. She started trying to talk me into going to school like that. I didn't want to, but she locked my clothes in the closet and hid the key somewhere. I was furious. I was ashamed to go out in the street, but eight o'clock was coming and what could I do? . . . We couldn't be late to school. I felt awful in the classroom, I thought that everyone was looking at me and laughing at me, but I got used to it very quickly.

After classes we were walking around the city and fooling around. We put scarves on our heads so we really looked like a bunch of Gypsies. We stopped ladies who were all made up and offered to tell their fortunes, but they ran away from us holding their purses. They must have been afraid we would rob them. Next to an engineering school we noticed a very strange woman. She was young and decently dressed, only she behaved so strangely.

WE'RE FOLLOWING HER and she's holding a stick in her hand like it's a microphone and speaking loudly into it: "Here's Zgorzelec, the towing service. The towing service? The cow pie service. Pie is, pie is, pie is, cow pie is service! Here's Zgorzelec, the towing service. The towing service? The cow pie service. Pie is, pie is, pie is, cow pie is service!"

The same thing over and over again, like a broken record.

She leaves. Kasia lifts a stick from the ground and speaks into it like a microphone: "Here's Zgorzelec, the towing service. The towing service? The cow pie service. Pie is, pie is, pie is, cow pie is service! Here's Zgorzelec, the towing service. The towing service? The cow pie service. Pie is, pie is, pie is, cow pie is service! Here's Zgorzelec . . ."

"Stop," I say, and cover her mouth.

She breaks away and repeats, "The towing service? The cow pie service. Pie is, pie is, pie is, cow pie is service!"

"I'm asking you to please stop making fun of her."

"I'm not making fun of her. I'm simply training. After all, this is my future."

"You're talking nonsense," I say. We look—that woman is returning with her stick. She passes us, constantly talking about this cow pie service. She's already gone. She's disappeared behind the corner.

"How is it," I say, "that some people are crazy?"

"There are two schools," Kasia says.

"Two schools for the insane?" I ask, surprised.

Kasia laughs. "No. But some think that this is an illness that has a mechanical basis, and others think that the basis is psychological. I personally vote for psychological."

"Meaning what?"

"That mental illness comes from thinking and not from organic changes in the brain. For example, Mateusz from Swiebodzice said—"

"What Mateusz?" I interrupt. "Who is he?"

"A friend of mine, a very good musician," Kasia replies. "But he's been dead for over a year."

"What happened to him?"

"Nothing much." Kasia laughs. "He wrapped himself in a wire and plugged it in. Before his death he wrote me a letter. You know how he signed it? 'Pork chop.' "

"Oh my God," I say.

"So Mateusz believed that there are no normal people at all, that the normal ones are just insane ones who very successfully pretend to be normal. And they call insane those people who can't pretend, or do not have the strength to pretend, and also those who don't care to pretend anything."

"Why did he do it?" I ask.

"Mateusz?"

"Yup."

"Because his guitar string broke and he didn't feel like replacing it. But actually he believed everything is an illness, life being the worst of them all, so in order to get well, you have to die. He'd had enough of this hospital, he wanted to get well soon. He did the right thing. Don't you feel you're dying, day in and day out?"

"No," I say. "I've never felt that way. But isn't it true that everyone has to die, only you shouldn't think about it?"

"And what *should* you think about?" Kasia asks.

At this moment some little boy runs up to us out of breath and asks, "What time is it?"

"What time do you want it to be?" Kasia replies.

"Thank you," the boy says, and takes off. Poor thing. He was in such a hurry he didn't even hear the reply. We're laughing at him.

I look at my watch and it's a quarter to five. Jesus Christ, it's a good thing God sent me this boy. "Let's go home quickly," I say to Kasia. "I need to change!"

"What happened?"

"What do you mean, 'What happened'? Catechism!"

And I start galloping toward the market square. Kasia runs after me and shouts, "You can't go in like that!"

"What are you talking about!"

Of course, she doesn't want to open the closet where my outfit is. She gave me the key to it only when I promised her that I would dress up like a Gypsy every day after school and that I would always dress like that at her house. I've kept my promise and ever since then I take off my stuff and turn into a Gypsy as soon as I get to Kasia's. I like myself in that outfit. It's beautiful and a hundred times more comfortable than what I'm used to. That Jigi had a great idea after all. I don't understand why Kasia doesn't like it, because as for me, if not for my mom, people and school, I could walk around like that for the rest of my life, and would do it at the drop of a hat. And to top it off, if I had pierced ears and could wear gold earrings, it would be quite wonderful.

That day I made it to church at the last minute. I sat at a desk and listened to the catechism teacher, who was quizzing people on Jesus' life giving one F after another. But instead of concentrating on the topic, I was thinking about Kasia. I always think about her. About her and Jigi.

Even now.

Why is it that although I'm so stupid and have only three dresses to my name, I'm satisfied and happy to be alive? And that when the sun is shining, I feel even more wonderful?

And Katarzyna is so smart and so rich. She can have everything she wants but is never happy. She's always thinking about all kinds of useless things. Somehow thoughts like those never come into my head. They don't come into anyone's head except hers.

When we're talking about something, for instance, and I say that I like it a lot, she immediately says what she doesn't like about it. "You didn't like that?" I ask, and she says, "No, what are you talking about, I liked it a lot." So what is it with her? Either you like something or you don't. But she both likes it and doesn't like it.

Take church, for example.

Katarzyna doesn't go to church at all. When I found out about that, I got scared, because maybe she's some kind of religious crackpot, the kind who go around to people's houses and pester them about the end of the world, and Mom always kicks them out. But no, it turned out that she's not. So then I thought even worse, maybe she's an atheist or a Satanist or one of those people who knock over gravestones in cemeteries. But it turned out she's not one of them either.

Because she believes in God, but she believes He exists more in the bathroom than in church. And then she kept blurting out even more horrible things. I tried not to listen, because I would have had to go to confession and confess for a long time everything I heard. I tried not to listen, I was praying to myself, but I heard. She was blaspheming so much I was afraid that thunder would strike her at once and kill her and me too. But it didn't strike, thank God. She even yelled at me because I covered my ears with my hands so I wouldn't hear. Then she called me a dumb sheep. I cried a little and told her I wasn't angry she'd called me a sheep, because all the people on earth are our Lord's sheep, and God is our shepherd and He is raising us.

To this Kasia said yes, He's raising us—for wool, skin and meat. So I ran away from her because I couldn't stand it. The next day we met in school and everything was fine between us, like nothing had happened. But Kasia doesn't talk to me about it anymore.

I know she holds me in contempt because I go to catechism. I feel very sad about that because I want her to like everything I do. Oh well. It's still good there's something she likes me for.

Why does she feel different about everything than everybody else? Everyone goes to church. Mom says that even party members go, even though officially they're not supposed to believe. At least if Katarzyna didn't believe in God . . . then maybe I could understand her. But she does believe, and one time she was talking about Him so beautifully, much nicer than the priest.

She also loves God. How can that be?

When she was talking about God, I practically had tears in my eyes and she did too. But suddenly she started to blaspheme that God is in me and I am God. I'm just an ordinary human being. Lord God is above us and rules us and it would be good and wonderful in the world if the devil wasn't always interrupting Him. How could I, Marysia Kawczak, be God? I'm stupid and don't lord over anything. Besides, Lord God is a man and I'm a girl. And I sin all the time, and then have to confess it later. I should confess that I listened to Kasia's blasphemies, but I'm afraid that if I was to repeat any of them to the priest, he would kill me and throw me out of the church on my ear. Or he would ask me who said these things and I would have to tell him it was Kasia, and then he could really do her some harm.

Or maybe he wouldn't harm her? Maybe he would call her in and convince her that you can't say things like that or else God will punish you. But I'm stupid, I can't convince her.

I'm worried about her. I'd really love to meet her after death in heaven, or at least in purgatory. Oh, if my Grandpa was alive . . . Grandma said that he was friends with the parish priest and that they even drank together. I would tell Grandpa about Kasia, and Grandpa would go and talk to his friend, the priest. Unfortunately, Grandpa's been dead for about forty years now; too bad he can't see us. Not me, or Tadzio, or Zosia, or Krysia. Or Zenus. He never even saw our dad, because when the Germans killed him, our dad was still in Grandma's belly.

But maybe he's sitting in heaven, and the whole time he's looking at us from up high, and he's happy when we're good . . .

Grandpa, tell me how to help Kasia.

Maybe it's Jigi who orders her to blaspheme. Yes, it's definitely him. He must blackmail her into thinking that if she doesn't blaspheme, he won't open the doors to the Land of Music. If I was in Kasia's place, I'd have driven him out altogether with his key and his music.

But Kasia can't live without music. She lives only for music. I understand her. Just like my mom says that she lives only for us. In order to bring us up and make people out of us. If somebody took us from her, what would she do?

She wouldn't have anything to live for.

ONE TIME DURING chemistry I came up with an idea.

"You know what?" I said to Kasia. "We should steal that key."

"How could we do it?" Kasia asked.

"We have to think about it."

We thought about it for a really long time and didn't come up with much. If Jigi was a real boy, it would be easy because Kasia says he's afraid of me and behaves better when I'm around. I'd grab him by his collar and take the key.

That left only one possibility. Kasia said she often dreams about him. So I thought that if I also dreamed about him, I could attack him in my dream and he'd have to give me the key. I'd definitely make him do it. Kasia told me exactly what Jigi looks like, so I could recognize him when I dreamed about him. Every night before falling asleep I thought, Jigi, I've got to dream about you, I must dream about you, I must dream about you . . .

But somehow I never dreamed about him.

Once I thought I dreamed about him, or maybe I really did dream about him, but I blew it.

It went like this:

I slept and slept, but then suddenly I woke up and couldn't open my eyes. I wanted to open them, but my eyelids were so heavy that when I tried to lift them, they closed. And the whole world was winking continuously. Finally I managed to open my eyes and everything in the room was cockeyed. I looked, I looked . . . but what did I see?

It wasn't that everything in the room was crooked, but that I was suspended in the air, tilted to one side.

I heard someone knocking at the window. I tried to turn around, but the moment I moved, I flew up to the ceiling like an astronaut in a rocket. I couldn't control my movements. The second I moved a hand or a leg, it immediately flew in some unexpected direction. Finally I managed to look out the window. It was dark—all I could see was a hand knocking at the windowpane.

I thought it was Jigi challenging me to a duel. My hair stood on end, but I gathered my wits and pushed away from the chandelier . . . I flew toward the window Jigi was lurking behind. But when I approached the window, I got scared I'd break the windowpane and Mom would yell at me. I jerked myself back and woke up again, this time for real.

Then I really regretted it and was angry at myself, because if I hadn't been afraid of breaking the window, I might have met Jigi. I would've had a word with him and taken the key to music. Kasia also regretted it a lot when I told her what had happened. Oh well, I thought to myself, maybe he'll knock tomorrow night. Unfortunately, the following night I dreamed about sunflowers. They seemed normal, but they were higher than the high-rise we live in. I leaned out the window, craned my neck, and they were not sunflowers but suns. A whole bunch of suns. I gazed at them so long that I forgot all about Jigi.

Now, whenever I fall asleep, I hope I'll finally dream about this boy with a hundred and twenty-eight teeth and seven fingers on each hand. He's skinny, has a large head and even bigger ears. Kasia says his face is tiny like a baby's, only his skull is huge and nearly bald, even though he's only fifteen.

It would be easy to recognize him.

I wonder how you can fit so many teeth into such a tiny mouth. They must be really tiny and thin as needles. I already saw his hand when it knocked at the windowpane, but I forgot to count the fingers. There must have been seven.

Today I went with Katarzyna and her mom on a trip to Sobotka, a tiny, pretty town in the foothills of Sleza Mountain. We took the car and Kasia's mom drove. We visited Kasia's grandma. She's only sixty. She's very happy and lives alone in a big beautiful house with a garden. Kasia was born there and lived there for a long time with her grandma. Her mom took her to Walbrzych when she was ten, but now every Sunday, or every other Sunday, they visit Grandma. There was also an elderly man who I thought at first was Kasia's grandpa, but as it turned out, Kasia's grandpa has been dead for a long time and this man is a friend of her grandma's. He was really neat. He had on a white short-sleeved shirt and a polka-dot bow tie. We ate dinner in the garden under a tree, and there was a lot of laughter and joy because the wind was blowing and Kasia and I were setting the table and the tablecloth kept blowing away from us.

If Kasia doesn't go visit her dad this year—and it seems she won't leave for another year—she'll spend her entire summer vacation at her grandma's and wants me to spend it with her. Her grandma and her mom asked me about it too. I hope my mom agrees to it. Mrs. Bogdanska promised that if push comes to shove, she'll plead on my behalf. Kasia'll bring all her electronic equipment from Walbrzych in a truck, and maybe she'll manage to write her grand opus in these two months. On the condition that I help her, of course. But how can I help her? I can only make sure Jigi doesn't get too out of hand. And we'll go on trips, swim in the bay, tan in the garden . . . We'll have a great time.

After dinner Kasia and I went for a walk. We were supposed to return right away, but we didn't come back for four hours because Kasia wanted to show me something on the slope of Sleza Mountain and we needed to go a long way up a tourist trail . . .

At first the path is wide and quite comfortable. Then the stones and rocks begin. Kasia goes up the hill like a deer. I'm not too shabby myself, and we soon reach a really strange place where two large stone sculptures stand, more than a thousand years old. It is cold and dark there, and the sculptures stand under a protective roof, surrounded by a chain-link fence, but on one side there is no fence and we can sit down and rest on a bear sculpture, which reminds me more of a giant pig.

Next to it, at arm's length, there is a statue without a head. Kasia tells me it's called *Maiden with a Fish*. This maiden, even though she has no head, is twice our size. Kasia read in a book that her head is supposedly in a museum in Wroclaw, but it isn't known whether it's actually the right head, because it's a man's.

Kasia likes to come here a lot because in this chilly half-darkness she comes up with her best musical ideas. The chain-link fence and the roof didn't used to be there, and then it was even more pleasant and strange. One day, though, she fell asleep and had the most terrifying dream of her life. She dreamed about the same place, but it was kind of different . . . There was no bear sculpture, the statue of the maiden with the fish stood alone, but it seemed larger and more angular, not so worn out and indistinct as it is now. Suddenly she heard a terrifying scream. She got scared and hid in the bushes. After a while a swarm of horrifying bearded people in clothes made of animal skins, with shiny studs, and armed with axes and bows, appeared around the statue. They brought a beautiful young girl with them. She was naked and tied up with rope. The girl was shouting in an incomprehensible language, pleading for mercy. A tall old man with white windblown hair stood over her. He hit her in the head with his club. The girl fell down. Then the bearded men quartered her body with axes and stuck the bloody bits on the ends of their spears and raised them toward the head of the statue, shouting in a chorus, *"Omni moa aaa! Omni moa aaa! Omni moa aaa! Ooo aaa!"* Petrified with fear, Kasia saw the face of the *Maiden with a Fish*, a monstrous face with bulging, gleaming eyes, horrible jaws full of sharp teeth . . .

I climb down the bear and slide away from the statue of the *Maiden with a Fish*.

"How many teeth did he have?" I ask. "Maybe a hundred and twenty-eight?"

"I didn't count," Kasia says, looking at me surprised. "You think it could've been him?"

"For sure," I say. We're standing and looking at the place where the head of the statue once stood. Kasia takes me by the hand.

"Do you remember when you had that dream?" I ask.

"A long time ago. Two years, maybe three . . ."

"Everything's falling into place," I say. "Soon afterward, he appeared in another dream and asked you to write a letter to your dad so he could send you all this electronic equipment."

"But it's a statue of a maiden and a fish."

"If she's a maiden, then I'm a man. I'm a hundred percent certain it's Jigi. You told me yourself that you come up with your best musical ideas here. Do you remember what our biology teacher said about tapeworms? That it's enough if its head stays in your body? The rest of it will grow back pretty quick."

"What of it?"

"His head," I say, feeling chills running down my spine, "his head went into you that day. It was you those bearded men sacrificed. Now you're his host."

Kasia lets go of my hand and runs away. I run after her. She stops by the tree and starts vomiting. Then she turns toward me all pale. She says with a snarl of disgust, "You pig! Thanks to you, I imagined a tapeworm in my mouth and I could almost feel it moving."

"I'm sorry."

"Forget it, it's just too bad about the dinner. Do you really think it was Jigi, or are you just joking around?"

"Believe me. It's him for sure. Now we know where to find the key to the Land of Music. I'll go look. You wait here and don't move." I turn toward the statue.

Kasia runs after me. "Mongoose, don't be crazy! You know this key doesn't exist in reality. It's a symbol."

"Say it is a symbol, I'm still going to look for it," I say. "It would be better for you not to come too close. I'm not afraid of him."

"Do you think I'm afraid? If that's the case, let's look for the key together."

We go under the roof and look around. I poke with a stick on one side, the *Maiden with a Fish* side, and Kasia on the other side. Suddenly I see something shining.

"Here it is!" I shout. Kasia's next to me already. I dig up a cap with "Coca-Cola" stamped on it. Kasia bursts out laughing and so do I. Kasia picks up the cap and puts it in her pocket. I examine the statue carefully. There are two grooves cut into the stone fish. "Something's engraved here," I say. "What can it mean?"

"It's a cult sign," Kasia says. "It means the sun. For the pagans the sun was the greatest god." I touch the crooked cross with the tips of my fingers and close my eyes. Something permeates me. The warmth, the light . . . the sun. I see the sun.

Omni moa aaa. Omni moa aaa. Ooo aaa.

"What happened?" Kasia asks.

"Nothing," I say, opening my eyes. I pull away from the statue and try to jump onto the stone bear's back. I raise my hands—I'm not going to reach it. I jump with all my might and grab the end of the body with my hands. I pull myself up, supporting my feet on the fish.

"What are you doing up there?" Kasia asks.

I stretch my chin toward the cut-off neck. There's something red on the top . . .

My foot slips, my fingers let go. I fall backward and—boom!—a grenade of golden stars explodes. Something bangs really loudly, as if in the depths of the earth. Oh, it's only my head on the stone.

Kasia's face appears from among the stars. "Mongoose!"

"Hush, I'm alright," I say, holding my head. Kasia leans over me, moves my hand away and pulls my hair apart.

"I don't see any blood. You could've killed yourself. Why did you climb up there anyway?"

"Because I thought the key would be there," I say, smiling. I get up and shake my head. Somehow it doesn't hurt. There's just an awful buzzing. I feel like an ant that got lost in an empty seashell.

Finally we emerge from the forest onto the highway. Beyond it there's a meadow sloping down and you can see the houses of the town. Kasia walks a few steps ahead of me. I've offended her. It's all because of my stupidity.

While we're walking down the mountain, Kasia tells me about the mysteries of the human mind. She says human consciousness is like a truck driver with a big load who doesn't know what he's hauling and can't stop and look in the truck bed, so he has to drive down all sorts of really rough roads and has to guess by the behavior of the truck what the load is, what it weighs and so forth. So you have to take risks, but at the same time you have to be very careful because a catastrophe threatens every minute. And she says that the comparison to the truck driver is a good one because it shows the difficulties and dangers of getting to know yourself.

So I ask her, Why bother? Can't you just keep driving and not think about what's in the truck? And Kasia says to this, Sure, go on ahead, go on a path made by the wheels of other trucks—a highway would be best—along with a million people just like you. But on that path I'd never know who I really was and I'd croak as stupid as I was the day I was born.

After shouting at me, she doesn't say a word for over half an hour. What am I supposed to do, seeing as I am so stupid and don't understand her? Kasia has read so many wise books and her mom is a doctor and her dad is a Frenchman in Africa. And me? . . . In my assigned readings at school I never read about things like that. There was a library at the school in Krzeszow, but how was I supposed to know which books to read and which not? You can't read them all. Besides, the librarian was almost never there. One time I took a book out and Mom yelled at me for reading fairy tales instead of studying . . .

"Kasia!" I call. "I would really want to know what I'm carrying, why and where!"

Kasia stops, waits for me. And smiles sweetly.

"I know you want that, Mongoose," she says. "I got carried away because I really wanted you to know everything I know. It's still not much, but it's better than nothing. But you have to understand that if you want to know yourself and the world, you can't wear so many blinders."

"I don't wear blinders."

"You wear a lot of them, and because of that, you're blind as a mole. I know it's not your fault that you let them be put on you, but eventually you're going to have to tear them off. No one's going to do it for you."

"So I'll tear them off," I say. "But how am I supposed to do it? I don't see them anywhere!"

"Let's take your faith in God . . ."

"Oh, Kasia, don't say anything about God. I beg you."

"But it's the stupidest of all your blinders."

"No, no, stop, don't say anything!"

"Why?"

"Because it's not allowed. You can really be punished for it. I beg you, don't say anything!"

"I'm going to tell you only one thing. If God is truly the way you imagine Him to be, how can you love Him, how can you believe in Him? He only deserves hatred and contempt. He's some kind of tyrant, a vengeful idiot, a bloodthirsty psychopath."

"Stop!" I'm trying to outshout her so God won't be able to hear her. I cover my ears. Kasia's still saying something. I run from the highway to the meadow. I'm running down, down the slope. I stumble and fall. Kasia catches up to me, she's saying something again. Screaming, I cover my ears. Kasia straddles me and pulls my hands away from my ears. I scream and scream. Kasia presses my hands to the grass, looks at me from above. I'm lying down, unable to get away from her, and I'm screaming.

I don't have the strength to scream anymore. Silence. The birds are chirping. And Kasia says with a smile, "Imagine that someone gave you a large and beautiful palace as a present. Bright, spacious and beautifully furnished. Think, wouldn't you offend the person who gave you the present if you crawled into a dusty cubbyhole under the staircase and stayed there for the rest of your life?"

"Yup," I say. "I would."

"The human mind is just such a palace, a gift from God. Wonderful, complicated, incomprehensible. And to you it seems like a rusty herring can. So it's not me who's blaspheming, it's you who's continually blaspheming!"

"I don't blaspheme, it's not true!"

"But you do! You treat God like He's a petty nine-to-five bureaucrat who's constantly on the take."

"I don't think like that at all, I don't give bribes!"

"So what do you call running to church every week for a Mass and rattling off evening prayers? What do you call collecting little sins in your pocket so you can pour them out in front of a priest onto the confessional counter once a month? What do you call your mindless recitation and regurgitation of ten Hail Marys for repentance, and then bye-bye!"

"What more can I do? The priest didn't say I should attend Mass every day! If he said it, I would have gone! What can I do if he never told me to do a thousand Hail Marys, always only ten? . . ."

"It wasn't the priest who created you, it was God. He created you so you could try to equal Him in wisdom. Above all, He created you so you could also be free from Him, do you understand? Free, free, free! Because freedom is the prayer that brings God the greatest joy. Pray to Him with your freedom."

"Let me go!" I say angrily. Kasia frees my hands, sits on the grass. She sighs painfully. She turns away from me. Her back begins to tremble. I touch her.

"Kasia, don't cry."

"I feel really sorry for you," she says through sobs, her voice breaking. "There's such tremendous goodness in you, and you're not even going to notice when you lose it . . ."

She sobs louder and louder.

"Don't worry, I'm not going to lose it," I say.

"You will, you will, because goodness is a huge and heavy burden, which you have to carry throughout your entire life. And you have to be really wise in order to know how to carry it. Because it's so heavy that even the best will run out of strength. Then you have to know where to lay it down so you can rest and carry it again."

"And do you know?"

"No, because I'm not good and I cast it off long ago. But you should know because one way or another you're condemned to it. I'm really afraid for you. One day you'll cast off that burden with a terrible thud and you'll lose everything because you don't know how to live without it."

"So what can I do?"

"You have to understand that you are the only proprietor of your soul. You can't give it to anyone. Or anything. Don't be angry with me for what I said, because I love you a lot, more than anyone in the world."

Kasia starts crying again. So do I. We're both crying and the sun is setting and everything turns orange—the sky, the bend of the road down there, Kasia's face and my hands. Everything's so beautiful. We've stopped crying. We're sitting and admiring the golden braids of clouds.

"I want to tell you something else about Jigi," Kasia says. "To you it seems like he's my enemy. It's not true. Jigi is a part of me, a messenger from my very being, from my soul. And though he really wants to eat me up, I can't get rid of him. I must fight him, defend myself against his teeth when he's strong and opens his disgusting jaws, but when he gets weak I have to take it easy on him. I can't defeat him, because if I kill him my internal world would perish together with him, and all that would remain would be an emptiness—emptiness, emptiness. I'd be an empty shell. And if he gobbles me up, I'd be a total schizo in a lunatic asylum. So I have to fight him ceaselessly and make truces and break them and . . . and so forth and so on, until the end of the ages, until the chain of my reincarnations comes to an end."

I rest my head on her lap and close my eyes. My thoughts fly around like those flies that Tadzio locked in a jar once. Kasia strokes me delicately.

"Why is Jigi so bad and ugly?" I ask.

"I don't know. Maybe because I'm like that somewhere inside. Maybe one day I'll manage to bring him up to be a good boy. You don't even know, my dear Mongoose, how much I've changed for the better, thanks to you. But I don't want to only take from you, I also want to give you something back. And maybe that's why I really want to wake you up."

"But I'm not sleeping," I say, and open my eyes. I look up at Kasia. She smiles at me and there is a lot of hair and clouds all around her face. There's less and less gold in them, and more and more red. Kasia lifts her face up to the sky.

"Oh, if you could only see the beauty I see," she says. She stretches her arms in the air and moves them slowly, like she's flying.

"Tell me about it," I say quietly.

"It's something very little, smaller than nothing, but also giant, giant like everything and even more than everything. I can't tell you anything more. I'd really like for you to get to know it on your own."

"But how can I if I don't even know what it is or how it looks?"

"No, no, you can't do it yet."

"How do you know? Maybe I already can."

"Only a few people can make it there," Kasia says. "This beauty could even kill if you saw it." She smiles beautifully. The halo of her hair is flaming red. She looks like an angel, or maybe she is an angel. I kneel in front of her and put my hands together as if to pray.

"Lead me there, I beg you. I want to see this beauty too."

WHEN WE RETURNED to her grandma's house, Kasia's mom examined my head and my eyes and said that it looked like it all ended well, but if for some reason in the evening or at night I felt bad, or if I felt like throwing up, I should call her immediately. Then we went to Walbrzych. They dropped me off right in front of my apartment.

It wasn't even nine and everyone was sleeping in front of the TV. Only Tadzio was really into watching. I carried the girls to their beds and I took a quick shower and went to bed . . .

Two hours have passed. It's after eleven.

Somehow I can't sleep. I'm lying in the darkness and I have so many thoughts in my head I don't know where to start. They're pushing their way in from everywhere. I can't even tell which is which.

I feel sorry for Kasia. She's so smart and brave, but if she's going to continue to take pity on that Jigi of hers, he's going to devour her in the end. If she could only see herself at night . . . but it was no longer her, but Jigi.

After all, it's better to be empty inside than to go crazy and scream and toss around for the rest of your life. Even if she doesn't go crazy, she'll have to suffer and argue with him all the time. It's terrible to have someone like that within you. It's like having a worm in your mouth and not being able to spit it out. And to be in such torment for the rest of your life? That's labor, not life. We have enough troubles, so why look for them in yourself? You need to go to school, clean up after yourself, take care of the kids and still do homework. The day just started, and now it's already ending. How are you supposed to find the time to look over and over at what's in the load? You can't even look back or stop. I'm curious whether I also have someone like Jigi. I guess I don't, because where would he come from? But if he did exist, what would he look like? Would he be as ugly as Jigi? I'd really like to see him, even for a second. What could I have inside? Of course, inside there are veins, there's the heart, the liver, kidneys and stomach. What else? In the stomach there is what I eat. There's also blood, but it leaks out only when you poke yourself. Oh, I have saliva in my mouth, but I can always spit it out. And what's inside the head? A brain. And there are thoughts in the brain. What could they look like? . . . They must be very small for sure because the head is no bigger than a ball, but there are so many of them in there. What could a thought look like, other than being so small? For example, you think of something and then you say it, but speech is invisible. If you write it down on a piece of paper, it changes into words. And you know right away what they look like. They consist of letters. I write small letters, straight and clear. Other people write them tilted. Some to the left, others to the right. Some write them big, others even smaller than mine, so small you can hardly read them. So if thoughts look like words, they must look different inside every person. Different in Poles than in Russians, and still different in French people. But there are also thoughts you don't know how to say or write down. What do they look like? Maybe they look like spilled ink? And where do they all come from? Maybe they're in the brain from the beginning, only they're asleep and sometimes some of them wake up, and then you start thinking. Or maybe they fly in from somewhere. But where from? It's only other people's thoughts that fly. When someone says something to me, they fly into my ears as words. And when I read something, they fly in through my eyes as sentences. Your own thoughts, I think, sleep inside, in the brain. What wakes them up? Because an alarm clock wakes me up. First it wakes me up when it rings in the other room for Dad, and then Dad puts it into our room and after two hours it wakes me up again. If I don't hear it, then Mom wakes me up, or Tadzio wakes me, but I wake Tadzio more often. And when I wake up, my thoughts wake up. But only some. And which ones do depends on all kinds of things. Different ones wake up when I get up for school, still others wake up on Sunday. But are my thoughts really asleep when I'm asleep? Maybe I sleep and they run around? Or else why would we have dreams? Maybe because when you fall asleep, your thoughts don't go to sleep and you don't think them, but thoughts think themselves and dreams are created. Some are so strange that I can't believe they're my own. Mom says that when you dream about fire, you have to be cautious with your apartment because thieves could rob you. But why don't you dream about thieves? And what do you dream about when your house is going to catch on fire?

Because when carbon monoxide leaked from the stove, I dreamed about this monster in the waiting room, in the cinema . . . and maybe it was my Jigi. Oh, I wouldn't want for him to turn out to be my Jigi. He was so terrifying that the minute I think about him, chills run up and down my spine. He also had a lot of teeth. But his eyes were the worst. Deep-set and small. Perfectly still. He looked at me like a snake. Even when he was chomping on other people, he was still staring at me like he wanted to eat me. That's because he did. He seemed small, but when he opened his jaws, he could swallow the heads of the other men that he crunched on later. And I think he was naked, because I didn't see his clothes. I didn't see his hands either. I think I remember his eyes the most. And he was flying around so fast, even though he didn't have wings. He flew low, close to the floor. But he was large, because I saw his eyes above people's heads, up high. He was gray and wet. Or maybe he wasn't wet, maybe he was dry. Gray, but a bit whitish. Disgusting. I wouldn't want to meet him again.

But he was good in the end. He was my friend. Because he was only terrifying me and chomping on people in a dream, but in reality he saved me and my whole family from death. I'm a pig. I shouldn't think so badly about my friend, no matter how disgusting he is.

My apologies to you, my monster. Don't be angry with me. Thank you so much for flying into my dream and warning me. Who knows, maybe you really are beautiful and you appeared to me in such horrifying form only because if I had found you to be as beautiful as you are in reality, I wouldn't have wanted to wake up, because I would have wanted to look at you for as long as I could. Even if you do look like you did in my dream, I like you a lot, because you have a good heart. You can visit me whenever you want—that is, if you want to. And please don't be offended by me. I swear I'll get used to you somehow. Maybe not right away, but in the end I'll get used to you.

Holy Mother! Now I know, it just came to me: he looked like a giant leech. Not quite like a leech, but a lot like one. And he was hard, not squishy like a leech.

I am an awful bitch after all . . .

I swear to you that I'll get used to you, my beloved Monster, only be patient and give me a little time. I'm curious to know what your name is, because my name is Marysia. But Kasia calls me Mongoose. You can call me whatever you want. You can call me Marysia, you can call me Mongoose. And you know . . . if it was up to me and you didn't have anything against it, I would prefer to call you "Pimpush." Do you like this name? If I see you again, can I call you Pimpush?

But Pimpush doesn't make a sound, not a word. Maybe he's rescuing some other girl from death. Maybe he's not just mine.

Because Jigi belongs only to Kasia. He's very musical, that's why Kasia composes and plays so beautifully. Maybe Pimpush has some exceptional talents too . . . Maybe he can sew really well, and if he belongs only to me, then I'll become a very good seamstress and all the clients will praise me and be happy with the dresses I've sewn. I'm not going to charge too much, but I won't do it for too cheap, because Mom says that when a seamstress doesn't charge much, then people say she doesn't know how to sew. Since if she knew how to sew, she wouldn't be charging so little. So I'm not gonna charge too much or too little. You can learn a lot in trade school in three years. You can learn to cut fabric and stitch all kinds of seams. I would like to be able to sew wedding dresses also. And to sew first communion dresses for girls.

Mrs. Kaminska sewed my communion dress. It was very nice, but she ran out of fabric, so my dress didn't go all the way down to my feet but was two inches short. Other girls showed only their shoes when they walked. But some other girl's dress was too long, and when she came up to the altar, she tripped and fell. Everyone in the church laughed, but she started to cry.

So it's better to have your dress too short than too long.

It was muddy right outside the church and the floor inside was dirty too. When she got up, it turned out her whole dress was dirty in the front. She wanted to run out of the church, but her mom caught her and forced her to go to the altar, all dirty. The priest put the Host in her mouth, but because she was bawling so badly, she choked on it and spit it out. Her mom smacked her on the head, but the priest said it didn't matter and gave her another Host and she swallowed that one all right, even though she was bawling even louder.

And my Host got stuck to my palate. I couldn't get it with my tongue, I had to lift it up with my nail, but no one saw me scratching it. I shouldn't have done it, because it's Jesus' body, but what could I do when it got stuck?

That was the most beautiful day of my life. Tadzio was four back then and he wolfed down a lot of cake. He didn't manage to make it to the bathroom and got his pants all dirty. Normally I would have smacked him . . . but instead, I took his pants off and washed him. I didn't shout at him or get repulsed by him. I vowed that I'd never shout at him or anything like that ever in my life, but then I forgot about it and have even argued with him a few times since then. And once I even talked back to my mom. That wasn't that long ago, just last year. She smacked me across the face, no doubt about it. On top of that, she didn't speak to me for a really long time, but she finally accepted my apology. It was lucky the way it turned out. One girl yelled at her mom and her whole face got twisted and stayed that way until she died. She became an old maid and didn't have any children, because who would want to marry a girl like that, with a twisted face . . . ?

Tadzio enters the room. He slips into the bed in the dark.

"Are you sleeping?" he asks.

"No," I say.

"You wouldn't believe the film I saw. It was about this bitch who killed guys. And then she got killed by this other bitch because it turned out this other one was a disguised cop. It's too bad you didn't see it. She had a cool gun. A small one, but when it fired, it blew the other woman's brains to bits. She whipped out a pack of cigarettes and offered it to the other one, but they weren't cigarettes, it was really a gun . . . and it went fucking boom."

"Don't talk like that."

"And she only had one bullet. If she didn't get her, that would have been it because the other one had a revolver in her hand, a big one with lots of bullets."

"Did you say your prayers?" I ask.

"Sure."

"When?"

"Before watching TV."

"Baloney," I say, but I also remember that I didn't say one either. I step down from the bed and take Tadzio by his collar. We kneel and begin to say in unison:

"Our Father which art in heaven, hallowed be thy name. Thy kingdom come. Thy will be done in earth, as it is in heaven. Give us this day our daily bread. And forgive us our trespasses, as we forgive those who trespass against us. And lead us not into temptation, but deliver us from evil . . . Amen.

"Hail Mary, full of grace, the Lord is with thee. Blessed art thou among women and blessed is the fruit of thy womb, Jesus. Holy Mary, Mother of God, pray for us sinners, now and at the hour of our death. Amen.

"Glory be to the Father, and to the Son, and to the Holy Spirit. As it was in the beginning, is now, and forever shall be, world without end, Amen."

Tadzio wants to hop into bed, but I grab him by the leg and say, "And what about the prayer to the guardian angel?" So we get down and say:

> *"Now I lay me down to sleep,*
> *I pray the Lord my soul to keep,*
> *If I should die before I wake,*
> *I pray the Lord my soul to take."*

Suddenly, on the very top of the *Maiden with a Fish*, where her head once was, I see a sign written in red chalk. I see it vividly, the same as before I fell down. When I fell down, it disappeared and I forgot about it. Now I see it again. It's glowing a bloody red in the dark:

KASIA, RUN AWAY! MARYSIA WENT TO HELL!

Am I dreaming that?

Chapter Four

KASIA AND I are sitting on a balcony. We're supposed to be study-ing, but the book is lying on the table and we're sprawled all over lawn chairs and don't want to do anything because it's hot.

In front of us is a fan that can swivel its head. It blows at Kasia and then at me, and on its way it ruffles the pages of the book. If it was alive, it would have grown bored with cooling off two lazy girls long ago. It's been three days since we did anything other than tan on the balcony. I'm brown and Kasia's golden. We have identical T-shirts on. They're yellow. One says GLIMP, and the other, GLUMP. When we put them on for the first time, Kasia called me "Glump" all day long and I called her "Glimp."

When I close my eyes, it's all rosy from the sun, and I'm having terrible pangs of conscience. An hour ago I sinned, really badly. Here's what happened:

I'm returning from school with Kasia. We're having vanilla ice cream in sugar cones.

"Katarzyna," I say, "what would I see if I was really brave?"

"What?"

"You know, the kind of beauty that could kill you when you look at it. What does it look like?"

"Please don't ask, because I'm not gonna tell you."

"But I am asking, so tell me."

"Stop, because then I'll tell you and you'll end up just like Eve."

"So you told Eva and you won't tell me?"

"What?" Kasia looks at me, surprised. "I? Told Eva?"

"You mentioned her," I say. "Eva Bogdaj."

Kasia laughs. "Stupid, I was thinking of Eve from the Garden of Eden. And besides, I don't know anything, I was only kidding back then."

"I don't believe you."

"Do you want me to swear?"

"Yup, swear."

"I swear on this ice cream I don't know anything. If I lied, it'll fall out of my hand."

So I go bang! Right on her ice cream and it's already on the ground. Kasia looks at it sadly. "What did you do that for?"

"Take mine," I say, giving her my cone.

"I don't need yours," Kasia says sulkily.

"You don't want it?"

"No."

"Then I don't want it either!" So I slam mine into the ground too. Now there are two ice cream cones on the sidewalk.

"Stupid idiot," Kasia says.

"And you lied—because it fell."

"You knocked it out of my hand."

"Katarzyna, I'm asking you to tell me about this beauty because I think I'm really gonna go crazy if you don't. I think about it all the time."

"I really regret telling you about it at all."

"But you did. Tell me."

"Understand, sweetheart," Kasia says softly. "It's a secret knowledge, only for the chosen."

"You mean I'm not as good as you?"

"I didn't say that."

"Tell me, even a little bit. Don't be such a—"

"It's something you have to reach yourself."

"At least tell me how I'm supposed to do that. Because I'm gonna go for it and reach it."

"It may turn out to be too difficult for you. Maybe you aren't cut out to see it . . . Maybe you were cut out simply to live."

"How do you know what I was cut out for?"

Kasia sighs. She's smashing the ice cream cones on the sidewalk with her shoes. The cones burst with a soft crunch. Kasia looks at me, biting her lip. Finally she says, "You want to find out?"

"Yes."

"Okay. See that old granny?"

She points to an elderly woman sitting alone on the bench next to the square.

"I see," I say.

"Go and tell her loudly, 'You pitiful old cow.' "

"What are you talking about?" I say, appalled.

"So you don't want to know."

"And if I tell her, I'm going to find out?"

"This might be the beginning of that knowledge," Kasia says mysteriously. "You have to start somewhere."

"In that case," I say resolutely, "I don't want to know or see anything."

"Great. That's fine with me," Kasia replies, taking me by the hand as we leave our wasted ice cream. But then I stop suddenly, because I really want to know.

"Wait for me," I say, and go up to the old woman in the square. Oh well, I'll say it. The worst that could happen is that she'll smack me with her cane and I'll get what I deserve.

I walk up to her. I take a deep breath and say loudly, "You pitiful old cow."

The old woman looks at me, furrows her brows and, smiling, puts her hand to her ear. "What did you say, sweetie?"

"I'm really sorry," I answer, and then I run up to Kasia. "She was deaf."

Kasia begins to giggle. She giggles and giggles. Somehow I don't feel like laughing.

"You're in luck," she says finally. "It was a warning. Apparently you're not supposed to know."

"I can say it to another old lady," I say.

Kasia turns serious. "I wouldn't advise you to. It's too easy for you. I underestimated your audacity. Don't you feel ashamed saying such a terrible thing to an old woman? She could be your grandma, after all."

"You told me to," I say angrily.

"I only told you that if you said that to her, you'd find out something. It was your choice, you didn't have to go over there. And guess what? Wasn't I right? Didn't you find something out about yourself?"

Kasia looks at me a little strangely, like she despises me. And I begin to feel ashamed. How could I do that? What happened to me? What a nice old woman and what an awful thing I said to her. So what if she didn't hear me. God, what have I done? I'm going to tell the priest everything and let him give me penance; I'm going to get on my knees and pray all day.

"Oh, what a sweet creature," Kasia says ironically. "First she's going to trip up an old woman, then she's going to confession right away so she'll have a clean conscience again. So clean she could lick it like an ice cream cone."

Once again she's been hearing my thoughts. I don't know where to hide. I lower my head and feel like crying.

"I know," I say. "I'm just a bitch—a pig. But I didn't trip her up."

Kasia bursts out laughing. She caresses me.

"My sweet little piglet," she says softly. "Don't worry, it's my fault. Let's go. I'll buy us more ice cream."

We lick the fresh ice cream cones all the way to her house.

Here's what it all boils down to. I didn't find out anything, and on top of that I sinned. And Kasia despises me. For sure.

I look at Kasia, shading my eyes from the sun. She looks so beautiful with her disheveled rosy-golden bun. I hope she hasn't fallen asleep.

"Katarzyna . . ."

"What?" she asks drowsily.

"You know, I lied to you about that woman on the bench," I say. "I didn't say all those bad things. I asked her what time it was and she told me she didn't have a watch on. I was only pulling your leg because I really wanted you to tell me about this beauty."

Kasia smiles without opening her eyes.

"I suspected that," she says. "Because, Mongoose, I know that such horrible words would never leave your lips. And I love you for that."

God, I'm so low. Kasia loves me and I lied to her. I don't deserve her love.

"Katarzyna," I say.

"What now?"

"I wasn't pulling your leg before. I was pulling it just now. Those horrible words *did* leave my lips. I'm a jerk and a liar."

Kasia turns her face toward me. She opens her eyes, looks at me and smiles.

"For that," she says, "I love you even more."

"For what?"

"That you can't even lie!"

And Kasia has a fit of laughter. She wriggles on the lawn chair holding her stomach and laughs and laughs and can't stop.

And the fan turns its head between us disapprovingly, like it's telling me, "No, no, you can't even lie. No, no, Kasia will never tell you about the beauty. No, no, you'll never see it."

I'M IN CHURCH and I'm kneeling, not in the pew but on the stone floor. A crumb pokes me in my right knee, but let it hurt, let me be in pain.

I was confessing to the priest and was about to tell him about the old woman, but I got scared and didn't tell him. Instead, I told him that I skipped two Sunday Masses. But that wasn't true. So the priest gave me a light penance, because how was he supposed to know what a rogue I really am? So I decided I would kneel for two hours and not a minute less. I'm not gonna move and I won't get up, no matter what.

But only twenty minutes have passed and I can't deal with this crumb under my knee. It's dark in church, only a few lights are burning on the altar. Occasionally an old woman will come in, sit for a bit, pray for a bit and then leave.

I'm kneeling behind a pillar. No one can see me.

God forgive me. I used vulgar words toward an elderly person and I'm a liar. I lied to Kasia, and even though I told her right away, I still lied. And I'm lying to my mom all the time. She struggles alone with groceries, with the kids, with the whole house, and I do nothing, just sit around the whole time at Kasia's.

I want to be with her all day and night and never be apart from her. Why wasn't I born her real sister? Then we would be together all the time. Take Zosia and Krysia, for instance. They were born twins and they're always together and they go everywhere together. Why can't Kasia and I be like that?

Why didn't Kasia's mom have me along with her? Or, why didn't my mom have her with me? But it would have been better for Kasia's mom to have me, because if my mom had had us, how would Kasia have managed to get money for all her synthesizers and computers? And maybe she wouldn't have been so talented?

Because I'm not talented. Maybe I am, only I don't know what in. I like to sew, but I only sew by hand and I don't know if I would know how to sew on a sewing machine. That will only come out in trade school, that is, if I pass my exams.

I don't know what's gonna happen to me when Kasia goes to Africa. I bet I'm gonna cry day and night. I really like my mom and Zenus, and the girls, Tadzio and Dad, but I love my Kasia the most. I don't know what it is, but even if she stops loving me, I'm never gonna forget about her and I will love her the rest of my life. Lord God, tell me what to do so she won't go.

Because Kasia's begun to compose again, and says that if she can pull it off, and write her grand composition, she'll give up the record idea and will bring her dad a cassette. But we were supposed to spend the whole two months of vacation at her grandma's house and my mom even agreed to it.

Oh God, I can't handle this. This crumb has dug all the way into my knee and I still have so much kneeling left to go. When this hour is over, there'll be one more left to go. God, help me stay true to my resolution. It hurts me so much, like it's never hurt me before.

Oh God, do something so that Kasia won't go to Africa this year. Let her wait a year. Give me one more year with Kasia and then I'll be good and will listen to my parents and never lie again or anything like that. If she doesn't go, I swear I'll kneel every day for an hour. I wish she wouldn't go. I'm gonna kneel just like I'm kneeling now, all straightened out, not sitting on my heels either, because it's a hundred times worse and I'm all shaky and I can't stand it, even though only half an hour of kneeling has gone by. But I'm gonna kneel to the end of this hour and I'll kneel through the next one, only please God make it so Kasia doesn't go and we can spend the school break at her grandma's in Sobotka.

I'll help her so she'll definitely write her grand composition, the most beautiful one in the world. Why is she in such a hurry? She's still young, only fifteen. And she'll be composing and playing for years.

And God, let me suffer through all this kneeling because I'm gonna go crazy soon from all this pain. I'm all sweaty. I've been kneeling for a full half hour. Half an hour is a long time, but I still have an hour and a half to go. God, help me get through it.

I really can't stand it any longer. If only I could sit on my feet . . . but you can't. At least take this crumb away from under my knee. It must be some kind of small pebble. Who brings little pebbles into church? And I wanted to kneel a little longer . . . but I can't!

What does "I can't" mean? I have to, that's all there is to it. I'm going to make it. God, if you give me this year with Kasia, I'm gonna take the pebble that's under my knee and I'll kneel on it every day. I'll get used to it. You can get used to anything. Some people are seriously ill, sometimes something hurts them for years, and they can handle it. I'd handle it too.

I hear footsteps behind me—it must be a woman, because I hear heels clopping.

I stop shaking, put my hands together and put my head down. The woman passes me by and sits in a nearby pew with her back toward me. I'm shaking again. I'm so sweaty, like I ran a hundred miles. I can't take it any longer, but I have to. Angels, save me! Time's dragging on so slowly. The woman turns around. I calm down for a moment. I shouldn't be breathing so loudly, because you can hear it throughout the whole church. Oh, Kasia, save me. Just give me one more year. Then I'll try to forget about you, because somehow I'll have to live and study in trade school. I can't! . . .

God forgive me, I can't do this any longer.

First I sit on my heels and then on my side. Now I'm sitting on the floor. I want to straighten my knees, but I can't.

You need to do it slowly. The pebble was so small, like the head of a match, maybe even smaller. I pick it out of my knee, put it in my handkerchief and place it under the belt of my skirt.

It's all over. Now God won't hear me. I promised Him and I didn't keep my promise.

Ouch . . .

It feels so strange to walk, like I have sticks, not legs.

I sit on the bench, but it's hard to. My legs feel huge, like puffed-up balloons, and they're full of pins and needles, though they look normal. Next time I'll make it for sure.

I'm gonna kneel on that same pebble, and you'll see, God, I'll be able to handle two hours. I'm gonna kneel in my room tonight after Tadzio falls asleep. Be patient, Lord God. I swear I'll be able to stand it this time. Tonight. I'll rest a bit, and tonight . . .

KASIA STOPS PLAYING in the middle of a bar and says angrily, "Why are you staring at me all the time!"

"I was just looking," I say. "Because I couldn't figure out how to solve this, so I got lost in thought and I looked up . . ."

"All right, quiet!"

She starts playing again. The whole room is roaring with music and I feel it against my body like a wind is blowing from the speakers. I lean over Kasia's notebook. I'll do my homework a little later, at home.

Since the beginning of the week Kasia hasn't paid any attention to school. On Monday she got an F in math. She would have stopped going to school if I hadn't been doing her homework for her and urging her to go all the time. I promised her mom I'd watch over her. I do what I can. At school I have to watch her all the time so she doesn't argue with the teachers. She's irritated all the time and picks on me for the smallest thing.

Yesterday our physics teacher called her to the board, and I knew perfectly well that she didn't know anything, and I was really afraid she was gonna argue with her, because Mrs. Zelenow is also very irritable. So suddenly I started moaning, gripped my tummy and fell to the floor. I was moaning so loudly and I was so bowled over in pain that the teacher wanted to run to call an ambulance, but luckily the bell rang and I felt better immediately and Kasia was saved this time.

I've learned how to forge her handwriting. It was very difficult because the way I write, I write uniform letters, and every letter of Kasia's is different, one leaning to the left, one leaning to the right, one large, and one so small that it's unclear whether it's a letter or maybe a period. But finally I've learned to the point where even Kasia doesn't know what she wrote and what I wrote.

When I am doing my own homework, though, I always forget and sometimes I make such a sloppy letter that I'm ashamed.

Only a few days are left till the end of the school year. Some teachers just shrug their shoulders and give us grades, but others squeeze things in to the very end. Like, for example, our physics teacher and our math teacher. Some things you've already forgotten and here you have to learn them again.

Mom asked me several times about the rehearsals, but I always come up with something and tell her all kinds of silly things. One time she wanted me to tell her the poem I'm going to read during the celebration. Luckily I remembered that poem about "the spit-out lungs that do not hurt" . . . and recited it loudly.* Mom liked it a lot and said she never would have guessed she had such a talented daughter. The girls and Tadzio liked it too, only Zosia spat and spat for the rest of the day, and when I asked her why she was spitting, she said she was spitting out her lungs. I had already forgotten about the poem and got scared that maybe she was sick. But she said not at all, that she was spitting just in case, because if she spit them out, they'd never hurt her. I laughed my head off, and I repeated what she said to Mom, and Mom said, "What a smart one I got."

---

*This is a prime example of first-rate socialist realist poetry. The poem, by Wladyslaw Broniewski, is called "Elegy to Ludwik Warynski."

Tadzio said that Dad's lungs must be all black, because when he spits, his spit is black. Then Zosia remembered the time I was cooking my "cream of tights," which was black, and said that maybe Dad ate it by accident and now he's spitting it out. Mom said it's because of the coal mine that Dad is spitting out the coal. So Tadzio said that when he grows up he's going to work in the coal mine too and he'll cover the entire balcony of our downstairs neighbor with black spit—the one who's always picking on us about our banging, which is why the girls are afraid to run around the house.

Mom doesn't let them go outside because recently this girl from our development got run over by a car and died. So the girls swear that they'll only play around the carpet rail, but Mom's afraid that now people drive their cars in such a way that it's not a big deal to run over a carpet rail. She's really unhappy we're living here. She says that if the Kaminskis hadn't joined their apartment to ours by knocking down part of the wall, she'd be happy to pack things up and return to Jawiszow, because though it's cramped and uncomfortable there, it's just different. She's already looking forward to September, when our whole family will go to dig up potatoes from our field. Dad has been there already on his bicycle once and said they're all right and they're growing.

Oh, it is so quiet right now. Kasia always calls it "that famous ringing silence."

Kasia rewinds the tape, plays it from the beginning, and plop, she sits beside me on the sofa.

"Listen up," she says. So I put down my pen, which I was only biting the whole time, and I sit comfortably. The music flies out of the speakers and we're sitting and listening.

"What do you think?" Kasia asks.

"Sounds good," I say.

"So listen, because soon I'm gonna spoil it," she says, and screws up her face. Suddenly she smiles. "No, that *was* good. Even that waviness came out pretty cool. Did you hear it?"

"Uh-huh."

The music ends. Kasia runs over to stop the tape.

"So maybe I can warm up dinner now?" I ask.

"No, no, I don't want to eat," Kasia says. "Just warm up enough for yourself."

She turns on the tape recorder and sits behind the synthesizer. There's music again.

I'm hungry, but I'm not gonna warm things up just for myself. I'll eat something when I get home. That's too bad because today Miss Zenobia was in a good mood, and when she's in a good mood, the dinner is always fabulous. She got a letter from her son in West Germany. She said he got a work permit and that her granddaughter is already sitting up. The granddaughter's name is Greta. Miss Zenobia's a little worried that she's going to be babbling in German from an early age.

Oh, the tea got cold.

I'm gonna go and make some more. I get up and leave. There was a time I was afraid to move when Kasia was recording, but now I know that the tape recorder records directly from the synthesizer and you can scream and jump and only the music will be recorded.

I pee in the bathroom and then wash my hands with a fragrant soap. I go into the kitchen and put water on for tea. I peek at the pots. I steal a cold potato with dill. Then another. And then yet another. There are cutlets in the frying pan. Oh, how soft. Very tasty—I just ate a whole one. I take the ladle and dip it in the soup. And it's a *chlodnik.* Delicious. I eat two huge ladles. That way, I've had my dinner. Oh, the water is boiling already. I make two cups of tea, I put them on a tray. There was supposed to be dessert . . . I peek in the fridge. There it is. Jell-O with fresh cherries and whipped cream. I place it on the tray and carefully take it to the room.

I walk in. Silence. Kasia is lying on the sofa, staring at the ceiling. I place the tray on the table beside her.

"You want some dessert?" I ask.

"Gimme."

I hand her the bowl and the spoon. She doesn't get up, she eats it lying down.

"Is it good?" I ask.

"It's okay."

I start eating too. It's very good. Kasia puts away the empty bowl on the table and says, "I came to an awful conclusion. I'm too intelligent to become a great composer."

"Why?"

"Because I think too much and feel too little. I don't even have anyone to talk about it with. It's too bad Mateusz is dead. Or that you don't know at least a little. You're constantly imagining something. Meadows, flowers, angels, birds . . ."

"Don't you imagine anything when you play?" I ask.

"What are you thinking!" Kasia gets upset. She takes a spoon and hits the bowl. "A sound is a sound. Isn't that enough for you?"

She throws the spoon into the corner and begins to moan. She whines like that a lot. She's lying down looking at the ceiling and moaning. It's okay—at least today she's not thrashing around on the bed or rolling on the carpet.

I don't say a word, I just sit quietly. Usually her whining ends with her hugging me, and me having to pet her.

"I can't, I can't," she says. "I can't! . . . Mongoose, what can I do, tell me, what can I do?"

"I don't know."

"Yell a little, come on."

"Okay," I say, and I start yelling. I yell louder and louder. My yelling also helps her every now and then. I yell and she looks at me. I'm running out of steam.

Oh, what a pleasant silence.

Kasia sits down, tucking her legs beneath her. I think she's over it.

"Because you see," she says, "the essence of music is its form. The form reveals the form. That's it—that's all of it. Crystal vacuum. Understand?"

"When you play," I ask, "why do I feel sad at certain times and cheerful at others?"

"It's all a matter of perception. Sound impulses travel through the ear to the brain and, depending on their properties, stimulate various areas there. Understand?"

I shrug my shoulders.

"Gee, you look wonderful today," Kasia says suddenly.

"Really?" I ask, smiling.

"You really look like a cross-eyed toad in a sauce made of squashed cockroaches."

"I am not cross-eyed."

Kasia laughs.

"I just showed you the impact of impulses on the frontal lobe," she says. "Speaking is like pressing keys in music. Each sentence is like a different key, though the path of verbal impulses is mediated, so it's a bit longer. The word must first make its way to the intellect, and then the intellect moves the emotional tones. But music gets by without intermediaries."

Kasia yawns.

"Why wasn't I born deaf?" she laments, lying on the sofa. "I'd like to be deaf, blind, mute and paralyzed."

"Spit out those words."

"I don't even have enough strength to do that. I think I'm going to go to sleep . . ."

"I'm gonna go home," I say.

"Uh-huh," Kasia mumbles sleepily.

"I didn't even finish doing your homework. That's okay. I'll take it with me and bring it to school tomorrow."

"Uh-huh." Kasia closes her eyes and buries her face in a sofa cushion. I stick her notebooks in my book bag.

"Take your clothes off," I say. "Don't sleep with your clothes on."

"Okay."

"Bye."

"How about a kiss?" Kasia asks. I come up to her and kiss her good-night. I put on my regular clothes, turn off the light in the hallway and leave, locking the lower lock on the door.

At that moment I hear the phone ring. If I hadn't left in such a hurry, I could have run out and gotten it, because Kasia definitely won't feel like getting up and it'll ring and ring until it stops.

I WALK THROUGH the empty streets. The minute they close the shops, people immediately hide somewhere. In their houses, in their nooks. Way up high, there isn't even a scrap of blue sky. A huge stone is suspended up above, all dark gray. The sun scratches from the other side, but it can't make it through because all the clouds made a pact and unite together into one giant stone.

If some bird flew too high, it would have to spend the night on the other side. Its mom would be worried all night. But it's much more pleasant on the other side because the sun is there.

It's so empty here, not a soul around. I'm walking along, skipping every third step. Huge houses tower over me; the street's so wide and so flat.

I'm skipping along, even though I have no reason to. I'm stupid, I don't know much, and I'm not gonna learn much more. Kasia, however, is smart enough for the two of us. I wish I knew as much as she does. And could see that beauty she can. I wonder what it looks like. I wish she could tell me how to get there before she leaves . . . But she'll be going for sure and isn't gonna tell me anything. Oh well. If that's the way she wants it, let her go to Africa. I'll miss her, but maybe I'll be calmer. I didn't used to be as nervous as I am now. It's something inside. There's something inside of me that's shaking all the time.

My mom says she's got the jitters too. She says it's all because of Walbrzych. Her heart hurts all the time now. I should help her more. As soon as Kasia takes off for Africa, I'm gonna help Mom with everything over the entire school break. I'll let her sit and boss me around. But knowing her, she won't be able to handle just sitting around and giving orders.

Suddenly . . . someone yells to me.

I turn around, there's no one there. Oh, someone's yelling from up above. I look up and they're standing on the roof of a brownstone. I can barely see them it's so dark.

They wave to me. Maybe it's a chimney sweep? But they're not black, just kind of gray. Wow, bit by bit they're leaning over. Oh my God, they're falling.

They're falling without a sound. Could it be a bag falling . . . ?

Clump!

They land right next to me. Why is it so wet? What am I stepping in? I see hands and a head with something gray leaking out of it. Even the blood is gray. A dead body's lying here. I look around to see whether anyone else has seen it. But there's no one else around.

I tiptoe away quietly.

THE SCHOOL BELL has rung already and Kasia isn't here. The teacher calls the roll. As usual, she starts with Bogdaj.

"Here," Eva says.

"Bogdanska."

"Here," I say.

"Daszkiewicz."

"Here!"

It's Zucharska already. After Zucharska always comes Kawczak, Maria.

"Kawczak."

"Absent," I say. The teacher makes a check mark and closes her roll book. A few people in the class give me weird looks, but I ignore them. I must have gotten confused.

It's probably because I couldn't sleep last night. I was afraid, I don't know why. And it seemed that as soon as I had fallen asleep, the alarm went off and it was time to get up. So here I am standing next to the elevator. Here it is. The elevator's going down, so I get in and all of a sudden I look down and I notice I'm wearing slippers. I go all the way down and then back up again to get my shoes. That's the way it goes. If you don't sleep at night, you sleep during the day. But I just don't feel like it now.

After school I go to Kasia's. When I ring the bell, Miss Zenobia answers. "Come in, sweetheart. Where's Kasia?"

"Isn't she home?"

"She wasn't home when I got here. She'll be back soon."

So I walk in. "Dinner'll be ready in half an hour," Miss Zenobia says, and goes into the kitchen.

Kasia's room is an awful mess.

Yesterday I left it straightened up.

I hurry and make her bed, straighten all the wrinkles and start working on the desk, which looks like a trash can surrounded by more trash. Postcards are scattered everywhere along with a few pictures and letters. Drawers are pulled out of the desk, and one is even turned upside down. Oh my God, what happened here? It looks like a thief went through it.

Quickly I pile up the loose papers and letters and put the photos in another pile. I put them into drawers. The drawers are a mess . . . A few colored sheets of carbon paper, a tangle of cables and wires, the head of a doll and an old pair of pliers. I would straighten things up, but with Kasia not here I'd feel funny messing with her stuff. So I'll just straighten it up a little so I can at least close the drawers and cabinets.

Hey, what's that sticking out? Something black . . . what is it? There's a long black tail sticking out of the bottom drawer of the left compartment. It's so long—more than twenty inches.

I'm so stupid, I got scared, and it's nothing but a braid of shiny black hair. What does Kasia need a black braid for? Maybe it's Kasia's hair, maybe she cut it, braided it and dyed it black the way I dyed my tights. The braid is tied with a blue ribbon at the end.

There's something scary about it—it's like a devil's tail. I throw it into the drawer, close the drawer and slam the compartment shut. Out of sight, out of mind.

Now I start to straighten up the mess on top of the desk. Again, Polish and French books are mixed together. Why is it so wet? I look and my whole hand is black. Ink or India ink was spilled here. I wipe my hand with my handkerchief. What have I done? My nicest handkerchief is now black. It probably won't come out. And I'm wiping the ink from the desktop with it. I run into the bathroom to wash my hands and rinse out my handkerchief. It won't be good for anything. A rag, at best. I come back to the room and wipe down the desktop with water. Oh no, one of the books got dirty. A small black figurine is making a face at me. It's that yucky devil—yuck, what is that he's holding in his hand? He's holding his pecker, yuck!

I've straightened up what I could. I threw out my handkerchief and washed my hands. Miss Zenobia has been gone for a while and I'm standing by the window, looking for Kasia. Why does she call Miss Zenobia "Miss" if she's married and her husband is retired and they have a son and a granddaughter in West Germany? A whole hour has gone by and Kasia's still not back yet. It's cold and empty without her. It's about to rain and it's getting darker and darker in the room. The dinner must be cold by now. I didn't eat any dinner; somehow I don't have any appetite. Where could she be? The synthesizers are standing in the corner, sadder and quieter than they've ever been before. I plug in the cord. Bright lights come on. I press a key.

Something blasts out of the speaker: I pull my finger back quickly. Silence. I press another key. Something rings. No, it wasn't this, someone must have rung the doorbell. I run down the hall and open the door. There's no one. I close the door and I hear a ringing again. It's the phone in Mrs. Bogdanska's room. It must be Kasia calling. I run in there and grab the receiver.

"Hello!" I say.

Someone is gabbing, but not in Polish. I can't hear it very well . . . maybe it's the wrong number. I put down the receiver. It's getting darker and darker. I go out onto the balcony. I look all around—Kasia's nowhere to be seen. And soon it's gonna rain. I have to go and look for her.

I grab my book bag and close the door behind me. I run, *clunk*, down the wooden stairs.

I GO TO one café after another, to the bookstore and everywhere else we go together, but Kasia's nowhere to be found. Maybe she's with her mom in that restaurant where we ate once, but I'm not gonna go there because it's far away and the bus doesn't go all the way there. Maybe something happened to her? No . . . What could possibly have happened? I'm running around Walbrzych, soaking wet because the rain keeps falling, but Kasia's nowhere to be found. Maybe she went home.

I run toward the marketplace, zip up the stairs and ring the bell, but no one answers, it's quiet behind the door, she's not home. She isn't back yet. Maybe she went out to the cinder waste dumps. She likes going there.

I jump onto the bus, riding without a ticket, since I lost it somewhere, and walk around the waste dumps, calling, "Katarzyna! Katarzyna!" She's not there either. Then I go back downtown; it's raining the whole time. The rain keeps pouring down. Again I'm at her door, again I ring. No one opens. Again I run to both coffee shops and to the bookstore . . .

Kasia's not there.

I have no feeling in my legs. Please God don't let anything happen to her. It's almost five. I'm running through the rain to church. I'm gonna pray a little, and dry off a bit.

IT'S DARK AND empty here, but at least it isn't raining.

I kneel, cross myself, get up and look . . . Thank you, Lord God, that's Kasia sitting way over there in a pew. I recognize her by her shiny silver overcoat and her hair glistening in the light of the altar. I thought about running over to her and kissing her, but no, maybe she's praying, maybe she got converted . . . Let her pray, I won't disturb her. I'll sit quietly in the back. When she's done she'll notice me on the way out. So we're sitting, her over there, and me here, praying. I like how the church smells. I like the sound of the bells when the altar boy swings the incense around. And the monstrance glistens so beautifully when it's taken out of the tabernacle. I've always thought there must be something hidden behind the monstrance, and wondered why the priest doesn't pull it out . . . there must be something there, something small, that would be big if you could pull it out. It would glisten like the sun, like a thousand thunderbolts. That's where it is . . . oh, Lord God, I know already, that's where the Mystery of Faith is.

I don't know how I know that, but I know it. Oh, how wonderful everything is turning, how bright. Only why is it so cold here? My teeth are chattering from the cold, I'm shivering.

Let's go home, Kasia, let's get out of here.

Maybe she fell asleep.

I'm gonna go up to her and see if maybe she's asleep. I go up quietly and sit next to her. She looks at me, totally unsurprised. I smile at her, but she doesn't react. Doesn't she recognize me?

"Kasia," I whisper. "I've been looking for you all day."

She doesn't say a thing, just looks at me like she's seeing me for the first time in her life and wants to take a good look at me.

"Do you still want to find out," she says, "the thing I never wanted to tell you about?"

"Yes. I do."

"Will you be brave, and not afraid?"

"I won't be afraid," I say.

She gets up and holds her hand out to me. I hold mine out to her. She grabs it tight and leads me to the door. I'm dying to find out and am really afraid, only I won't admit it—I've got to see It.

We stop at the entrance. It's raining out. Kasia says, "Work up a lot of spit in your mouth."

"Why?"

"Just do it. Hurry up!"

So I do.

"And now, spit."

"Where?"

"There!"

She pulls me hard, turns my back toward her. I spit. What have I done? . . .

My spit is floating in the holy water in the stone basin. My God, what have I done? I can't believe what I see. It's my spit floating there. My spit floating in the holy water. I hear laughter. It's Kasia laughing.

"It's the same water as anywhere," she says. "It's the same as in a bathtub, it's the same as in a toilet."

I sink to my knees, press my face to the ground and sob in despair. I moan and howl. She tugs at me.

"Calm down, Mongoose, calm down!" She covers my mouth. "Calm down!" she shouts.

I bite her hand. She lets go of me. I moan with my face against the floor. "What have you done to me?" I howl. "What have you done?!"

She pulls me up from the floor, slaps me across the face once, then again, and yells, "Shut up, you idiot!"

I'm kneeling and moaning quietly. She kneels next to me, hugging me and kissing me on the lips.

"Stop, sweetie," she whispers. But I don't do a thing, I just moan. It's all over, all over.

"Go away," I say. "Leave me alone." I'm crying and moaning. She gets up.

"What did you think?" she asks, standing over me. "That it would be easy? You wanted to catch a free ride to hell?"

I look at her in shock. She's got a smirk on her lips.

"Have you forgotten?" she asks. "We promised. You swore you wouldn't hate. Now you suffer alone. My Be Kind to Animals Week just ended. It lasted far too long as it is. I've had enough of you."

She pulls on her hood and leaves.

Kneeling in the vestibule, I watch her leave. She walks through the stripes of rain.

"Kasia!" I shout. I leap up and run after her. "Kasia!"

She stops, turning toward me. Her raincoat and hood are slick from the rain. Her wet eyes glisten. "What else do you want?"

"Kasia," I say through the tears and rain. "Tell me . . . Was it Jigi that asked you to do it? Tell me, was it Jigi?!"

She laughs sarcastically and raises her brow.

"What Kasia? What Kasia? . . . A year has already gone by since I devoured your Kasia. I can't even remember anymore whether it tasted good."

She picks her sharp white teeth with her nail, trying to taste between her teeth.

"I think it might've even tasted good." she says. "Too bad you didn't get a chance to try it."

She leaves, shimmering in the rain. Vanishes.

My dearest Kasia. She's gone. I know I'll never see her again. She only befriended me so she could hand me a ticket to hell.

So Jigi was HIM. I felt that he was hanging around, but I had no idea I'd find him so close, in a person I'd come to love so much.

Good, so now I know.

GESTURES ARE ONLY gestures. Words are only words. They're only there so you can press keys in the brain. A key with the sign FRIENDSHIP, a key with the sign HAPPINESS. Bang . . . The sounds are over. You have to leave because you don't have anyone to love and you have to die, though you'll live on and on and on and on and on.

My God, I know now that You aren't mine. I thought You were good to everyone on earth, but it turns out You're only good to some. I forgive You, but You should also forgive me, because Your daughter must leave You. I don't know the name of where I have to go, but I have to go because there's nothing left for me to do.

I don't know whether I was ever good. Maybe I was only thirsty and trying to win over the well. I only pretended to be nice because I wanted You to like me. And maybe You have punished me for that, Father. There's no longer a place for me in Your house, which is a house for everyone, but some have to leave to find a home elsewhere, at the bottom of hell. But I have a long way to go to get to the bottom and a long time before I get there. A long time.

A minute ago I wanted to go and soak up all the blessed water and my saliva with my own sweater like a floor rug in order not to dirty the crooked fingers of some old granny with my sacrilege. Now, my bad Father, let Your servants take care of it.

Farewell.

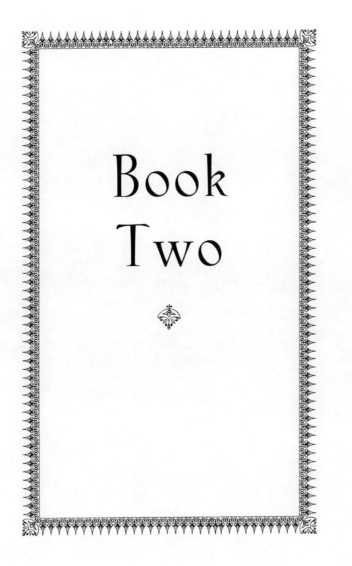

Book
Two

Chapter Five

I HAVEN'T BEEN to school in two days. On the third I show up
with a note from my mom in her own handwriting that says, "My
daughter Maria Kawczak felt sick in connection with her health. Sin-
cerely, Slava Kawczak."

Slava is my mom's name.

I watched her to make sure she didn't make any mistakes, but
there were only four possible spots to make them, so the checking got
by without a dictionary.

I'm sitting alone at my desk. Of course, Kasia isn't in school. I
don't know how I know, but I know she won't be coming, not even
once these last couple weeks before the end of school, and will send
either her mom or maybe Miss Zenobia for her diploma.

Well . . . why should I care? During the long break Eva Bogdaj
comes up to me and asks what's going on with Kasia. I tell her she's
sick.

"That much I know. Yesterday her mom came in with a note. I
saw her talking to Mrs. Turska. But what's wrong with her?" Eva says.

"We still don't know," I say. "Something very complicated."

"I guess so," Eva says, smiling faintly. "You know . . . I'm really
worried about her."

She puts her hands behind her neck. I've always liked that gesture of hers.

"Maybe you'd rather she died?" I ask.

"You just make up all kinds of things about me," Eva says. "You know, I'm not like you think."

"How do you know what I think?" I ask, gently imitating her earlier smile.

"What do you think?"

"Maybe the same thing you do . . ."

"Yeah? Because I was thinking you were really cool."

"That's strange," I say. "Because I was thinking you were really cool."

Eva bursts out laughing.

"It turns out we're both cool," she says.

"It turns out we're both cool," I repeat.

Eva looks at me suspiciously. "Are you being a copycat?"

"Are you being a copycat?" I repeat.

Then Eva turns serious. She starts biting her lower lip, not saying anything. I also start biting my lower lip, not saying a word. I puff my lips up just like hers. So which of us is which? Just then the bell catches up with us. The hallways start to empty. There's just the two of us standing, facing each other.

How's this going to end?

Not just any old way. Eva shrugs her shoulders and leaves. She's halfway down the hallway when there's a loud whistle. It's me that whistled. Eva stops and turns toward me, looking at me from far away. I smile. She smiles back with an unsure, shy smile. This is the Eva Bogdaj I've been so afraid of?

I burst out laughing, my laughter made even louder by the echo.

Eva disappears through the classroom door.

I'm standing here alone, surrounded by thin air.

DURING PHYSICS CLASS I could feel her gaze on me. When I turned around, her eyes darted away.

I'm walking along Maria Konopnicka Street when I hear a whistle.

I look and it's her. She's sitting on her big black motorcycle on the other side of the street, waving at me.

I walk up to her.

"I'll give you a lift home," she says. "You want a ride?"

"Sure."

I get on behind her and look for the footrests. She tells me, "Hug me tight, and when we're turning, lean with me, and if I'm going too fast, poke my back with your chin. It usually works."

With a loud noise we take off.

We're gone already.

One street, then another . . . we're already at the marketplace.

Eva parks her motorcycle in front of Kasia's house.

"But I don't live here," I say.

Eva jumps off her seat and puts the kickstand down. "I know. But you must want to see what's up with Miss Katarzyna Bogdanska."

"Great, thanks. So, bye."

"I'll wait for you here."

"But it might take a really long time, I might not be out until after dark . . . I don't know."

"It doesn't matter. I got nothing better to do. I promise I'll take you home."

"I'll manage. Some genius invented buses."

"He wasn't as smart as the one who invented motorcycles." She smiles. "I'll wait."

"Okay, I'll be back in half an hour," I say. "See you."

I enter the doorway and walk up.

I'm already on the third floor, but I'm not going to ring the bell. Fourth floor, fifth floor. I'm going up to the roof.

The roof is flat here. It's a large terrace, fenced in by a stone balustrade. I was here once. Kasia and I made twenty paper airplanes, ten each, and had a competition.

The airplanes circled above the marketplace. At least three of them flew into the same open window on the other side of the marketplace. All three were mine. One of Kasia's landed in the open bed of a pickup truck. Another one went up high and we lost sight of it in the clouds. None of them made it to the window where my three went.

Later, when I was going home, I saw some children playing with our planes. I was very happy they weren't wasted, that they were still flying, and that there might even be one flying tomorrow and the day after that.

I go over to the balustrade and look down at Eva, so tiny from here next to her tiny motorcycle. Half an hour passes, forty minutes pass, and she hasn't left yet.

I go down.

"KATARZYNA DIED," I say, dead serious. Eva looks at me, her eyes as still as a doll's, her open lips frozen in mid-sentence.

Oh my God, what happened?

Where did Eva go?

Oh, she's lying at my feet.

"Excuse me, sir." I stop a passerby. "A girl just fainted here."

The man takes her in his arms and carries her to the fountain, with me following behind him. A whole crowd surrounds us. I splash her face with water and she opens her eyes. She sits on a stone bench and wipes the water off her face with the hem of her cotton shirt.

By now everyone is gone. Eva isn't quite herself. I need to get her going.

"Did you believe me?" I ask.

She lifts up her large eyes. The whites of her eyes are white, almost blue, the pupils are black, almost navy. I was wrong about her: she's a perfectly nice ordinary girl.

"Everything is okay with Katarzyna," I say. "She went to her grandmother's house in Sobotka."

Eva takes a deep breath. Her face livens up.

"You really led me on," she says. "Your jokes are just great."

"That's a game called "Pressing the Buttons." Did you like it?"

"A lot. You have to teach me how to play."

I snap my fingers. "You already know how."

Less than five minutes go by and we're already on my street. The bus would have taken half an hour.

"This is my apartment complex," I say. Eva brakes, rides up to my door. I get off.

Eva says, "If you have the time . . . we could ride around for a while."

I sure do. Lots of it. Because now I'm doing the rehearsal and later I'll be looking after Kasia, who's sick.

"I do," I say.

"Aren't you afraid to ride with me?"

"Why?"

"Aren't I driving too fast?"

"I was about to ask you what the holdup was."

"Do you know what kind of motorcycle this is? Look."

Eva points to the golden letters on the shiny black fuel tank: YAMAHA. It's amazing how everything comes in pairs. The fountain glistening in the sun already happened twice. Let a second icy cloud crumble and we can slowly close the shop.

"Yamaha," I read aloud. "Does that mean 'turtle' in Japanese?"

"You're going to regret that," Eva says, and slides her dark rubber-framed glasses down over her eyes.

"Hop on!"

I get on and hug her tightly. I can feel her ribs under my fingers, and the delicate beat of her heart, silenced after a while by the vibration of the engine.

Slowly we reach Wroclawska Street. Suddenly Eva revs the throttle and weaves back and forth between lanes going in opposite directions.

WALBRZYCH IS ALREADY far behind us. We're flying, with the engine humming, and I can't even tell whether the highway is still under the tires or whether we're already flying up above it. Deaf and blind, I rest my head against the black leather of Eva's jacket.

The trees flash by like fence posts.

The cars bursting from the opposite direction explode with the noise.

Oh, let it be right now. Right now, now, let it be right now.

Bang, and that's it! So I can be there right now!

What's happening . . .

She brakes, slows down and stops on the side of the road. I see two angels in uniforms, in white caps, looking fierce, the way only on-duty policemen look, buckled up, strap under the chin.

"Well, dear ladies, that's the end of the ride," one of them says.

We get off. Eva puts the kickstand down. The angels come closer. One is blond with a light mustache, the other brown-haired with a dark mustache.

"Please, boys, give me a break." Eva smiles. Out of her pocket she pulls her driver's license inside a plastic cover. She gives it to the dark-haired guy. He reads and raises his eyes at her.

"That's real nice, Miss Zdzislawa," he says. "We confiscate vehicles for these kinds of things."

"What kinds of things, what kinds of things?" Eva asks sweetly.

"A hundred miles an hour and no helmets. Those kinds of things."

"Your radar must be broken." Eva laughs. She takes off her dark glasses, darting her eyes first to one, then to the other. "How did you guys turn up here without me knowing you?"

"You're gonna get to know us better in the courtroom," the blond says.

"Oh, you cops, even when you're kidding, you're not kidding," Eva chirps.

"Miss, can we have the key?" the dark-haired one asks.

"Just a sec, let me concentrate," Eva cries, taking the key out of the engine. The blond extends his hand. Eva jumps back.

"Just a second, I have to part with it tenderly," she says, and kisses the key. She throws it into the top pocket of her jacket. She places her hands over it so it looks like she's holding them over her heart and says sadly but flirtatiously, "Guys, please, is there anything we can do about it? . . . My husband is gonna kill me. He's color-blind, and I have to drive him everywhere and you're gonna take my driver's license for such a trifle."

"Give me the key, miss," the dark one says.

Eva puffs up her lips. "Guys, please have pity on a pregnant elderly lady."

The policemen laugh.

"Don't worry, ladies," the blond one says. "I'm gonna give you a ride to the police station in my car and my friend is gonna try out the bike."

"Too bad," Eva says. She searches in her pocket, takes out the key and gives it to the blond one. He clenches his fist, and Eva takes away her hand. I look . . . she still has the key. What's the blond one holding? The other cop comes up to him, holds out his hand.

"Come on, gimme," he says. "I've never ridden one like that."

"I don't know whether you'll like it," the blond one replies, and shows him what he has in his hand.

The dark-haired one raises his eyebrows and looks at Eva. She makes big, sweet eyes, and flashing them, she chirps, "And it comes with a kiss."

"Okay," he says. "The kiss seals the case."

"What case?" Eva acts surprised. "There was no case."

She comes up to him and kisses him on the lips. Then the blond one. He tries to embrace her, but she's already slipped away.

"Thank you, boys, until next time," Eva says. "They call me Zdzisia. And this is Eva, my little sister."

She cocks her head toward me.

"Franek," the blond introduces himself.

"Edek," the dark-haired one says, adding, "Doesn't your sister like to kiss?"

"She's still a virgin," Eva replies.

"Oh yeah," Edek says. "All the ladies are virgins."

Franek waves his finger. "You might be in trouble next time."

"Next time it's gonna be a French kiss," Eva says.

And Edek says, "Maybe we should rehearse the French kiss?"

"Only if you can keep up with us." Eva laughs. She mounts the motorcycle, I sit behind her.

"With this corpse?" Edek points to the car standing under the tree.

Eva turns the throttle. We take off, leaving our guardian angels in a cloud of blue smoke.

ON THE WAY back we go to a country inn. Eva orders two Cokes. We sit at a table.

"That was nice, wasn't it?" Eva says.

"It was."

"That 'nice' cost me twenty bucks."

"Twenty zloty?"

"Get real."

"Twenty thousand?"

"Twenty dollars. It's not much, but you can always buy something with it. But I thought I knew them all."

I lift up the glass and take a sip. Oh, I forgot something. Something very important. Last night I felt it slipping away. I was lying wide awake, like I was sick, and I was daydreaming about some things, some people who wanted to do something to me . . . I was so close, all I needed was to connect that to another thing.

There were all these rooms there, and people were playing billiards. Men in checkered shirts. They . . . I wanted to escape, but I had an extremely narrow skirt on. There was a child there . . . Was I his mother? Me and some other girl. And her—I don't remember anything else.

"What are you thinking about?" Eva asks. She puts her hand on mine. She pulls it away immediately. She's all movement, and each of her movements is like a star in the sky.

I was so close, so close.

A longing that never ends.

What was it?

Eva looks at me. I smile. She smiles back.

"Oh, how you came out of the woodwork," she says. "You're wonderful. I always wanted to meet someone like you. I was such an idiot not to realize it right away. Kasia was faster and stole you away from me. Can you forgive me?"

I look around and say, "This is a very pleasant place."

"Yes, it really is."

"It's horrible."

"It's horrible and repulsive," Eva seconds me. "You should understand I was only acting up because of those idiotic friends of mine. I get bored, so I act up . . ."

"It's still a pleasant place."

Eva sighs and says, "Please give me a chance."

I shrug my shoulders. "What do you want from me?"

"Nothing. Only . . ."

"It's too much," I say. "I can only give you half as much."

I get up, take my glass and drop it on the floor. Bang. Splinters of glass. Everyone is looking at us.

I leave.

I'm walking in the parking lot; there are trees behind it. I can't disentangle myself from these dreams, these words. I sit on Eva's black motorcycle. I grasp the handlebars.

Eva comes out of the inn. She comes up to me. Wherever I look, she's there. She's all over the place.

"Do you want to drive?" she asks.

"I don't know how."

"I'll show you."

I shake my head and slide back. She sits down in front of me. She doesn't turn the key, just sits there, her hands on the handlebars. I wrap my arms around her. I hug her. "Eva . . ."

"Yeah?"

"Take me to hell."

Eva tilts her head back, touching my face. I feel her soft, fragrant hair on my lips.

"I thought as much," she whispers. "I'll do anything you want . . ."

"Let's kill ourselves," I say.

"Okay," she whispers. "But not yet."

I close my eyes. When I open them, I see a huge white fairy-tale mansion through the lush green of the trees. We're in Szczawno Zdroj.

"HOW DO YOU like my little gingerbread house?"

"It'll do."

"Wanna stop in?"

"Maybe for a minute . . ."

In the hallway by the phone stands a rather pretty bleached-blond female in a minidress.

"Hi, Mimi," Eva says. "I want to introduce you to Maica, my new girlfriend."

"Hi," the blonde says. She smiles at me as she says into the phone, "Okay, I've got to run now."

She puts down the phone and does a double pirouette.

"How do I look?" she asks.

"Great," Eva says.

"Have a good time, dolls," this Mimi person says. "I'm outta here."

She disappears, she's out of here. Eva takes me by the hand and leads me up the stairs into a huge bright living room. At the other end of the room a handsome dark-haired guy is sitting by a round table. He's eating and reading the paper.

We walk up to him.

"Hello, Dada," Eva says. The man raises his head. He glances at Eva, then at me.

"Hello, cuties," he says.

Eva points at me. "Dada, let me introduce you to my best girlfriend. Her name is Maica."

The man gets up. He extends his hand to me and I shake it. He says, "Bogdaj. My pleasure."

"Likewise."

"Excellent soup," he says. "I recommend it to you ladies."

He looks at his watch.

"I'm gone," he says. And he's gone. We're alone.

"This way, you got to meet the folks," Eva says. She points to the chair next to the table and we sit down. Eva calls out, "Miss Zenobia! Two sets of plates!"

The doors open slightly at the end of the living room. I look . . . the same Miss Zenobia is standing there.

"At your service, ladies," she calls, disappears and reappears again, pushing a cart with plates in front of her. She sets everything she has brought on the table and ladles the soup from a large bowl. She glances at me, doesn't recognize me and disappears.

Something strange is floating in the soup. I scoop it out. It's a blue, transparent piece of pasta. Miss Zenobia appears again. She bustles around us, serves the second course onto our plates and disappears.

"Why did you look at her like that?" Eva asks.

"Because she reminds me of someone."

"I even know who."

"Who?"

"Herself."

"So that's her?"

"Who?"

"Um . . . Miss Zenobia."

"That's her name." I pull my plate over and pick up a knife and fork. The knife bends when I try to cut the meat with it. A ladybug walks on the table. Eva laughs. We're sitting in Eva's room, sunken into the blue, transparent love seats. And we're drinking something good and cold in tall glasses. It might just be tea . . .

Eva jumps up and runs over to a tape player. "Any requests?"

"I don't know."

"Cue, then."

She looks for the tape and puts it in the deck. Jarrett starts pounding on the keyboard.

"Darn, I got my tapes mixed up," Eva says.

"Leave it on."

Eva runs back. She plops down on the love seat.

"Do you really like that idiot?" she asks.

"How about you?"

"It's not my tape. But I can live with it."

"I like it," I say. "I picture him rolling a golden ball on a never-ending staircase."

"You put it so well," Eva says. "I have a great lipstick. I'll give it to you if you want."

She runs to her dresser and then comes back. Quickly she puts on the lipstick.

"Look, it's gold," she says. She puckers her lips. They're gold. She hands me the lipstick. I paint one of my nails with it. It's gold.

"Cool," I say.

"Are you a virgin?" Eva asks.

"All the ladies are virgins," I answer.

Eva gives me a pearly smile. "If you want, I'll dance for you."

She jumps up from the love seat and starts dancing to Jarrett's music. The golden ball tumbles down the never-ending staircase. Should I run after it or stay put and look at Eva?

I stay.

She dances like a real ballerina, only she's a hundred times prettier. I look at her in awe. Hey, she must be Jarrett's sunny ball.

"You're completely different than I thought," I say.

"It's because you didn't know me," Eva says. She jumps up high, touching her head to the ceiling, shimmies a bit and slowly sinks into the turquoise carpet.

I lower my eyelids and can't open them.

"I don't know why, but I feel really sleepy," I say, barely moving my lips.

"So lie down." Eva's voice comes from far away. I lie down on a transparent sofa. I sink into it. I feel Eva covering me with something light, I can feel her taking off my shoes.

"Shall I turn off the music?"

"Leave it on," I say quietly, so quietly I can't even hear my own words. I only hear Jarrett and see Eva dancing—his sunny ball. I grow light and now I can follow her. She runs down the never-ending white marble staircase. I follow her.

Winding underbrush and snakes and stinky ponds full of silent frogs and their stupefied eyes are all around us.

Running, running. Diamonds sparkling in the sun.

Suddenly I trip and vanish in the darkness and silence.

E . . . E . . . E . . .

Earthworm. I, the blind and deaf earthworm, wind down along the very bottom of an underground lake.

Aaaaaaaa. Oooooooo . . .

Something's moaning here. Some being without body or thought. A bubble of air in a vacuum.

Wyyyyy . . . dooooo . . .

Ooooooooodyyyy . . .

Eeeeeeeee.

Give me something I can touch.

Hereeeeee . . .

Vacuum. In the va . . . cuum of va . . .

Mmmmmm.

Mprr . . .

A

Mprstv . . . mine.

I GOT SO scared. But it was me. Mom was asking me to empty her ashtray . . .

I walk around the apartment complex looking for the garbage dump. Some guy's running after me on wobbly legs. He has a billy club in his hand. It's a fluorescent tube that shines the whole time. He wants to hit me with it. I run away. There are two boys walking. They run away with me. They turn left, I turn right. The drunk with the fluorescent light comes after me. A policeman walks down the other side of the street. He's young and handsome. I'm gonna show him the ashtray, I'm gonna tell him everything. I run out into the street. A bicyclist makes a last-minute turn. Boom, bang, he gets run over by a car; everyone's dead, blood comes gushing out of the car. I jerk around suddenly. A tall man in a gray sweater and glasses is standing in front of me.

"Marysia," he says, "don't run away, I want to help you."

I jump into an elevator and run down a hallway. I walk through a doorway. It's so empty here. What a small window. What a dirty windowpane. I'm going to plug myself in, I'm gonna wash myself.

"Eggy!" someone cries. "Eggy!"

Chapter Six

I OPEN MY eyes. A pretty olive-skinned girl sits beside me in a white robe. I already know who it is. It's my friend, my classmate Eva Bogdaj. What am I doing here? What am I holding in my hand?

Oh, the corner of a blanket.

Eva smiles at me.

"Maica," she says gently. "It's very late, it's almost twelve."

Oh, gee . . . I sit up on the couch.

"I've gotta go," I say.

"What are you talking about?" Eva asks. "You're gonna sleep with me—the bed's already made."

"I can't," I say. "I have to go. Mom would kill me."

"Call and tell her you're gonna stay at my place."

"We don't have a phone there." I get up. I'm a little off-balance. That's how sleepy I still am.

"Please stay," Eva says. "I drew a bath for you."

"I really can't."

I'm looking for my shoes. Here they are. I squat down and put them on.

"Too bad," Eva says sadly. "I was so happy . . ."

"Where's my book bag?"

"It's somewhere." Eva screws her lips up into a horseshoe shape. "Do you really have to go?"

"I really do."

"I can't give you a ride, since I just took a bath. I'm gonna call you a cab."

"No, I don't have any money on me. I'll take the bus."

"The buses aren't running now," Eva says. "I'll pay for it. Sit down, I'm going to call a cab."

I sit down. Eva picks the phone up off the table and comes over to me on the sofa. I look over and see that it's not a whole phone; it doesn't have a cord.

Eva presses the buttons. It starts ringing. It rings again. We wait about a minute.

"This isn't gonna work," Eva says. "No one's picking up. You'll have to stay."

"I can't," I say. "I'm gonna walk."

"In that case, wait. I'll be right back." Eva puts down the receiver and leaves the room. I take the phone without a cord. So it really is a phone. I press the buttons.

Beep . . . beeep . . . beeeeep . . . beep . . . beeep . . .

I put the phone down like I just got burned. What did I do? I dialed Kasia's number—the only one I know.

It's really pretty here. A plush turquoise carpet—looks like a meadow or, even more, like a sea. And these transparent chairs must be inflated. What would happen if I poked them with a pin? . . . And these neat white cupboards made out of slanted boards. The pictures on the walls. They're of pretty girls with wide eyes. The sofa's fairly low to the ground, somewhat round and really big. It's big enough for me and my whole family. And the bedding is so nice, but I have to go.

The door to the balcony is ajar. I get up and head over to it. I poke my head out. It's not a balcony, it's a terrace. You can see trees in the yard. It smells so nice.

I turn around. Eva walks into the room followed by a tall dark-haired guy.

"Allow me to introduce you to my brother Michal," she says. "And this is my Maica."

"Good evening," I say.

"Hi." He really looks like Eva, but he's older and looks a little different, since he's a guy.

"Michal will give you a ride," Eva says.

"No, I don't want to cause any bother. I'll walk. It's such a nice night—"

"Another time. Tonight I'm giving you a ride." All three of us leave the room. My book bag is in the hall. I pick it up and follow Michal.

Eva kisses me on the cheek. "See you tomorrow." She's warm and fragrant.

"See you tomorrow."

We're standing on the front steps, watching Michal bring a large white car around. He waves at me and I run over. I get in. It's very comfortable in here.

"Where are we going?" he asks.

"To Piaskowa Gora."

You can hear the roar of the engine. We pull out slowly. Eva's standing in the doorway in a white robe, waving at me. I wave back.

We're on our way. The streets are empty, and there's music playing since Michal has turned on the radio. He doesn't say a word and I don't say anything to him either. There goes some lady with some man. They look like they're drunk, because they're walking crooked. The neon lights glow; it's warm. The window is open a crack and the wind flies in. I feel it playing with my hair gently, like it's petting me.

"Here," I say. "To the left."

We turn.

"Rabiegi Street," I say. "Oh, I think it's over there . . ."

MICHAL'S ALREADY GONE. I'm standing alone in the empty street looking up. There's a light in the kitchen. They're not asleep yet. I wonder what's going to happen? Right above our apartment complex there are a lot of stars.

I'm not going into the gate. I sit on the bench in front of the apartment complex and look at the stars. They're winking at me. I think of Eva in her white bathrobe, all tanned. I see her eyes . . . If it's all true, and not a dream, she's going to save me. She's good. You think all kinds of things about people because you don't know them. Then you get to know them and it turns out they're good.

It turns out that Eva likes me. And I like her too. I wanted her to kill me, but she's gonna save me. I don't know how I know it, but I know it.

She's going to defend me. She's not afraid of anyone.

Only I can't let on what kind of person I am . . . that I'm only average and stupid. I'm going to have to always come up with something strange. Something she'd like.

But what?

Kasia would know how to do it . . . but Eva doesn't like her, she likes me. And she smells so nice. And she's so pretty and sweet, like a doll.

But maybe by tomorrow she won't even be talking to me.

Too bad I went to sit with Kasia. Instead, I could have been sitting with Eva right now; the four of us—Klaudia, Magda, Eva and I— chitchatting and fooling around. But how could I have known then that Eva was so good . . .

Too bad I gotta go home, because the light in the kitchen just isn't going out.

I TURN THE key and walk into the apartment. Mom's sitting in the kitchen.

"Good evening, Mom," I say quietly. I'm standing in the kitchen doorway. Mom doesn't say anything, just gets redder by the minute. I hope her heart doesn't burst from all this anger. She's breathing so hard and so fast . . .

The whoosh of running water comes from the bathroom. Dad comes out in his long johns, his hair all messed up. He looks at me and goes into his room.

"I'm sorry," I say to Mom. She beckons to me with her finger. Slowly I walk over to her. She's gonna whack me now. I'm standing in front of her with my eyes closed. I lean forward so she can reach my face with her hand. But for some reason she doesn't whack me . . .

Dad comes into the kitchen with his belt folded in his hands.

"I couldn't get home any earlier," I say quickly. "I'm really sorry, it'll never happen again!"

"You better get yourself over to the window," Dad says. Which I do, since the kitchen's small and there's more room by the window to get spanked.

"Get your skirt hiked up."

"Daddy, no . . . I beg you, I'll never do it again. I really couldn't make it home any earlier. Kasia got sick and I had to keep her company."

"She's lying, to boot. She's lying through her teeth," Mom says. "I saw you from the balcony on the back of some guy's motorcycle right in front of our apartment complex."

"That wasn't a guy, it was Eva. But she had jeans on and has a short haircut. I swear!"

"Get your skirt hiked up, I said." Dad stretches his belt in his hands. I pull my skirt up slowly, gathering the pleats in both hands and gritting my teeth. Dad says, "Turn around some."

I stand facing sideways. My skirt falls down because my hands start shaking. Dad loses patience, and without waiting for me to pull my skirt up again, he whacks me with the belt across my calves. Whack, it goes.

"Get your skirt hiked up!" Dad shouts.

"Quiet," Mom says. "You're gonna wake up Zenus."

"One more time, get your skirt hiked up and show your ass, or else I'll whack you in the goddamn face," Dad says, just a bit quieter.

I lean over. My legs start shaking and they feel so hot, like someone is burning them with an iron. Dad takes a swing, hits the sink and knocks a glass off of it. The glass goes clank and the belt goes smack! At the last minute I jump out of the way and grab the belt with my hand.

I pull on it and yank it out of his hand.

Dad sticks out his lower jaw. He walks up to me all mad. Suddenly all the heat from my legs moves up into my head. I start yelling.

"Shut your face, you little asshole!" Dad runs up to me and whacks me on the head. I push him away with all my might. He trips and falls to the floor, gets up again and comes right back at me.

"If you touch me," I shout, "I'm gonna turn on the gas at night and poison everyone! I swear on Christ's wounds, I'm gonna start the gas and then light it all up! I'm going to make the whole place explode!"

Dad looks at Mom all frightened. Now both of them are looking at me.

"She's gone nuts," Dad says. I feel my whole face screwing up into a grimace.

"Just try," I say through my teeth. "I'll leak the gas, I swear."

Dad shakes his head.

"That's it," he says to Mom. "I can't take this. I'm gonna kill the little whore."

"Go ahead. Grab an ax and kill me. Tomorrow you can have meat for dinner! Better than rabbit meat."

Dad runs up to me. Mom grabs him by the waistband of his long johns.

"Leave her alone," she says. "She's gone nuts."

"I'll beat the brains back into her. Let go!"

Dad tries to pull his long johns away from Mom, but Mom holds them tight and won't let go. "Drop it, Jasio. Don't touch shit, you'll get yourself dirty. Look at her. This ain't our daughter."

Dad looks at me closely, and Mom says, "It's some weird little snot, some artiste straight outta crazyville. Our Marysia didn't have such long hair. And her nose was different, kinda flatter. And she was shorter."

"That's right," Dad says. "So why is she in our kitchen?"

"How the heck would I know?" Mom says. "She musta wandered in . . . You better go to sleep. Just make sure the gas is turned all the way off at the pipe."

She gets up, pulling Dad by his long johns.

"Leave me alone." Dad's getting angry. "I'll leave on my own."

They leave. I hear Dad ask for a monkey wrench. Then I hear the scraping of a stool in the hallway and the banging of the wrench on the pipe.

I turn my face to the window, to my night mirror.

There is no reflection of me there.

Someone's standing behind the window. I draw my face close to the windowpane. The other girl does it too; she wants to take a look at me too. Who is that?

Kasia, is that you?

She doesn't say anything, just looks at me with her eyes wide open. No, that's not Kasia. She looks a little bit like Kasia, but she's very different.

Oh, it looks like she's saying something to me, because her lips are moving. Yeah, she puts her face up to the window and speaks, looking me straight in the eye. I don't hear anything, because there's a windowpane between us . . .

I open the window. She's disappeared, she's gone.

I lean out and she's there, way down on the ground, nine floors down. She's standing in front of the apartment complex, waving her hand at me. Is it Eva . . . ? No, it's not Eva. It's someone else. I'd recognize Eva.

I have to lean out quite a ways to see her, since she's stepped onto the grass. She's squatting by the wall of the house, gathering something. She gets up and looks up at me. I look . . . she has a bunch of flowers in her arms. She shows them to me and tosses them in the air. They fly nine floors up to me. There are so many of them, so colorful, so beautiful. I lean over the windowsill, stretch my arms . . . and suddenly someone grabs me by my clothes and pulls me in from the window.

"Ain't gonna be no jumping for you, girl," Dad says. He leads me by the collar into my room. He sticks me in there and shuts the door. "Sleep," he says. "Night is for sleeping!"

I hear him closing the window in the kitchen.

Now he's talking to Mom about something . . .

Do I really care?

I sit on the chair and lean my elbows on the table. Something's making smacking noises. Oh, it's Tadzio, smacking in his sleep. Maybe he's dreaming he's eating a chocolate elephant.

I just sat down, and already a whole hour has gone by. The lit face of my watch shines in the darkness. The whole house is quiet.

SUDDENLY I LOOK up and see it's already bright out, it's almost seven. I slept the whole night sitting at the table. I didn't do any of my homework, and I'm not gonna be able to get it done. I pack my books and notebooks when I hear the ring of the alarm clock, but it's far away, in the living room. Now I need to wake Tadzio up. He just stuck his leg out from under the blanket. I tickle him with my finger. He pulls it back.

"Tadzio, get up."

He says something and turns over.

"Tadzio . . ."

"Yup, yup, I'm getting up," he says, and falls asleep again. I go to the bathroom and wash up quickly, only my face and hands. I walk into the kitchen and Mom is heating up milk for Zenus.

"Morning, Mom," I say. Mom doesn't say anything, like I'm not there. Suddenly I remember everything I did yesterday, pushing my dad onto the floor, shouting at him. He should have killed me. If not for Mom, he would have killed me and it would have been a good thing.

"Mom," I say quietly. "I'm really sorry."

Mom doesn't say anything. Oh well, better get to school. I grab my book bag, jostle Tadzio and leave. It's ten after seven.

IT'S EIGHT-FIFTEEN already. Sweaty and out of breath, I run through the school hallway; it's way past the bell. How did I lose so much time?

I was riding the bus, got off too early, then I stared at something . . . I run into the classroom. I want to say something, but I can't say a thing because my mouth is really dry.

Ms. Trauman smiles.

"Sit down. You don't need an excuse. I can see there's been a problem."

I run to my desk, I look . . . Eva is sitting there, wonderful and smiling.

"You're not gonna kick me out of your desk?" she asks. I pant and can't say a word.

"What are you talking about?" I say finally. "I'm really happy. But I didn't do any of my homework."

"Don't worry. During the break we'll give Magda your notebooks; she'll copy from hers quickly."

"I'll copy it myself."

"Why should you work so hard?"

"Miss Bogdaj and Miss Kawczak, what are you doing over there?" the teacher asks. Eva opens her notebook and slides it over to me. She gets up.

"We're arguing over Mickiewicz," she says. "Maica claims he was tall, and I'm almost certain he was really short."

"You know, girls," Ms. Trauman says, "I haven't the vaguest idea. He simply might be of medium height." She bursts out laughing. "Did you hear how that rhymed? When you talk about a poet, the rhymes just come to you."

"He was tall," Zbyszek Karpiel says.

"How do you know?" the teacher asks.

"Because in the picture he looks just like my uncle. And my uncle is really tall, about this tall." Zbyszek gets up and lifts his hand up over his head.

"I'm not changing my mind," Eva says. "Because even though I'm not the Mickiewicz sort, I still think he was short."

Everyone laughs at the new rhyme, including Ms. Trauman. Eva turns to Zbyszek and says, "Even if he was tall for real, he was no bigger than a seal."

More laughter. Eva motions to the class to quiet down. "But seriously speaking, I think everyone knows that short people always look for a chance to advance. There are a lot of examples from history."

"Napoleon!" shouts Edek Skala.

"Balzac was short too," Rita Salomon says. "And fat," she adds.

Nag gets up and points to Zenek. "Zenek is small too." The whole class laughs. Except for Zenek. He looks at Nag and makes a fist.

"Someone ought to write a book about the influence of height on achievement," Eva says. "It would be really interesting."

"Hitler was tiny too!" someone cries.

"Not so short," Florek Gamburowicz points out. "Hitler was of medium height."

"Just like Mickiewicz," Marlena Brycko says in a high voice.

"You're stupid," Ziebinski says to her. "Mickiewicz was a hundred times taller than Hitler."

"I'm sure he wasn't," Florek says. "Hitler wasn't that short."

"And I'm telling you he was a hundred times shorter than Mickiewicz." Ziebinski gets redder and redder.

"I wouldn't be so sure of it," Florek says. "Who knows whether he wasn't even taller."

"Oh yeah? You better watch it!" Ziebinski gets all worked up.

"What you're saying is that if Mickiewicz was over six feet tall and Hitler was supposed to be a hundred times shorter, Hitler would be less than an inch tall. That's all." Florek shows the class how big an inch is.

"Now you see what all the fuss is," Eva says. "And it's all because in our textbooks next to the birth date and death date there's no height listed. In all the Western magazines and articles about famous people, everything is listed. Age, height, weight, wife's name, how many children they had . . . everything you could ever want to know. And what about us?"

Eva shrugs her shoulders and plops down. She glances at me.

"Why aren't you copying?" she asks.

"I did it already," I say. "Remember, we have Polish every other day."

"So what was I monkeying around for?"

Just then I catch on. Meanwhile, the discussion between Ziebinski and Gamburowicz gets louder and louder.

EVA, KLAUDIA AND I are sitting on the windowsill, swinging our legs and chewing gum. Magda is in the classroom copying homework for me. I didn't want to give her my notebooks, but Eva said she's not doing it for free, so I shouldn't ruin her living. I told her I don't have any money to pay her, and Eva said it's already been paid and Magda's just paying off the debt, and if I take that much pity on her, then I can go and lick her feet out of gratitude, or some other part of her body, since she really likes to be licked.

So I keep on sitting and swinging my legs.

"You know what?" Klaudia says. "Something strange is happening to me these days. I don't want to do anything. I don't want to go to bed, and when I wake up, I don't want to get up. And now I really need to pee, but I don't feel like going . . . God, if I could just find someone who could carry me and help me relieve myself . . ."

"I don't see any problem," Eva says, and cries, "Julek!"

He's a big guy who is in eighth grade just like us but in a different homeroom.

"What's up?" he asks.

"We heard you're a bodybuilder. Is that true?"

"It's true," Julek replies, straightening up and sticking out his chest.

"Let me feel your biceps," Eva says. Julek pulls up the sleeve of his shirt, bends his arm and flexes his muscles. We all take turns feeling the small, hard ball in his arm.

"My brother told me," Eva says, "that bodybuilders aren't as strong as they look and their muscles are just puffed up."

"What are you talking about?" Julek protests. "Get your brother over here—he'll find out in a hurry."

"He knows karate."

"Good for him. I don't care if he brings friends. One bodybuilder could take care of three karate guys."

"You're pulling my leg."

"Come watch if you want. You'll see with your own two eyes."

"Are you saying you could carry a hundred and twenty pounds to the end of this hallway?"

Julek brushes it off with a snicker. "To me that's nothing."

Eva looks at Klaudia and says, "You weigh a hundred and twenty pounds."

"Hundred and twenty-six," Klaudia corrects her.

"Even better," Julek says, grabbing Klaudia. He takes her in his arms and bolts to the other end of the hallway. But our school has a really long hallway—you can't even see the end of it. By now they're pretty far and Julek has stopped running. He walks slower and slower, but doesn't let go of Klaudia.

"Oh yeah, bodybuilders are really strong," Eva says, lost in her own thoughts.

A fight breaks out right outside our homeroom. Ziebinski versus Gamburowicz. It's over already. Gamburowicz holds his face and moans, "He knocked my eye out . . . he knocked my eye out!"

"Hitler oughta give you one of his," Ziebinski says.

"Come here, fatso!" Eva calls.

Ziebinski comes up to us. "What do you want?"

"I'm giving you a medal for patriotism," Eva says. She pulls a nickel out of her pocket and gives it to Ziebinski.

He takes a look at it, puts it away and says triumphantly, "Yeah. That's what he gets for his *Hitlerjugend.*"

"Bring me his eye and I'll give you five bucks," Eva says.

"I didn't punch him that hard," Ziebinski says, suddenly frightened. He runs after Gamburowicz, who has gone with Marlena into the bathroom to wash his eye.

The first-aid squad passes Julek the bodybuilder, who's carrying Klaudia back. He sets her on the windowsill beside us and, panting heavily, he gasps, "How's that?"

"You've convinced me," Eva says. "You could kill any bodybuilder."

Julek looks at her severely. "I don't kill bodybuilders."

"Gee, I messed up. I meant karate guys. I'll tell my brother and his friends to avoid you when they see you."

"That's right," Julek says, smiling nonchalantly. "And if anyone starts hitting on you, you girls can count on me."

"Zenek!" Eva suddenly calls.

Zenek runs up to us. "What?"

"Are you hitting on us?" Eva asks.

"Me? . . . No."

"You're lucky."

"Why?"

"Because if you were hitting on us, you would have to deal with Julek."

Zenek cranes his neck and looks up at Julek. Julek takes a look at him, then at us, and then starts to get it, that Eva was making fun of him.

"Uh," he says, waves his hand and leaves. And we burst into pieces from all the laughter we've been holding back.

AT FIRST KLAUDIA and Magda were following us on their East German motorcycle, a Simson, but we lost them long ago, weaving through the streets of Szczawno Zdroj. I have a large shiny black helmet on, and so does Eva. We keep knocking them against each other.

I go knock and she tilts her head back and knocks against mine. Knock, knock. Knock, knock.

The helmets entered the picture when Eva decided she'd had enough of charming the cops all the time and lining their pockets with green.

I finally found out why that policeman called her "Miss Zdzis-lawa" yesterday—because Eva has her older sister's driver's license, the one who's been in London for the past year. Their pictures really look alike. Thanks to that, even though Eva's only fifteen, she can ride a regular motorcycle and drive a car.

We sat together at the same desk for every class. During the breaks Klaudia and Magda joined us and we monkeyed around, all four of us. I've never laughed so hard in my life as I did today, not even back when I was with Kasia. Eva's always coming up with new ideas about how to make a monkey out of someone. She's not trying to be nasty, she's just joking around so we can have a laugh.

Knock. She knocks against my helmet again.

I knock against hers too. I look through the visor and here we are, approaching the white fence surrounding Eva's house. The gate is open and we pull in. A car's parked in front of the garage and Eva's dad is just getting out of it.

We get down off the Yamaha and take off our helmets.

"Hi, Dada!" Eva calls, and I say, "Hello."

"Hello, cuties," Eva's dad says. We enter the house together.

"How's business?" Eva asks.

"Okay," her dad replies. In the hallway we go our separate ways. Her dad goes upstairs and we go to Eva's room. She throws her bag in the corner, and soon after, my book bag lands there. We sprawl out on the puffed-up transparent love seats on opposite sides of the glass-topped coffee table. Suddenly Eva snaps her fingers.

She jumps up from the chair and heads straight to her closet. She pulls out a turquoise denim dress with shiny buckles and throws it to me.

"Try it on," she says.

"No, why should I?"

"Just hurry up and do it."

"I don't want to."

"I'm gonna jump out the window if you don't try it on," she threatens, and takes a step in the direction of the window. I laugh, because the window leads onto the terrace.

Eva comes up to me and pulls off my polyester blouse.

"I'll do it myself," I say. I take off my skirt and take the dress from her. I step into it feetfirst because I can't get it over my arms. I pull it up. Eva zips up the back.

"It fits you great," Eva says. "Check yourself out." She leads me to a large mirror.

Gee, I look so nice. The dress is tight and narrow at the bottom, with a slit in the front. It has a very nice neckline. I put my hands in the pockets.

"Do you feel comfortable in it?" Eva asks.

"Yup."

"It's yours."

"No, come on . . ."

"It's a great dress—it cost fifty-nine dollars and sixty cents."

"I can't pay you for this," I say, and glance in the mirror one last time.

"I'm giving it to you for free."

"No, I can't."

"Don't be silly. The foolish give, the wise take. It's yours and that's it."

"What's your mom gonna say?"

"Why should she say anything?" Eva wonders. "She doesn't know my dresses, she's only interested in her own."

"Somehow it doesn't seem right," I say quietly. "Such an expensive dress . . ."

"Just remember one thing from now on," Eva says. "Never pity the rich, because they'll never pity you. See how beautiful you look in it? It matches your hair and your skin tone. It's too small for me anyway—look how my boobs have grown."

"Well, thank you so much." I try to smile at her, but I can't, since I feel so stupid.

"I have a lot of supercool clothes I don't wear," Eva says. "But if I have to beg you on my knees . . ."

"Come on," I say. "I'm not a beggar."

"You're my friend, and it just turned out that you have little and I have a lot. It's not to my credit, nor is it your fault. So, are you gonna try some more things on?"

"No," I say. "I don't want to."

"Because I don't have the patience to see you struggling with your two skirts and two blouses. And your underwear . . . It breaks my heart in two. So, are your parents normal? Your father works in a mine, and miners make pretty good money."

I shrug my shoulders.

"Not that much," I say. "There are seven of us on one salary. Count for yourself. You really need to use your smarts not to die of hunger. It's a good thing Dad makes a little money on the side. Besides, it doesn't pay to buy anything for me, since I'm still growing . . ."

Eva bursts out laughing. She hugs me.

"You're wonderful," she says. "I simply adore you. Every word you say is sweet. I wish I could be like that."

"Like what?" I ask.

"So sunny and so strong. I could look at you for hours on end. If I had a million dollars, I would buy you forever. Would you like that?"

"No," I say. Eva hugs me even harder.

"Oh," she sighs, "where in this stupid world did you come from? What star did you fall from? You know, yesterday I was lying in bed listening to music and I was thinking about you the whole time. I remembered everything you said . . . Come on, let's plop down."

We sit down on a love seat, the two of us. Eva cozies up to me.

"Are you comfortable?" she asks.

"Yes."

I look at her ear. It's as pretty as Eva herself. I touch it, it's warm. Eva starts purring, just like our Tabby, who we left in Jawiszow. I miss him a lot. He always used to come over to me wanting to be petted. So I would pet him, and when I'd ease off, he'd lift his head up and look me in the eyes. So I'd start petting him again and he'd start purring again. He purred just like Eva is purring now, when I pet her hair. It's so soft and black, almost navy.

"Tabby, Tabby," I say sweetly, and Eva goes "Purrrrr!" and looks me in the eye, just like Tabby.

"I've always dreamed of having a real girlfriend, just like you," she says.

"What about Klaudia and Magda?"

Eva screws up her face. "They're idiots. Klaudia's an icicle and Magda's self-centered. Whenever I lend her money, she never pays me back. I forget and lend her more. Then I have to get paid back in favors."

"What do you mean?"

"She runs errands for me," Eva says dismissively. "You know, she's in love with my brother."

"What about him?"

"He couldn't care less. She constantly asks whether he said something about her, so I make up all kinds of idiotic things to get her excited. She thinks she's gonna latch onto the family. Too bad Michal is such a loser . . ."

"Why do you call him a loser?"

"Because he has a requited love affair with his computer disks. I would marry you off to him, but unfortunately, you're not a diskette. You know what an idiot he is? One time I couldn't sleep and I got up at six in the morning. I heard him rustling around his room. I come in and he's parked in front of his computer playing this video game where you fly a jet. Just think about it . . . This guy is twenty years old, almost twenty-one. Everyone's a bit nuts at our house. Dada has his business deals twenty-five hours a day. Even when he's making love to Mimi, I'm sure he's thinking about business. Mimi never has any time either, she's always running around, always half a minute late, tongue hanging down to her stomach, clocks in her eyes. She has about thirty watches. Shopping for them is her hobby. She makes all these appointments with people and she runs from one to the next, with the hairdresser, beautician, massage therapist and tanning booth all squeezed in. She comes home at night exhausted and immediately runs to the phone to make a thousand two hundred thirty-seven appointments for the *next* day. Michal, you already know, total computer masturbation. And if only you met Zdzisia . . . She's a total joke. She's only been in London for two years, but when she calls us, she speaks English, because she can't remember how to speak Polish anymore."

Eva laughs. She puts her hand up to her ear and jabbers at it like it's a telephone: "Helloeve, howdoyoudo, mydee . . . !"

"And what about you?" I ask.

"What about me?"

"So . . . what are you like?"

"Me? I don't know. Could be I'm a little monkey, with a family made of wire."

"Why of wire?"

"Because once I read an article about a monkey who was separated at birth from its mom, and locked up in an isolated cage with two artificial mothers. One was covered with plush, the other was made of wire. The one made of wire had tits with milk. The little monkey hugged the plush one all day, but it would go to the wire one to suckle."

"Poor little monkey," I say.

"It's me who's the poor little monkey," Eva squeals pitiably, and she nuzzles her face into my breast. I embrace her and stroke her hair. She takes some of the fabric of my new dress into her mouth and starts smacking, pretending she's sucking on it.

"But I'm not made of wire," I say.

"You're made of plush," Eva says, "but you've got the nipples *and* the milk."

So WE SAT hugging each other, until dinner. Miss Zenobia served us again, but it might not be the same Miss Zenobia that Kasia has, because she doesn't recognize me. Or maybe these are twin sisters and one cooks at Kasia's place and the other at Eva's?

After dinner we went for a walk.

And we are walking right now. Szczawno is wonderful. Each house is different and they all look straight out of a fairy tale about distant ages long ago. Whenever some guy passes by, whether he's young or old, Eva shoots him a glance, and immediately he turns around. Eva calls it "the hunt" because she collects guys who stare at her so hard they trip and fall. Since the beginning of the year she's managed to collect five of them. We've been walking for half an hour and not a single one has tripped and fallen down. There was just one who bumped into a woman with a stroller and apologized like crazy, but she still screamed at him. It's not that easy to get someone to trip and fall, since Eva spares cripples. Sometimes she hunts for a whole month, then another, and nothing happens. But once she had a good day and got two, only one of the guys didn't fall down all the way, since he caught himself.

It's best to shoot a glance at a guy just as he gets to the curb or any other obstacle. It's also great to give those walking with their wives the eye, because when their heads turn to Eva, their wives make hellish scenes, if not right away, then later, at home. Sometimes the hunt ends kind of stupidly because of guys who are hard to get rid of. And if they're trashed, that's it. You either have to run or look for a policeman.

One time she hopped into a cab and the guy she made eye contact with went after her. She got the cabby to go after him, because he didn't want to leave. The cabby pulled him out of the taxi and punched him, then he punched back, and they started fighting, so she ran away.

"I would be afraid," I say.

"That's what the hunt's all about," Eva explains. "It's dangerous. If you shoot at a tiger and miss, you're a goner. But I've never met a real tiger."

"And what if you did?"

"I'd let him eat me." Eva laughs. Then she stops and says, "I have an idea, let's play 'Orders.'"

"What's that?" I ask.

"We take an oath of obedience, you follow my orders, and I follow yours. Do you want to play?"

"Uh-huh."

"But it's not really a game."

"Why not?"

"Because the oath counts for your whole life."

"So be it," I say.

"And what if I order you to do something horrible?"

"For example . . . ?"

"Well . . . I might order you to throw yourself under a train."

"I'd do it," I say.

Eva grows serious. "Are you for real?"

I nod my head.

"You'd really throw yourself under a train?"

"If you wanted me to die, then too bad for me."

"I don't believe you," Eva says.

"Tell me to throw myself under a train. If I threw myself under one, would you believe me?"

Eva looks at me for a long time, biting her lip.

"I believe you," she says, finally. "Remember, you can order me to do whatever you want too."

"And if I order you to throw yourself under a train?" I ask.

Eva doesn't answer right away. She looks at me funny, breathing quickly.

"Yes," she says. "I swear on everything, I'll carry out every one of your orders. You go."

"I swear on everything," I say, "that I'll carry out every one of your orders."

"They might be some bad things," Eva says.

"Too bad. An oath is an oath."

We look each other in the eye. Eva shivers a bit, and her shivering affects me. I'm as scared as she is, but at the same time I feel sweeter and more wonderful than I ever have before. Eva takes me by the hand.

"One day you'll regret this oath," she says.

"And you'll regret it too!" I say with sudden anger. "If either one of us doesn't keep it, that's the end of our friendship."

"I'll keep it."

"So will I."

We look at each other, shivering, terrified and happy—and somehow closer to each other than ever before. What's going to happen to us now?

"There is no taking back an oath," Eva says. "Even the one who orders can't revoke it if she says the word 'order.'"

"But we take turns giving orders," I say.

"Who goes first?"

"You can."

"Come on—don't be so nice," Eva protests, and turns to a guy passing by: "Do you have any matches?"

The guy stops and searches his pockets. He pulls a matchbox out of his pocket and gives it to Eva. "Glad to be of service, ladies."

Eva pulls out two matches and gives the rest back to the guy. "Thank you."

The guy walks away, looking back a few times. Eva stretches her hand out to me.

"Heads goes first," she says. I draw a match. It has a head. Eva sighs.

I smile. "What? Are you afraid?"

"No, but remember that I'm going to take revenge," Eva says.

"I know," I say. "Hop on one leg to the end of the street and then back to me."

Eva sneers. "No, that's stupid."

And I say, "That's an order!"

She bends one leg behind her and hops away from me. Before long she's halfway to the corner. People look over their shoulders. I look to see whether she's cheating.

She turns around at the end and starts hopping back. Some guy zeroes in on her and starts hopping behind her, also on one leg. By now Eva is standing next to me, on two legs. And the guy says to her, "If you want, I can hop with you all the time."

"Get lost, buster," Eva says, "before your varicose veins burst."

She takes me by the hand and pulls me behind her. She's mad and out of breath.

"Don't be mad at me," I say.

"What are you talking about? An order is an order."

We look up and see the guy's already gone.

"My turn," Eva says. She looks around and points her finger. "See that fat bald guy?"

"I see him," I say, looking at an old fatso standing on the other side of the street in front of a grocery store. He's holding flowers in his hand.

"Go up to him," Eva says slowly, "kiss his hand, spit on his bald spot and take the flowers away from him."

"No!" I'm horrified. "He'll catch me and take me to the police station. Please think of something else!"

Eva smiles ironically and says curtly, "That's an order."

I sigh in despair and step into the street. It's like I'm going to my execution. I wish a car would run me over so it would all be over with. But tough luck, there are no cars.

But how am I going to do it?

It's no big deal to kiss someone's hand, it's just a little embarrassing. But how can I spit on his bald spot and, on top of that, steal his flowers . . . ? I won't be able to pull it off.

I look around. Eva's standing under a tree, watching me.

What a lowlife. All I asked *her* to do was hop on one leg . . . Why did she have to take such revenge? And why did I take that oath?

I have to do it. If I asked Eva to do what I ordered her to do, she'd do it. Only I'm such a scaredy-cat. Oh, if I can pull this off, just watch me get her back . . .

The guy is really fat and bald, in an elegant suit . . . he's probably some kind of executive. Maybe I should ask him for the flowers? He won't hand them over. He must be waiting for some lady—otherwise, why would he have the flowers?

Whatever happens happens.

I circle around and come up to him from the back. He hasn't noticed me yet. I look around to see whether anyone else is looking, and suddenly I spit upward with all my might, kind of to the side. My spit goes splat on the guy's bald spot.

He claps his hand on his head, turns to me, and I wipe my cheek with a handkerchief, and looking up, I say, "I saw him. It's the guy from the second floor. Did he spit at you too?"

The guy looks up, backs up to the curb.

"Hey, you over there!" he shouts. "I'll be back with a cop! You asshole!"

Across the street Eva is doubled over with laughter and I still have the flowers and the kiss left. I come up to the guy and wipe the lapel of his suit.

"You still had something on here," I say sweetly.

"Thank you," the guy says with a smile. He's really nice . . . maybe he's not an executive. I look at his flowers.

I clasp my hands to my heart.

"Oh gee, those are just really wonderful flowers!" I say in awe. The guy looks at his three carnations with withered ferns, choked to death by a paper ribbon.

"You really like them?" he asks hesitantly.

"Wonderful. I like the arrangement!"

He examines the flowers carefully. "I really don't know much about it."

"I'd really love to get flowers like that. I'd give my life for them . . ."

But he's not about to give them to me. What a jerk! Here I was cleaning the spit off his lapel with my own handkerchief and he doesn't do a thing in return. I sigh.

"Why are you sighing?" the guy asks.

"Because if I had such pretty flowers, I'd take them to my little sister in the hospital," I say, doing my best to sound pitiful and trying to shed a tear. "She's all burnt and we're not even certain whether she'll live."

I raise the handkerchief to my eyes.

"How did she burn herself?"

"Boiling water," I say. "On top of that, she caught fire from the gas."

"My friend also got burned," the guy says, "in his car. The gasoline caught on fire and it was a miracle they saved him. Nowadays you have to be careful all the time. When they're not spitting at you, they're setting you on fire. When they're not setting you on fire, they're robbing you."

"Excuse me," I beg. "Could you give me these flowers, so I can take them to the hospital to my poor Kasia? Let her enjoy their fragrance before she dies."

"But why *my* flowers?" the guy puzzles.

"Because they're so pretty."

"I saw much nicer ones at the flower stand. Go and buy some. I'll tell you where."

"I don't have any money."

"Okay, I'm going to give you some," the guy says with distaste, and reaches for his wallet.

"I don't want money, I want flowers! These flowers! Something tells me that if Kasia gets these, she'll get better. Don't you have any pity for a poor, burnt girl?!"

"Leave me alone," the guy says. "I'm waiting for a lady, so I can propose to her. How am I supposed to propose without flowers! If you want, I'll give you two hundred zloty."

"I beg you, please give me these flowers."

"Here's three hundred. Now get lost."

"Please . . . I'll adore you for the rest of my life. I must have those flowers."

"Let's do it this way," the guy offers. "I'll give you some money, you run to the stand, bring me some new flowers, and you can have these."

"I can't," I moan. "I have to have them now!"

"No means no. Get lost, kiddo, or I'll kick you!"

He walks away a few steps. I follow him. I'm about to grab the flowers, but first I have to kiss his hand.

"If you don't give me these flowers right now, I'm going to wait for your fiancée and tell her that you got me pregnant."

The guy turns red. "Screw you, you little shit, or I can't say what will happen next!"

"I'll tell her I'm having your baby!"

I say that really loud. Some guy turns his head, and a few women leaving the store look at us.

The fatso laughs nervously. "Sure she'll believe you?"

"You'll find out soon," I answer coolly.

The fatso gives me the flowers and says, "Take them and get lost!"

I take the flowers.

"Well, let's at least be polite," I say. Suddenly I grab his hand and kiss it. He jerks it away. He looks at me with fear. I curtsy elegantly. "Thank you very much."

I take the flowers to the other side of the street. I walk up to Eva and hand her the bouquet. "For you, my dear."

"Oh, what wonderful flowers!" Eva gushes, and—bang—feeds them to the mouth of the penguin-shaped trash can. I turn to look at the fatso. He's watching, he saw the whole thing.

I take Eva by the hand and we run. We peep from the corner and the fatso pulls his flowers from the trash can. We burst out laughing.

"You reversed the order," Eva says, "but it came out even better. That's great. You spit at someone's bald spot and he gives you flowers for it. That's how one should deal with men. I thought you'd chicken out. You're wonderful."

"You'll find out how wonderful I am," I say. "Now it's my turn."

"No, that's enough for today."

"That's not for you to decide." I pull her along with me. I'm looking around thinking what order I should give her.

Eva resists. "I don't want to anymore!"

What shall I order her to do so she'll remember it for a long time, like I'll remember this bald idiot with the flowers . . . ?

I'd order her to kick someone, but that's nothing to her.

I'd order her to steal something, but that's nothing to her.

Now I know, my pretty doll, what I'm going to do.

I pull her into the doorway of a low building. We walk into a small dirty courtyard. It fits my plans better than I thought. All the Dumpsters are overflowing, there's trash everywhere. It smells horrible. Big flies are buzzing around.

I push Eva toward the Dumpsters.

"Here," I say.

Eva looks at me, frightened. "Here what?"

"You have to kneel here for an entire half hour."

"Please, don't order me to do that!"

"You have to kneel with your hands up," I say slowly, taking full pleasure in her horror and disgust. "You won't be allowed to sit on your heels or put your hands down for even a second. You can't move for half an hour, no matter what happens."

"Maica," Eva pleads with me, "don't do this. I'll give you whatever you want. I'll give you ten bucks, you can buy whatever you want in the dollar store . . . I beg you, take it back, don't say 'it's an order'!"

"No way," I say with a smile. "I asked you the same thing."

Eva cozies up to me. "Please . . . not today. I'll do it tomorrow. I don't have time now, gotta run. I made an appointment with—"

"No way," I say. "Kneel! It's an order!"

I point to the place where there's the most garbage. Eva fusses and frowns and moans in disgust, but she kneels. I lift her hands up.

"Not so high," she pleads.

"That's how high it's going to be," I say. I back off a step.

"Show me your watch," Eva says.

I show her. "It's four thirty-five. You have to kneel here until five after five."

"I never knew you were so cruel," Eva says, kneeling with her hands up.

"There are lots of things you still don't know about me," I say, putting my hands in the pockets of my new dress.

"The sun's blinding me. Can I kneel facing another direction?"

"Too late. The ball's already rolling."

"You're gonna regret this."

"Concentrate on being able to make it."

"Don't worry, I will. But you won't be able to stand what I order *you* to do. You'll see."

She's mad.

I smile ironically. "I still have a whole half hour."

"Yuck, it smells so bad here," Eva says.

"You're right, it's really disgusting. Bye, darling. I'm gonna leave you alone with the sweet smell."

I hold my nose and go to the other side of the courtyard. I sit on a low wall. I'm watching Eva from here. She's still kneeling calmly. Let a few minutes go by. Yup, soon her martyrdom will start. I know something about that. Oh, she's starting to move her head . . .

"Flies!" she shouts in despair. I don't say a word. Sure, they're flies. I selected this place especially because they'd be buzzing. She shouts, "Maica, can I shoo them away from my face?"

"Not allowed."

"They're landing on my face!"

"Too bad!" I cry. "You can only move your head!"

"Come here, chase them away!"

"I don't feel like it!"

I watch her tossing her head from side to side.

"You bitch!" she shouts. "I hate you!"

I laugh loudly so she can hear.

Let her yell a little. Only seven minutes have gone by. There are still twenty-three left. I sit on the low wall a bit farther down so the sun can reach me. I'm not going to pass up this opportunity to get a tan.

"How much time is left?" Eva asks.

"Twenty-three minutes!"

"I'm kneeling on something! May I move over?"

"Not allowed!" I shout back. She's moaning loudly. I jump down from the low wall and come nearer so I can see her martyrdom close up. I stand in front of her. Flies sit on her sweaty face, which is twisted up in pain. She shakes her head. They fly away, then sit down again, like they know they can go unpunished for so many minutes.

"Poor thing," I say. "I feel very sorry for you."

"My knees hurt," she complains. "And my spine. I can't stand it, I'm gonna faint . . ."

"Calm down," I say. "There are only twenty minutes left. You'll be okay."

"No way," she moans. "Please call off your order."

"Sorry, poor girl. We agreed, there's no taking back orders."

"At least chase the flies away. I beg you."

"I don't feel like taking my hands out of my pockets," I say, standing in front of her and watching her misery.

"I'll go crazy," she moans. Tears well up in her eyes.

"You look wonderful," I say.

"Fuck off!"

"Yuck, why are you using such foul language?"

"Dirty pig. Idiot, piece of shit! I hate you!"

"Kiss, kiss." I smack in the air. And I say, "I haven't heard such nice compliments in a long time. Thank you."

"Maica," she moans. "Do something, help me."

"Only fifteen minutes to go."

"I won't make it . . ."

She sobs. The sobs get louder and louder. I feel awfully sorry for her, but what can you do, an order is an order. I squat in front of her and say sweetly, "My itty-bitty Eva, my poor baby, my unhappy girl."

"You'll see," she says. "I'm gonna order you to kneel until dark."

"Big deal, so I'll kneel. I'm not afraid, because you're not gonna be able to stand the fifteen minutes that are left."

"I'll be able to stand them."

"You should be thankful that I only ordered you to kneel for half an hour." She spits at me.

I jump back—she didn't get me. I work up some spit in my mouth. I spit straight in her face. "There! An eye for an eye, a tooth for a tooth, a spit for a spit."

Eva lowers her head and sobs powerlessly. My spit trickles down her face. She's crying and her whole body is shaking. She sounds so desperate that my heart breaks. I take out a handkerchief, I wipe the tears and spit from her face.

She brushes her face against my hand. "Maica, dearest, do something, help me. I really can't take it anymore."

"What do you want me to do?"

"I don't know. Let's not play 'Orders' anymore."

"We have to," I explain, stroking her face. "We swore for life. Remember?"

"I do," she moans. "But at least hold my hands a bit . . ."

"Not allowed."

"I can't take it."

"So you'll break our oath and that'll be the end of our friendship. And you'll never be able to take revenge on me."

"You'll see, I'll take revenge!"

"I know, darling, I know," I say, and I kiss her pretty, sweaty face. An old woman comes out of the doorway carrying a trash can. She empties it in the Dumpster next to us. She looks at Eva.

"What's wrong with her?" she asks, surprised.

"She's atoning for her sins," I explain.

"Why near a Dumpster? Let her atone in church."

"The church doesn't smell as bad," I say. "And it doesn't have as many flies."

The old woman giggles.

"What a weirdo," she says. She disappears in the doorway with the empty trash can.

Eva shakes off a fly.

"Soon they're going to eat me alive," she says. "Chase them away . . ."

I pick a large piece of newspaper off the ground and wrap Eva's head in it. I twist it in back and it holds. I say, "I've done this so you know that I take pity on animals. Thank me."

"Shit!" Eva says from under the newspaper.

"Oh, don't say that or I'll take it down and leave," I threaten.

"No, no, thank you very much."

"There's still ten minutes left," I say. Eva shakes and moans softly. Suddenly there's this very loud music. It's coming from the window on the second floor. Violin and drums. But here, by the Dumpsters, among the scattered trash, my Eva is kneeling with a newspaper for a face and her arms stretching up toward the sky.

I leave, tiptoeing.

By now I'm on the street.

People are walking. Everything is so ordinary, boring and normal. No one knows that over there, in the courtyard, a girl is in agony. No, I'm not gonna run away, although a minute ago I wanted to. I'll go back to Eva, even though I'm in for a terrible revenge. She's all I've got in the world. What would I do without her? . . . I'm going back to the courtyard.

Eva is shaking and she doesn't even know I was gone for so long and wanted to leave forever. The music coming from the window is so loud that I can't hear Eva's moans until I'm very close to her. I look at my watch. It's two after five; Eva only has three minutes left. I turn the knob and set the time back by about four minutes.

I take the newspaper off Eva's head. Her whole face is covered with sweat and tears.

"How much longer?" she mutters through her teeth.

"There's still seven minutes left."

"I can't . . ." she moans. Her body is twitching in spasms. She's turning her head back and forth.

"Just a little bit longer. You can do it, darling."

She's crying. "Help me . . ."

"How?" I ask, feeling tears coming to my eyes.

"Touch me," she pleads.

I begin to stroke her hair.

"No, not there . . . Touch my boobs. Stroke them. Please."

I touch her boobs, I stroke them. They're bigger than mine. Eva shuts her eyes tight and begs, "Harder."

I stroke them harder. Under my fingers I can feel two hard buttons hatching.

"Grab them . . ."

I grab them and squeeze them. Eva calms down and purrs quietly.

"Feel better?" I ask.

"Yes." Eva smiles through her tears.

I'm playing with her buttons. At some point I lift my head and see the old woman in the window, the one who was dumping her trash. She's staring at us. At another window a guy's peeping at us from behind a curtain.

I let go of Eva's buttons.

"Please, just a little bit longer, please . . ." she says, without opening her eyes.

"Enough. That's enough. Only two minutes to go. I have to get the most out of your suffering."

She opens her eyes.

"You're a witch," she says.

I smile. "Uh-huh . . ."

I look at her face. Again it's twisted in pain. I look at my watch.

"One minute left." I get up. Eva is wriggling in her final spasms next to me . . . "That's it," I say.

Her hands flop down. Eva's lying on her side now in the trash, not moving, moaning quietly. Her suffering is over. Soon mine will start. I lean over and grab her under her arms.

"Don't touch . . . it hurts . . ." she says.

I lift her up.

"I can't straighten my legs," she squeals.

"That'll go away soon." I lead her slowly toward a low wall. She's walking like a cripple and moaning painfully with every step. I help her sit down.

"Poor little thing."

"Ohhhhh . . ."

I squat and kiss her kneecaps. There is a hole in her tights on one of them.

"I'll never forgive you for that," Eva says.

"As you wish. But I have my book bag at your place. I have to get it."

She reaches over and messes up my hair. "What's that got to do with it? An order's an order. I'll never forgive you, that's one thing. The other is, I adore you, you nutty girl."

She straightens her legs and notices the hole.

"Shucks," she says with regret. "Ten dollars gone."

"Why didn't you tell me they were so expensive? I would have put some cardboard down."

"Calm down. My order is going to cost you a thousand times as much."

"I don't have anything that expensive. My tights only cost 350 zloty. All I have is that dress from you. If you want, I can cut it into pieces."

"What do I need your dress for? You'll soon find out how you're going to pay for my suffering. The only thing that helped me make it through to the end was the thought of sweet revenge."

At this point the loud music from the window, all the racket, stops. Over the radio a powerful voice says, "The piece you have just heard was an Antonín Dvořák concerto!"

Eva laughs. "I'll remember Dvořák for the rest of my life."

"Me too," I say.

"You?" Eva exclaims. "You weren't the one kneeling near the Dumpster during this concerto . . ."

"But I finally came to realize who I really am," I say, feeling my lips go slightly numb.

"You *are* a monster," Eva says.

"Yup."

"One of these days you're going to kill me."

"Yup."

Eva gets down off the low wall, takes off her shoes, quickly takes off her tights, rolls them up into a ball and throws them away. She looks at me.

"So?" she says. "Do you want to kneel down next to this Dumpster until sunset?"

At first I feel hot, then suddenly cold. But I don't say a word. Eva takes me by the hand and leads me to the Dumpsters. She points to the same place she was kneeling.

I kneel down, I lift my arms.

"That low? Higher!"

I lift them up higher.

"And now . . . if you ask me nicely, maybe I won't order you to kneel until sunset," Eva says. "You're only going to kneel for an hour."

"Please," I plead quietly.

"Nicer."

"Pretty please."

"Come on, a little bit nicer."

"Eva, I beg you, don't order me to kneel until sunset. Please, pretty please . . ."

She looks at the watch on my up stretched arm. And says, "All right. You asked me so nicely . . . that I've decided . . . that there are more fragrant places to get my revenge. Get up, silly, we're going home."

I jump up from the ground and I throw myself into her arms. "My sweet, dear, wonderful Eva!"

WE'RE LYING ON the sofa in Eva's room, looking at foreign catalogues and fashion magazines. We're chitchatting about the dresses and everything else.

I turn to the next page of the catalogue . . . There are a lot of watches there, the same time on every one of them, ten after ten. I automatically look at my watch.

It's ten after seven. I sigh.

"What's the matter?" Eva asks.

"I have to go home."

"I still haven't given you my order."

"You'll have to do it tomorrow, because now I've got to go. Really."

"How about sleeping over at my house?" Eva says. "Tomorrow's Sunday, we can sleep till noon, and then I can take Dada's car and we can ride around."

"I can't," I reply, getting up from the sofa.

"I order you to stay."

"No, no, no," I say quickly. "They'll kill me if I don't come home."

"Who?"

"My mom and dad. If only you knew what happened yesterday when I got back from your place. Dad wanted to beat me with his belt. I pushed him and he fell down and hit his head on the gas stove. It was a miracle he let me off. But now I'll get it three times worse. I have to go now. Believe me, I have to!"

"You're not going anywhere."

"So when you see me at school on Monday, I'll be all bruised."

"You're making that up."

"I swear I'm not. My dad doesn't joke."

"He must be some kind of psychopath," Eva says.

"No. He's really nice when he isn't angry or drunk."

"Oh yeah, he sounds really nice," Eva says sarcastically.

I turn my back to her.

"Undo my zipper," I say.

"Why?"

"Because if I go home in this dress, my mom's going to ask me where I got it."

"You can tell her you got it from me."

"She'll yell at me for being a scrounge. Undo it."

"Undo it yourself."

"I think it's stuck," I say, my hand behind my back. I yank harder on the pull tab—nothing happens, it's stuck.

"Please . . ."

"Anyway, you're not going anywhere," Eva says.

"Please understand, I have to. I had to go on forever just so she'd let me spend the night at Kasia's. After what happened yesterday, she's never going to believe me. She saw us from the balcony and thought you were a guy."

"You slept at Kasia's?" Eva says, growing angry.

"She was sick and her mom was on call that day."

"How do you know I'm not sick? You can stay at her place but not mine? Oh no, I'm not going to let you off the hook that easy! You have to stay at my place until Monday. That's an order. You hear? An or-der."

Suddenly I let go of the zipper. I sit down on the sofa because I'm starting to suffocate, I can't get any air, I feel like I'm choking. What's happening to me? I wriggle like an earthworm that's been stepped on, I wave my arms and my legs. I'm choking! I'm dying . . .

That thing, whatever it was, lets go of me, I can breathe now. I strain for breath with heavy gasps. Eva's leaning over me. "What's wrong with you?" she asks, frightened.

"I'm fine now," I answer.

"Is that epilepsy?"

"No. I felt something choking me. It might have been out of fear."

"I hope you're not gonna die on me."

"Don't worry," I say. "Shit don't sink."

"Was it because of my order?"

"I don't know. But I don't have a place to live anymore. They won't let me in there again."

"Good," Eva says. "Why would you need a home like that anyway? You can live with us and we'll never part. Everyone here liked you a lot. Mimi and Dada . . . and Michal thinks you're out of this world."

Eva lies down on her side, pulls me toward her and snuggles up to me.

"You'll see," she whispers. "It'll be wonderful to be together. Why are you crying? Don't cry . . ."

I don't feel like crying, but I'm crying.

"Maica, don't cry," Eva pleads. But it's not me crying, it's that stupid Marysia inside of me who's crying. She must be crying for Mom, for Zenus, for Tadzio and for the girls. And for Dad, though he's never home, and when he is, he's asleep.

"I'm sorry," I say. I can't stop crying, even though I really want to. Stop blubbering, I say to Marysia. Go sob at your place, leave me in peace, I want to laugh with my Eva.

"Are you that frightened?" Eva asks.

I don't say a thing. I press my face to the pillow. Eva gets up from the sofa and says, "Cry a little. I'll be back in half an hour. I have to run an errand downtown and I'm taking your shoes with me so you can't run away."

"Where are you going?" I ask. I raise my head and she's gone. All I can see is the door closing. My wire sister has gone away and the second, plush one keeps on sobbing. What can I do?

I wipe away my tears. On the bed lies a catalogue filled with beautiful girls, all smiling at me.

Join us, they say. Smile, look, maybe you want that dress? $48.

That one's cheaper, but it's pretty too. Only $42.

Maybe you prefer the little suit? $66.

Or that one for $120.

Isn't that pullover with sequins pretty? Only $100.

I'll let you have these pink jeans for twenty-five bucks.

Check out this skirt for $40; it's really neat. It goes with a blouse for $19.

Flats for $34.99.

Purse: $28.

The other one for $31.99.

Undies, seven pairs for the whole week, only $19.99.

Try on these bathing suits: 100% lycra!

Two-piece swimsuit: $24.99.

One-piece: $22.

Anyway. Buy it all, let it all be yours.

Now it's all mine. On Monday I'll go to school in this dress. I'll wear that one to church tomorrow and that one in the evening if it turns cold. I'll tan in this suit and I'll wear that one for skiing. And I'll order these precious pearls for my precious little girls.

And for my boys these corduroys.

Those are my pots and those are my plates. Oh, here's my living room and my TVs. I'll put this carpet in the bedroom and I'll give that one to my mom as a gift. I'll ride to my wedding in this car. This guy'll be my husband. No, this one's cuter. No, not him, because what kind of a husband would he be wearing only his underwear? Oh, I'm going to take this one. He'll always have a tan.

Mikael will be his name. Maica and Mikael.

Here we are on vacation. And here we are again at a party at the Persian Embassy. Oh, this watch is just right for me. And I'll give this one to Mikael. No, I'll give him that one, for $210.

"Stretch your hand out and close your eyes," I say to Mikael. He closes his hand and stretches his eyes. "The other way around, silly!"

I put his watch on.

He looks, and laughs with great joy.

"Great watch," he says. "Thankyouverymuch. Iloveyou!"

He kisses me right next to our set of garden furniture and pull-out table. Grand total: $400. Plus our umbrella for $30.

"Say, let's have a seat, why should we stand?" I say. We're sitting down. I speak English so well. Mikael understands everything I say.

"And where are the children?" I ask suddenly. Mikael points to the swimming pool, a glistening new watch on his wrist. They're splashing in the blue water.

"What time is it?"

Mikael shows me his watch. Oh, it's ten after ten. The maid's walking through the garden carrying a tray with drinks. She sets it down on the table. I look at her watch. It's right. It also says ten after ten.

Here come the guests. They're all nicely tanned, just like us, only not quite as deeply.

"Hello!" they say, making themselves comfortable. I look . . . their watches are also running well: it says ten after ten on every one of them.

There's only one guy who doesn't come up to me. He's standing under a palm, somewhat pale, a little frightened, in a gray sweater and without a watch. And he's wearing glasses. Oh, he might be a Pole.

I grab two glasses of "Orange Blackmail" and I go up to him. I'm walking, the ice is clinking in the glasses, and my heels are knocking on the marble tiles.

Quite young, but somewhat balding.

"Howdoyoudo?" I say. Gee, what does "Howdoyoudo" mean? The guy takes me by the arm and pulls me into the bushes.

"Marysia," he says quietly. "I want to help you."

I hand him the cocktail and the watch. "Welcome, my countryman, what's new in the old country?"

He empties the cocktail in one gulp, like it's straight vodka, puts the watch into his pocket and says quickly, nervously, constantly looking at Mikael and the guests, "Maria, run, I have a bike."

I pull myself away.

"Mikael!" I cry. "Helpme!"

"Be patient, Maria, please," says the guy in glasses, and again he grabs me by my arm.

I cry, "Mikael! Mikael!"

Attentionplease, the jerk is gone. He dove into the bushes and ran away. Mikael comes up to me; he must not have seen anything. Maybe it's a good thing he didn't.

"Comeonbaby, sitdown," he says, unzipping his smile. I quickly count his teeth. One hundred and twenty-eight, okay, not a single one missing. We return to the guests and sit down. We eat and drink and talk about the weather . . .

We finish drinking the cocktails, the guests have gone, the orange sun is hiding behind the white mansions. I've already put my children to sleep, now I'm going to our rosewood-lined bedroom. I have on a pink shirt, gleaming, for $35. Mikael's wearing a pair of $30 pajamas. What time is it? What? . . . Ten after ten again? I glance at Mikael's watch, and yes, his also says ten after ten.

I turn off the TV. The picture goes out. It's also dark outside the window.

What did that jerk in the glasses want from me?

We'll need to lock everything because he might break in at night. Right away, tomorrow, I'll buy a mean dog and at night I'll let him out into the garden. I wonder how much a dog like that would cost? I get into bed, lost in thought, accidentally bumping into Mikael.

"I'msorry," I say.

This Mikael is a little weird. He's looking at a picture book and grinning. Why doesn't he grin at me instead of the book?

"Night is for sleeping, not for reading!" I say, all angry, and turn off the light. I stretch gracefully and fall asleep.

I wake up and look . . . the sun is shining through the glistening blinds into our bedroom. Mikael's brushing his teeth in the bathroom. What time is it? What, ten after ten *again*? Oh yeah, after all, it is morning. The children run in in their pajamas and hug me, smiling and squealing.

So . . . we're done playing, we've eaten our breakfast, what else is there to do? What time is it? Come on, ten after ten again? Such an expensive watch and it's stopped. I call the kids in and their watches also say ten after ten. Mikael's says ten after ten too.

Time is so strange. Sometimes it moves like a rocket, at others it freezes like a sculpture. Well, we need to go to the beach, soak up a little sun, tan some and so on. Why walk? Better to go by car. We drive and drive . . . and reach the sea. All of us—the whole family— are walking on the beach, fooling around. The sand is yellowish, the sea sapphire, the sky blue and my Lycra swimsuit red, glistening in that way that only Lycra can glisten. Awesome.

"I think I'm gonna go for a swim," I say.

"Attentionbaby, Iloveyou," Mikael says, pulling out his picture book.

"YesMikael, yes."

I kiss Mikael and the kids. Something just flashed on the dunes. It's the four-eyed guy. Something tickles my heel. I jump away. A giant spider, all hairy, burrows into the sand . . .

"I'll be right back," I say to Mikael quickly. "You watch the kids and don't let them onto the dunes. And if you see this guy in a gray sweater, call the police for help."

Splash!!!

I jump into the sea. The water's warm and I know how to swim, so I do the breaststroke. I swim and swim and swim and swim . . . It's a little boring to be swimming that much. I turn my head and can't see the shore, the sea is all around me. I've swum out too far. I need to go back.

Something's floating on the surface over there. I'm pretty sure it's a buoy. I'm gonna rest alongside it I'm so tired.

I swim up to it, but it's not a buoy, it's a corpse, horrifying, all puffed and gray, even black in places. I jerk backward and the corpse comes after me. It grabs my leg, pulls me underwater, embraces me and holds me close. Air . . . I need air . . . or else I'll be choking on water soon.

I hear a scratchy whisper in my ears: "Mary . . . Mary . . ."

Or maybe it's only the sea whispering?

The corpse holds me in its clutches. Its swollen, somewhat decomposed lips are moving; its face is horrifying, black, balloon-like. It's saying something . . . but instead of words, little fish jump out of its mouth. These aren't fish, they're letters, they're whole words. But they're not Polish—I think they're English. I don't understand anything, though I understood everything perfectly when Mickael was speaking to me.

I'm choking! I need air!

I open my mouth, water starts pouring in, along with the fish and the words. They crowd into my lungs. I'm about to explode. The corpse brings its mouth to mine. It drills me with its eyesight—there's a snail in a shell where its eyes should be. I push it away from me and jump up crying.

I'M HERE, I'M lying on the sofa.

Eva stands over me, furrowing her brow and staring at me.

"Did you sleep?" she asks.

I'm panting heavily. I still see the corpse's face. I look around the room and say, "Where's my book bag? Give me something to write with! Quickly!"

Eva passes me a pen and a large green notebook. I sit down, place the notebook on my lap and quickly begin to write so I don't forget.

"ABANDONED HOPE AND love that turneth to hate; / And self-contempt, bitterer to drink than blood; / Pain whose heeded and familiar speech; / Is howling and keen shrieks day after day; / And Hell or the sharp fear of Hell . . ."

I'm finished.

Eva looks over my shoulder and says, surprised, "You really know English well."

"Only I don't understand any of it. Read it to me, please. Translate it."

"You wrote it, you must understand it."

"I don't understand any of it, I dreamed it up. Those were the fish and I swallowed them."

"Unbelievable." Eva laughs. "I don't believe you."

"I swear," I say. "Translate it for me."

Eva takes the notebook and starts translating slowly: "Abandoned hope, and love, which turns into hate . . . self- . . . self-contempt more bitter for drinking than blood. Pain . . . which something or other, I don't know, the familiar speech is horrible . . . and shrieks, piercing shrieks day after day. And Hell, or real fear of Hell . . ."

Eva looks at me. "Hell . . . *pieklo.* That's the last word. Don't look at me that way."

"How?" I ask.

"So strange . . . I'm afraid of you."

"I'm afraid too," I say. I get up and walk around the room. I sit down in a love seat. Hell. Everything is clear. I'll never be able to escape. There's no one to defend me.

Eva comes up to me. "Did you really dream that up?"

"Yes."

"That's awful . . . Stop making such big eyes, please."

Hell, *pieklo*—how did I end up deserving it? I hear something in me whispering, You didn't. So not yet. But will I in the future?

"Maica," Eva says. I look at her, smiling. I'm not really smiling, I'm only stretching my lips in a smile. But Eva sees a smile.

"I have good news for you," she says. "I went to your house. I talked to your mom."

"You talked to my mom?!"

"Yes. I lied to her. I told her you started bleeding at my house and that we called in a doctor who determined, after examining you, that it's caused by an imbalance of the nervous system that has something to do with adolescence. And that you must lie down quietly and mustn't be moved. So I told your mom you'd be staying at our place until Monday."

"What did she say?"

"She was worried."

"Poor Mom."

"I calmed her down, though. I told her that here in Szczawno you're in good hands, and the doctor who examined you is our neighbor, which is actually true. Your mom made me some tea. We talked for about twenty minutes."

"What'd you talk about?"

"Everything. About you too. Don't worry, I have a method so that if I want, I can make anyone like me. All you have to do is just say what they want to hear. Oh, and I met your sisters too. They'd just finished taking a bath. I said all sorts of silly stuff to make them laugh. You know, your sister Zosia is quite smart."

"That's just because Krysia is much more shy. Did you see Tadzio or Dad?"

Eva shakes her head. "I didn't have the pleasure."

"Dad must've been sleeping and Tadzio was probably running around outside. But tell me . . . did Mom really fall for it?"

"What do you think I am? An idiot? She swallowed it hook, line and sinker and chased it down with tea. When we said good-bye to each other, she even told me how glad she is you have such a responsible friend, and that you'd become even more responsible if you stayed with me."

Eva puckers her lips and folds her hands like she's praying. Standing in this noble pose, she shoots a glance at me and says with a sudden scratchiness in her voice, "If one day I go really ballistic, I'm going to join a convent. But one for men."

She jumps up and screams, "I'm so happy!" She runs over to the tape recorder, puts in a tape and turns the volume up all the way. A blast of heavy metal knocks her into my seat. A wave of sound crashes over us.

IT'S A WARM, sweet evening two hours later. It's almost ten after ten. I'm sitting in my chair with my back facing the mirror. I'm wearing a pretty dress made of white silk with crimson polka dots. It's short and tight with straps. I'm also wearing panty hose, as smooth as glass. And high heels, really tall ones, which make it very easy to trip and fall.

Eva straddles my lap, putting shadow on my eyelids. She puts lipstick on me and covers it with a special gloss.

Yuck, that doesn't taste good.

"Don't you lick it or I'll pull out your tongue," Eva says. She gets up, steps back and checks me out. She breaks a bud off a white rose in a vase and pins it to my smoothly pulled back hair.

"I'm done," she says. "Now check yourself out in the mirror."

I get up from my chair, turn and face the mirror.

A girl is standing there.

Is that me?

This beautiful, serious, grown-up girl . . . Is that me?

Eva appears behind me in the mirror. She's all made up and dressed up too. Oh, we look so much alike. So pretty.

"You're much prettier than me," Eva says.

"No," I say. "You are."

"You're much more unique-looking," she says. "Look how far apart your eyes are set. Uncovering your forehead brought them out."

I look in the mirror.

My forehead . . . so weird, so high. And eyes, even more bizarre and strange. I turn back to Eva and look at her pretty, delicate face close up.

"You're the prettiest girl in the world," I say.

"No, you're the prettiest," Eva says. "You're so pretty I'm gonna eat you up."

"I'm gonna eat you up too."

We smile in awe of each other. Our pretty eyes wander over to the mirror again. I stare and stare, and still I can't recognize myself in it. If I saw this girl on the street, I'd be too shy to talk to her. But she's me. I open my lips, and this girl opens her lips too, because she's me.

Me.

I could stand here and stand here and look at myself until the end of the world.

Eva pulls in her cheeks and puckers her lips. I do the same and I become even prettier and more of a stranger to myself.

"What do you think?" Eva asks. I hug her, but carefully, watching my makeup.

"I love you," I whisper.

"And I love you, princess, I love you even more," Eva whispers.

"You'll see—we'll conquer the whole world. But you have to listen to everything I say."

"Yes," I whisper. Pearl clip-ons delicately poke my ears.

"Our pictures will be on the covers of all the important magazines. We'll be making half a million dollars a year. I promise. But remember, you have to stick with me."

"Yes," I whisper, shaking somewhere inside. I'm going to die any minute now, I feel so wonderful.

"Let's go to the garden and show off," Eva says. "The girls'll die with envy."

I grasp her hand. "No, I'm too shy . . ."

"Oh, don't be coy. Let's go."

She pulls me behind her. I resist a little—but only a little. We leave the room for the terrace.

Lights shine into the garden down below. Quiet music, voices and laughter come from over there. We go downstairs and, holding hands, walk down a narrow tiled path through the trees. My legs are made of Jell-O and I have to be careful the whole time not to stumble on my heels. Over there, in the gazebo, there are a lot of people. About ten of them. Men and women, all very elegantly dressed. They're sitting in lounge chairs by a white table. They're talking, drinking and laughing.

Eva and I enter the ring of light. We've been noticed. Eva's dad whistles.

"The princesses have paid us a visit," he says. "Welcome, Your Majesties."

"We're like moths," Eva says. "We came to burn our wings in the fire of your glances."

At this point we're in the gazebo. Eva greets everyone. She kisses the ladies, and the men kiss her hand. They laugh and joke.

"This is Maica," Eva says, pointing to me. "My fellow troublemakeh."

"Good evening," I say quietly, almost curtsying. Now everyone's looking at me.

"Mind if we sit with you for a minute?" Eva asks.

"You could even lie down with us," one of the guys responds. Everyone laughs. Eva sits down on a white bench next to the banister.

She gestures to the place beside her, so I sit down, holding my knees together. I lift my eyes, and lower them right away because no one is saying anything, they're all just looking at us.

"What are you staring at us for?" Eva asks. "Get us a couple of drinks, we're sober and shy."

"Grzesio, pour them a drop of gin in a pitcher of ice," Eva's mom says, smiling at us. She looks young and pretty in a shimmering white blouse and white miniskirt. When she laughs out loud, it sounds really cool, like she has a frog in her throat.

"You really are very pretty," a lady in glasses tells us. "The two of you should compete in the beauty pageant together."

"We don't want to compete against each other," Eva says. Mr. Grzesio, who is completely gray, but really handsome, pours something out of one colored bottle and something out of another into a couple of short glasses. He throws in some ice and hands them to us. He looks at me closely.

I say, "Thank you," but I don't know what happens next, since I've lowered my eyes, and although I am quite uncomfortable, I feel strangely ecstatic.

I feel good here.

Soon I'm going to be an adult. I'll be discussing various topics with other adults. Just like my Eva, who's not the least bit inhibited. She just answers something and they laugh. It's so great to sit like that with your friends on a summer evening in an illuminated gazebo and talk to them and laugh. They're saying something, I don't know what. I'm not really listening, because it feels so good to be with your own thoughts . . . I wish Tadzio could see me now, or Kazio Kaminski. He'd really be surprised. Or if Mom saw me . . . she'd dart in right away, smack me on the ear and drag me home. Nah, she'd be too embarrassed to come here.

In three years I'll be eighteen. I'll still love my mom a lot, but I'm not going to let her mess with my life. The ice clinks in my glass. The transparent cubes are melting slowly. I look to the side and see that Eva's almost done with her drink, so I lift the glass to my lips and take a sip. It's a little bitter, and a bit sweet. It's some kind of vodka mixed with something. At Zenus's baptism party, Dad got drunk and told me to drink a glass of vodka. The minute I brought it to my lips, I had to vomit. But now I don't feel like vomiting, even though I took a big sip. My tummy's growing warm and pleasant and the same thing's happening to my head. Well, here goes nothing. That's what Marysia, Mr. Krzysiek's wife, would always say when they were drinking in the garden by the chain-link fence with Dad and Mr. Kaminski. Dad would say, "Down the hatch" or "Bottoms up . . ." And Mr. Kaminski would say, "Past the teeth, through the gums, look out stomach, here it comes . . ." And then Mr. Krzysiek would say, "To the Commies, that they will not outlive us." Then everyone would sing "Tonight the bottle let me down / And let your memory come around / The one true friend I thought I'd found / Tonight the bottle let me down . . ." And finally, they would sing about drowning sorrow in a bottle of wine.

Here at the Bogdajs' we're also drinking alcohol, but there's something different about it. Everyone has their own glass and drinks when they want and no one shouts at anyone else, nothing like that, they just talk politely.

Suddenly Eva grabs me by the arm.

"I'm so stupid," she says. "Mr. Grzesio can give us an exact translation."

"What do you want translated?" Mr. Grzesio asks.

"We have a really strange English passage that Maica dreamed about. I'm going to get it right away."

Eva gets up.

"No, no," I say. "I'll go get it!"

"All right, go."

I leave the gazebo and plunge into the darkness of the garden. What would I have done if I'd been left there alone, without Eva? Someone would have asked me something and I wouldn't have known how to respond. Luckily I was able to stop her. Oh, I brought the glass with me, and there's still so much in it . . . I stop on the path and gulp . . . drinking it all down. Very good. I'll leave the glass here. On the way back I'll pick it up and take it with me. I just almost tripped. It's these heels, it's time I learned how to walk in them. Eva put ones on just as tall and she floats in them, like she's walking bare-

foot . . . Instead of turning left, where the terrace and Eva's room are
. . . I turn right. I'm going to circle the house on the stony path, so I
can practice walking a little.

I'm walking and clacking . . . clack, clack, clack, clack. You have
to take small steps, otherwise you can't manage, and it helps a lot
when you swivel your butt. That's right, Eva was doing that. And
that's why all the models on TV move their butts like that. I always
thought they were being silly, but they simply have to, to keep from
falling over.

Clack, clack, clack . . . I've already got it down.

"Hi, Maria!"

I look over and see someone standing behind the white fence,
some soldier. I walk over.

"Oh, Kazio, good evening. What brings you here?"

"I'm on leave. What about you? What's up with you?"

"I just got back from London. I'm flying to New York tomorrow.
I'm doing a fashion show there."

"You look great. How'd you like to take a little walk with me? My
leave ends soon . . ."

"Oh, you know, you'll have to excuse me, the guests are waiting
for me. Good-bye."

Clack, clack, clack . . . I leave. I am walking by the front gate
. . . and who should happen to be standing right there behind the
fence? Mom and Tadzio, two shadows in the darkness.

"Mom, it's so good to see you. I was about to mail this to you . . .
here it is, a check for a hundred thousand dollars. A professor in Vienna's already waiting to hear from you. He said that in two weeks
Zenus will be able to see. Twenty thousand for Zenus's operation, the
same for your heart and varicose veins. With the rest, why don't you
buy yourself a house in the country, with a garden? If there's anything
left, use it for pocket money. And tell Dad not to drink vodka, it's a
yucky thing. Let him drink gin. And Tadzio, here's a hundred dollars
for ice cream. Remember to share it with the girls. So, good-bye, darlings. I would give you a ride in my car, but I have so many things to
do . . . I'll call you from Bombay! Bye!"

I swim away on my heels . . . clack, clack, clack, clack.

Clack, clack, clack . . . on the stairs leading to the terrace. Now the clacking stops, because I'm walking on the carpet toward the mirror, swaying my hips. Dolled up in slick silk, shiny, pretty. I smooth my hand over my dress and touch the string of pearls on my neck. It's all me.

I came here to get the notebook. It's lying on the table, open, just as I left it. I go over and pick it up and suddenly electrical needles go through my head.

The sheet where I wrote stuff down is torn out. The ragged edge is sticking out. On the bottom, only the word "hell" remains. I feel someone's eyes on me. I turn around quickly. There, behind the window . . . is my reflection in the windowpane. No, it's not my reflection.

Who's standing there?!

I want to escape, but I can't. My legs are frozen. The tinny, gurgly buzzing in my ears grows louder. Dirty, beet-red and gray mist descends on everything. I push through toward the armchair. It's not an armchair, it's a reddish clump. I curl up in deathly fear. Goose bumps rise on my naked arms. There's water everywhere, thick as soup. A disgusting glug, bubbles bursting, and something emerges slowly. Cold, sunken eyes are staring at me dully.

They're coming toward me. Relentless, unstoppable.

It's dark, I can't see a thing. Something touches me and enfolds me in slimy tentacles and dry, hard claws. It pushes inside me until my bones creak. It's already in me. It coils inside my stomach, in my limbs. Now I'm only somebody's shell.

There's the sound of laughter and footsteps . . . some people just came in, two of them. One of them says something and a huge face slides toward me. Then it shrinks away. Two agile skeletons covered with flesh and fabric dance around my head. Their words ring in the air.

They've disappeared, they're gone.

Am I inside or outside . . . ?

Hands are moving. Her hands? Or my hands?

Fingers. Mine?

We turn the periscope. Oh, on the belly the skin's smoother than on the hands. White and crimson polka dots.

Legs, you walk on them. Everything is called something, every-thing serves a purpose. Armchair's for sitting. Oh, I almost know it all.

Only tell me, Spirit, what is my name and what purpose do I serve? And whom do I serve? . . .

There, behind the glass door, is an answer. Let's go there. I go.

Someone's coming toward me from over there. A girl, somewhat familiar. We come toward each other. I look for the doorknob and she looks for the doorknob, but there are no doorknobs on these doors. There's a glassy touch of our hands.

"What's your name?" I ask.

"Maica," she says. "And yours?"

"Ya? Maica."

That's some kind of rum. Yamaica rum. So *that's* my name. Ja-maica. It's some island. So I'm an island and the sailors drink me by the gallon? I already know everything, thank you, Spirit. I peel myself off the mirror and walk away. I turn around and wave good-bye to her. Will we ever see each other again?

I walk out onto the terrace.

I hear a quiet moan. I walk over to the banister. In the darkness, under the tree, under the moon, stands Eva. She's kissing Mr. Grzesio and moaning. Mr. Grzesio's hands move down her butt, under her dress, which is lifted up.

I look at them, but I'm invisible.

What they're doing is kind of repulsive and kind of beautiful. And that moan is like music. Distant, endlessly distant. And sweet as a plum.

The white head goes down, Mr. Grzesio kneels. He kisses Eva on her tummy. She moans quietly and sweetly. So sweetly I'd almost like to lick that moan.

Enough of that. That's enough. I call, "Eva!"

They start. Mr. Grzesio gets up, Eva looks at me. I see her face in the darkness, a little dazed . . . now both of them are laughing. Mr. Grzesio disappears in the darkness. Eva pulls her skirt down and runs up the steps to the terrace. She sits beside me on the banister and, swinging her legs, says, "I sometimes make love with him, you know . . . I lost my virginity to him. He taught me lots of interesting positions. He's old but cool. How about you—did you get drunk on the gin?"

I'm standing in front of her, close. I put my hands on her thighs. She smiles at me.

"Maica," she says. "I'm so happy you're here with me."

"Don't call me Maica, my name is 'Yamaica.'"

"How wonderful! It's pronounced 'Jamaica,' you know? I can tell by your eyes that you got drunk, after all."

I take her by her hands, I back up. She jumps down from the banister. She follows me without even guessing that she—this whole house, the whole city, everything—exists thanks to me. If I didn't exist . . .

"Don't grab me so tight," Eva says, and tries to yank her hand out of my grip. "Leave me alone, it hurts! Don't be an idiot, let go!"

I let go of her left hand and with my right I slap her face.

"That's for calling me an 'idiot,'" I say. "You want more?"

She's frightened and would like to escape, but she can't—both her hands are trapped in my claws again. Helpless, she starts crying. I hug her, not letting go of her hands, which are twisted behind her back.

"What do you want from me?" she asks, fear in her voice. "What did you hit me for? Let go of me before I call my dad."

I lick the tears off her face. They're good, salty. "I just wanted to taste your tears."

"Please leave me alone," Eva begs, producing a flood of new tears. I smile, feeling the saltiness of the sea on my lips.

I say slowly, "If I want to, my pretty one, I can turn you into a frog. Or I can order you to disappear and you won't be anywhere. And if only I wanted it to, the whole world would disappear

In the Kingdom of Dead Hours

THE YOUNG PRINCE screws up his face. "Mom . . . that's the fashion now, you wear it to the side."

"It's my birthday. Do your mother a favor."

The prince moves his crown to the middle of his beautifully styled hair and sighs. The next instant three parroting princesses, my daughters, do the same to their crowns. A noise goes around the room. That's the sound of my courtiers' caps moving to the centers of their heads.

One more ambassador bearing gifts slips into the hall. Yet another fat ambassador unrolls yet another parchment with yet another birthday greeting. At this instant I re . . . something . . . something . . . something. But what? Oh, I know. I *remember* something. I lift my hand.

"Silence!" I say. "Don't move, be silent for a while, because I am re . . . something . . ."

I bend my finger and tap it on my forehead.

Re . . . what? Oh, I remember. But what was it? I remembered something and then forgot it right away.

Why isn't anyone moving or saying anything? A statue of a fat ambassador with a raised parchment stands in front of me, his mouth ajar, a golden tooth shining silently. There are lots of statues of courtiers all over the place, and the statues of my little ones stick out like molding here. Oh yeah, it was me that ordered them not to move or talk . . . Good, now I've remembered one thing. But what about the other? What was it that just disappeared now?

Outside the window, fireworks are painting zigzags in the night sky. This music has been blaring from over there since this morning. It's this crown that's squeezing me so hard that I can't remember anything. I lift my head and the crown slides to one side—oh, now it's much better. On the ceiling is a huge "M" made of gold and a number "$£" made of diamonds. It's a strange number—maybe it's not a number? These diamonds shine so brightly you have to squint your eyes to read the number. Then you can make out that it is "50."

That's right, it's my fiftieth birthday. A high-pitched chorus of fat eunuchs comes from outside the window. "Long live Her Majesty, oh, long live Her Majesty!"

. . . What was it that was on the tip of my tongue . . . Did I swallow it or what? I know, now I remember.

"Miranda!" I call. I look over and my youngest daughter comes running up to me and kneels at my feet. No . . . that's not it, it's not her. I know, it's Marika, yes, Marika.

"Marika!" My middle daughter leans down two feet away from the youngest. No, no, no, no, it's not her either, it was . . . Oh, now I remember.

"Marcelina," I call. Yes, that must be Marcelina. No, it's not her either, it's just my oldest daughter disappearing in an elegant curtsy, and right after her all the courtiers and ladies-in-waiting suddenly bend their elegant attire toward the mosaic on the floor. Suddenly I snap my fingers in the rattle of my rings. I know, I know, she had eyes like diamonds.

"Maria!" I call with a triumph. It's Maria!

Maria—that's it, it's Maria. It's been on my mind for years, it was hiding under other names whenever I wanted to re . . . re . . . remember. Maria.

I look around the hall. "Where's Maria?" I ask. Why isn't my dearest Maria by my side?

She's nowhere to be found . . . That jokester hid somewhere again.

"Has anyone seen Maria?"

The courtiers and ladies-in-waiting shake their heads, lift their eyes to the ceiling and spread their hands in resignation. What parasites. They're always the first to arrive at the table, but when the Queen asks a simple question, there's no one there to answer.

My first minister drapes the pleats of his golden robe around him and prepares to bow. Soon he'll say where he saw Maria. Yup, he's already bowed, about to open his mouth . . .

"Your Majesty," he says solemnly. "In the court, besides the princesses of highest honor, Marcelina, Marika, Miranda, there are six Magdalenas among the ladies-in-waiting, eleven Malvinas, two Maryannas, forty-seven Matildas, twenty-four Michalinas, three Monicas, one Maura and even one Modesta . . . but there is no Maria, we don't know a single Maria, Your Honor."

He finishes his speech, bows and carefully folds his robes around himself.

"How is it possible you don't know Maria—my favorite lady-in-waiting, my adopted sister Maria???"

I'm asking, at this point only rhetorically, for no reason. We can now move on to the next item of the celebration: the ambassador with his scroll is waiting for the signal to start his proclamation . . . But no, I won't give him the signal yet, because my old chambermaid is waving in the crowd, like she wants to say something but is hesitating. I beckon to her. Now she's running toward me at the speed of six yards an hour. I'm gonna buy her roller blades for her hundredth birthday. She finally makes it and, bang, she falls at my feet. The step up to my throne helped her a little.

"Your Highness," she gasps, breathless. "I know, I remember, how could I not remember Maria, Your Highness's favorite?"

"What's with her? Why isn't she here?"

"Because it was on Your Majesty's birthday, on the fifteenth."

"Fifteenth???"

"Yeah, on the fifteenth. Your Highness got angry at Maria for something or other, but about what I can't recall . . ."

"What do you mean 'for something or other'?!" I say, and suddenly I remember everything, and a flush comes over my face and shows through the powder. Now I know! It was because she ate the last raisin in my ice cream, just when I was blowing out the fifteen candles of my birthday cake! But what happened next? I did get angry at her, that I freely admit, but then Maria disappeared somewhere . . .

"Be . . . uh . . . be . . . cause . . ." the old lady stutters. "Your Majesty ordered her to be put in the dungeon and chained."

"Oh yeah. That's right," I say, slapping myself on the forehead. "That's right, I did that because I got really angry. Bring her to me at once!"

Two courtiers take off for the dungeon, along with a cupbearer and swordbearer. I clap my hands in joy and say, "You know, memory is a strange thing. On each of my birthdays something would always bug me, but somehow I was never able to figure out what until now . . . oh, that Marysia, what a jokester she was. She had plenty of raisins in her own ice cream, but she had to pick the last one out of mine! What was I supposed to do? I had to punish her, frighten her a little and throw her in the dungeon for five minutes so she'd become more responsible, so she'd remember the raisin . . . You can't imagine how happy I am that I finally remembered it and that I'm going to see Marysia, my favorite, and hug her."

A terrifying scream is heard from behind the door of the throne room. The two courtiers who went down to the dungeon bring in some old witch, toothless, in filthy rags and almost bald.

The witch thrashes around, howls and jiggles the chains.

I look and see that my son the prince, my daughters the princesses and all the courtiers and ladies-in-waiting are holding their noses. What smells so bad in here? Yuck, the stench is coming from the witch.

"Who did you bring in here?" I ask, laughing. "Bring me Marysia. This is some kind of mistake. She must be in another dungeon."

"This was the only tenant of the dungeon," the cupbearer says. "Besides her, there is not a soul in the dungeon, dead or alive."

"But this isn't Marysia. Marysia had eyes like diamonds, and a nice face, quite pretty. This is some kind of toad, a crazy witch. Throw her in the dungeon again so she won't spoil the air of my kingdom."

The witch starts screaming at a high pitch, raises her twisted claws at me and sinks her festering eyes into me. The cupbearer and swordbearer drag her out of the hall and I wave my perfumed handkerchief in front of me . . . It's noisy now, everyone's fluttering their handkerchiefs, creating a cocktail of the scents of many flowers.

"Dear," I say to the old chambermaid, "look who these screw-ups brought in instead of Maria." She nods her head, sniffs some salts, rolls her eyes, turns completely pale—like she's about to faint any minute.

"Don't you remember our Maria?" I say to her quietly. "Wasn't she sweet?"

"Oh yes, Your Majesty, I remember. She was the sweetest creature in the entire court, besides Your Majesty, of course. And she looked so much like you, Your Majesty, that when Your Majesty switched clothes with her, no one even noticed. Do you remember, Your Majesty?"

"Is that right? I don't remember," I say. Oh well, once there was a Marysia and now there's no Marysia. Well, memories are pleasant, but duty is the most important thing.

I lift my eyes to the embassy.

"Mr. Ambassador, don't interrupt yourself," I say graciously. "Read Our Majesty your master's greetings."

The ambassador bows splendidly, sweeping the floor with his chin. He looks at the scroll and in a voice like a horn he states, "In the name of His Highness, my king, O lowest of ladies, I declare war on you!!!"

Suddenly he pulls out a whistle and blows it with all his might. With that signal, some strangers in armor run into the hall. At that point the whole court begins screaming and yelling. All sorts of swords and daggers glisten. I see my daughters the princesses falling under the sway of spiked bludgeons. The prince, my favorite son, tries to draw his tiny sword, draws it halfway . . . and keeps drawing it, even though his sweet head is rolling on the floor like a ball, smearing his own blood in his hair, so perfectly arranged.

The ambassador himself is aiming at me with his pistol.

I draw a thin dagger out of my sleeve. I send it on its way, and soon it's sticking out of the ambassador's eye. I draw another little dagger out of my other sleeve and, taking advantage of the commotion that's come over the room, I draw the blade like a bow across the strings of the old lady-in-waiting's plump throat, fattened on court pastries.

The only witness has expired at my feet. The poor old woman has died of asthma.

I escape this butchery through the secret doors behind the throne. I run up to my tower to fetch my wonderful, magic diamond. I hear a jangle behind me, and a patter. I look back. The witch from the dungeon is running after me, jangling her chains.

Hocus pocus dominocus. There is not a single poisoned pin in my topknot; I've already used up all the vials of acid from my belt. I'm fleeing up the spiral staircase when I feel a tug. The witch has caught me by the train, ripped my dress off . . . I run up naked as a jaybird.

I run through the iron door at the top of the stairs.

It's my astrologer, the eccentric, wringing out a giant book like a wet garment over a huge washtub. Whimpering, he says to me, "I'm wringing tears from each page of this book. The salt stinging my wounds is making me cry."

"My magic diamond!" I shout. "Where have you hidden it? Give it to me at once!"

"Look through the telescope, my queen, I gave it to the sky."

I run up to the telescope. I look . . . a new star in the navy blue sky glistens like a rainbow. Suddenly I hear a shrill cackling in my ear. I turn around. The witch is standing in front of me. Out of her rusted face only the shine of her eyes seems familiar . . .

"Forgive me, Your Highness," I whisper, my lips numb with fear. I back away from her. I'm completely pale, naked and shivering. Oh, I've stumbled over something. It's the washtub. I fall straight into it.

"They're my tears," she screeches. "Drown in these dead hours of mine!"

And she bangs me on the head with her chains.

WE'RE SITTING NAKED on the edge of the bathtub and we're drying each other's hair with two dryers: one pink and one yellow.

"You have very thick hair," I say. "Why don't you wear it long?"

"Do you want me to?" Eva asks.

"Yes."

"Okay. From now on I'll never cut it again."

I turn off the dryer. I look at Eva and imagine how she'd look with long hair. She lowers her eyes and says quietly, "Jamaica . . ."

"What?"

"I have a strange whim . . ."

"Yeah?"

"Kiss me . . . there . . ."

"Where?"

"On my pussy."

I lean over and kiss her curly hair, soft like down, at the bottom of her stomach.

"And now I'm gonna kiss you," Eva says. She kneels in front of me, spreads my thighs and kisses me there. She raises her head, looks at me and sighs.

"You know," she says, "we're some kind of lesbos . . ."

"What does 'lesbo' mean?"

"Don't you know?"

"No."

"Lesbians are girls who love each other."

"So we're lesbians because we love each other," I say.

"Did you feel disgusted when you were kissing me there?"

"What are you talking about? Not at all. I could kiss you anywhere. I could lick you like ice cream, so much there'd be nothing left of you but a stick."

"Oh, so that's how you are," she says. "I never know when you're pulling a fast one on me . . ." Kneeling, she touches my thigh with her cheek and, smiling sweetly, shoots her eyes at me. I love to see the whites of her eyes flashing on her tanned face. A white belt from Eva's bathrobe hangs on the towel rack. I take it and wrap it around her neck. I pull in the ends; the belt digs into her neck. I pull even harder. Eva parts her lips, looks at me, and though she begins to choke, there's no fear in her eyes. There's something in them, something really strange.

I loosen the grip of the belt a bit.

"What are you trying to do to me?" she asks.

"I'm thinking about choking you . . ."

"No."

Again I pull on the ends of the belt. I see the blood flushing her face, but instead of trying to free herself, she just keeps looking at me with those huge eyes. I already know what's in them. I don't know how I know it, but I do. I let go of the ends. Eva moans quietly.

"Did it hurt?" I ask.

"Yes."

She embraces me. She snuggles her face to my belly and says, "Please don't choke me. I'd look ugly if I died."

"So you would," I say, and again I tighten the belt around her neck. Again she doesn't do anything, she only hugs me tighter and tighter. I loosen the grip and unwrap the belt.

She whispers, "Why are you so bad to me?"

"Because I am."

"But you love me."

"I love you."

"So why do you abuse me?"

"Because."

I grab the belt and tie it around her neck, making a bow. Eva gets up, glances in the mirror and, making a pirouette, says coquettishly, "Modest, but very fitting evening wear. We recommend it in particular to practical ladies not yet in their eighties."

I pull the belt from the yellow bathrobe hanging on the door, tie it around my waist and also make a bow. Swinging my naked butt, I announce, "An equally modest ballroom dress for girls of tender ages. Highly beneficial for virgins in pregnancy's later stages!"

Eva puts her hand on my tummy.

"Oh, it's already kicking," she says. "What month is it?"

"You mean, what second?" I say. We burst out laughing.

WE STEAL THROUGH the darkness of the garden holding hands, wearing the same modest yet fitting evening outfits. It's Miss Eva that came up with the idea, but Miss Maica had nothing against it. It's getting brighter and brighter. In the lit-up gazebo, people are playing cards. We stand naked behind the bushes, looking at them and elbowing each other quietly.

"Shall we do a fashion show?" says Eva.

"That would be a little too—"

"If there were only men there, then why not?"

"I would be especially embarrassed in front of men."

"Because you haven't slept with any."

"What do you mean I haven't slept with any? Every day I sleep in the same bed with a man."

"You're lying."

"I'm serious. With my brother Tadzio."

"Brothers don't count. Tell me, would you ever wanna?"

"What?"

"Make love to a guy?"

"I don't know . . . I don't think so."

"Why?"

"Yuck, they pee with that thing . . ."

"Don't be silly. We do the same thing."

"Have you made love a lot?"

"Sure."

"And?"

"And nothing. It's fantastic. It's like you're dying, only a hundred times better. It's the greatest thing in the world. It's even better than hang gliding."

"Have you ever flown?"

"Sure."

"So have I, but without a hang glider."

"Everyone and their dog has flown on a plane."

"I wasn't on a plane. I flew without anything."

"How?"

"When Kasia played for me, I flew a lot."

"What do you see in her? She's crazy, and a mythomaniac."

"What does 'mythomaniac' mean?"

"It's an idiot who makes up all kinds of stories, and on top of that believes in them herself."

"She's not making up anything. It's really true her dad's in Africa. I heard it for myself when she was talking to him on the phone, and I saw letters from him."

"It's no big deal to have a dad in Africa. If my Dada fell in love with an African woman, I'd have a dad in Africa too. Tell me . . . did she ever show you a picture of her dad?"

"No."

"He's a hunchback. A hunchback midget."

"You're pulling my leg! Really?"

"I thought you knew about it."

"How do *you* know about it?"

"Someone saw a picture and told me. I don't even know who."

"You know, it might be true . . . Once she was joking around and said she's the daughter of a siren and a hunchback horse . . ."

———

WE DRANK MORE than half a bottle of red martini and I think I might be drunk, since I feel a strange spinning in my head. The lights are out. We're lying in bed. I hear Eva's quiet whisper in the darkness. She's snuggled up against me.

"Are you going to kill me?" she asks.

"Yes," I reply. "I will."

"In that case, before I die, I have to teach you how to kiss. Give me your lips . . ."

I slide lower down and search for her lips with mine. She kisses me. Or maybe it's not her. Maybe it's the sweet darkness kissing me, and the distant music from behind the window, and the murmur of the trees in the garden . . .

I swim through the darkness on a silky ribbon.

Everything is darkness and the murmur of trees. My dark daughter sucks on my nipple. I touch the sweet darkness of her body. She moans softly. I want to hear her moan and feel her shiver. I touch her hands, which are tied behind her back. Oh, my poor thing. How will she make it through the night . . . I only tied her up because she begged me to. I didn't want to, I felt terribly sorry. Then she ordered me to do it, so I had to, since it was her turn to give orders. And no matter how much she begs me, I can't untie her until morning . . .

"When are you going to kill me?" the shivering darkness whispers.

"Soon," I say, listening to the rapid beating of her little heart.

"I'm going to tell you how I lost my virginity . . . Do you want to know?"

"Yes."

"It was late in the evening, almost a year ago . . . I was coming home from Klaudia's, taking a shortcut through a few backyards. Suddenly someone grabbed me by the hair. You know, it was long back then—down to my waist. There were three of them, and they were drunk. I began to scream . . . They threatened to cut up my face with a pocketknife. I was really afraid of them. They tore off my undies . . . they argued about who would be the first to do it. I begged them on my knees not to do anything to me. They just laughed. They surrounded me and pulled out their . . . and told me to put them in my mouth. They made me lick them; they smelled of piss. I didn't want to

. . . they were pulling my hair and beating me. So, I did it and cried. They were pulling me back and forth between them. I had to do it to one, then another . . . Suddenly one of them pulled my head toward him. I felt him in my throat. I was beginning to choke, but I couldn't tear myself away. Something hot squirted in me and he let me go. I threw up. They started hitting me again, and told me to drink vodka to wash my mouth out. Then they made me lie down and they mounted me, one after the other, and they pounded into me. It was fairly fast for two of them . . . but the worst was when the third one got on top of me—the one who made me vomit. He told me that even if the first floor turned him down, the basement wouldn't. The other ones were sitting next to him drinking vodka, laughing and making jokes . . . and he kept pounding into me and pounding into me . . . By that time the other ones got bored and left . . . but he wouldn't stop. I was moaning from pain, writhing under him . . . I don't even know how long it took—an hour, maybe longer. It didn't even hurt me anymore. I was lying there kinda distant . . . I think I fell asleep. When I woke up, he was gone. I was lying there alone. I wanted to get up, but I couldn't. Clouds were hanging above me . . . Then I saw a light . . . and guess what happened?"

"What?"

"Someone came to me."

"Who?"

"The moon. I made love to him and it was wonderful. I swear it's true. Don't you believe me?"

"I do."

"You must think I'm crazy . . ."

"I'm crazy too," I say. "We all are crazy."

IT'S SO QUIET. I must have been asleep. I was dreaming of something . . . Now I know. I was a model, and Eva and I appeared on TV. In a commercial. And we had on these really dirty, scrappy rags. It was in London . . .

Gee, it's really hot. Eva's sleeping right up against me. She's all sweaty, and I am too. I wish I could open the door to the terrace, but I don't want to wake her up.

I'm happy. Finally I found someone really close, someone who needs me. Everyone needs someone who really needs them. Oh, I know, she needs me so I can kill her. Well, that's too bad . . . I'll kill my most beloved daughter. Then I'll kill myself and we'll go there together, holding hands. Oh, what strange light . . . it's my skeleton glowing green under the lampshade of my skin. My skeleton, the frame on which a kite is stretched.

Tied to a sausage, I'm shivering on the end of a string. The wind will come, it'll break the string.

Where will it take me?

Chapter Seven

MOM'LL REALLY BE surprised when she finds out I'm not going to be a seamstress. I'm going to take the entrance exams for college prep along with Eva. I was really afraid of the exam, but there's nothing to be afraid of thanks to Eva. We have all the questions and all the topics for the written exams.

Where did we get them?

It's Eva's secret.

After high school I'm going to study philosophy. I'll become a professor of philosophy—I'm going to be even smarter than Kasia Bogdanska. Then we'll have another conversation about the mysteries of the human mind and about trucks and their loads.

Rich guys are terrible snobs. It would be an insult for them to marry a seamstress. You need to study some exotic field for them—the stranger and less comprehensible the better. Is there anything stranger in the world than philosophy?

A rich guy is only an emergency exit, sort of like a booster engine. Because you need to become self-sufficient and liberate yourself from the family, from the poor flock of ducks paddling in the pond struggling to make ends meet. I have to be sly in order to deceive them because I know they'll do their best not to allow me to spread my wings and fly away. Who's going to give them a cup of tea when they get old, after all?

Don't worry, I'll send you a whole gallon of tea from far away—and, to top it off, in a thermos made of gold.

Maybe someday they'll understand I was right. Though . . . knowing Mom, I don't think she'll ever forgive me for not following in her footsteps, for not making my life a carbon copy of hers.

It'd be really easy to get rid of a rich guy like that right after the wedding. It'd be enough to send Eva after him, and when the moment was right, snap a beautiful color photo with a hidden camera. Eva could even pick up a cardinal in his late eighties, not to mention my future balding husband. The divorce would be his fault, so the property would be split up half and half, and then so long—see you later. But maybe I wouldn't like being divorced . . .

Eva's mom went after her dad for his money too, and now they really love each other and are really happy. Sometimes when they meet for dinner, you could split your sides laughing. It's really fabulous how they talk to one another; it's really great. We all sit around the table and say whatever comes to mind. I never thought I knew how to talk to adults. But it's so simple. I don't even know where I find all the words that I'm saying. I never knew I was so witty and intelligent. Sometimes I say something so funny everyone is struggling not to choke from laughter.

I think the secret to a good sense of humor lies in looking at everything from a distance and not worrying about anything at all. When the five of us are sitting around the table, the words fly like sparks above it. I never knew there were such happy and upbeat families in the world. Whenever I'm at Eva's house, and I spend most of my time here, I feel like I've been with them forever, like I was born into the family. And they treat me like their own daughter and sister.

Mimi and Dada are really wonderful. They're always smiling, always relaxed. To Eva, Michal and me, it feels like they're the same age as we are. And the reason we respect them is not because they're older, or that we're supposed to . . . but because they're smarter than us and always a little quicker. That's what real respect is all about. It's really lucky to have parents like that. You can tell them everything and ask their advice about anything. I can't understand why Eva doesn't like them. I'll never understand her. As for Michal, he must have a crush on me. I like him quite a bit too; he's trim and handsome. Only a bit spacy. Eva says he's a flake and he'll never get it together. So I'll only use him to practice picking up guys, because that'll come in handy in the future. When I think that he used to look down on me like I was nothing but a teenybopper, it makes me want to laugh. Now he's the one with nothing to laugh about. I'll make my face number eight and he'll turn all pale. Eva gave numbers to all my faces. She said number eight would make anyone drop to their knees, no matter who they were. I let Michal kiss me only once, but now I keep him at a slight distance so he'll get a bigger and bigger crush on me, and I'm a little afraid that I won't know how to back out, but Eva says you can back out of any love. I wouldn't want to hurt him, I wouldn't want him to be sad on my account, because I like him a lot. For now, I'm just balancing things a few feet away from the edge of the roof. Poor thing.

But in general it's fun and he doesn't complain. We play on his computer a lot. I've learned a lot of cool games. Kasia had a computer too, but she didn't like to play with it.

I've also learned how to ride a motorcycle. Not a computer one—a real one. Eva's Yamaha. Of course, I don't ride it on the roads . . . but the minute we go into the woods, we switch places and I go so wild on the trails that Eva pokes her chin into my back to get me to slow down, slow down! Then I go faster, even faster.

It's really a miracle we're still alive.

It's so easy to rev the engine to the max.

Because that's how I see it. If we're gonna live, then we're gonna live, and if we're gonna crash into a tree, then we're gonna crash. In principle, Eva shares my point of view on these matters, but she's really afraid of disfiguring her face. I console her that as a rule the passenger dies instantly. Eva says it's best to put off dying until after the third facelift.

Facelifts are great. You can be fifty-odd years old and still look like a young girl. So we have forty years of youth ahead of us. Of course, only on the condition that you have money, lots of money, and not zloty. So unfortunately, we'll need to learn English, because really rich guys don't speak Polish or Russian.

If we ever do manage to become sought-after models, then let all those big fish eat their pounds and dollars. We'll have our own money we earned ourselves. Then they can only lick us through a TV screen or on a magazine cover. The most important thing is to get the hell out, and if you have to sell yourself, get the most you can. If you have to escape, better to do it with a bag full of money.

Eva's absolutely right. Money isn't the most important thing, but that's true only when you have it. The most wonderful thing about that is that I know it now, at age fifteen, because if I came to that conclusion after forty, like a lot of idiots do, then I could only bite my pussy and stay with a good-for-nothing husband on my back and a whole bunch of kids, all of them wanting jeans for forty bucks or so, and meanwhile I have fifty thousand zloty until the first of the month and I have to make sure we don't all croak from hunger.

It's enough for me to look at my mom—Miss Varicose, two hundred pounds of fatback. But twenty years ago she was a pretty, thin girl. What happened to her? Where did the pretty girl go?

Oh no—I'm not going to run in the same relay she did. No one's going to make me. Everything I know, I know thanks to Eva, though I have a feeling I always knew it. Is it so hard to figure out if you're the least bit intelligent, and beautiful on top of that? If I don't think about myself, who will?

Even if I have to swim the breast stroke through all the seas and oceans, I'll reach that island where the rich live. Rich and intelligent, because everyone who's rich is intelligent, and if someone is intelligent and poor, then apparently he's not that intelligent.

Lucky for me I met Eva and befriended her family, because I finally understand how this world really is. The rich and intelligent stick together and help each other, because there are only a few of them and the billions of stupid poor people stand in lines everywhere fighting among themselves. That's the way it's always been and always will be in this world. And it's only going to get worse, because there are more and more people on this planet and there's less and less for them to share. So you have to stuff yourself while there's time, because you only have one life, and maybe a very short one on top of that.

Who knows . . .

Who knows . . . it could be in five minutes or it could be right now. Will I turn the wheel to the left and head straight for some tree at seventy miles an hour? And where there's now the roar of an engine, there'll be nothing but silence, and birds chirping, and two pretty girls in a red puddle. Dead and naked.

Because we're riding through the woods naked, completely naked.

Two naked she-devils on a black Japanese broom with a covered license plate are flying through the village accompanied by the hellish roar of an engine, in clouds of dust and blue smoke.

IT'S INCREDIBLE THAT you can be such a realist and at the same time be so wild. Because Eva is totally wild, now I know it . . . and to prevent her from going way too wild, I must be wilder than her.

Maybe every girl our age is wild.

Kasia was really wild too.

And isn't Magda wild? She sneaks away to one man, who's seventy-six. He's such a repulsive, elegant old geezer in his white suit, hat and cane. When Eva pointed him out to me on the street, I couldn't believe Magda goes to his house, dresses in a pink slip, stockings and a garter and lets him lick her pussy.

It all started two years ago, when she was running a school store and ate more chocolates than she sold and had a huge cash shortage, and then one of her friends from a higher grade secretly told her there was this guy who pays two dollars a lick if a girl lets him. She took her to him. He liked Magda right away and she went to his place three times a week. In a month the shop had surplus cash. Then the old man got poorer because his brother in America died and his sister-in-law stopped sending him money. So for the past six months he hasn't been able to pay Magda, but she goes to him anyway and lets him lick her for free.

And Klaudia . . . isn't she wild?

Maybe a little less, or just in a different way, since she's a year older than us.

And Bogusia, whom I don't know because she's in the hospital . . . she was really wild. She ski-jumped from a big Krokwia and might be a cripple the rest of her life. She was Klaudia's best friend— the one who came up with the infamous "Moments When Girls Can Truly Be Themselves."

I really wanted to know what this game was all about, so one day Eva took me to Klaudia's house. She has a great-great-grandfather who's a retired colonel. He's ninety years old and fought at Tobruk and Monte Cassino. He's blind now and sits in a wheelchair all the time. He really likes people visiting him in his room so he doesn't get bored and telling them stories about the war. So the three of us went to his place and were drinking hot chocolate and he was telling us very interesting stories. I felt sorry I didn't bring Tadzio, because he really likes listening to war stories. Then suddenly I look over . . . and I see Eva pulling up her blouse and shaking her naked boobs. And the great-great-grandfather keeps telling his story and doesn't see a thing, since he's blind. He tells Klaudia to bring his sword and medals from the cupboard. So Klaudia brings him the medals and the sword, but takes her jeans and underwear off on the way. She's walking along, sticking her naked butt out at us. Her and her naked butt . . . Eva with her boobs showing . . . what was I supposed to do? I took everything off. The great-great-grandfather was feeling one medal after another and was saying he got this one for this and this one for that, and I put on his military hat and buckled his sword around my waist. The sight sent Eva and Klaudia into such a fit that they made some kind of excuse and fled the room so they could explode with laughter. On top of that, they took all my clothes, so I was sitting with this great-great-grandfather completely naked, wearing nothing but his cap and the sword dangling from a leather belt on my side. And he was talking about his three best friends, who all died on the same day. As he was telling this, tears were trickling from under his dark glasses.

That's how I found out what these "Moments When Girls Can Truly Be Themselves" were all about. I mean, isn't Klaudia wild? Making fun of an old man . . . and your own great-great-grandfather to boot? Either she's wild or she is nothing but a bitch.

And I'm not the least bit better. I'm just as much of a bitch. Not long ago, I said something bad about my mother to somebody . . .

Here's how it went:

A buddy of Michal's came to visit him. At one point they'd gone to school together, and then Julek went to Austria with his parents and didn't go back to Poland for seven years. He had a great car and wasn't bad himself. So Eva and I made a bet as to which of us would pick him up first. But to the point where he'd be really into it. And I won, because before Eva could even open her mouth, I'd already taken him by the hand and led him into the garden. I was really blunt and told him my greatest and only dream was to go for a ride in his car, just the two of us. Right away he felt really important, since I was going after him, so he generously invited me for a short ride. So we went, though Eva and Michal were really mad at me. Julek had only one hand on the wheel and was holding my knee with the other, so he must have been wondering in which ditch he was going to do me. But I wasn't the slightest bit afraid, because I know I'm stronger than any guy in the world and it wouldn't take more than a snap of my fingers to make him disappear. I told him I was in the mood for a piece of cake. We stopped off at the closest coffee shop, which was in Walbrzych. As we were getting out, I heard someone call, "Marysia!"

I looked over and it was my mom and Tadzio, going to the market. It was right after the first and Mom was going to the city to buy sandals for Tadzio. I pretended I didn't hear her, backed off toward the car, and we took off quickly. Julek figured from my face that something was wrong and he asked who that woman was who called me.

So then I told him, like it was just a passing comment, "That was our maid."

I said that about my own mom. Then we went toward Ksiaz and we walked around in the woods. Julek became really shy without his car. Or maybe he got that way because I'd turned serious, since I was thinking about my mom and what I said about her. Finally I remembered my bet with Eva and, boy, did I have to work hard before he decided to kiss me. And while he was kissing me, I slid my finger along his jeans at the spot every guy considers most important. Then he got bold and I had to cool him off, because the bet wasn't about sex, but love. A little sarcasm, a cutting word, a glance with raised brows, and again he got shy, clumsy and a little angry. Then I became delicate and sweet again.

"I like you too much," I said mysteriously, and went back toward the car. As we drove back, I felt happy and extremely sharp, so just as we were reaching Szczawno, Julek must have felt like a complete idiot next to the most intelligent girl in the world. Then right in front of the Bogdaj mansion I touched him there again and bit my lips . . . and my whole body shivered.

"I'm so afraid of you," I sighed, and I knew he was mine. Had I continued any further, he would have been a doormat in front of my coal bin by the end of the week.

The moment we entered the house, Eva looked up and knew she'd lost. Michal drank his fourth can of beer without saying a word.

"I don't know about you," I said, "but I could eat a whole tub of ice cream right now."

At that, Julek ran into the bathroom, grabbed a huge plastic tub, jumped into his car with it and in ten minutes, risking his life on turns, was back with the tub filled to the brim with ice cream from the best café in Walbrzych.

Michal greeted him warmly, since Eva and I had enlightened him on the crux of the bet. We ate some of the ice cream, brought the rest to the garden for the dogs, and Eva took our sponsor into her hands, since we'd made another bet in the meantime. This time it was whether Eva'd be able to win him away from me. She told him she needed to show him something in her room . . . He gave me a long, loving glance, but he couldn't refuse and went with her. Michal and I had managed to squeeze in a computer game by the time they got back. Strangely enough, Julek was no longer looking at me, only gawking at Eva with eyes like saucers through a magnifying glass, since he had fallen in love with her forever and left with the firm resolution that next year, when Eva turned sixteen, she would come to Vienna to visit him and they'd get married. Later on, he sent her three telegrams that said, "No one but You, You, You. Julek," but Eva didn't answer a single one, and when he called, she told him over the phone it had only been a bet between us and he left her alone, his heart completely broken. On top of that, he broke things off with Michal too.

And to think that she didn't even let him kiss her. For half an hour all they talked about were all kinds of terrible perversions, that is, Eva was talking and he was listening all pale and sweaty at the thought of strange things like that running through her mind . . . Eva, you know. She really knows how to talk about all this stuff very concretely, but at the same time, you don't really know what it's all about. In the end, you don't know anything but one thing: that it's all wonderful.

It doesn't pay to pick up young guys like him. Not a month passes without them thinking that if such a pretty girl likes them, then they'll be liked by a million other pretty girls, and by the time they learn it's not so easy to find a smart and pretty girl, they start to go bald and grow a beer belly. That's the best time to shoot one like that down and snare him for the rest of your life—that is, until the divorce. Eenie meenie miney moe, catch a tiger by the toe, if he hollers let him go.

Eenie meenie miney moe!

IT DOESN'T PAY to be honest.

In the past I told everyone about everything, I told the whole truth, no matter what it was. But that was in the past, and now I'm not so stupid anymore.

I was good, and told the truth, and Mom never said a single good word, didn't praise me even once. And now . . . now she's in awe of me because I'm always serious when I'm around her and I utter life maxims from the guidebook of the practical idiot. The other thing is, I'm almost never home. I leave in the morning for school and don't come back until late evening.

The exams for trade school are supposed to be very difficult, because there are a lot of candidates, but since my friend is rich and has tutors at her place all the time, I'm seizing every opportunity and grabbing what I can. So, unfortunately, I've even had to give up rehearsals for the end-of-the year assembly . . .

Now, what kind of financially strapped mother wouldn't want to hear something like that coming from her level-headed daughter? I don't like coming home because I feel so sorry for them. That's not life, that's nothing but bare survival. Maybe one day I'll manage to rescue them. But I'll have to be really, really rich.

I love them all. Well . . . do I really? There's love for your family, and then there's the obligation to love your family. One has nothing to do with the other, and then all of a sudden one day they become the same thing without you ever knowing what it's really like. Better to accept the first one and not have to worry about it.

An underground river's flowing through me. It's pearly and cold. It's glistening with happiness, and happiness is the light that can illuminate the darkest and biggest of caves. I'm only gonna do what I want to do. And I'm gonna live my life on my own—I won't let anyone parasitize me. And I'm only gonna come to shore where I choose.

When a man is born, the world is born with him. The world exists for him. No one but him.

So I have to force the world to serve me. I can't let myself be brainwashed by all these morals, because the strong invented them for the weak so they could dominate them. I must be strong and wise. And sometimes I have to give in, but only in order to strike even harder the next time. Never looking at anything, never looking back, just striking with all my might and fighting until the worms feed on me.

THE COLD BLADE of my bowie knife. Eva gave it to me as a present. Me and my knife slowly slide along the naked body of my friend. Here's her little heart, here's her tummy.

We go back and forth. Again we're by the heart. The tip of the knife sinks into the body. Eva's lips quiver. Will it be now?

She doesn't know, and neither do I. Only Pimpush knows. My Pimpush, who lurks in me, pretending to be asleep. I know he's pretending, otherwise why would I constantly feel his glassy, motionless eyes in me . . . I feel them in my stomach, I feel them everywhere. Sometimes I even feel them in my eyes. At that point it's not me looking, it's him, Pimpush, looking out at the world through me. Sometimes I even feel him in my thoughts, and I no longer know whether it's still ME thinking or HIM thinking for me. Yet, as long as I think "he" and "I," that probably means it's still just me . . . I'm afraid of him, because I know that when he sees fit to pretend he's woken up, I'll have to obey him in everything.

What will he order me to do? How am I supposed to know?

Eva's even more frightened of him than I am. She doesn't know him the way I do, though I know him only a tiny bit, so little it's almost nothing. She only guesses he's here when she's kneeling in front of me, hanging on to the blade of the knife.

Snap!

"Done!" Eva yells, running up to the camera, which took the picture on its own.

Then Michal makes a color enlargement of it.

In an empty meadow a naked girl is kneeling. Above her stands a figure in a black leather uniform and a black helmet with a darkened visor. The meadow's grayish, the sky reddish, with smudges of dark smoke. The edge of the bowie knife glistens on the girl's breast.

We sit admiring what a beautiful photograph it is.

"I'd rather it was Maica kneeling down naked," Michal says.

Eva replies, "Sausage isn't for the dog."

"She's insulting you," I say to Michal.

"Ruff, ruff, it doesn't matter, she insulted you too." He licks his lips and looks at me like I'm a sausage.

"She simply stated a fact," I say. "I am but a sausage. Walbrzych summer sausage, nineteen hundred a pound."

"I'd gladly buy the whole shipment," Michal says. "How much do you weigh?"

"A hundred and twenty," I answer.

Michal grabs the calculator and tells me after a second, "Two hundred twenty-eight thousand. I'm buying."

Eva laughs. "That's two hundred twenty-eight thousand dollars, jerk. In this store we pay only in bucks. Go away, old beggar, and take your bag with you, you're blocking the counter!"

"In that case, I'd like six pounds of these spare ribs." Michal points his finger at Eva. We burst out laughing.

"That's what you get," Eva says. "See what happens when you let a jerk into a store?"

"Actually, I only weigh a hundred and ten," I say.

"That's because you're a stick," Eva says.

"And you're a barrel," I say.

"And me? What am I?" Michal asks.

"You are an intrusive bolt," I reply.

"You're a nut."

"I'm bored." Eva yawns ostentatiously. "We took some other pic-tures too . . ."

"Just one," Michal says. "But I made it into a postcard, since it's nothing interesting."

He hands us a small print. A bunch of girls are in it, in white dresses for first communion. Eva took that picture in Swiebodzice when we were stopped by a procession.

It was the holiday of Corpus Christi.

We had to wait for the town's entire population to roll through. We were sitting on a black motorcycle in black leather, in shiny hel-mets, our faces hidden behind the veils of the dark visors. Thousands of people paraded in front of us and they were all staring at us. They must have thought we were two devils, but actually they were looking at two witches. They were walking in front of us, walking and walk-ing. I knocked my helmet against Eva's and said, "They're cowards. They're walking here like that because they are afraid of hell."

Eva smiled quietly and knocked back.

"Fools," she said. "In any case, they wouldn't even all fit in heaven." She turned on the engine and we backed away with a roar. We tried to circle the procession, but the procession was faster, and by the time we reached the front of it, little girls were just walking and tossing flower petals from their baskets. Eva took off her helmet and took a picture of them with her Nikon camera. I took off my helmet too, since it was such a hot day and the procession looked like it would never end.

I looked at the girls in long white dresses, and in my mouth I could taste the day, six years ago, that I walked in a procession just like that and tossed rose petals on the road. I could hear the rustle of my white skirt. I remember I wanted to keep going and going like that, that I never wanted it to end, that I just wanted to go on and on in the white dress, tossing rose petals for the rest of my life to the sound of bells and the choir.

We sat on the black motorcycle in our black leather uniforms, with all the guys staring at us, but in a very different way than they had before we took our helmets off. They were sweating in their suits, singing and staring, with their women giving us grim looks from beneath their brows. Suddenly there was a break between groups. Eva turned on the engine and we flew with a roar across the intersection. A few minutes later Walbrzych appeared in front of us with a sky cloaked in dark smoke, one of the twelve dirtiest cities in the world. Being among the twelve, it is not in bad company. There's Lodz and Warsaw, and Manchester and Detroit . . .

"You forgot Zabrze," Michal says. I kiss him on the ear and ask him to get lost because we want to study a little. We have to memorize our written exams for the college prep entrance exams. Michal just wrote the math one out for us, and his buddy, who is a literature major in Wroclaw, wrote out the Polish lit one.

I GET HOME well after eight. Tadzio looks up from the TV and says, "You got a letter, express, but local."

"Where is it?" I ask. Tadzio nods his head toward the shelf in the wall unit. I take the letter and run to my room. There's no return address on the envelope. I tear it open . . . it's Kasia's scribble.

My dear, sweet Mongoose,

If you can forgive me, I'd like to ask you to forgive me. I've never missed anyone as much as I miss you. I'm begging you to come see me as soon as you get this letter. I'm back from Sobotka, but Karolina won't let me get out of bed because I'm still sick, so I can't come see you myself. I know I did a horrible thing to you, but please, don't be angry with me. I was really unhappy, and maybe that's why things went the way they did between us. So please forgive me, and if you can't forgive me, at least come and tell me. I really want to see your sweet face. I miss you, and this whole time I've been waiting for you.

Katarzyna.

P.S. Please, come.

I was up half the night crying because of that letter.

I took it with me to school and had it in the pocket of my dress during every class, and I kept putting my hand in there and feeling the envelope . . . but I never went to Kasia's. I didn't go, and that's that.

In the evening we got made up like dolls and Michal drove us to the disco. We each drank two glasses of wine and started joking around, so Michal got angry at us and asked some gloomy, quiet idiot with messed-up purple hair to dance. A couple of workers from a cheap motel wouldn't leave us alone. They wanted to dance with us and they spoke in a really weird dialect.

"Beggin' your pardon," Eva said, mimicking their pronunciation. "But my prosthesis done come loose."

"Don't fuckin' bullshit me," one of them said, grabbed her by her hand and started pulling her. I took an empty Coca-Cola bottle from the table and smashed him right in the face with all my might. He fell down, and by the time he got up, Michal was next to us. There were a lot of guys from the motel and they couldn't just stand there and watch some guy beat up on their buddy. So we had to save ourselves by running away, because there was no way in the world one beginning karate student was going to handle ten young miners.

Eva drove the car and Michal and I sat in the back and I kissed his black eye. And he had his hand on my thigh underneath my skirt and was really happy about the whole outcome. And all the while I kept thinking about forgotten gestures. I hadn't the slightest idea why I suddenly remembered that . . .

Forgotten gestures.

Kasia was reading about it in one of her smart books one day and told me about it right away. These were all human activities that were really popular at one point, but now no one does them anymore. For example, the gesture of shielding a candle with your hand when you walk down a drafty corridor . . . or drawing a sword. Or tipping your hat . . . gathering up a long dress when you ascend a staircase . . . All these gestures had been with people for hundreds of years. Some of them have been completely abandoned and others are heading that way. There must be a lot more of them, but for some reason Kasia and I couldn't bring them to mind, though we both had the impression they were on the tip of our tongues. Kasia said that faded memories from prior incarnations meander in our heads. In any case, I feel sad about the passing of all these forgotten gestures. They're like flowers that no one waters, so they wilt in forgetting and silence . . .

On the second day I don't go to Kasia's either. I just keep that letter of hers on me all the time until Eva pulls it out of my pocket because the edge of it is showing.

She reads it right away. "When did you get this?"

"The day before yesterday."

"You didn't go see her, did you?"

"No."

"What did she do to you, that she's begging you for forgiveness?"

"She didn't do anything, she just . . . she turned me into a real person. Both of you did."

"I don't understand."

"You don't have to understand everything."

"You're not going to go see her?"

"Are you crazy?"

"You're wonderful."

Eva laughs and looks at the letter and declares with great feeling:

" 'My dear, sweet Mongoose,

" 'If you can forgive me, I'd like to ask you to forgive me.' "!!! . . .

She grabs her heart in exaggeration, hanging on my pleading look. I laugh and yank the letter away from her. And my eyes watch my hands tear the letter into tiny pieces and throw them into the garbage.

I open a closet and take out the belt of a dress. I turn toward Eva, commanding her, "Come here!"

She comes over, scuffing her feet. "No . . . please. No . . ."

"Turn around."

I twist her arms behind her back and bind her wrists. Hard, with lots of knots, so she can't get loose. I push her onto the carpet and straddle her belly, slowly undoing the buttons of her blouse. Looking at me unconsciously, she shivers and moans quietly.

"Jamaica," she whispers. "Jamaica . . ."

I pull out the bowie knife. Consciousness returns to her eyes and they widen in fear. She squirms beneath me.

My lips say, "It's going to happen now."

"I beg you, not yet! You promised me it wouldn't happen this year!"

"Promises, promises," I say with a sad smile. With my free hand I stroke Eva's face. "Good-bye, Eva."

She bites her lips in despair and freezes. "I hope your aim is good . . ."

"Don't worry, it is," I say. "Now close your eyes."

"Good-bye," she whispers, and lowers her eyes. I lick the blade of my bowie knife and, tasting the blood from my cut tongue, I lift my arm. Suddenly Eva starts shaking, looking at me, and it's too late, I can't strike. I throw the bowie knife down and lean over her. The blood from my lips drips onto hers and she starts licking it and swallowing it.

I kiss her. She's drinking blood straight from my mouth now, like a nestling picking a worm out of the open beak of its mother.

"You chickened out," she whispers.

"So did you," I say.

"Next time, I'm not going to."

"Neither will I."

MY WOUNDED TONGUE hurt me all night, and when I get to school, I am lisping badly. So to keep me company, Eva starts lisping too. Then Magda starts lisping and so does Klaudia. Soon the whole class is infected and everyone's walking around lisping. Before long the lisping plague spreads throughout the entire school and even the teachers are lisping. These are the final days of the school year and everywhere you go in the classrooms and hallways it smells like summer vacation.

It's the long recess. I'm sitting alone in the classroom, reading a book. I hear someone come in. I look up . . . and see Karolina Bogdanska, Kasia's mom. She comes over to me smiling and I say, "Hello."

"Hi, Mongoose," she says, and sits down at the desk next to me. "Don't you want to visit Katarzyna?"

"I was going to," I reply, and my heart starts pounding like a hammer.

"Don't be angry with her. She was extremely upset. She waited to see him for so many years and she never got to . . ."

"What happened?"

"Her father died."

"When?"

"You didn't know about it?"

"No! How was I supposed to know?"

"We found out about two weeks ago," Mrs. Bogdanska says.

Two weeks ago . . . then that was it. That was when I was looking for her all over town, in the rain. So that was it, when I found her in the church. God, that was it.

I get up and start packing my books.

"I'm going over right away," I say.

"You don't have any more classes?"

"I do, but it's okay, we're not having any quizzes."

"In that case, I'll give you a ride."

We go down the corridor filled with screams and I'm looking everywhere, to see if Eva is there. I don't see her—that's good. She must have gone to smoke cigarettes with Klaudia.

MY HEART POUNDING, I enter Kasia's room.

She's sleeping. Sleeping in her red, flowered pajamas. I sit on the edge of her bed and look at her. Her thin face is all freckled.

So this is my Kasia. So funny, so pretty. She's pretty, even though she's not good-looking. My little Kasia. I can hear her breathe. What could she be dreaming of right now? Could she be dreaming of me? My pretty one, my Kasia. I sit and watch. So many nights I've thought about her. And now she's right next to me, sleeping. I could stretch out my hand at any moment and touch her.

Poor thing, how much weight she's lost.

Or maybe she's always been like that, only I never saw it. I didn't know the right way to look, even though I did look. What's happened to me, that I'm not the way I was in the past? The past, the past—a whole two weeks ago.

So that's the way you look, Kasia darling.

She wakes up, opens her eyes and looks at me, and I can see that her eyes are getting wetter and wetter. Suddenly she's screaming for joy and throws herself at me and embraces me, all sweaty and hot. I hug her tight. So that's what true happiness looks like. We weep in each other's arms and can't stop. Five minutes pass, maybe ten. Maybe it's only a minute, maybe a hundred years.

Kasia wipes my eyes with the edge of her blanket. Then she wipes hers. We look at each other and can't stop.

"You're so beautiful," Kasia says, "and so strange."

I smile. And Kasia says, "How you've changed. You're the most beautiful creature in the world. You put me to shame . . ."

She buries her head in her blanket. "Mongoose, is that really you?"

"Yes, it's really me," I say. Or maybe it's no longer me? How am I supposed to know?

Kasia cuddles up to me. "Forgive me."

"It's nothing. I forgot about it a long time ago. It's like ten years has passed . . ." I say.

"Did you hear he died?"

"I know." I start stroking her hair. My sweet little one. She waited for so many years to meet her dad, and now they'll never meet.

"He was sick for about a year, but he didn't want to worry me, so he never said anything or wrote anything about it. That's why he really wanted me to come."

"Kasia, I really missed you."

She looks at me, her eyes like buttons. As usual, there are circles under her eyes. She stretches out her hand and touches my face.

"Mongoose," she says. "Mongoose."

"If only I'd known . . ." I say.

"I don't know how I didn't go totally insane. Maybe my composition saved me. Because I decided I had to compose it before going to the hospital for the rest of my life."

"And did you do it?"

"Yes. And on my own, without Jigi's help. I killed him—I killed him for good."

"And the music?"

"Now the music is completely mine."

"That's wonderful."

"I didn't sleep at all for five days and nights. And everything got mingled . . . dream and reality. And you were with me the whole time . . ."

"Me?"

"Yes, Mongoose. I felt your presence all around me and everywhere. What I played was you. Even I was you. I looked at my hands and saw your hands. I heard your voice, even though it was me speaking." Kasia strokes her face with my hand and kisses it. "Forgive me."

"For what?" I ask. "I've already forgiven you everything."

"No, you don't know anything," Kasia says quickly. "Because you see, I'm so evil, so cold, I don't even know how to suffer. When my dad died, I didn't even suffer, I was just angry at him for dying and for never being able to listen to my composition. Angry that I didn't have anyone to write it for. And I felt so empty, so empty . . . I didn't have anything in me except anger—powerless, empty anger. And it wasn't until I saw you in front of the church, on the ground, squirming in pain . . . when I understood what I did . . . the anger disappeared in me. Your suffering saved me. I ran away from you because I couldn't bear to look at your tears. But your cry followed me and I could hear it all the time. There was no longer any anger left in me, but only your cry. I went over to the keyboard and started to play in order to block it out . . . and I scared myself because what I was playing was so beautiful, so beautiful . . . so powerful . . . and this was the beginning of my composition. I called my mom and asked her to come right away and take me and all the equipment to Sobotka, to my grandmother's. Then there were those five days and nights and then I got really sick. I was in the hospital, then I was in bed at home . . . and the whole time I was really worried about you and couldn't do anything because my mom didn't want to let me get out of bed . . ."

Kasia stops short. She sits in front of me with her legs tucked beneath her and sways gently back and forth. Tears flow from under her closed eyelids.

I look at her and feel like I was her great-grandmother. I look and I can see everything. I see Kasia, but I also see the stain on her bedding and all the folds of the blanket. The bedposts, my own knees, the rays of sun on the carpet. Everything's so clear . . . I could never see things that way before.

"Finally, I understood," Kasia says, "that I only created this piece because I hurt you. It was as if I'd locked a butterfly in a metal candy tin and was recording the flapping of its little wings on sheet music. There, inside, in the tin darkness, until it died out . . . No, this composition isn't mine."

Kasia opens her swollen eyes. She reaches under the pillow, takes out a flat box with a roll of tape inside and passes it to me.

"It's yours," she says. "Do whatever you want with it. Throw it out the window—burn it. But forgive me, if you can. I'm begging you."

I take the case from her hands and smile.

"Don't worry," I say, "you didn't do me any harm. On the contrary, I'm really, really grateful to you. Thanks to you, I understand who I really am and can finally stop deceiving myself, which of course doesn't mean that I'm not deceiving others . . . but that's another can of worms. Oh . . . about that butterfly . . . you must have had me in mind, didn't you?"

Kasia nods her head.

"If you did, don't worry about it. It only seemed like you imprisoned it to you, but really, you set it free. Now don't cry, because I can't look at your tears. You told me once yourself that every artist makes a mountain out of a molehill."

I take my handkerchief and carefully wipe her face. She snuggles up to me. I hug her tight.

"Mongoose," she whispers in my ear, "you'll see. I'm going to change. I'll never be bad. I swear."

"I know, Kasia, I know."

I look at the box with the tape inside, which I hold in my right hand. On the transparent Plexiglas it says in red marker: IN THE KINGDOM OF DEAD HOURS.

"What a pretty title," I say. "I can't wait for you to play it for me."

"Do you really like it?" Kasia asks.

"A lot."

"Because you know I have no idea when I wrote it. I must have had a fever . . ."

"Poor little thing," I say, and touch her forehead. "You still do."

"Not much of one," she says. "Ninety-nine point nine."

"And that's supposed to be not much? Get under the covers right away! And I'll play your composition."

"I'm going to play it for you!"

Kasia jumps out of bed and, barefoot, runs toward the window. So tiny, tousle-headed and childish.

I LISTENED TO the whole composition—it lasted an hour, five minutes and twenty seconds—and then I had to go back to school because Mrs. Zelenow had threatened last time to quiz me on a few things, and if I'm afraid of anyone in that school, it's her. I told Kasia I'd come after school, so we could talk about her wonderful composition and things in general.

I run into the classroom and sit at my desk. Eva's pouting. "You were at her place?"

"How did you know?"

"I have my own intelligence service."

"What if I was?"

"What was it, then?"

"She's sick, but she's feeling better now. She simply caught a cold."

"You're despicable. You promised you wouldn't go."

"I had to."

"Because?"

"Her dad died."

"So what?"

"What do you mean, 'So what'?"

"I mean I knew about it for a long time."

"How did you know?"

"I simply have my own intelligence service."

"Why didn't you tell me?"

"How was I supposed to know you were interested? What, did she tell you how many thousands of dollars she inherited?"

"No, she didn't—I couldn't care less."

"Yeah? Don't pull the wool over my eyes."

"Idiot."

"Moron."

"Well, great."

"Are you going to see her after school?"

"None of your fucking business."

"Please tell me."

"I am."

"Don't go."

"Don't be jealous."

"Me? Jealous? Over an idiot like her? Choose. Either me or her."

"Leave me alone."

"So you don't love me anymore?"

"Quiet, stupid. I do. But she's sick. I promised her I would come."

"In that case, it's finished between us."

Eva takes her bag and goes to Magda's desk.

I go up to her after the break. "Eva, come on."

"Buzz off."

So I buzz off.

AFTER CLASSES ARE over, she's waiting for me right outside the school.

"Hop on," she says. "I'll give you a ride to that damn Kasia."

She brings the motorcycle to a halt, but we're in Szczawno—in front of her house. "I'll take you there in an hour. Okay?"

"I can even stay for two, you naughty one," I say.

AFTER DINNER WE sit in the garden on the swinging bench. "Tell me, what do I have to do to stop you from going to her place?" Eva says.

"It shouldn't matter for us that I'm going. I promised, and she's waiting for me."

"It's an order. You can't go to her place, today or ever. That's an order!"

"Has the little thing forgotten that it's my turn to give orders?"

"Okay, then give me one quickly."

"Okay. I order you to let me go to Kasia's and not be angry with me about it."

"You'll see, she's gonna destroy you!"

"If you don't stop, I'm gonna go right now!"

I jump off the bench and walk away. Eva runs after me. She snuggles up to me. "Maica, don't go. If you do, I'm gonna go crazy."

I sigh.

Eva pulls me by the hand. She says, "Come here—I'm gonna show you something."

We go into her room. Eva rummages through her wardrobe and finally pulls out something small. It's a vial, with a small pill inside. "Do you know what this is? Cyanide. If you go to Kasia's, I'm gonna swallow it and die in agony."

I sit down on the sofa.

"What am I supposed to do?" I say in despair.

Eva sits down next to me. "Just don't go visit her, and that's that."

"Give me that vial," I say.

She shows me her empty hands. "I don't have it anymore."

Eva kneels and takes off my shoes.

"Hug me . . ." she says.

We lie down on the sofa. Eva jumps up, runs to the window and closes the door leading to the terrace. She rolls down the shades and locks the second door, leading to the hallway.

"No," I say.

"You have no say."

She comes out of the darkness and lies down on top of me. She kisses me and strokes me. All over my tummy and everywhere. A sweet feeling overcomes me and I disappear in a salty wave.

LIFE.

You can do nothing, say nothing, think nothing . . . and it'll still be life just the same. The same in me, in an ant, in any plant.

No matter what I may become, I will always be alive. For as long as I exist. And what about when I no longer exist? What will I be when I'm no longer alive?

The air?

Because right now I'm a body.

A skeleton dressed in meat, skin and other extras. My body lies on the sofa, in the reddish half-darkness, breathing and thinking. My body lies here, and there lies Eva's body sleeping. She is she, and I am I. But I . . . am also my thoughts. So, am I everything I think about? And am I everywhere my thoughts are?

And my thoughts, wherever they may go . . . could they stay there, or will they always come back to me? Because if I stick my hands out to the side, I stretch as far as they stretch. And if I clasp them across my chest and then tuck my legs under me, I'm no longer there, I'm here. But then thoughts are something completely different from arms and legs.

Maybe it's much better for them not to be at all? And if they're supposed to be, they should be like arms and legs—very close. If I was to lie down, they would lie down with me and we would jump around here and there. And if I was to eat, they'd eat with me.

Oh, look what they do, how they flee what's directly in front of them. I look at Eva sleeping and think about Kasia, waiting for me all flushed with fever and worrying that she sacrificed me at the altar of her composition.

It's no big deal, it doesn't bother me.

So I'm living for nothing. At least I was useful for something. And not just for anything, but for creating a great masterpiece.

Maybe that's the way it always has to be? Maybe behind each wonderful symphony, behind each wonderful book, stands the victim of a sacrifice made of someone unknown, someone just like me? Maybe in five hundred years someone will listen to Kasia's composition and say, "How beautiful!" And what if this beauty contains a trace of the flapping of my wings in a tin candy box? Back when Kasia was telling me about reincarnation, I dreamed that in my next life I'd like to be reincarnated as music. Maybe the time has come. Maybe this is the way I become music.

I'm horrible. As usual, I'm thinking only of myself. Kasia's waiting, and she doesn't even know whether or not I like her composition.

I reach my hand over to the telephone, lying by the sofa. I press the buttons. After a second I hear Kasia's voice: "Hello?"

"It's me," I whisper, so as to not wake up Eva.

"I'm waiting for you."

"Kasia, your composition is wonderful. Really. It's a masterpiece. You'll see, you'll be a part of music history."

"What are you saying?" Kasia laughs. "How soon can you come over?"

"I can't today," I whisper. "Zenus is sick, I have to take care of him . . ."

I look and see Eva raise herself up on her elbows and listen to everything. Her lips are shaking and she's looking at me so sadly that my heart is breaking into pieces. I hear Kasia's distant, distant voice in the receiver: "Maybe I can come to your place. I'm feeling better."

"No, no, don't come!"

"Why?"

"Because I lied to you," I say in sudden anger. "Zenus isn't really sick. I'll never come see you. Bye, Kasia."

I can hear her start to cry. Eva takes the receiver from me and holds it up to her ear. Hearing Kasia's crying, she smiles at me and hangs up the phone. She puts her hand on my shoulder. I listen to her breathing.

"Are you happy with me now?" I ask.

"I'll never forget you did that. You're sweet."

"Gonna make me some tea?"

"I'm on my way."

Eva jumps into her bathrobe, runs up to the window, rolls up the shade and leaves the room. I dress quickly. From the cushion of the chair I fish out the vial with cyanide, because I saw her hide it there. I struggle with the cap.

Eva comes back.

"I put the kettle on," she says, and sees me with the vial in my hand. She shouts, "Leave it alone!"

She runs up to me. Too late—I already swallowed it. She looks at me and I look at her . . . Nothing is happening to me.

"I fooled you—it was an aspirin," Eva says.

I put on my shoes, pick up my book bag and leave. Eva runs after me. "Don't be silly! Maica!"

I close the gate behind me.

I'm going down the street.

The sun's shining, the wind's blowing . . . it's wonderful.

I CALL KASIA from the first telephone booth and apologize to her, but she isn't angry, so I jump onto a bus and in half an hour we're together. We talk about music and philosophy until evening. We have to be patient. There are so many mysteries in life whose existence we can't even guess . . .

When I get home, Dad's drunk and acting up. Mom's heart is hurting, the girls are crying, even Tadzio's angry, because he can't watch television with all the noise. I bring things to order in a split second. I put Dad to sleep on my bed together with Tadzio, I tell the girls a bedtime story, and finally I even calm Mom down by making her tell me stories from her childhood.

Now everything's all right at our house. Everyone's asleep, only I can't fall asleep because I'm sleeping with Mom and she's snoring so loudly that even the painting on the wall is shaking. Okay—maybe I exaggerated about the painting, but it really is impossible to sleep with snoring like that.

I walk out onto the balcony.

It's warm, the stars are shining.

The earth seen from afar is a little star just like they are. A little light in the darkness. That's what we all are here, on this earth. Somehow I feel comfortable with that thought.

IT'S FIVE IN the morning. I managed to take a little nap. Now I'm making breakfast for Dad.

I wake him up. He gets dressed and comes into the kitchen. It breaks my heart to look at him. I put a mug of tea in front of him and stroke his head. First time in my life I've ever stroked my father's head, like he's my little brother, or even my little son.

"I made a mess of things, didn't I?" he asks.

"A little," I answer. "Buy Mom some flowers on the way home from work. You never buy her flowers."

"What do you mean? What do you think I brought her for Mother's Day?"

"Buy her some today."

"Sure . . . I'll buy them and she'll raise hell that I spent money on such stupid things."

"Maybe today she won't. Take a risk."

Dad laughs. "All right. What the heck, risk schmisk."

He's by the door, about to go to work, when suddenly he turns around, winks at me and says quietly, "Risk schmisk."

I wink back at him and smile. Boy, does this house need a grown-up daughter.

"HI, MAICA."

"Hi."

"Listen, something stupid happened. Mimi lost a ring. The diamond one. You know—the one that cost over a thousand dollars. She wanted to wear it yesterday because they were going to a party. I looked for it all night. Remember . . . we were playing with it."

"I do. But we put it back in the box. Together with the necklace."

"You were the last one to have it. Did you maybe forget to take it off?"

"No, I didn't. You don't think I stole it, do you?"

"I'm not thinking anything. But you could have forgotten. Then you took it off at home, put it somewhere and forgot . . . It happens."

"Not really, I would have remembered. I swear to you I don't have it."

"Please try to understand. You're the only one who's been coming to my place lately. If we don't find it, the blame's gonna fall on you."

"But I don't have it."

"Even so, look for it at your place. We have to make sure. And if you find it, call me right away. I'll look too."

"I'll look, but I know for sure it's not at my place."

"Look anyway. Bye, I'm going home."

And she was gone. And the last day of school was poisoned by thoughts about the ring.

I try to remember everything that happened the day we played with Eva's mom's jewelry, but the more I think about it, the less I can figure out what could have happened to the ring. Suddenly a thought comes into my head: the ring wasn't lost at all and Eva came up with this so she could torture me, so she could take revenge for yesterday.

Yes, I'm positive that's what it is.

Almost positive.

No—totally positive. I've gotten to know Eva a little and I know what she's capable of. No one knows her the way I do. Maybe she doesn't even want revenge. Maybe with this ring she wants to some-how cancel out what happened between us yesterday. I'm not even angry with her; I can completely understand her jealousy toward Kasia. Maybe if I was in her place, I'd be jealous too. I think everything'll fall into place between us. Oh, it would be wonderful if she wanted to befriend Kasia. Then I could have the two of them. Maybe we could manage to talk Kasia into taking a high school exam together with us. The three of us could be together until the end of high school . . .

Kasia in a regular dress is a completely different person than Kasia in a Gypsy dress, only now can you really see how thin and pretty she is. And so carefree. It's because she got rid of Jigi. That's good, pal.

She feels okay now. She doesn't have a fever or anything, but she still has to blow her nose a little. She got the cold because after those five days and nights of composing she went to the garden and lay down in the grass and slept on the ground for five hours before her grandmother found her there.

She put her composition onto a cassette and sent it to a very good music critic with the request that he write her what he thinks about it, and she runs to the mailbox all the time now to see whether there's a letter from him. But how could there be if she only sent him the tape a few days ago?

We took a long walk and bought almost forty round-trip tickets to Sobotka at the train station. Now we're sitting at home stuffing them into envelopes.

The tickets are for the day after tomorrow and we're writing down the time of departure on each one.

Why are there so many?

That's a secret.

TWO GIRLS IN our class are missing from the elementary school graduation ceremony. Kasia and Eva. Kasia is already in Sobotka, preparing everything for tomorrow. And Eva? Magda takes her report card and I take Kasia's. I look . . . she passed, only she has C's all the way down.

Magda comes up to me. She asks me whether I've found the ring. I say I haven't, and I give her two envelopes with tickets for Eva and her. I pass them on to the rest of the kids in the class and I skip the rest of the ceremony because I don't want them to ask what's with the tickets. I should go to Eva's. Maybe that ring really did get lost?

But no, I don't feel like talking to her today.

DAD GAVE TADZIO two paddles and a Ping-Pong ball for passing to the next grade. We set up the table in the large room, but instead of a net we stood some books up, and we're playing. Tadzio and I are the only ones home, because Mom and Zenus and the girls went outside to get some sun.

I totally lost the first two games—I didn't even score a point—but in the third one I slowly started to get the hang of it, and now I am leading five to three. The doorbell rings. Tadzio runs to open it.

It's Eva.

I can tell right away it's about the ring. I take her to my room and tell her I looked and couldn't find it. Eva waves her hand and smiles.

"Did you find it?" I ask.

"No . . . but Mimi must have put it somewhere herself. Don't worry."

I sigh in relief. Eva sits on the sofa, extending her hand to me. I sit beside her. She sighs and says, "I came to apologize for everything. I'm a stupid, jealous bitch. Please don't be angry with me."

"I'm not."

"For two days I've felt completely out of sorts. I think about you all the time."

"I think about you too," I say. "I'm so happy."

We throw our arms around each other.

"What I really want is for you two to become friends," I say. "You can't even imagine how much she's changed. You'll see—you'll like her now."

"For you, I'd even marry a dog catcher," Eva says.

"Don't say that. Kasia's no dog catcher."

"I know. It's me who's the dog catcher."

"You're no dog catcher either."

"So what dog catcher were you talking about?" Eva asks.

At this point Tadzio opens the door and peeks in and asks whether I'm chickening out. Eva and I burst out laughing.

All this joy makes me lose the last set fifteen to five. Then Eva plays with Tadzio and loses too. So Tadzio gets the gold medal and Eva and I fight for the silver.

Tadzio referees.

"What's with the tickets to Sobotka?" Eva asks while serving.

"It's a secret," I say, and slice the ball. I'm leading. "But I'll tell you. Kasia's preparing a huge garden party at her grandmother's. She'll be waiting for us at the train station."

Eva serves. I slice the ball and I already lead by two points. Eva serves again. We rally for a long time.

"You know," I say, "she understood she was being silly, cutting herself off from her peers. She's decided to become an ordinary, normal girl."

The ball hits Eva's racket and, instead of hitting the table, hits the chandelier. I'm leading by three points.

"It's good she wised up," Eva says. "Maybe we'll wise up too someday."

"Sure we will," I say. It's my serve. Eva returns the ball, I return it, Eva returns it, I return it . . . and I win.

Tadzio gives out the medals. He gets the yellow butterscotch, I get the almond one, and Eva, for a bronze medal, gets a toffee. I think it was a mistake beating Eva, because the bronze medal is the tastiest.

TRAIN STATION, WALBRZYCH City Center.

It's almost nine o'clock. Everyone's here. Nag grabs Zenek by the arms and swings him around on the platform.

"Let go!" Zenek shouts, flapping his legs in midair.

"I love you, I love you, I love you!" Nag calls out like she's singing. Finally she puts him on his feet and he can't walk, he's staggering like a drunk.

Ziebinski, the fatso, says, "What are you doing, Zenek, drinking vodka this early in the morning?"

We all start laughing.

The train arrives. It's almost empty, and it's really cool because it's a double-decker. The boys are running back and forth between the two levels and Klaudia's organizing a disco, since she has a boom box with her.

Eva and I run to the other end of the train because she really feels like going to sleep. I sit by the window and she puts her head on my lap. I stroke her head and she falls asleep.

We've already passed Swidnica. There are green and yellow fields all around. Far, far away, you can see Sleza Mountain. Me and the train are slowly getting closer and closer to it. Kasia's somewhere near Sleza Mountain. She must be bustling about in the garden doing last-minute preparations with her grandmother.

The mountain basks in the sun. It's a good thing, since it was about to rain in Walbrzych. A path runs alongside the mound beneath the tracks that our train trudges along. Some guy on a bicycle is trying to outpace us.

He must not have kept up for long, because we can't see him anymore. Here comes the conductor. I pull out my ticket and he waves his hand.

"How far is it to Sobotka?" I ask.

"It's the fourth stop," he replies, and disappears.

Eva wakes up. "What did he say?"

"Sobotka's the fourth stop."

"Gee, I really need to pee," Eva says, yawning. "I'll be right back."

So she runs to the bathroom. I look out the window: Sleza Mountain is so close now you can see every tree on its slope. Can you see Kasia's grandmother's house?

Only three stations to Sobotka.

WOW, WE'RE ALREADY in Szczepanow. Grass is growing on the platform and chickens are walking around. Even flowers grow here. I could jump out quickly and pick a few, but I'm afraid I wouldn't be able to jump back on in time.

Jeez, a poor little dog is dragging along, limping. It has a dirty, sticky coat. It must be sick and sad . . . and there go three drunk guys. One of them kicks the dog. The dog jumps away with a howl.

The train starts moving.

SOBOTKA WEST.

What's going on with Eva? Maybe she fainted. I go to the bathroom and knock. Silence. I open the door—it's empty. I go to the next one. I turn the knob—it's locked.

"Eva?" I call.

"What do you want?" a gruff voice answers. I run through the whole train. Maybe she went to see what the rest of the class is up to. I hear their voices from the upper level. I climb the steps.

Everyone's there and Eva is with them. They're discussing something loudly.

"They might not sell it to us," Florek says.

"What, do I look like I've never bought wine in the store before?" Eva asks. "I'm going with fatso. They'll sell it to us."

"Twenty bottles? You'll never pull it off."

"Don't be silly," Eva says. "When they sell it to us, we'll whistle over to you."

"Good thinking," someone says.

"But I don't have any cash," Marlena says.

"Neither do I . . ." says someone else.

"I already told you, it's on me," Eva says. "Okay?"

"Okay!"

I go up to them and Magda elbows Eva. Eva turns toward me. She takes me by the hand and pulls me back down to the corridor downstairs.

"What's going on?" I ask.

Eva puts her hands on my shoulders and, looking into my eyes, she quickly says, "Listen. We've all decided not to go to Kasia's party."

"Why?"

"Because. You're not going either."

"Eva, what are you trying to do?"

"That's my business," she says coldly. "Now listen. Surprise! If you don't come with us, I'm taking a cab straight to Walbrzych and telling my mom you stole her ring. Magda and Klaudia saw it on your finger."

"That's not true!"

Eva runs up the stairs and calls, "Klaudia! Magda!"

She comes back to me. Magda and Klaudia appear after a second.

"Did you see her wearing that ring?" Eva asks.

"I did," Magda says.

"So did I," Klaudia says.

"Would you be willing to tell that to the police?" Eva asks.

"We would," Klaudia says. Magda nods her head in agreement.

"You couldn't have seen it!" I shout. "When did you see it? Where?"

"We saw you downtown in Grunwaldzki Square on Monday," Magda says. "Don't you remember?"

"You're lying!"

Eva gestures to them and they go back upstairs.

"The police will search your apartment today," Eva threatens.

"Don't do it," I say in despair. "My mom will never survive it. You know she has a bad heart!"

"Okay, but on one condition. Stay with us, and you don't say a word to Kasia—not a single word. Now choose."

"No—you can't do that to me!"

"I guess you still don't know me by now, baby. I swear to you—one word to Kasia and I immediately get in a cab with Magda and Klaudia and we go straight to the police station at Walbrzych."

"But you know I didn't steal it!" I say.

Eva smiles. "Of course, it's hard to imagine you stealing anything. I know you—but the police don't."

"I beg you," I say, "don't do it. Don't destroy Kasia; she'll break down. I swear to you, after tomorrow I'll stop being friends with her, I'll never see her again. But let me be with her today. I'm begging you!"

My tears begin to flow. I kneel in front of Eva, I clasp her legs. "Eva, I beg you, don't be so evil."

Eva lifts me up.

"That's pointless now," she says. "It's too late. So you better think quickly. What's more important to you—that idiot, or your mom's health? And stop sniffling. You better be smiling."

She wipes the tears off my face.

The train slows down and everybody from our class runs down the steps. The building with the big logo is coming closer: SOBOTKA CITY.

And there, on the platform, stands Kasia.

"Oh, won't the prima donna be surprised." Ziebinski laughs, opening the door. Everybody pours out of the train. Eva and I get off last.

Kasia approaches us. She's dressed in shorts and a yellow shirt with the word GLIMP on it and has a straw hat on. She looks like a little girl.

She smiles at us sweetly.

"I'm so sorry I troubled you," she says loudly, "but I thought we should celebrate the end of elementary school together, so I'm inviting you to a huge garden party. There's going to be music, candy and all kinds of other attractions."

"Is there going to be ice cream?" Ziebinski asks.

"Is there going to be cake?" Kawczak asks.

"It'll all be there, everything's going to be there." Kasia smiles.

Ziebinski makes a worried face and says, "Too bad, because I'm on a diet."

Klaudia steps up front.

"Sorry," she says, "but we're not here to visit you at all. We're simply using the free tickets."

"Stop making a fool out of yourself," Kasia says, smiling.

"You'll see who's made a fool of himself," Ziebinski says with a sarcastic smile. "Let's go, guys. Come on, girls!"

And everyone leaves Kasia. No one's left but me. Kasia's staring at me, and Eva cries, "Maica!"

I swallow, and walk away from Kasia.

"Mongoose!" she cries after me. "Mongoose!"

I don't look back, I just keep on walking. That's the end. I have to do it like that, I can't do anything else. Mom would never survive our house being searched.

Eva's waiting for me. She hugs me and we walk along together, embracing each other. Kasia and the train station are far behind us. We're all trudging toward the marketplace.

"I know what you're going through," Eva says. "But it's time for you to grow up. Because once you're an adult, you have to stick with one group or another. And remember—from now on, for the rest of your life, the enemies of our friends are our enemies. And I'm the one who's your friend. Someday you'll understand I was right. The only way to wealth and fame is the road I'm on. If you want to make it to the top, you have to be like me. Could it be I came up with all of this especially for you? So you could practice a little? There'll be plenty of times you're going to have to choose. If you want to raise yourself and your family out of the mud, you're going to have to learn to choose. And choose wisely. Kasia is an egomaniac, and she's totally crazy. Sooner or later she's going to the nuthouse. One day you'll thank me for saving you from her. She'd only suck you dry and throw you away. But I need you, and you need me. You can be really strong—I've learned a thing or two about that. I need your strength. But if you're going to deal with weaklings, your strength will evaporate. So I'm asking you, accept my help now so I can accept yours someday."

"You're right," I say, "you're right, you're right! But don't say anything to me right now."

Eva smiles.

"Okay," she says, and runs up to Klaudia.

WE'RE SITTING ON the benches in the market square around a huge concrete map of the area. Eva and Ziebinski and the boys have gone to the store to buy wine.

The girls start singing. It's a familiar melody, but the words are new.

"*Strata fata parampa faita, lura kota larento data. Trucia fucia dakore borita, elo heto nuciamo perke. Silo heto saramo merone, into pinto pulpecia siusia sentrufale coloretto mamlone, niesierono lunapa kuka!*"

I look at my watch. It's ten after ten. The second hand's not moving . . . it's stopped. The girls are shouting another verse. They're all singing except me.

So that's what my adulthood will look like. I've made my choice. I chose wisely. It could have been different. And I'll be making decisions like that for the rest of my life. I'll watch evil people destroy good ones and I won't even lift a finger.

One day I will have my own children . . . But sometimes, in order to be good to your own children, you have to be bad to other children. There'll never be enough for everyone.

How can that be? To be good and evil simultaneously.

No, they must be separate.

To either be evil.

Or be good.

I DART FROM the bench and run away.

I RUN TOWARD the station. Kasia isn't there anymore. I look around. Where can her grandma's house be? It must be over there.

I run.

YES, THAT'S THE house. I'm standing, breathless, by the gate. In the garden, by the tables, Kasia's grandma is walking around. But Kasia isn't here.

Her grandma is quickly collecting the plates from the tables. She looks up.

I look too. Oh, what horrible, dark dragons are gathering up there, spreading their tentacles. They must have followed us from Walbrzych. The grandmother runs into the house carrying the plates.

"Kasia!" I shout. "Kasia!"

Suddenly I get an idea and start to look around. There, far away, on the road by the slope, I see a yellow spot. Oh, it just disappeared into the woods, on the road leading to the top of Sleza Mountain. It's Kasia, in her yellow shirt.

I have to catch up with her, but it's so far away.

I run through the fields.

I TRIP AND fall, because I stepped into a molehill. I get up right away.

If Eva fulfills her threat, if something happens to my mom . . . I know what I'll do. I'll take a screwdriver and gouge Eva's eyes out. I swear.

Why didn't I say that to her right away? I should have said, I'll gouge your eyes out, I swear!

I'm right by the highway, but it's still a mile to the road on the mountain. I don't have the strength to run.

A taxi's approaching. I don't have any money—too bad. I flag it down. The cab stops. I get in.

"There." I point.

He turns around and we go uphill.

Wait—that's where I saw her.

"Stop here," I say. We stop.

The driver turns to me. "Two hundred."

I put my hand in my pocket. "Hold on, I can't get it out. Just a minute . . ." I get out and pretend to search in my pocket . . . and suddenly I start to run and head into the forest.

Behind me I hear doors slamming and footsteps pounding. He's chasing me.

He's caught me. Tugging my clothes, he pulls me back.

"Wait, you bitch!" He wrenches my arm behind my back and leads me back to the car.

I begin to shout.

"You can shout all you want in the police station," he says in a rage. I kick him and fall down. He picks me up and wrenches my arm behind my back again.

At this moment I see the tourists coming down the mountain.

"Help!" I shout. "He's raping me!"

The tourists run over to us. I keep shouting like that so he won't be able to explain a thing to them. I think he must have got it, because he lets me go and runs back to the cab. They run after him.

I flee between the trees and keep running uphill. No one's running after me.

I lie down in the bushes and catch my breath. I have a lot of it to catch.

IT GETS DARKER and darker, and steeper and steeper. I hear footsteps pounding right in front of me. A group of boys and girls with backpacks are running down the rocky path.

"Did you see a girl in a yellow blouse?"

"Don't be stupid," they say. "Run away with us. A terrible storm is approaching. There's a lot of uranium on that hill. It'll be hell here any minute."

I'm alone again.

I CLIMB HIGHER and higher in the thickening darkness. A strap on my shoe has broken, so I'm going barefoot. It's so dark here you can barely see a thing.

The sky above me creaks.

Someone's walking behind me.

I turn around and listen. No, no one's there.

Bang.

It must be from the sky.

Someone's here . . .

It must be the rocks, or the trees.

"Kasia!" I cry. Oh, what an awful silence. I must have gotten lost, there's no path anywhere.

Where did this mist come from?

"Kasia!" I shout in despair. "Kasia!"

She's standing there. I see her light hair and something yellow—it must be her blouse. She stands there motionless . . . Is she looking at me?

I approach her slowly.

No, she can't see me, because she has her back to me. She's wearing really strange clothes. That yellow—it's not a blouse, it's . . . tights. Red shoes and red vest, embroidered with gold.

She turns toward me. But it's not Kasia. It's a boy. I think I know him. The long golden hair, falling in curls, the hat with feathers, this sword . . . some strange guy in a costume.

"Excuse me," I say. "Did you see a girl in a yellow blouse? It had 'Glimp' on it . . . and she had a straw hat on."

Didn't he hear me?

He looks at me strangely and smiles. "So you've come to the conclusion that evil and good can't be in the same box?"

"I'm looking for Kasia," I say louder. "Yellow blouse and straw hat!"

"And I'm looking for Marysia."

"That's me. I'm Marysia."

"I thought your name was Mongoose, or Maica."

"That's me too. Kasia and Eva call me that."

"Do you recognize me?"

"No," I say. "Yes," I say. I don't know . . .

"So are you Pimpush?" I ask suddenly.

He laughs. "Pimpush? . . . I didn't know I had such a pretty name. I brought you a letter."

"From whom?" I ask.

"Maybe from yourself?"

"How could it be . . . from myself to myself?"

"That's beside the point," he says. "I ate it anyhow. Nothing satisfies your hunger like stationery paper. Don't worry, I remember everything it said."

"What did it say?"

"If I were to repeat everything, I would have to speak from now till yesterday. I can only tell you what was written on the last, unfinished page . . ."

"What was written there?" I ask.

"Did I say 'was written'?"

"Yes, you did."

"That's a typo. I meant to say there was a drawing of a map, something like a labyrinth . . ."

Pimpush looks around.

"Yes," he says. "That's right, looks like it's right here. Do you see these stones? They're the remains of the walls."

I look back . . . stones are sticking out of the ground and glowing faintly. How beautiful it's become here. It's dark everywhere, only it's light around us.

"Yes," Pimpush says. "Because we're in the middle right now. Do you see this path?"

I follow his finger. "I see it."

"It's Maica's path. If you follow it, you'll turn into an icicle from the heat. Now look there . . ."

"Uh-huh," I say. "I see."

"This is Mongoose's path. It's so cold there you're gonna burn like a moth. Marysia's path starts here. It winds like a spiral around the hill. It's a very long path, but if I were to advise you, I would say, follow it, Marysia. With this path you will make it."

"To where?" I ask.

"That's obvious." Pimpush smiles. "All the mountain paths lead to the top of the mountain. There's also another . . ."

He turns around and shows me the fourth path with the tip of his shining sword.

"What is this path?" I ask.

"No one knows. It could be the longest of all the paths, or it could be the shortest. Could be the most wonderful, or could be the most horrifying. Could be it's only the shadow of the path in the negative of the mountain. I won't tell you anything more, because I don't know myself . . ."

I look at the fourth path. It's no different from the others in any way, but everything in me pulls me toward it. I take a step in its direction. I take another step. Then I stop.

"If you're gonna take that path," Pimpush says, stepping behind me, "I'll have to lend you my sword." I've already stretched out my hand for the sword when I hear, as if through cotton, the sound of thunder.

The storm . . . Kasia . . . where's Kasia?

I turn my face toward Pimpush. "I have to find Kasia!"

Pimpush's pretty face twists in disgust. "She didn't take that path, that's for sure."

"Please tell me where Kasia is!"

"In order to help others," Pimpush says, "you first have to help yourself. What a comic sight, when a blind man leads a blind man. Think about yourself, Maria."

"I beg you, tell me how to find Kasia."

"Kasia took her own path. You should take your own too. And as for that path . . . don't you want to go on the path of surprises?"

"I really do," I say, "but I have to find Kasia. The storm's gonna be here any minute and I have to be by her side . . ."

Pimpush turns sad and puts his shining sword back into its sheath.

"Well," he says, "I won't impose on you with my sword. And as for the storm, it's been going on for a long time."

Suddenly I'm surrounded by lightning and thunder. I'm all wet, I shiver from the cold.

"Pimpush!" I shout. "Tell me where Kasia is!"

From the rain and darkness a hand emerges.

"There," a voice sounds. "Farewell, Maria."

IN THE THUNDER and lightning bolts I run in the direction he showed me.

"Forgive me, dear Pimpush, I know I'll never see you again. But I have to save Kasia," I say.

———

I CLIMB THE wet rocks in the sheets of rain.

I lift up my head.

There, on the very peak of Sleza, on top of the viewing tower, a little Kasia stands with her arms raised up toward the inflamed ocean of sky.

I hear her wailing pleas, even though I'm too far away to hear them.

"Daddy! Take me out of here!!!"

There's lightning and terrible thunder. The hill just shook.

The glittering cocoon of a spider web of lightning encloses Kasia.

I CAN'T REMEMBER anything else . . . How did I get down? How did I wind up here?

This is a train station, this is still Sobotka. Someone next to me folds a red umbrella. I'm sitting on a bench in the house by the tracks. Someone's looking at me, someone else is saying something about me. Bells are ringing. A husky voice comes over the loudspeaker. I'm sitting completely soaked through, glued to my dress and to the bench.

There are a few squeals, and some boys and a girl run in here, dripping wet. It's them. Stealthily I run onto the platform. Maybe they won't notice me. I'll sit on the bench by the wall.

The door squeaks.

A dark-eyed, dark-haired girl comes up to me. She's sitting in the rain right next to me.

"Didn't you find Kasia?" she asks.

"She's already in heaven, with her dad," I say.

"What are you saying? What happened?"

"We killed her. You killed her, and I killed her. We all killed her, the whole world killed her!"

She grabs me by the shoulders and shakes me. "Maica, what's wrong with you?"

SHE DISAPPEARS. THE train's moving and I'm on it, my back to Walbrzych and my face to Sleza. I watch it get farther and farther away from me. It's as small as the molehill that little dead mole was lying next to. Now it's covered by a blanket of rain.

"Why are you crying, young lady?" a woman asks.

Magda and Klaudia pass by. "Have you seen Eva?"

In front of the apartment building I see Dad.

"Quick, lie down," Mom says.

"Gee, she's shaking," Tadzio says.

And Zosia: "I wrung out her dress. Two gallons of water came out."

I push off the comforter.

But it's a rock. I can't push it off. Oh well, I'll have to leave my legs there. But how can I go without legs? Well, I can always do the breast stroke.

I start to swim.

Why so many crosses? Crosses all the way to the horizon.

It's some kind of line. There are crosses everywhere, with people on them. They're moaning, crying, wriggling like earthworms.

"Where do you think you're going, bitch?" they scream at me. "Get the hell out of here! Go to the end of the line!"

"I'm telling you, the blood splashed all over the ham and pastrami."

"Don't push, don't push, I say!"

"Is there much left?"

"She wasn't here!"

Oh, it must be the line to heaven. Don't worry, sweethearts, I'm not gonna cut in, I'm looking for a different line. Slowly I swim to the very end. There are more and more children on crosses. They're crying and my heart is about to break.

Oh, there's an old man in a glistening raincoat walking along with a cane. His silver beard sweeps the ground. I swim up to him and put my hands together. "Help them, God, they're innocent."

I look over and the old man's pointing a finger at me. He shakes it at me and cries in a thin voice, *"Fucku shitaku!"*

Giggling, he skips and flees. *"Fucku shitaku! . . . fucku shitaku! . . ."*

Shedding bay leaves on the way, he hides behind the crosses.

I hear bubbling and turn around.

Here, on a platform of white marble, a beautiful rosy kid is mixing something in a cauldron with a ladle. He smiles at me with porcelain teeth.

"Try it," he chirps like a nightingale. "It's a very GOODBADSOUP."

He ladles out the soup and lifts it to my mouth. I take a gulp and it explodes in my stomach with an icy fire, a fiery ice.

I WAKE UP only to find myself immediately in a new dream. I'm sitting on the sofa in blue pajamas. The room is as small as a canary cage. I quickly take off the pajamas and put a dress on.

I leave.

Some clothes are hanging here. There, in front of the TV, a family is praying. It's bright, the sun's shining, and something is frolicking around on the screen. I run into the street. The tall buildings around obscure the view of everything. There was something important I had to do . . . Oh, I know—I have to find out how far back this dream goes. I need five zloty. Oh, something's glistening on the sidewalk. I lean over—it's five zloty. And there's a phone booth over there. Everything's been prepared for my next move. I take the five zloty to the phone booth. I put the coin in the slot of the talking piggybank. I dial. Something beeps in my ear. Suddenly I hear a voice.

"Hello?"

It's Kasia's voice, Kasia's voice loud and clear.

"Hello, hello?"

It's Kasia's voice. I hang up the receiver. Oh, I'm a total fool. She's alive, she's at her place. I have to see her with my own eyes, to convince myself, because now I only heard her with my own ears.

The bus is moving. I'm inside.

Everyone's staring at me.

I'm smiling at everyone. I feel so wonderful. But maybe I'm dirty . . .

I look myself over . . . Oh, I'm barefoot. That's why everyone's staring at me. And what did I put on? A housedress, covered with holes. Kasia will laugh when I show up like this.

I run through the marketplace.

The fountain blossoms in the sun with a golden glow. In front of her doorway I run into a limping postman.

"Do you have a letter from Warsaw to Kasia Bogdanska?" I ask.

He browses through the bag and says, "Yeah, certified. You have to sign. You're a godsend. I would have had to drag my leg all the way to the second floor."

I take the red pen and make a blue signature.

I run up the stairs. Oh, what if there's something bad in there? Because if it's bad, Kasia will break down. I look . . . the glue's barely holding up. Well, I'm gonna open it.

Dear Ms. Bogdanska,

As you requested, I am responding promptly and right to the core of the matter, so you won't worry unnecessarily. There's no doubt that you have talent, and taking into consideration your young age (being only twenty), quite a considerable one. I listened to your tape with great joy. To tell the truth, there are a lot of . . .

IT'S FROM THAT CRITIC; he's praising her. Wonderful. Kasia's gonna die of joy. I moisten the rest of the glue with my tongue. The envelope's closed and holds even better than before.

I'm about to press the button when the door opens, without my even having touched it. It's Kasia's mom, who's just leaving. She looks at me surprised.

"Good morning," I say. "Is Kasia home?"

"She is. Come in. I'll lock the door right behind you." I walk in and hear the click of the key in the keyhole. I go over to the honey-colored curtain. Kasia's behind it . . . Laughter, I hear laughter. But it isn't Kasia's laughter.

I bring my eye to the crack.

On the sofa, in the sun, sits Eva. Eva Bogdaj . . . Here?

Kasia sits beside her, with her back to her. I see her in profile. Two profiles, silhouetted by the sun.

Eva brushes Kasia's hair.

"That's a bit of an exaggeration," Kasia's saying.

"You know I never lie," Eva says, and they both burst out laughing.

"Ouch! You're pulling my hair!"

"I'm sorry. You have brilliant hair. I think I'm gonna grow mine long again."

"I told you not to cut it. I really liked your braid."

"But what you really liked to do was to pull on it. Do you still have it?"

"Sure I do. If you want, I'll loan it to you. A dollar an hour. You want it?"

"I was afraid you threw it in the garbage," Eva says. "It's already been half a year since our terrible argument."

"What are you talking about, it was only last February, four months ago. I don't even remember what started it."

"Don't you remember?" Eva wonders.

"No."

Eva embraces her and whispers something in her ear.

"Oh, you little bitch!" Kasia cries. "No, it was the other way around! It's a good thing you reminded me. I'll never forgive you for that."

"I'll never forgive you either!"

They're giggling. Eva starts to brush Kasia's hair again.

"Coming back to that," she says, "you know what I think?"

"What?"

"She's really nuts. You know . . . she took every game seriously."

"Sometimes I thought so too," Kasia says. "At first she was so quiet and sweet . . ."

"She was just hanging around. She wanted to use us to make a career."

"No. I don't believe that."

"I'm telling you. Look how many things I gave her. She's walking around in my underwear, my tights, my bras, my dresses, and on top of everything, I arranged for her exam to prep school. Is that nothing?"

"I wanted to give her an entire wardrobe too," Kasia says. "But somehow I felt stupid—I didn't want to make her uncomfortable."

"She's quite comfortable. You just needed to try. Then you'd have seen. She'd have carried off two suitcases, a bundle, and come back with a cart for the rest."

"Yuck, you're repulsive," Kasia says.

"Be the holy one if you like—I prefer to be the repulsive one. Every truth is repulsive."

"I felt some mystery in her," Kasia says. "But it was simply naiveté, shyness, fear. But that's beside the point. If only she was good . . . but she wasn't even that—she really disappointed me. Yuck! Yuck!" Kasia shudders.

"She's just a little cuckoo, and that's all there is to it," Eva says.

"Mystery schmystery," Kasia says. "I've come to the conclusion that there is no mystery in people."

"I don't like mysteries."

"Mystery exists only in music. Now I know it. Only in music. You'll see, one day I'll discover it."

"To top it off, she wanted to marry into the family," Eva says.

"Oh, stop talking about her! She's nobody—she doesn't even exist."

Eva laughs. "Nicely put. You're right. She's Miss Nobody."

I back away from the curtain. I hear their voices, their laughter. I am Miss Nobody.

THE DOOR SLAMS behind me. I'm running down the stairs. Snow falls on me from above. It's scraps of the letter torn by Miss Nobody one floor up.

OH, I WENT too far. It's the basement. Someone's standing here in the darkness. His glasses are glistening.

"Marysia," he says, "if you want, I'll scrap the whole thing—it'll be the way it used to be, like nothing ever happened."

"Get lost! You have no rights. It's my story, not yours."

I run away and stand in the sun, in front of the doorway. I left a remote-control bomb there. I take the watch from my wrist. I throw it on the pavement. The crystal shatters. I quickly turn the hands to nine after ten. *Tick-tick-tick-tick* . . . The house is about to collapse right on their heads.

Bang. Is it now?

———

NO, IT'S A shiny black car pulling in with the roar of three hundred horsepower. The chauffeur, red in the face, jumps out and opens the door in front of me.

I get in and my glove falls. A young man dressed in a silver waist-coat is already reaching for it. He kneels and passes me the glove. With reverence he kisses the hem of my dress, made of gold silk. He snaps his fingers at the chauffeur.

We're under way.

"Who are you?" I ask.

"I'm your page and personal secretary, Your Highness," the young man says, raising his silver-blue eyes to me. "The princess made us wait so long that we, too, lost hope. But persistence pays. Oh, much waited for, our princess, the sweetest of ladies . . ."

I hear a murmur from the back and turn around. The car is huge inside, like a ballroom, and as pretty as a ballroom, with a fountain in the middle. A group of young men and esteemed maidens bow to me. Everyone's pretty and dressed greatly, stately, as if for a disco.

"We're ready, Your Highness, to fulfill your every wish," my sweet page says.

"Can I ask you to do anything?"

"You do not ask—you order, Your Highness. You are our sovereign ruler."

"In that case," I say, "make every critic ridicule Kasia Bogdanska's composition, and make the critic who praised it go deaf. And make sure that Kasia never writes anything and is always tortured because no one appreciates her compositions. Let her live for a long time and make sure she isn't appreciated until after her death. And when she dies, let her compositions perish with her."

"Oh, Your Highness, that's a piece of cake," the page says with a porcelain laugh. "I can do that without lifting a finger. So many won-derful works throughout history have perished together with their creators without anyone asking for so much as a chord from the coun-try church. So that's done. Another wish? I have a strange premonition that Eva Bogdaj will also be in for a surprise . . ."

"Yes," I say. "Make sure Eva becomes a fat, prematurely aged sow with seven children and a drunk for a husband hanging on her back."

"Oh, that may be a little bit more complicated," my sweet page says, looking at my courtiers.

"I'll do it. I'll gladly do it," says a pretty thing in a stole, with a live peacock in her hairpiece. "I'll do a number with her hormones. And her metabolism. Would two hundred pounds and elephant legs satisfy Your Highness?"

"Sure," I say, and burst into pearly laughter. My whole pearly court bursts into laughter with me.

"And make her poor," I continue. "Let her lug pails loaded with coal all the way to the attic, where they'll be living as squatters. And arrange it so that the whole last week of the month she'll have nothing to feed to her ugly, moronic children."

"I have a great idea," says a fashion buff, extremely elegant in snakeskin shorts, with a hat made of a gold-plated rooster. "We'll get hold of her father's business. There isn't a business on earth where you couldn't find a few shady bills. I'll make sure the family is hit with penalties and loss of property. Is that enough?"

"I think that would be just fine," I reply, clapping my hands, which are studded with rings. My group of courtier club-goers claps along with me. Rings roll across the mirrored floor.

"Next wish?" my page says.

"How many can I have?" I ask, suddenly anxious.

"As many as you wish, my dearest lady. A hundred, a thousand, a million, a billion . . ."

"Billions, grillions . . . !" The courtiers are all shouting at once.

I sigh with relief, I proudly straighten my posture. "Make me rich and famous. And make sure everyone's jealous of me. Let them see me in newspapers, on posters, in movie theaters, on TV. Let them talk about me in buses, subways and trains. And make sure that Eva and Kasia in particular are jealous of me."

"Done!" the page calls out in awe.

"What else?"

What else? I'll think about that later . . . For now . . .

"For now, all I want is simply to be happy," I say.

"Oh, how beautifully you put it. Simply happy." The page turns to the court. "Did you hear it, darlings?"

"Oh yeah, we heard it!" the whole court cries. "You put it so beautifully. 'Simply happy'!"

"Think about it, that's just so deep," says a young man with his hair done up high and a diamond eye.

"And on top of that, of such broad sweep!" goes a chorus of two women black and pretty, accompanied by their faces sweet and velvety. Oh, what a great court my court is. It all falls into rhymes.

"Bravo!" the page cries.

"Bravo!" the whole court cries.

"Bravo for the princess!"

"Bravo! Bravo!!!"

They clap and clap, and each time they clap, the pearls and diamonds roll on the mirrored surface, resounding.

"Oh yes, a truly never fully completed bravo," my page says, placing his hand over his heart. "That's what we call a princely wish. Simply happy. Retail sounds like loose change. Wholesale glows with the stars. It's wholesale the princess evinces."

"Oh, thanks, we send thanks, our twinkling lady!!!" the courtiers cry in unison.

"What are they thanking me for?" I ask, surprised.

"They're thanking you for your trust," my sweet page and personal secretary explains. "Because a wholesale wish is held to our retail responsibility, by a pigtail. And we cherish above all our self-reliance, of course not counting you, Your Highness, whom we cherish above all."

The page falls gracefully onto his knees and kisses my golden high heels. Suddenly there's a grating noise.

The squeal of brakes.

"WHAT THE HELL kind of driving is that, asshole!" the page shouts at the chauffeur.

"But, master, I ain't drivin', I'm standin'," the chauffeur says, bending his red neck toward us. "I was tryin' not to hit that guy . . ."

I look . . . I look, and see an old man—drooling, toothless and lichened, pressing his furrowed face to the window on my side of the car. He clutches the crack of the window with his skinny, twisted fingers.

He stares at me, mumbling quietly, "Mom, Mom . . ."

"Who's that?" I ask.

"It's Pavelek," the page says.

"What Pavelek?" I ask. "I don't know any Paveleks."

"Your son, Pavelek."

"My son? My small, beloved future son, like that??? How come?"

"I'm sorry, Princess, but that's him. In just some eighty years."

"Oh yeah, in eighty years . . . Go," I say to the chauffeur, and then to my page, "I need a cigarette—fast."

The car jerks forward and the old man falls backward, smack, onto the road! I hear him mumbling, "Mom, Mom . . ."

The page whips out his golden cigarette case and flashes his golden lighter. I'm smoking a cigarette in a golden cigarette holder, chasing each golden puff with a golden cocktail. My sweet page snaps me out of my reverie. "And there, O Princess, turn your pretty head over there—there lies Zuzanna, your daughter."

I look to the side and see the cemetery. There, in the cemetery . . . my Zuzia?

"How is that possible?" I ask. "I haven't even had her yet, and already she's biting the dust?"

"Unfortunately," says my page, turning sad, fanning his silver-blue eyes with his eyelashes in embarrassment, "you can only suck on a candy until it's gone. And when you suck it in your mouth, no matter how sweet it is, it goes into other regions, other fragrances, as my Aunt Eufemia said. It's Time showing you its mean face, O our greatest, greatest, greatest lady. It's stronger than us."

"So go ahead, do something," I say, turning to the whole court. But, well, they don't hear anything. They're behind us, riding in a luxurious string of limousines.

"Unfortunately," the page says, "we only work in Time. Without Time there wouldn't be us or our work. Idiotic, cursed Time!" My secretary grinds his porcelain teeth, and as he grinds them, pearls flow.

"So what's gonna happen to my happiness?" I ask, chasing that question with the sip of a cocktail.

"Oh!" the page cries, a smile coming over his pale face. "If you eat one candy, you can go on to the next. No, you won't run out of gold-wrapped candies."

"My children aren't candy," I say. "I don't want to suck on them or eat them. I want only to have them and I want them never to die. I want only to have the same two children, not to have new children constantly! You have to figure out in your own head how to make it the way I want it. I command you!"

The page is on the verge of tears. "Unfortunately, O Lady, if you're going to have children, it can only be in Time. There's nothing we can do about this matter."

"In that case, you're fired!" I shout. "You'd best take your leave."

Wham! Bam! Kablam! My sweet page and secretary disappears. In his place another page and personal secretary is turning on his charms. As pretty as the other one, maybe even prettier. "What's your order, Your Highness?"

"You have to come up with something so Time doesn't mess with my happiness."

"Unfortunately, Your Highness . . . umm . . ." the page stutters. I show him the door.

He's gone—another's already sitting in his place. Supposedly he's different, but he's just the same as the other two. "What's your order, Your Highness?"

"I see that the whole children thing came to nothing," I say. "At least you can quickly get me a beloved husband. Do you know my taste?"

"We do, Your Highness," my page says to me, and yells to the driver, "Stop, you asshole!"

We stop and get out.

Down the country road there's a whole cavalcade of courtly limousines. Courtiers and ladies-in-waiting get out. Silks and diamonds swarm and glitter. Here he is, here's my boy.

There he is, sitting by the side of the road looking stupefied, his eyes glowing at the sight of my royal beauty.

He's sweet and handsome, yes, that must be him, that's the way I've always pictured him when I planned my marriage. I walk up and look . . . Some snotty girl is putting her head on his knees staring,

frightened, at my regal figure. And he—my beloved, my future husband and lover—strokes her mousy hair.

Oh, that'll be the day!

"So that's the way it is?" I ask, turning to my secretary, to my
court, glistening on the country road.

They shrug their shoulders, looking to the sides. One pretty girl
kneels and pretends to fix her shoe. Another lady-in-waiting pretends
to brush dust off the shoulder of another . . . My page sighs and lowers his eyes in embarrassment.

"What's that girl doing with him?" I say, enraged. "Take her
away!"

A bunch of courtiers immediately run up, and two of them cap-
ture the girl . . . But then what? My beloved doesn't let go of her. I
like him—he's really strong.

Either that or my people are really weak.

Finally they tear them away from each other. Two are holding her,
six are holding him. I approach her first. What does he see in her? She
might be pretty, she might even be very pretty, she might even look
like me, she might even look just like my reflection in the mirror . . .

But after all, that's not me, it's her. Maybe there was a day, before I
ascended to the throne, when I was as absurd and stupid as her . . .

We stand in front of each other. Tears flow from her eyes, pearls
and diamonds from mine.

She lowers her head, not even looking at me. Is she afraid, or
what? I take her by the chin and forcefully lift her mousy face toward
me.

"Little one," I say kindheartedly, "what's your name?"

She's silent and looks down, sobbing.

"You feel stupid, don't you?" I say. "You don't know what to say,
do you? Your head is spinning, isn't it? . . . Well, if it's not, it's about
to."

And I whack her on the noodle. And whack her yet again. She
doesn't shout, she doesn't shield her head, just swallows her tears silently.

"Hang her from that willow tree," I say. "Turn her into a pear.
When she ripens, she'll fall down."

"Ha, ha, ha!" the courtiers laugh, and clap their hands, splashing the dust of the country road with pearls and diamonds. They elbow each other, chattering among themselves: "Oh, ah, our princess is so witty!"

"Oh, ah, and so brilliant!"

"Oh, ah, someone like her is so hard to find."

"Oh, ah, oh, ah! . . ."

I approach my beloved.

"Let him go," I say. They let him go.

He's wonderful. He has just the hair he should have, his eyes are just right too, and his hands, all of him is like that, just like that, exactly like that.

"Sweetheart," I whisper softly. I embrace him and he embraces me. But somehow he's not holding me tight. But wait a second, boy, I'm going to fire you up. And I raise my rosy face and I touch his sweet lips with mine. I'm shaking all over, I merge my sweet breath with his, our lips become one coral lip. And with my tongue I'm luring his.

"Oh, ah, look, our princess is a master kisser! Deserves a gold medal! Bravo!!!"

They sure got that right.

There's no one better than me in the kissing category. My love, of course, kisses me back, but when he does it's like he's just kissing me back. On my tummy his magical snake flexes, but it flexes like it isn't flexing for me, but just flexing, flexing in general.

"Oh," I whisper, looking into his eyes. "I love you, I love you, I love you more than life. And what about you, do you love me?"

"I love you," he says, adding, "I love you more than life."

It felt sweet, but why did he have to add that? Just like a parrot.

"He doesn't love me at all," I say to my courtiers.

"He loves you, he loves you, we all heard it, Your Highness! He said he loves you, loves you more than life!"

I take three steps back.

He may have said it, but he doesn't love me.

I stick out two fingers for a cigarette. Snap! Golden flash and I'm smoking.

"I want him to love me," I say. "Make it happen! He has to love me! He must love me so that I believe it!"

Suddenly the chauffeur butts in, uninvited: "Maybe I should smack him upside the noggin just for the heck of it? I know he'll come around right quick."

"Shut up, you boor! I want love, not obedience!"

My love is such an idiot!

He stares longingly at a pear growing on a willow tree when he has a golden pineapple right in front of him.

"What about you?" I say to my court. "What about your promises, promises?"

Suddenly one of my courtiers, the one in leopard skin, with a wig made of silver plated leeches, curtsies nicely in front of me and chirps, "May we sing you an old Chinese peasant song?"

"You know where to put your peasant songs!" I shout, enraged. "You have to do something to make him love me!"

My page leans toward my ear and whispers, "Let them, Your Highness. They haven't sung for you yet. And it's a superb chorus, a royal one. It won all the court festivals."

"All right, sing," I allow benevolently. "But run through it quickly, because I don't have much time, I'm in a hurry to be happy."

Instantly the court forms four rows at the edge of the ditch. The page picks a branch off the ground; he'll be the one conducting. The basses begin and the tenors soon join in, then the sopranos and altos. Is this called a canon?

> *"Lali lo lali lo lali lo haida ho*
> *haida ho lali lo lali lo lali lo*
> *Lali lo lali lo lali lo haida ho*
> *haida ho lali lo lali lo lali lo . . . !!!"*

"Get on with it!" I cry. "Faster!"

They go faster, but it's the same thing over and over. The same thing again, only faster and faster.

They squeal so fast, like someone is rewinding a tape played over a loudspeaker.

"Why so fast?" I cry.

They start to slow down. They're singing so slowly now you can't even tell that their lips are moving. Again they start to speed up.

Oh well. They got going and nothing will stop them now. I call in the chauffeur. "I need a chair!"

He falls onto all fours, stretches out his back, and I sit down. The chair's shaking under me a little because of the *"haida ho lali lo"*s from under my behind—that's how much a peasant gets into courtly singing. Only that idiot, this moron, my love, neither sings nor walks nor does anything.

He's standing, staring at the pear tree.

I'm going to wait. Maybe he'll get tired before the court stops singing. What, are they done already? No, it's one of my ladies-in-waiting, the one wearing tights artistically mended with golden thread, who leaps in front of the choir and with her soprano voice crows so sweetly you could sweeten an entire city's tea with it.

"As thou canst not the course of time reverse, so canst my princess fair not love purchase!!!"

Again the chorus sings its *"lali lo haida ho"* . . . What a bunch of nerds. Why do I keep them here? Finally there's silence. Only a fly buzzes without permission. My court is sad, pale and wan, though still a bit shiny.

"Not much of a song," I say with disdain. "Any earthworm can chirp like that. And do I want to buy the love of this snot?! I simply want him to love me. I simply want to be happy."

The court does nothing—it glistens in silence by the road. No pain, no gain. For the last time, I'm going to put my royal authority on the line. I go up to that dolt and say, "Do you love me? Be honest—because if you lie, if I don't believe you, I'm going to smack you so hard you'll remember where moles go in winter!"

"I love you," he replies in a shaky voice. He's lucky he told the truth.

I wave my hand to the courtiers.

"Get this male prostitute out of my sight," I say. "Take him to the other side of the world and turn him into parsley."

And already they've taken him, and come back.

And that one is nothing but a pear on a willow tree.

"They got what they deserved," I say. "One is a pear here, the other one is a parsley there. Now let them try to love each other."

I roar with laughter and the whole court roars along with me. Suddenly I stop laughing. At the same instant the court turns silent. Good court, well drilled. I come up to the chauffeur, straddle him, slap his ass and cry, "Giddyup, to the car!"

He starts to gallop, good old chauffeur, and, neighing with laughter, he shouts, "Ha, ha, ha, neither from parsley, nor out of a pear."

"Ho, ho, ho," the courtiers laugh.

"Hee, hee, hee," go the ladies-in-waiting.

Bang, bang! A whole cavalcade of limousines hits the road. I'm at the front.

"Great," I say to the page. "You really set up some great wholesale happiness for me."

The page fearfully raises his eyelashes; his ugly, flattering gaze stabs me. His ugly eyes smear me.

All of a sudden I slap the chauffeur on the back of his red neck. "Get out of here! I'll drive myself."

I sit behind the wheel. Here's the gas, here's the brake.

I put the pedal to the metal.

The ladies-in-waiting screech and squeal with fear, the courtiers squeal and screech. What's it to me, let them screech, let them be afraid.

Here comes a turn. Good. You'll see, cowards, how the princess cuts a turn at full speed. Eeee! Ahhh! The wheel no longer obeys me. We're flying through the fields, through the woods. I look up . . . the car, racing at a wild speed, slams sideways into some barracks covered with corrugated, tarred metal, then into a small building with the paint scraped off, with a crooked chimney. All I see is a sign, beat up by the wind and rain, bleached in the sun:

EENIE MEENIE MINEY

MOE

LTD. INC.

BANG!!!

A blinding flash.

I sink into a thickening darkness . . .

I want to get up, but I can't. Oh, Tadzio's piled all the blankets on me in his sleep.

I get up. In front of me the road slobbers slickly in the light of the moon. I'm gonna get on that road. They're waiting for me over there with pitchforks.

Oh, here's Daddy sleeping, and there's Mommy. They're snoring.

Don't be angry with me, don't cry. I'm not worth crying for. What do you need such a wicked Hydra with a wrinkled brain for?

Quiet, Zenus, quiet. Come here, little one. They won't let me in without you. I swore on your life that I wouldn't hate. You'll never see anything here, and in heaven you'll see the stars, the sun, everything. You'll only walk with me for a bit, the angels will take you right away. Grab tight on to my neck. It's so warm here on the balcony, so beautiful. Can you see? I put my legs over the railing. Oh, that's right, you don't see anything. You'll see everything soon. You'll fly there soon.

We're flying now.

Zenus's lighter and lighter, and I'm lighter and lighter.

Zenus is no longer with me.

AND I . . . THERE'S less and less of me. I'm lighter and lighter, already lighter than air. But somehow heavier and heavier. The more I'm not there, the more I'm here.

I'm flying through black emptiness, spherical and heavy, pregnant with the heat that rises within me. I press my legs together closely, so the shout of the embryo won't come out of me. What kind of a birth is that, when you give birth again and again, though you never do give birth and constantly fight with the heat that rises within you. In the glow of the Father, in the circle of the Father, I orbit as an obedient star among dancing stars, my sisters. Full of impudent humility and joyous suffering, calmly shivering, I'm silent